STARTING OVER

STARTING OVER

Bob McCurdy

Prairie Viking Press
Westby, Wisconsin

Starting Over
Copyright © 2011 by Bob McCurdy

Published by
Prairie Viking Press
E7409 Sherpe Road
Westby, WI 54667

ISBN 978-0-9789332-6-5
ISBN 0-9789332-6-5

Printed in the U.S.A.

Starting Over is distributed by:
Prairie Viking Press
www.sherpe.com

Cover Illustration by Jeanne Whilden

ACKNOWLEDGEMENTS

The author would like to extend immense gratitude to Jeanne Whildin, who offered a great deal of solid editorial and grammatical advice to this project. Jeanne also brought her artistic talents to producing the cover illustration for the book. It has been a joy to work with this gracious, intelligent talented lady.

Thanks to my friend Howard Sherpe who took on the role of producer. He has applied his expertise as an author and self publisher to getting this book print-ready and arranging for it to be printed.

I wish to dedicate this book to my life partner Nancy K. She is my biggest hero. She endured a terrible depression that lasted for years and almost ended her life. We went through much together. There were times when both of us wondered if it would ever end. I feared that I would lose her. It is a story unto itself. Happily she has been doing very well for the past several years. I thank her for the many major contributions she has made to the final editing of this book.

Many thanks to Billie Johnson. She loaned fresh eyes to the proofreading process. Her energy, insights, ebullience and friendship have been invaluable.

Door County is a very special place. It is both rugged and at the same time fragile. Its scenic beauty owes to its geologic formation during the last Ice Age. It is rock, etched by ice and water. Nothing and no one has found it an easy place to thrive. Perhaps, that is what makes it so appealing to those who have chosen to be here. I am grateful for having found my way to this place and for the confidence that its challenges have instilled in me.

Chapter 1

Sometimes events occur in a person's life that are life-changing. Often it isn't until later on that that one comes to realize that such a thing has happened. It was a cool, sunny morning in early May. Andrew McLeod was outside hanging wash on the clothesline when he heard the phone ringing inside. He abandoned the task and rushed into his circa one hundred thirty-five year old farmhouse. When he answered the phone, a vaguely familiar woman's voice asked, "Is this Andy McLeod? " He affirmed that it was. The woman said, "This is a voice from your past. I don't know if you even remember me. I'm Stephanie Fitzpatrick. We worked together at a mental health clinic in Illinois a few years ago." He did remember her. She was a psychiatric nurse. She was married to a former Jesuit priest. He remembered her long, flaming red hair and her seemingly boundless energy. "I'd heard that you moved up here, but I didn't know where for sure. I also heard that you left being a social worker all together." He asked where she was calling from. "I'm here in Door County with a girlfriend for the week." She told him that she was staying at a motel in town. He knew the owners. It wasn't far from his gallery. She asked how he liked being away from social work, how he liked living here, what he was doing to make a living now and if he had ever gotten married again.

"You'll probably find this hard to believe," he said. "I've got a small business of my own now. I'm a wood carver and I also make rustic furniture. And 'no', I don't miss being a social worker at all. And 'no' I'm not married. Over the years I've discovered that I'm allergic to rush hour traffic and marriage."

She laughed. Your sense of humor hasn't changed much, McLeod. "She asked where he had his shop and if he would be there today. "I'd love to stop by to see you. It's been a long time."

"That would be great." He gave her directions. For some reason he decided to ask, "How's Michael? That is your husband's name, isn't it?"

"I have no idea," she answered coolly. "We've been divorced for over five years now. I've gone back to using my maiden name of Brandt. The last I heard he was living in Seattle." Her tone changed to cheerful again. "Hey, Andy, I'll see you this afternoon. Is there a time that would be best?"

"I never know. Sometimes there's nobody around. It's usually pretty slow this early in the season. Why don't we shoot for around four o'clock?" She agreed to the time.

After hanging up he went back is laundry. He used an old wringer washer that he'd picked up at a garage sale years ago. As he resumed hanging the load on the clothesline, he found himself wondering several things. How had Stephanie found out where he was living? They had been friends, as well as colleagues, when they worked together. They had both left the mental health clinic within weeks of one another. She leaving before him. He hadn't heard from her since. It had to have been over ten years ago. Why was she making an effort to contact him? Why now?

Stephanie arrived at the gallery at three o'clock that afternoon. He had no trouble recognizing her when she came up the walkway toward the shop. She looked very much the way he remembered her. He had forgotten what a great smile she had. She was by herself and she greeted him warmly with a long hug. "God, Andy, you look terrific. I like you with a beard. You're tan and svelte. You look like you still take good care of yourself. This way of life must agree with you."

"You look good too, Steph." There was no one around. He offered her some coffee. She declined.

It was a warm, sunny day. They sat down outside his shop on benches that faced one another. Andy introduced her to his dog, Lucy, a golden retriever/beagle mix. Lucy had been snoozing out on the deck that fronted the gallery entrance. Stephanie asked about his previous dog. "As I recall you had a big, old, loveable, three-legged golden retriever. What was his name?"

"Buck," he told her. "He died awhile ago." Andy felt a slight sense of awkwardness. He felt like he was being scrutinized. They asked a lot of questions of each other about what had happened in their lives since they had worked together years ago. They talked for nearly two hours. Finally she asked him what time he closed up for the day. "Anytime, Christ, there've only been six people in the shop all day."

Stephanie leaned forward and looked at him. She seemed to be searching for something. "Andy, I've kind of fibbed to you. I'm not up here with a girlfriend. I came up by myself. I've heard a lot of good things about Door County and I wanted to see it for myself. I guess I'm a little early. Spring is in full bloom in Illinois. Things are a good two weeks behind us up here." She looked down at her hands, "Andy, I also came here looking for you. I wasn't sure what to expect. I mean, I didn't know what your situation would be. I decided to take a chance."

"Steph, let me close up the shop. I live just a couple miles up the road from here. Why don't you follow me to my place? It's a beautiful piece of property, with a not-so-beautiful old farm house. We can pour some wine and go for a walk." She accepted the invitation showing visceral relief. "It's good to see you again, Steph."

When they arrived at Andy's house he took her on a quick tour of the run-down, old farm house he lived in. He explained many of its primitive features, starting with the fact that he heated with wood exclusively. He explained the lack of a conventional plumbing system. The house had no septic which necessitated the use of a self-composting toilet. He devised a system of diverting his gray water to the garden area. Water was available only when the outside electric pump was turned on. Hot water required directing the flow through an on-demand water heater. He didn't bother explaining the complicated details of that procedure. She helped him take down his laundry. He pointed to the old wringer washer he used. "I was in the process of doing my wash when you called this morning," he told her. She recalled as a young girl helping her mother do laundry using just such a machine. He also explained that the house had little insulation. "On windy nights I can't keep a candle lit because of the drafts." He decided not to tell her about the flies. They were a problem mostly in the winter when they came out of dormancy in the warm house."

Before they started for a walk Andy got Stephanie a sweatshirt. "This time of the year it can get downright cool in the evening. You'll probably need this." He poured them two full mugs of inexpensive box wine.

As they walked out across the meadow to the north of the house, Stephanie took his arm. Lucy was roaming out ahead of them, stopping occasionally to sniff whatever attracted her interest. Andy explained the property to her. "I've got a little over thirty acres. It's an elongated swath of land that extends up through those mature hardwoods." He pointed to the north to a tall forest. There's a bluff in the woods that drops some forty feet. It's part of the Niagara Escarpment that extends across the northern Great Lakes basin, all the way into New York State." They walked into the woods to see the bluff he was referring to. "According to the abstract, my property was part of a hundred-and-forty acre section that was granted by President Fillmore as payment for military service to the original settlers in the 1830's. Over the years it's been broken into smaller and smaller parcels being willed or sold off."

As they made their way back to the house, Stephanie asked if

Andy had ever considered renovating the farm house. He chortled. "Look at that tired old place, Steph. The asphalt, shingle siding was probably installed at the turn of the last century. The metal roof is probably just as old. The foundation is stone. Most of the mortar that held the stones in place has long since crumbled and disappeared. I've patched most. What amazes me is that the place it still standing. My guess is that the electrical wiring dates back to the late nineteen thirties or early forties. I'm told that one of the families that lived here had eleven children. Can you imagine thirteen people existing under that roof?"

Andy pointed to the ancient concrete silo the stood to the east of the house. "There used to be a good-size barn that stood next to the silo. I'm told that it collapsed from neglect a couple of years before I came here." He pointed to the fifty-foot barn that stood just south of where the old barn had been. "That barn was built in 1950. It's in decent shape. I put a new roof on it the first summer I was here. Part of it houses my studio/workshop. The rest of it I use for storage." They stopped in the yard. "I've thought many times about trying to renovate this old house. It has a lot of history and even a fair degree of charm. I could probably put up two nice houses for what it would cost me to salvage the old one. Fixing it would be an exercise in futility. My goal is to put up something else. I even have a good idea of what I'd like to build. Maybe someday I'll be able to do it. It's a matter of money. I'm working toward that."

"Andy, it took real guts for you to leave what you were doing and start all over like this. I always saw you as being a rugged individualist. Bailing out of your profession and coming here to live must have been an almost overwhelming challenge. Weren't you afraid?"

"I was too stupid to be afraid."

"No, stop that. Give yourself credit. I know of very few people who would have the fortitude to give up everything familiar to them, like you've done. You're a real adventurer. I admire that."

"I don't think of myself as being an adventurer, Steph. There've been moments when I was ready to throw in the towel. It's been a real struggle to make a go of it. There was so much I didn't know in the beginning. I felt so stupid. I think it was my masochism that kept me going."

"I don't buy that Andy. Tell me the truth about why you've chosen to hang in there."

They stopped walking and he turned to face her. "I love this place. I fell in love with it the very first moment I saw it. Call it good karma or whatever. I just knew right then, that this is where I wanted to spend the rest of my life. That hasn't changed for even a second over the years. Well, maybe for a few seconds now and then."

"It isn't just this place, Andy. What else?"

"I like what I'm doing. At the end of each day I can see results from my efforts. That's not something most people in the helping professions can say. I love being my own boss, even though I work a lot harder than I would if I were working for someone else. I love going to bed physically tired at the end of the day instead of mentally exhausted. I get to breathe clean, fresh air. The stars are brighter. The local folks here are genuine and honest. I never feel like I have to lock my doors. The only time I take the key out of the ignition on my truck is when I go to the city. I can walk down the street and wear my arm out waving to all the folks I know going by. I could go on."

Stephanie reached up and slipped her hand behind his neck and pulled him toward her. She kissed him gently but sensually. "You're beautiful, McLeod. I'm glad I found you." Lucy lay down and patiently waited for them to finish embracing.

It was nearly twilight when they got back to the house. "Can you stay for supper? I'm a half-way decent cook," he offered.

"Is there a restaurant close by? I'll treat you to dinner," Stephanie offered.

"Yeah, there's a nice family-owned restaurant close to where my shop is. The food is good and the prices are reasonable." He put on a sweater before leaving. Stephanie offered to drive. This is a pretty fancy set of wheels," he commented about her expensive SUV.

"I'm sorry now that I bought it. It's loaded with all kinds of extras, most of which I don't even know how to use. It's got four-wheel drive. In the two years I've had it I've never had it in the four-wheel mode. One of the few things I do like about it is that I sit up higher and can see more of what's happening up ahead. I see you still drive a pickup."

"I need a truck living up here and doing what I do. Old Rosinante is over ten years old and has almost a hundred and fifty thousand miles on it. It still runs good."

As she drove, Stephanie asked, "don't you ever get lonely?"

He thought about the question. "I hate going out to eat by myself. Even though the place we're going to is close by, I never go there by myself. Sitting alone in a restaurant is, to my way of thinking, a really lonely endeavor." He looked at her. "But to answer your question; no I seldom feel lonely. I've got a few friends. For the most part I'm too busy to feel lonely, even during the winter."

Andy found himself relaxing during the course of dinner. Stephanie had numerous questions about what it was like living here. She seemed genuinely interested in this place and his way of life. He noticed that she tended to deflect several of his questions about her. She would either change the subject or offer some vague answer. At one point in the conversation she said, "my life has been pretty dull and uninteresting these past few years, Andy. I feel like I'm ready to make some changes. I just haven't figured out what direction to take."

When they got back to the farm she asked, "How would you feel about me staying here tonight?"

He looked at her. "I'd like that, Steph, but maybe you need to see how I live first. I won't hold you to anything. If you decide to go back to the motel, I'll understand."

The only thing Stephanie seemed a bit squeamish about was the self-composting toilet, but she decided to stay. She had brought an overnight bag, 'just in case'. His earlier sense of awkwardness at the shop was beginning to make sense to him. It was becoming more and more evident that Ms. Stephanie Brandt was on some kind of mission. However, that didn't interfere with their lovemaking that night. When Andy blew out the candles close to midnight, they snuggled together.

The next morning Stephanie stood in the doorway of the small kitchen watching as Andy dished up Lucy's dog food. He offered an observation about Stephanie's previous husband, Michael. "I used to wonder about you and Michael. He seemed to be wrapped pretty tight. I saw you as being more impetuous. I wondered what kind of chemistry was going on between the two of you."

"You're right, Andy. Michael was almost obsessive-compulsive. Everything he did had to be just so. Our sex life was like some kind of sacramental ritual. If we missed a step he would lose it entirely. I mean that literally. He would lose his erection and the show was over. It drove me crazy. After I left the clinic we moved to Portland. I ended up having a couple of affairs. They weren't anything serious. It was mostly sexual attraction. When one of the men began to get serious about me, I broke off the relationship. The weird thing is that I pretty much stopped messing around after Michael and I split up." Stephanie moved to Andy and snuggled up to his back, slipping her arms around him. "I haven't been to bed with anybody since I left the west coast nearly two years ago, Andy. I've only gone out once since I've been in Chicago. I don't know what I want from a relationship. I used to think I did. I'm sure you're wondering if I'm just testing the waters by coming here. I suppose in a way I am. I don't know if I can commit to anything or anybody at this point in my life."

"Why did you look me up? How did you even know where to look?"

"I called Gene Eckert. He's still the director of the clinic where we worked. He told me that you moved up here. I called information. There's only three other McLeods in this whole area code. I decided to take a chance. I like what you used to say about a certain chemistry between people. I've always liked you, Andy. I wondered if you ever remarried or if you were involved with anybody. I hoped you were free. I wondered what kind of chemistry we might have."

"What would have happened if you had come here and found out that I was married?"

"I've heard a lot of nice things about Door County. Like I said, I wanted to come here to see it. If it had turned out that you were not free, I would have done the tourist thing and gone back home."

Stephanie asked what Andy had planned for the day. He told her, "I usually go for a run. I come home to bathe before opening the gallery. In the summer, when the lake warms up enough I take a swim/bath at the beach."

"I'd go for a run with you, but my running gear is back at the motel."

"I run on the beach. You don't really need shoes. It's sand the whole way. I've got a sweatshirt and shorts you can use." Because she was not used to running in sand, she only went a little over half the distance. "Go ahead and finish your run, Andy. I'll see you back at the truck." Later at the farm he showed her the drill for taking a bath. While she bathed he made breakfast for the two of them. After breakfast he took a bath. Before leaving for the shop Andy asked what Stephanie had planned to do today. "I was hoping you could steer me to some of the things I should see while I'm here."

"Sure, stop by the shop. I've got some visitor maps that the chamber of commerce puts out. I'll make a list of places and mark them on the map for you."

"Andy, today is Thursday. I was planning to leave on Saturday. How would you feel about my staying here the next couple of nights?"

"I'd like that. I guess I figured after last night you would prefer the creature comforts of your motel. I've never invited anyone to stay here over night except for my sons. I have to admit that I'm embarrassed to have anyone see the way I live. Life is much simpler here this time of the year. It gets much more challenging in the winter."

She did not respond to his apology. "I'll go to the motel to get my things and check out. I'll see you at the shop in awhile."

When Stephanie showed up at the shop, close to noon, she looked fresh and almost radiant. He commented on how nice she looked. She took the compliment graciously and repeated what she had said to him yesterday about how healthy and fit he looked. As promised he had a map and the list of places he thought she would enjoy seeing. "Andy, I know you work hard to make a living. Are you ever able to take some time off during the season?" She looked down, "I was kind of hoping that you would close up for the afternoon and take some time to show me around."

"You know what, Steph, that's a good idea. If this were the peak of the season I would probably refuse to close up. I need to loosen up. If anybody comes by who's that interested in my stuff, they'll come back tomorrow. Besides, I don't want to be accused of being like Michael."

Just as he was about to close the shop, a middle age couple came in. They spent almost twenty minutes looking around. It appeared that they were about to leave when the wife said. "We really like this bench. It would be perfect in our entry way. We're not leaving until Saturday. If we paid you for it now, could we stop by Friday afternoon to pick it up? We just don't want to haul it around with us for the next day or so."

"That's fine," Andy said, "but let me show you something about this bench. It's what's called a trestle bench. It can be completely disassembled and reassembled very easily. I make them this way intentionally so that they can be transported without taking up much space." He showed them how simple it was to take apart and reassemble. They bought two of them. One of them was going to be a present for their daughter.

After they left, Stephanie asked if he had any more of them. He had four more. "I'll buy one of them, too. I didn't realize it could be taken apart. I have just the place for one of these. What a brilliant idea!"

"What can I say? I'm a damn wizard and this is my lucky day."

"You are a wizard, Andy and it's my lucky day." In her car they kissed. "Andy, I don't feel like going to see a bunch of shops and galleries. I can do that by myself. I can do that back home. Take me to your favorite place. Take me to some place that you regard as special."

He smiled, "I have just such a place and it's not very far from here. The only caveat is that we'll have to park the car and hike about a mile to get to it."

"Perfect, let's go."

He was sure that the gods were smiling on him that day. He had made more money in half-an-hour than he had made in the entire time he had been open thus far this season. The day was cloudless, and there was no cold, east wind off the lake. He was with a beautiful woman and now he was about to take her to one of the most enchanted places he had ever experienced.

To get to Thorsen Point one had to turn off the paved road and drive a distance of a quarter of a mile on a primitive gravel road to a barricade. From there, they began strolling along what had been once the driveway to a remote long abandoned resort. "Not many people even know about this place. The locals prefer to keep its existence a secret, lest it be spoiled by hordes of tourists." The unpaved drive was canopied by mostly old growth white pines, cedars, hemlocks and spruce. The bugs were not bad yet because of the cold nights, plus it had been a fairly dry spring thus far. Lucy disappeared and reappeared into the forest. Her nose was always on over-load whenever she came here. When they reached the site where the resort had once stood, Stephanie stood in awe.

"Andy, this is incredible. You're absolutely right, this is an enchanted world." He led her around the extensive grounds. She continued to be astounded by the beauty and the feeling it gave of having stepped back in time. At a point looking out on the lake she said, "Let's get naked and go swimming."

He laughed, "Okay, you go in first." She squinted at him and asked what was behind his expression. "Sweetheart, that water is so cold your beautiful nipples will freeze and break off instantly. Maybe in August we can go skinny dipping but the lake is barely above freezing right now." She went to the water's edge and put her hand in. She agreed. "Oh, ye of little faith," he said.

"Andy, I have never known what to believe coming from you. I've always felt like you were up to some kind of prank. They were never mean pranks. It was more like you took some kind of pleasure in taking advantage of people's gullibility. I was always a sucker for your antics."

"Is that a compliment?"

"It wasn't at the time. Come on, let's go over there." She pointed to a rock promontory." They climbed on top of it. She slipped her arm around his waist. "I enjoyed being with you last night, Andy. I'm glad you let me stay. I'm already discovering why you like being here so much." They stood together for awhile. She turned to face him. "I don't think I've ever experienced much intimacy with anyone as what we've shared over the past twenty-four hours. There's a lot of sexual energy that flows between us."

"That's an interesting way to put it," he said. "I've never thought in those terms. I like that better than 'chemistry'. It really is a kind of energy. I've been by myself for a long time. I've forgotten what it's like to share genuine closeness. I feel like my energy level has been given a real boost." He smiled at her. "That's a compliment."

They went out for dinner the next two nights and went home afternoons to make love by candle light. On Saturday morning over breakfast, Andy asked, "What happens now? Am I going to see you again?" She asked if he wanted to. "I do, very much. But there's a lot of physical distance between us. I'm not going to be free for the next few months to go anywhere. Steph, this has been a fantastic three days together. I'm just afraid that by the time you're a mile down the road you're going to begin to come to your senses and question everything about this place and me. You're going to wonder what on earth possessed you to come here. Why would any sophisticated, urbane, beautiful woman want to have a relationship with a hermit who lives somewhere back in the nineteenth century?" He paused. She remained silent. "Look, maybe this distance thing is positive. It will give both of us a chance to decide a few things. You have to know that I have no intention of ever leaving here or ever moving back to the city. I love my little corner of the world. That needs to be a big part of your decision making." He had deliberately avoided telling her about a previous relationship he'd had with a woman named Josie. Being here and living the way he did, had proven to be more than she was willing or able to endure.

"I know you're right, Andy. That's one of the things I didn't like about you. You were always so damn practical." She put her arms around him. "I think I'm falling in love with you. That scares me. I don't know what I expected to find. I think I half expected that you had turned into some paunchy, bald headed, boring, old fart. That's not what I found, not at all. I'll call you when I get home to let you know I got there safely. Let's see what tomorrow brings."

"Fair enough," he patted her butt. "Travel safely, and thank you for everything." They held one another.

Chapter 2

Andy spent the next several evenings in his workshop making up for the time he had taken off to be with Stephanie. She called him every other evening at 9:30 and they would talk for close to an hour. She told him how much she liked the bench she had purchased from him. She had orders for two more for friends of hers. She asked about coming up to see him on the Memorial Day weekend, which was two weeks away.

"You're welcome to do that, but it's usually a madhouse up here that weekend. Plus, the traffic heading north on holiday weekends is always bumper- to-bumper. I'd rather you come up the following weekend. Early June is still quiet. It will be more relaxing for both of us."

"There you go being practical again. I miss you. I don't know if I can wait another whole week."

They talked about his sons. He asked her if she had ever thought of having kids. She said that she had but was glad that she hadn't. "Not given the way things have turned out in my life. Besides, I don't think I would've made a very good mother. Kids tie you down. I think I would have resented that. I felt that way with my own mother. She divorced my father when I was very young. She became the head surgical nurse at a children's hospital in St. Louis. We're friends now but I felt like I was a burden to her the whole time I was growing up. I don't want to put any kid through that." She paused. "Sometimes I think I'm a selfish bitch. Seeing you and the life you've made for yourself has had a real impact on me. You seem content. You've learned to do without a lot of stuff in your life. I feel like I've been running around frantically trying to find happiness in all the wrong places. You seem to embrace solitude. I feel lonely most of the time. I hate that feeling. You seem confident. I put up a good front, but underneath it I'm scared a lot of the time. I think that's why I've avoided any kind of commitment. Underneath my façade I'm pretty fragile. I don't trust myself to make the right decisions when it comes to what's best for me." There was a lapse in the conversation. "Hey McLeod, this is where you're supposed to say, jeez Stephanie, you're beautiful and intelligent and vivacious and scintillating and irresistible, blah, blah, blah."

"Jeez Stephanie, you're almost as cynical as me. Freud never talked about that as a defense mechanism, probably because it was one of his personal favorites. I'm just as afraid of being hurt as you are. You'd think that having been in business for myself for a few years now I would have gotten to where I don't take things personally. Christ, when someone comes in and doesn't like my work, it can damn near ruin my day." She was silent. "You left out a few things from your list like sensitive and caring and sexy and curious. You're a great kisser and snuggler too."

"Thanks Andy. I know I'm my own worst enemy at times. I feel like reaching out to you is the best thing I've done in a very long time, maybe ever."

Over the course of their continuing telephone conversations during the next three weeks, they gradually opened up more and more to one another. They both agreed that it was easier to reveal things about themselves via the phone than 'face to face'. She took Friday and Monday off from work, the first weekend in June, to give her a four day weekend. By leaving early she arrived at Andy's shop just after noon that Friday. Despite the fact that there were people in the shop when she arrived, Andy gave her a big hug. He closed the shop at 4:00. She said, "Let's go back to that place you took me to before." He agreed but not until they went home to get a bottle of wine and some mugs. As they walked the road with Lucy disappearing and reappearing she said, "I'm curious to find out if this place has the same magical effect on me as it did the first time we came here."

"I discovered it a few years ago. I still find myself captivated by it every time I come out here, but with subtle differences. Maybe it's the mood I'm in. I also think it has something to do with the time of day and the light. I should come out here at dawn. I haven't done that yet."

"I wonder if we could get permission from somebody to camp here one night," Stephanie said. They found a secluded spot and ended up dropping their jeans and making love on top of a boulder. As they were beginning the trek back, another couple arrived. They greeted one another in passing. Stephanie broke out laughing after the other couple was past. "That was close. Another five minutes and we would literally have gotten caught with out pants down."

"It's probably going to be this way until mid-fall. Even though this place is a fairly well kept secret, there are still a lot of people who know about it."

Back in the car she said to Lucy. "I brought something special for you, Luce. Your master is going to appreciate it too." She unveiled a horse grooming rake. "This will make brushing her coat a lot easier for you and easier on her. I met a lady who does pet grooming and she told me about it. When they got back home, Andy tried it. He was amazed at how much easier it was to use and how much more hair it got out of her coat. Lucy was one of those dogs who seemed to shed hair perpetually.

"That was really nice of you Steph. We both appreciate your thoughtfulness." He made dinner for them that evening. They took another walk afterwards. She took his arm. They stopped in the middle of the meadow to kiss.

"There are times when I would just like to curl up in your lap and have you wrap your arms around me and protect me from the world."

"I would do that if I felt you really needed it."

"What about you? Don't you ever have times when you feel weak, like you need someone to step in and take care of you?"

He smiled, "when I first came up here I had quite a few times like that, when I asked myself 'what have you gotten yourself into, McLeod'?" I felt I was in over my head. I wasn't sure I could make it. I wondered if it was worth the struggle. I thought about going back to the city and maybe even going back to social work.

"What kept you from doing it?" she asked.

"I guess I knew that if I did, I would end up feeling a terrible sense of failure. It just wasn't an option I could live with. I clung to the phrase 'this too shall pass' and it always did. Things always had a way of working out and in time I began to have more and more success. Nothing builds confidence more than success. I know I'll never end up getting rich. That's okay. I make a living and I'm happy. I'm better off than a lot of the poor schmucks that traipse through my shop every summer."

"You really do seem happy with your life, Andy. I envy that about you." As they neared the end of their walk, Stephanie asked, "what about you and me? Do you see yourself being able to ever include someone else in your life?"

He stopped and turned toward her. "I have to say that so far this feels very good, Steph. I admit that I'm still pretty timid about this relationship. Every time you call I anticipate that you're going to tell me it's over, you've changed your mind. Adios McLeod. Have a good life."

"I go through the same thing Andy. I feel like this is too good to be true and that something is going to come along to ruin it." Just then Lucy spotted a deer and started to chase after it. They watched the deer bound away. Lucy gave up the pursuit after the deer disappeared into the woods. "I've never seen a deer in the wild before. I can't believe how graceful it is." She turned back to their conversation. "So what are we going to do about all of this uncertainty?"

"Hang in there and see what happens."

"That's it? You don't have any wizardly advice?"

"Nope, I just attempt wizardly things with wood. I've given up trying to work magic with people. It almost never works."

"I think you work more magic with people that you even realize, Andy. I don't mean this to sound like I'm looking for a guru. I feel pretty confident about you. You've found yourself. I see you as being steady and sure of yourself. It's me I'm worried about. I think I feel a lot better about myself than I used to but I still have my days. The thing I'm the most concerned about is that you may get tired of having to deal with this flaky lady. You haven't seen that side of me yet."

"Look Steph, neither of us can make any promises. Hell, you may decide next week that you don't want to continue on with this single-minded, anachronistic, workaholic. My life isn't all that exciting. It's probably one of the things about me that drove my girlfriend, Josie nuts. You haven't experienced the frustration and aggravation that sometimes comes from dealing with the public. The tempo of the season is starting to pick up. There will be lots of evenings that I'll be out in my workshop trying to fill orders for signs or some other quick, easy-to-crank-out project. I hate to turn anything down. It's probably because I've had such a struggle just to get to where I am. I have the goal to try to get enough money together so I can put up a livable house in the not too distant future. I've started over several times already in my life. I'm getting to a point that I don't know if I can or want to do it again."

There was a long silence. "What if you didn't have to do it alone? What if you had someone helping you?"

"Is that a proposal?"

"It might turn into one but for now just answer my question."

"I can't think in those terms, Steph. I need to operate as though it's just me. If things work out between us and we end up together, maybe that will change the equation. For now I can't allow myself to indulge in that kind of fantasy."

"I understand. I guess I'm trying to push the river. I'm impatient. I don't want to let it flow by itself."

When they got back to the house Andy made a fire in the rock-lined fire pit he had constructed. They roasted hot dogs. He had made some potato salad the day before. They sipped wine and talked. "How would you feel about it if I were able to find a job up here and came here to live? I'm not saying move in with you. I could look into finding a place to rent?"

"I don't know. A part of me would love to have you close by. This distance thing has already worn thin. It would be an awfully bold move on your part. Have you ever not lived in a city?"

"No, but you hadn't either when you came here." She was studying him. "Look Andy, the only reason I wouldn't make the move is if you told me that you didn't want me here. I have nothing to lose. I know I can find a job just about anywhere. Nursing jobs are a-dime-a-dozen. There are things about the city that I used to enjoy. I'm sure that living here will require some adjustments on my part. I want to close the gap between us. I want to see what happens; if we're a match or not. I've done nothing but think about you and this place for the past three weeks. I may be kind of ditzy at times but I'm not stupid. Nor am I as impetuous as you seem to think I am. The clock is ticking. We've both wasted too much time already." She smiled. "Just say yes." He did. They finally retreated to the house and to the bedroom.

Andy awakened a little before three. The wind had come up strongly. Thunder and lightening were approaching from the north-west. He got out of bed just as the rain began. He lowered the windows on those two sides of the house. Minutes later the rain became torrential. Stephanie got up to use the toilet. The two of them stood watching the storm. "Well, in the morning you'll get to see an unpleasant reality about living here." She asked him what that meant. "With a downpour like this, half the damn driveway will be washed out into the road. I'll have to go down with a wheel barrow and repair the driveway first thing in the morning."

"I'll help you."

"It's brutally heavy work."

When they got up at six, she insisted on helping. He found her a pair of old work gloves and a rake. He filled wheel barrow after wheel barrow, dumping the wet, heavy gravel into the ruts. Stephanie raked the gravel to fill in and smooth the surface. It took them over an hour. Andy was drenched with perspiration. He got his old Ford 8-N tractor out. Stephanie got on with him and watched while he drove back and forth over the repair work packing it in. Afterwards he suggested that she could take a quick bath while he tended to some chores and made breakfast. She called to him from the bathroom. "Andy, what's wrong with the water? It's brown."

He went into the bathroom. "I'm sorry Steph. I forgot about that. When we get real heavy rain, the water makes its way down through fissures in the bedrock. It leaches sediment into the well. The water will be like that for a day or so. It will clear up. The lake is still way too cold to bathe in. I don't know what to tell you. I know it looks terrible. The only other alternative is to go over to the YMCA in Fish Creek and pay to take a shower. It's up to you. It's another one of the realities of living here." Stephanie asked him what he did. He told her he bit the bullet and bathed here. He omitted telling her about the two or three week period during the spring thaw when the water was like that.

She finished her bath. While they were eating breakfast she said, "Andy, don't apologize, please." He said nothing. "Tell me about the other realities, all of them. Don't leave anything out."

He reluctantly started down the list. She listened. She asked a few questions if she was not clear about what he was telling her. She asked about remedies. Most of them revolved around putting up a livable house, drilling a new and deeper well and putting in a conforming waste water system, something that would be mandatory if he built anew. The only solution for the driveway was to pave at least the steeply inclined lower portion of it. She asked what kind of cost was involved to do all those things. "I haven't got the slightest idea Steph. I'm not in a position to even consider doing part of it, so I haven't bothered to look into the costs."

"How would you feel about my doing that? I've never done anything like this before, but I'm willing to call around and talk to a few people to get some idea about prices."

"Be my guest. It should prove interesting."

Because it was Saturday the only person she was able to contact was a well driller. She made an appointment with him to come to the farm on Monday morning. She called her place of employment and left a message. She told them she had car problems and wouldn't be able to be back to work until Thursday. She said the parts couldn't be ordered until Monday. Her car wouldn't be operable until sometime on Wednesday at the soonest."

Stephanie and Andy had several lengthy discussions over the weekend about where to build a new house and what kind of place to consider building. On Monday she systematically began calling builders. She had three appointments scheduled for Tuesday. "Oh Andy, this is exciting. What a neat experience." He tried to temper her exuberance by reminding her that she was collecting data only. "I know; I realize that this is just the first step but I'm excited just the same."

When she left late Wednesday afternoon to return to the city, they had exact figures on the cost of a well and a waste water system. Three different builders were going to submit bids to build a house. Andy had sketched out a basic design for both the shape of the exterior and interior floor plan. All three of the builders encouraged him to consider increasing room sizes. They advised that he would be sorry later on for having sacrificed space. He wasn't saving that much by 'under building'. They were also willing to submit bids on both constructing an exterior shell that he could finish himself, and a completed house.

The estimates for the well and the waste water system totaled what he had managed to save thus far. He tried hard to hide his disappointment about those figures but when Stephanie called him that night, she picked up on his frustration, "I know you were disillusioned by the cost of a well and a septic Andy. I was too. I had no idea getting water and getting rid of it could be so costly. I won't ever bitch about my water and sewer bill again. If I left my faucets on twenty-four/seven for the next twenty years, my bills still wouldn't add up to what it's going to cost you. Hey wizard, I love you. It was a wonderful 'almost week' we had together. I enjoyed every minute."

Chapter 3

Stephanie made an appointment the next day with the hospital's personnel director where she worked. She told him that she had met someone special and she was going to relocate to be closer to him. She gave him two weeks notice. He was sorry to be losing her. He wished her well and assured her that she would be welcomed back 'if things didn't work out'. He asked where she was going to be moving to. She deliberately told him that she was moving to the Galena area in the northwest corner of Illinois. He was familiar with the area. "My wife and I go there just about every year. We just love it. Maybe we'll see you the next time we're there."

Stephanie's roommate was upset about her leaving, mostly because of having to find someone else to share expenses with. "Here's what I'm willing to do Margaret. If we can't find an acceptable replacement for me by the time I leave here at the end of the month, I will give you my share of the next month's rent. That will give you an additional month to find someone. Two days later Stephanie found a nurse who worked in a different unit who was looking for a place. Everything worked out so that the other nurse could move in the same day that Stephanie moved out.

"How auspicious," Andy said in their phone conversation that night. "Devout skeptic that I am, I keep waiting for the sword to drop. This is either a very good omen or the gods are messing with our heads."

"I know. I keep thinking this is all going too smoothly; something is going to go wrong. So far so good."

"How are you going to get all your stuff up here?"

"I don't have very much to move. The girl who is replacing me wants to buy my dresser and bed. Margaret said she would buy the rest of my furniture, which isn't all that much. I'll keep my television, my stereo and my bench. I'm letting both of them have their pick of a lot of my clothes. It's not stuff that I would have much occasion to wear living up there anyhow. I feel like I'm about to begin a whole new way of life. I can't wait to get started. I'll be there the night of the thirtieth. I'll start looking for some place to rent the next day."

Andy hesitated; then said, "Steph, how would you feel about living here?" There was no response. "I've been afraid to ask. You know how embarrassed I am about this place. It's probably not a very good idea. I'm sorry, I shouldn't have asked."

"Yes Andy. I'd like that. I'm sorry. I wasn't expecting that question." He started to say something. "Andy, I've been so lost for such a long time. I had just about given up. I've just been going through the motions for the past couple of years. I knew that first night we spent together that this was what I was looking for. I love you so much." The remainder of their conversation was devoted to some of the ramifications of the move. They acknowledged their individual trepidations about entering into a fulltime relationship. They agreed that, should either of them decide it wasn't working, they would be forthright in addressing the issues.

Toward the end of their conversation Andy said, "Steph, we've both made mistakes in the past. We've both been around the block more than once. We won't know if this can work unless we give it a try. I trust you more than I trust myself. I suspect you feel the exact same way. Let the adventure begin." He added, "you're absolutely right, Steph. You're about to start a whole new way of life."

Lucy announced Stephanie's arrival a week later by barking and running down the driveway. Andy was in his workshop putting the finishing touches on a corner cabinet. It was almost nine o'clock in the evening but it was still light out. They held one another for several moments. "Welcome to my humble abode." He carried a couple of boxes into the house. He had placed a blue glass vase filled with wild flowers on the dining room table. "I found this vase for you at that resale shop down the street."

"I love blue glass Andy. It's supposed to have healing powers. It's beautiful. What a nice welcome present."

They put on insect repellent and went for a walk. Stephanie asked, "Is the lake warm enough to go swimming yet?"

"It's getting there. A lot depends on wind direction. There are days when it's pleasant. I've taken a couple of baths after running already."

She smiled at him. "I want to go skinny dipping. That's why I'm asking."

"Well, it's probably warm enough for that, but the mosquitoes might suck us dry before we could get our clothes back on." They were already beginning to swarm.

When they got back to the house, neither of them were hungry. She took a quick bath and they went into the bedroom. They were lost in the act of lovemaking when something flew by. "God damn it," Andy said.

"What, what's wrong?"

"A bat, a goddamn bat." He got out of bed; turned on the bedroom light and picked up a tennis racket. After swatting at it several times, he finally hit it. It took a couple of minutes to find its corpse. He picked it up by one wing and left the bedroom to dispose of it. When he came back in the room Stephanie had turned out the light and lit a candle.

She giggled. "Does this happen often?"

"Not as much as it used to. It's down to maybe once-a-week now." She was still smiling. "What's so amusing?" The candle flickered.

"That's one of the 'realities' you overlooked telling me about." He sat down on the bed. "I feel sorry for the poor bat. The thing must have been terrified when you turned the light on. It must have said to itself, 'holy shit, I really screwed up this time'." She patted the pillow. "Come on, lay down." They lay next to one another. "I don't know when I've ever been this happy, Andy. I was prepared to find my own place to live. I wouldn't have minded doing that. You really did surprise me when you asked me to come to live here."

He chuckled. She asked what that was about. "I'm just amazed at you, babe. You not only weren't pissed about having a bat in the bedroom with us, but you even empathized with the stupid thing."

Within three days Stephanie found a job at the same clinic Andy went to. She soon took over most of the mowing which required more than an hour using a riding mower. She planted a couple of flower beds. It was too late to start a vegetable garden. Andy told her, "I had a garden the first three years I lived here. The deer and raccoons took turns coming through every other night to raid it. I finally gave up. It wasn't worth the effort. It was cheaper just to go to the store and buy the food than to try growing it." She was going to find a way. She would do that next year.

By mid July they had received bids for building a new house using a basic plan that Andy had drawn. He thought the estimates were high. She thought they were dirt cheap compared to what building costs were in the city. They chose a builder named Dan Lundquist that they both liked. Dan had taken the time to draw up detailed plans. He was a small independent contractor who told them straight out that he would not be able to start on the project until the next spring. His schedule was full for this year. That gave them the time they would need to get permits and to arrange financing. Stephanie was excited. "Andy, I've never had a house of my own before. I've never even lived in a house before I came here. I've always lived in apartments."

He smiled. "Home ownership is a myth. All of us are down here on the planet for a brief moment. Even if we pay off a mortgage, we're really only leasing a piece of property for the time we're here. The Canadians have it right. We could go to Canada and rent an island for a hundred years. We couldn't buy it even if we wanted to. Who's ever going to see a hundred year lease to its conclusion? There's a famous quote by Chief Seattle, 'The earth does not belong to man; Man belongs to the earth.' The Indians were baffled by our government wanting to purchase the land they lived on."

She didn't care. "For the first time in my life I'm going to have a place to call home. I don't care if I die a week after we move into it. I will have had that wonderful week."

Andy apologized. "I'm sorry, Steph. I do that without realizing that I'm sometimes raining on peoples' parades. I'm with you. It will be a pure joy to return to a civilized way of life again."

The summer raced by. Andy was having the best season he had ever experienced. As always there was a brief, much-needed lull after Labor Day. It gave all the people involved with tourism a chance to catch their breath before the final push associated with the fall colors and close-out sales. For Andy, the season had been financially rewarding but physically and emotionally draining. Stephanie helped out as much as possible by taking over many of the mundane tasks of daily living. Still, he worked long, seven day weeks without a break. When the end of the season arrived at the end of October, Andy had a large number of Christmas orders. He also had a number of commissions that he could do over the winter.

With a great deal of encouragement from Stephanie, Andy decided to go in with his friend Rob to purchase ten cords of firewood. Rob had a shop of his own in the village of Fish Creek. Both of them were just too busy during the fall to spend time in the woods logging anymore. It made more sense for them to purchase the wood, both in terms of time and money. The wood was scheduled to be delivered by mid-November. It would arrive via a semi truck at Andy's place. It would be delivered in eight-foot lengths. It meant that it would need to be cut into sixteen-inch stove lengths. It was going to require a good deal of physical labor but not nearly as much time as logging it themselves. Andy's younger son, Corey, who was a jet engine mechanic in the Marine Corps, offered to come help cut, split and stack. He scheduled ten days of leave from his post at Cherry Point Air Station in North Carolina. He arrived at the airport in Green Bay the day the wood was delivered. Late that afternoon Rob came by to have a look at the wood. Now that his shop was closed he was working as a carpenter for a large construction firm. On his way from work Rob had purchased a case of beer. He offered Andy and Corey a bottle. When he handed one to Andy he refused it. "Where did you get this stuff?" Andy asked. Rob told him. "I'm not one to turn down a free beer but this is peacock piss. As desperate as I was for money in college, I wouldn't buy this stuff. I didn't know Kingsbury was still being brewed. I'd have thought the free-market would have driven this brewery out of business a long time ago."

Rob and Corey had already opened their bottles. They both took swigs, thinking he was trying to put one over on them. They both immediately spit it out, making faces. Rob used his hammer to tap the caps back on. "This is the worst swill I have ever tasted," Rob said. "Your description demeans peacocks." Corey agreed.

It was Wednesday. Rob wouldn't be free to help cut the wood until Saturday. "I can borrow a large trailer from work. Can I use your truck Friday? I don't have a trailer hitch on my car." Rob drove a beat-up, rusty, old Subaru that probably couldn't have pulled the trailer anyhow.

"Sure, the weather is supposed to be good. Corey and I will get going on it tomorrow. Maybe we can have my half cut and stacked by Friday evening. If the weather holds, the three of us ought to be able to get your half done over the weekend."

Rob put the two bottles back in the case. "I'm going to see if I can return this and get a case of decent stuff. God, this is just awful."

The days were much shorter now and it was well after dark when Stephanie got home that evening. She seemed tense and on edge. Andy poured her a large glass of wine and mixed himself a martini. Corey had a beer. They sat down to relax and visit in the living room. She had not met Corey before. After a few minutes she got up saying that she had a splitting headache and she was going to lie down for awhile. The bedroom was right off the living room, so Andy and Corey retired to the dining room so as not to disturb her. After awhile Andy decided to start supper. "I thought I'd put together some Spolish rice tonight. It used to be one of you and Brian's favorite meals."

"I remember it." Corey said. "It was a combination of Spanish rice and Polish sausage. That sounds really good." He helped his father by dicing up the sausage and chopping an onion.

When dinner was ready Stephanie got up and joined them, saying that she was feeling somewhat better. She asked Corey about his job in the Marine Corps and what the area surrounding his base was like. She asked if he intended to make a career of the Marines and where he eventually wanted to end up living. Andy listened. Corey asked her where she had lived and where she thought she'd like to end up living. "I like it here but I confess I haven't experienced a

Wisconsin winter yet. Ask me that question in the spring." All of them went to bed at 9:30. Andy thought it was odd that Lucy chose to go upstairs with Corey that night. Since Stephanie had moved in she'd taken to sleeping on an old comforter next to Andy's side of the bed. The strange behavior didn't stop there. It had become routine for he and Stephanie to cuddle with one another before turning over to go to sleep. Tonight was different. Stephanie was already curled up with her back to him. She fell asleep without even saying goodnight.

It was sunny and cold when they got up the next morning. There had been a hoar frost that night. The outside thermometer read twenty-two degrees. There was no wind. Stephanie left for work after a quick breakfast. Andy found an old pair of lined bib overalls for Corey to wear over his other clothes. They were dressed in layers. After showing Corey the safety aspects of using a chainsaw, the two of them set to work cutting the logs.

It warmed into the mid-thirties by noon. By mid-afternoon they were both feeling the exertion and their pace slackened significantly. They quit for the day at four o'clock. After servicing the saws Andy mixed a drink and Corey opened a beer. Along with Lucy they took a walk up to the woods.

"It feels good just to stand up straight again," Corey said. "I don't know how you did it for all those years, logging your own wood. Doing it this way is hard enough." Corey looked at his father. "Are you going to be able to stay awake long enough to make dinner?"

"I'll be okay. I love being outside. I like doing this physical work. I can't begin to tell you how much I appreciate your help. We'll probably be able to finish up my half of the load tomorrow. If so, we'll be able to get a start on Rob's half." When they got to the woods the sun was close to setting. The bright tangerine light filtering down through the bare branches made the forest feel ethereal. They stood absorbing the scene as the intense glow faded into violet; then purple.

When Stephanie arrived home she seemed even more out of sorts than she had the previous evening. She poured a large glass of wine which she drank in minutes. She poured another before she went in to change out of her uniform. By the time dinner was served she was half way through her third glass. Two glasses was her normal self-imposed limit. Andy asked if it had been hectic at the clinic today. She said that it had. "Mostly it's John. He drives all of us crazy with his constant micro-managing. The other thing that drives our receptionist, Linda and me bonkers, is all the old people who just drop by expecting to be seen. John can't bring himself to insist that they make appointments. He refuses to send any of them away." Andy had not heard Stephanie criticize John before. She joked about his unorthodox management style from time to time, but tonight she seemed downright negative. He wondered what was really going on.

When they went to bed that night, Lucy again went upstairs with Corey. Andy remarked about it to Stephanie as they lay in bed. "I don't blame her," Stephanie commented. "Maybe she likes it up there because it's warmer. The floor gets so damn cold down here at night." He didn't disagree but it hadn't seemed to ever bother Lucy before. He reached over to touch Stephanie. She already had her back to him and she did not respond to his touch. She said 'good night' and within a short time her breathing slowed and deepened with sleep.

The next day was even nicer than the previous day. It was above freezing when they got up. Stephanie seemed preoccupied as she readied for work. She left without even saying goodbye. Andy felt like she was fleeing this place or maybe him. He tried to dismiss her seemingly sudden withdrawal by saying to himself 'Christ McLeod, you're blowing this way out of proportion.' Still he could not let go of the abrupt change in her. He tried hard not to indulge in speculating, but fears were beginning to invade his thoughts. 'Has she met someone else? Is she preparing to leave here? What have I done or not done to piss her off? Was this just an interlude? Has the novelty of being here finally worn off? Has she decided that this is not what she really wants after all? Is she pissed off about Corey being here? To some extent he could understand the 'why' of her not wanting to be here. He was baffled by the 'why now'. 'What had brought about this sudden change at this particular point in time?'

Before he and Corey started cutting wood he said, "Let's slow the pace down today. We busted our asses yesterday. We don't need to drive ourselves that hard." Corey agreed. Even working at a steady, slower pace, they completed cutting Andy's five cords by mid-afternoon. There were a lot of larger stove-length pieces that they had set aside to be split later. Andy would rent a log splitter to break them into manageable chunks. They stacked the rest and were done by walk time.

Rob showed up just as they were about to leave for their walk. He took Andy's truck to go get the trailer. Andy, Corey and Lucy were on their way back to the house when Rob returned with the trailer in tow. He had difficulty backing the trailer. Andy started to explain the trick to backing trailers. "I know what the trick is but I can't get my brain to think in those terms," Rob said. Andy ended up backing the trailer into position. Andy invited Rob to stay for dinner. He was making venison stroganoff. Rob had never tasted venison before and he accepted the invitation.

Stephanie arrived home a short while later. She seemed in a better mood tonight but Andy couldn't help wonder if that was because Rob was here. After he had dinner underway the four of them sat around the dining room table visiting. Rob had succeeded in trading in the terrible Kingsbury beer he had purchased yesterday. He and Corey were drinking the higher quality Bush Bavarian beer he now had. Rob left shortly after dinner saying that he would be back by eight tomorrow to cut his wood. Because it was Friday night, Corey wanted to go into town to see if any of his acquaintances from the past were around. Stephanie offered to let him use her car. Andy's back was hurting from bending over all day. He decided to take a hot bath and soak in the tub for awhile. Stephanie took care of doing the dishes and cleaning up the kitchen. Afterwards she came into the bathroom and sat down next to the tub. Her demeanor was pleasant but somewhat distant. Andy asked her if she was alright.

She shrugged. "I'm okay." After a brief lapse she said, "I have a difficult question to ask." Andy braced himself not knowing what to expect. "How would you feel about my going to Florida at Christmas to see my mother? I haven't seen her in over five years. I'd leave a couple of days before Christmas and be back before New Years Eve."

"It sounds like you've already looked into travel plans." She said that she had. She told him that because the holidays were a busy time for travel, she felt she needed to make her plans well in advance. She needed to make a decision as soon as possible in order to insure her booking. Andy flipped open the drain on the tub. She handed him a towel after he stood up. As he dried himself he said, "To be honest, I have to say that I'm somewhat surprised. I was under the impression that you and your mother were not very close to one another." He finished drying himself. "As a matter of fact you made it sound like you were pretty much estranged from one another."

"It's true. There was a period of several years when we weren't on speaking terms. We're still not what you would call 'best friends'. My stepfather, who I couldn't stand, died last spring. She's all alone now and she's getting old. I feel like I need to try to mend some fences before it's too late." He stepped out of the tub. "I hate leaving you here by yourself at Christmas. I know that we can't both go. Maybe Brian can come up to spend a few days with you."

"Steph, Christmas is just another day. It's highly overrated. Too much is made of it in my humble, jaundiced opinion. The fact is the holidays are more a pain in the ass than they are a time of joy for the majority of people."

"You're disappointed aren't you, Andy."

He admitted to being surprised. She pressed him about his feelings. "Yeah, well I guess I do feel some disappointment. I was really looking forward to Christmas this year. I was looking forward to sharing it with you." "We still can; just a few days later," she apologized. She instructed him to go lay down in bed and she would give him a back rub. She had him lie on his stomach and she straddled his legs. After she finished massaging his back she laid down next to him. He took hold of her hand. "My timing is probably way off Steph." He hesitated. "I've been thinking a lot lately about asking you to marry me." She gave no response. "As you know I have some real reservations about marriage. I'm pretty sure you do too." She remained silent. "I guess now is not the time to be discussing that subject." She rolled toward him and kissed him. It was only then that he realized she was crying. She got on top of him and they made love. Nothing more was said.

Everybody was up early the next morning. Andy prepared a large breakfast. Stephanie left afterwards to run errands and grocery shop. Before leaving she said, "I'll try to get everything done this morning so I can help you guys this afternoon. It sounds like the weather is headed south by tomorrow afternoon." Andy watched her get into her car thinking, 'she really is a beautiful woman', wondering if their relationship, like the weather, was heading south too.

Rob arrived at 8:00 and the three of them set about cutting his wood. When Stephanie got home, she and Rob loaded the trailer and left to dump it at his place. He lived about twenty minutes away. Andy and Corey kept cutting. They had close to two-thirds of it done by late afternoon. The four of them were back at it by eight the next morning. The sky was cloudy. It looked like it could begin snowing at any moment. They pushed themselves hard and had the rest of the wood cut and moved by early afternoon. Andy and Rob followed the last load in Stephanie's car to Rob's house. With four of them working they got all of Rob's wood stacked neatly by the time it started snowing. They stacked the large chunks separately for Rob, so he could split them at his convenience later on. By the time they started back home the snow was coming down in huge wet globs. Stephanie drove while Andy and Corey drank the beers that Rob had given them. "Rob's a sweet man," Stephanie remarked. "He really appreciated our help with the firewood. I can see why the two of you have gotten to be such good friends."

The snow continued. Andy decided to clear the driveway before it got to dark to do so using his ancient, underpowered snow blower. Stephanie had to be at work by 8:00 the next morning. Andy got up with her. He made some breakfast for her before going out to clear the snow off her car windows and start the engine. She waved to him as she started down the driveway. He thought about her departure. A week ago she would have hugged and kissed him goodbye even if it meant stopping and getting out of the car to do it. Something had shifted. 'What the hell is going on?' It had seemed to him that things had improved between them over the weekend. As the surge of fears began to rise in him again, questions began to surface about this proposed visit to her mother. One of them was about the mother's last name. According to Stephanie, her mother had married four times. He had no idea what her most recent husband's name was. Stephanie had no pictures of her mother. She and her mother didn't correspond with one another to his knowledge. How did they maintain contact? He wondered if her mother was even alive. 'Christ McLeod, you're turning into a full blown paranoid. You're imagination is getting the best of you. Is this what being crazy is like.'

Corey was scheduled to leave to return to his base on Wednesday. They would just have today and tomorrow together. Corey was still not up when Andy came in the house. He fed Lucy; then the two of them went out to his workshop. He started a fire in the stove and went upstairs in the barn to get boards for a couple of projects he needed to start on. Corey came into his shop a little after nine. Andy had his radio tuned to the classical music station of public radio. Andy asked if Corey had gotten some breakfast. He had not. "Let's run into town to get some. It's going to take an hour for the shop to warm up."

They talked about a number of things over breakfast, especially pertaining to Corey's future plans. Corey was pretty much decided that he was not going to reenlist in the Marines. Andy was surprised. He had gotten the impression that his son had planned to make a career of the Corps. "I'm about as far as I can go with the Marines. Unless I get a college degree, I'm ineligible to become an officer." Corey had always struggled with school. He had gone into the Marines because he did not view himself as being college material. Andy was fairly certain that Corey had been mildly dyslexic, and, therefore, had fallen through the cracks in school. By the time his sons had come to live with him it was too late to request remedial help from the school. There simply weren't any programs for secondary school learning disabled students. Andy couldn't afford to send him to a special private school. Even if he could have, he was sure Corey would have refused. By the time they left the restaurant, they both decided to give the matter more thought. Corey had a year before his enlistment was up.

The sun came out by noon. Andy suggested that the two of them take a hike out to Thorsen Point. Corey had never seen it before. The snow was melting and slushy as they walked the road to the point. Lucy was in overdrive as usual, crisscrossing in and out of the woods. Andy had never come out here during the winter. There was a light breeze off the lake which made it feel a bit colder. Corey was taken by the place. He had a number of questions about it. Andy was beginning to feel like a docent. On the way back Corey commented, "You know Pops; you really are living in a paradise. Your place is one. This place is another. I can see why you love living here so much. Now, if you can just manage to build something livable."

The way things were going between he and Stephanie, Andy wondered if that was going to happen. He chose not to say anything about the plans to put up a house in the spring. He was beginning to have doubts about whether they would still be together by then. The possibility of that saddened him deeply. All he said was, "I'm working on it."

Stephanie was back to being tense and remote when she arrived home that evening. She barely made eye contact and avoided even hugging him. After dinner Corey went upstairs to begin organizing and packing. He was required to travel in uniform and he brought his shirt down to iron it. The flies were out in full force, banging off the lampshades and light bulbs. Corey had never witnessed this aspect of living here. He made a comment. Andy peered at him over his reading glasses. "Welcome to paradise, son." Stephanie wondered what that was about. "It's an 'inside joke' between us," he explained.

Chapter 4

Everyone was up early on Wednesday morning. Andy and Corey departed for Green Bay at the same time Stephanie left for work. It was overcast and looked like it might start snowing any minute. It was a two hour trip to the airport. Corey talked about his visit. He said that several of his opinions had changed over the past ten days. He raised concerns about Stephanie's mood swings. Andy said, "You caught that, too. It just started last week. I don't know what it's about. I feel like I'm walking on eggs with her. She's planning to go to Florida just before Christmas to visit her mother. I don't know if that's triggering her moodiness or what. I've decided to cut her as much slack as possible for the time being."

They arrived at the airport half an hour prior to Corey's scheduled flight. Andy asked one of the airport staff to take a couple of pictures of the two of them together. Before they parted, Corey gave his father a hug. "I hope things work out for you, Pops. Thanks for everything. I'm glad we had this time together. I'll call you when I get to Raleigh."

Andy made a couple of stops in Green Bay before heading home. One of them was a jewelry store that had been recommended to him. He found a simple band wedding ring that he liked. It was in his price range. He asked the gentleman who waited on him, "I'm taking a chance in buying this. If things don't work out, can I return it and get a full refund?" The man smiled and assured him that he could. He hoped for both of their sakes that wouldn't be necessary. Next he went to a department store where he found a thick, royal blue, terrycloth robe and some lined slippers for Stephanie. Finally, at a sports store he bought a cross-country ski package for her. He had gotten her shoe size by checking her small collection.

He was pleased with his shopping success as he started the drive home. He had almost all his Christmas shopping done. He was undecided about the ring, as to whether he should give that to Stephanie before she left on her trip, or wait until she returned. It began to snow as he drove north. Lucy was curled up next to him on the seat. It was growing dark and the snow kept increasing in intensity. His mood started sinking until he felt so much melancholy he was nearly in tears. It reminded him of how he felt each time he had parted from his sons after weekend visitations when they were very young. This felt even sadder. It was more of a sense of grief, he thought. He tried to attach his sadness to having had such an enjoyable time with Corey. He hated goodbyes. In truth it kept coming back to Stephanie. Things had been so good between them. It felt like some kind of inexplicable, irreparable, cosmic shift had occurred. By the time he was about halfway home the snow was coming down so hard the visibility was like driving in dense fog. He slowed down hoping that he wouldn't be rear ended by some jerk in a hurry to get somewhere. It continued like that until he was about fifteen miles from home, when he suddenly drove out of the snow entirely. The sky was so clear he felt like he could reach up and touch the stars. There was some snow on the ground but he had apparently been driving through an intense band of it. It was almost six o'clock when he drove up the driveway. He parked next to Stephanie's car. Before he could get out of the truck Lucy jumped over him. He could hear the clicking sound of contracting metal coming from Stephanie's car. The hood was still warm. He concluded that she must have just arrived home herself. In the house, Stephanie was working to stoke one of the stoves to get it to burn. It was cold in the house. After giving Stephanie a peck on the cheek he went to the other stove to do the same thing.

"How come you're so late?" She asked.

"I did a little shopping while I was in the big city and I drove through a terrible snow storm coming home. It was almost a white out. I had to drive at less than twenty miles per hour for about thirty miles."

She sounded like she didn't believe him. "We just had a light dusting here. That's incredible."

He defensively invited her to drive fifteen miles down the road to see for herself. He asked, "how come you're so late getting home?"

"I needed to get a few things for my trip and I did some Christmas shopping. I wanted to get a couple of things for my mother."

They had a light dinner of soup and crackers and cheese in the living room. As the house began to warm, the flies began ricocheting off lampshades. "Where are the goddamn bats when you need them?" Stephanie said.

They talked about Corey's visit. "I don't think either of the boys was thrilled about my moving up here, Corey liked it even less than Brian. He came right out and said that his spending this time here has given him an appreciation for this place. I think he understands now why I chose to live here."

They went to bed a little after nine. Andy was almost asleep when the phone rang. It was Corey letting him know that he had arrived safely in Raleigh. He was about to board a bus to complete his trip back to the Cherry Point Air Station. "Thanks again, Pops. It was a great visit. Say hi to Steph."

After Stephanie left for work the next morning, Andy went to his truck to get the presents he had bought the day before. He wrapped them while he waited for the workshop to warm. Thanksgiving was a week away. He thought about inviting Rob to join them. Maybe Stephanie had someone she'd like to invite. A week ago he had been looking forward to Thanksgiving and the holidays. A feeling of numbness was starting to set in. He knew it from past experience. He likened it to emotional Novocain. It had happened to him years before in Viet Nam. It was a means of survival, a way of protecting the emotional self from the constant assault of loss, grief, fear, and physical degradation. He sensed that he was losing Stephanie. He was confused. He couldn't figure out what had happened, or what he could to do to try and reverse it. He hated feeling so helpless. Maybe some miracle would happen to turn things around. Maybe it would simply pass. Maybe she would return from Florida and things would go back to the way they had been. Maybe she'd found someone else. Maybe she decided that this way of life was just not her cup of tea. He tried to stop his ruminating. He'd just have to wait and see what happened when she returned; if she returned.

Saturday was the opening of the gun deer season. Even though the weather was clear and mild and the forecast called for more of the same, he decided not to hunt this year. Shots could be heard throughout the entire day. Some of them were close by. He took his deer rifle to the workshop in the event that some hapless deer should walk by. That had happened a few years back and he had not been prepared for it. He remembered watching the deer amble across the meadow to the south of his studio. It passed within fifty feet of the barn.

Because the days had gotten so much shorter he stopped work at 3:30 to go for a walk. As Lucy and he started out across the north meadow, two large does took flight bounding away toward the woods. Because the breeze was southeasterly, Luce hadn't caught their scent. The tall brown weeds and grasses prevented her from seeing them. About half way across the meadow Lucy stopped and started barking furiously. She was facing in a southeasterly direction toward the woods. Andy scanned the woods but couldn't make out anything. "What is it Luce?"

He took a few steps in the direction she was facing. Suddenly he saw the outline of a person moving just a few feet within the edge of the woods. The person was headed away from them, deeper into the tall hardwood forest. There was a road that ran through the forest about a quarter of a mile away. Andy quickened his pace and then broke into a run. He knew that he couldn't catch up with the interloper but if the person was headed toward the road he probably had a vehicle parked there. Maybe he could at least catch up enough to see what kind of car it was. He reached the woods and began weaving his way through the trees. He was to where he could make out the road when he heard a car door slam shut, an engine start and then the squeal of tires on pavement. He caught a glimpse of the vehicle through the trees. It was a dark sedan. He was annoyed that his initial reaction had been so slow. He decided to see if he could locate where the intruder had been when Lucy had first spotted him. In the years that he had lived here, a couple of people had driven up his driveway. In both instances they had backed down and departed. He had regarded it as strange that someone would drive into what was obviously private property. Both times he had been present. There probably had been others when he wasn't around. This was not the same. Andy sensed that he was being deliberately observed. The light was fading but he did find a place where he was fairly certain a person had been standing. It didn't make sense that someone was spying on him. He was doubtful that it was a hunter. He didn't like this. It was triggering all sorts of paranoia. He was puzzled by Lucy's behavior. She had alerted him to the person's presence but she hadn't charged off in that direction. She had stayed close to him. He wondered if she had sensed some kind of danger.

Stephanie had been gone for the day attending a continuing education workshop in Green Bay. When she arrived home, she looked tired. He asked how it had gone. "I don't know if it was worth it. There were only three of us signed up for the class. The instructor was knowledgeable but she kept getting side tracked. I guess I shouldn't care. I get credit for the class whether it's useful or not." He poured her a glass of wine.

She went into the living room. He came in and sat down to join her. She had her shoes off and her feet up on a hassock. "I'm making some Swedish Meatballs. They need to simmer for awhile," he told her.

She said that she needed to pick up her airline tickets. She planned to do that during her lunch break on Monday. He asked where her mother lived in relation to the airport. "I'm flying into Orlando. She lives about an hour-and-a-half from there on the east coast. She's not far from the Kennedy Space Center. She's going to pick me up at the airport." He asked her several questions about her mother, a subject they had only touched on occasionally before. He asked if she had any photographs of her mother. "I do, but they're packed away somewhere." She said that the two of them looked a lot alike. "We even had the same red color hair." He asked her what her mother's last name was. "Her last husband's name was Daniels. I don't know if she's gone back to using her maiden name of O'Hara or not." He wasn't sure why, but he had decided not to say anything to her about the trespasser this afternoon. He told her about seeing the two deer.

They awoke in the morning to snow on the ground and a light snow was falling. The temperature had dropped into the low twenties. After breakfast he and Lucy went to the workshop. He planned to get started on a special bench order today. A lady had called him from Illinois and ordered six of his trestle benches as Christmas presents. Her sister, who lived in Green Bay, would pick them up when they were ready. After he had a good fire going he started to go upstairs to get the lumber for the benches. He normally covered the top of the stairwell with a four-foot by eight-foot sheet of rigid Styrofoam insulation. The purpose was to prevent the warm air from the shop from escaping into the loft area. He noticed that the sheet of insulation had been moved aside. He remembered specifically putting it back in place the day before. He climbed the stairs cautiously. In addition to storing lumber in the upstairs of the barn, both he and Stephanie had several boxes full of personal items, books, photographs and business records. He looked around. He found several boxes that had been opened. The tops had not been folded back down. One of them was his business records. He looked through the contents. Everything appeared to be there but some of the envelopes were out of sequence.

All three of Stephanie's boxes were left standing open. One of them contained summer clothing. Another had personal records. It was obvious that the boxes had been gone through. It appeared that everything had been removed from the boxes and then dumped back into them helter-skelter. His experience with her was that she was meticulous about keeping things in order. This was not something she would have done. It was impossible to know if anything had been taken. She might not even know the answer to that. He decided to leave things as he had found them. He felt angry about this patent invasion of his, their privacy. It appeared to him that she was the one being targeted. 'What the hell is going on here'? He wondered if this was somehow related to yesterday's intruder. 'Was the person he'd seen in the woods the person who had done this'? He went to the house with his senses on alert, wondering if he was being observed. He took some comfort in having snow on the ground. Whoever was sneaking around here could now be tracked. He went to his dresser and lifted up a stack of shorts and t-shirts. He extracted a .45 caliber semiautomatic pistol. It was a colt 1911 that he had carried in Viet Nam. He examined the weapon. He withdrew the clip to make sure it was full. He drew back the receiver enough to see that there was a round in the chamber. In his sock drawer he pulled out a box of cartridges. He took a dozen of them from the box and put them in his coat pocket. Andy stuck the gun in his belt and returned to the shop. He had forgotten to put the upstairs covering in place. He went up to do that. He asked himself, 'was the intruder sloppy and careless or was he in too much of a hurry to put things back the way he found them'? A third possibility occurred to him. 'Maybe this was all done deliberately to let me know that someone has been here. If so, why?'

He was preoccupied the rest of the day with what was going on. He debated several times whether he should tell Stephanie about any of it. He considered calling the Sheriff. He knew two of the deputies personally. He had the parts for the benches cut out by the end of the day. He put the gun into his inside coat pocket. It both saddened and angered him that he felt the need to carry a gun. On the way to the house he considered putting a padlock on the shop door for the next several nights. It had stopped snowing before noon. He decided that there was not enough snow to warrant clearing the driveway. Stephanie had spent the day cleaning and working on knitting a sweater that she said was for her mother. He mixed his drink and invited her to join him and Lucy for a walk. "If you don't mind I think I'll take a pass. I know I should get some fresh air and I could use the exercise." He didn't pay attention to the rest of her excuse. It was just as well that she not be with him if there was another encounter. He deliberately took a different route. If he was being observed he wanted whoever it was to know that he was not completely predictable. During the walk he thought about all of the ways they were vulnerable and what he could do to counter any of them. He had to remind himself that, 'paranoids imagine their threats, this is not imagined'; except he didn't know what kind of threat this represented.

When he and Lucy returned from their walk he sat down in the living room where Stephanie was working. She asked, "Are you okay Andy?" He asked what she meant." I don't know; you just have a really serious expression. You get these deep frown lines on your forehead when something is bothering you."

"I'm just practicing my curmudgeonliness. I get out of practice during the off season."

He asked her when the last time that she had the oil changed in her car. She was sure it was overdue. "Why don't you take my truck

in the morning and I'll take care of getting it changed tomorrow."
After dinner they spent the evening reading. As they often did, they
would interrupt the other to carry on brief discussions; then they
would resume whatever they had been doing. It felt like a normal
pleasant evening.

The next morning shortly after Stephanie left for work, Andy got
in her car following after her. He had gone about a mile when a car
pulled onto the highway from one of the side roads. It was a dark
sedan. He kept track of it in the rear view mirror. He turned onto a
side road five miles later and the car turned onto the same road. His
suspicion that Stephanie was being followed was beginning to
appear valid. He made another turn and so did the car behind him.
The road he was on now intersected another highway a few miles
north. He remembered that there was a branch office of a bank on the
corner of that intersection. He decided that he would pull into the
bank and drive up to the night deposit. The bank wouldn't be open
for another hour. He set the pistol on the seat next to him. The sedan
kept a constant distance behind him. He could not identify its make.
To him they all looked alike. As planned, he turned into the bank. The
car that had been following him went by the entrance and came to a
stop at the intersection. He hit the accelerator and made a tight U-
turn. He drove out the exit. The car had made a right turn at the intersection and was headed north. Andy was driving well over the speed
limit in pursuit of the sedan. He soon came up behind it. He closed
the distance enough that he was able to get the car's license number.
Then he slowed putting some distance between the two cars. The car
pulled into the parking lot of a restaurant that was closed for the season. He slowed even more to see the car turn around in the parking
lot. After he passed the restaurant, the driver exited onto the highway
and headed south away from him. He was undecided about what to
do. He pulled into a service station that he did frequent business at.
He got out of the car and went inside. "Dave, I know it's early. Can
you do an oil change? I should have called ahead."

"Sure, pull into the first bay."

As Andy was about to get back into the car he saw the dark sedan
go by. Knowing that it would seem strange to take off in pursuit, he
pulled up to the bay door that was being opened. It took fifteen minutes to complete the oil and filter change. When he left the station he
drove to the clinic. He took Stephanie's car keys in and left them with
the receptionist. He got into his truck and drove back home. There
was no sign of the sedan. When he got home he let Lucy out of the
house and they went to the workshop. He called one of the deputies
he knew. "Marty, this is Andy McLeod." After a brief exchange he

stated his reason for calling. "Marty, I have reason to believe Stephanie is being followed. I'm wondering if it would be possible for you to run a check on a license plate number for me." Marty wanted more details. Andy told him what he had done this morning in order to come up with the number. "Yeah, we can run a check, but this sounds like a police matter. If I come up with a specific name, department regs prevent me from giving you that info. You'll have to file a complaint and then it will be up to us after that." Andy reluctantly agreed.

He looked around the shop and the upstairs again to make sure no one had made a repeat visit. He went to the house and walked around it looking to see if there were any footprints. He was becoming angrier about the situation. He devised another plan for the next day. He would follow Stephanie at some distance to see if she was being followed. He decided to try to get a hold of Rob to see if they could exchange vehicles. Whoever was following Stephanie would most likely know his truck. If Stephanie wanted to know why he had Rob's car, he would tell her that Rob asked to borrow his truck to haul some stuff; a perfectly plausible explanation.

Marty called later that morning to report that the car was a rental. "I'll contact the rental agency to find out who they leased it to, but like I said before, I can't share that information with you. Besides, nine times out of ten when some nefarious person rents a vehicle, they use an alias. What do you want me to do?"

Andy thought about it. "What's the name of the rental agency?"

Marty laughed, "Nice try, Andy." He asked, "How sure are you that she's being followed? It could just be a matter of coincidence." Andy decided to give him more details of what was happening. "That casts a different light on the matter. What do you think is going on?"

"I haven't got the slightest idea Marty. It pisses me. I don't know if she's in some kind of danger. I've been around and around with myself about it. I've gone from thinking it might be some nut-case patient from the clinic, to an ex-boyfriend. A person can drive themselves bonkers speculating."

Marty agreed. "Tell you what, with your permission I'd like to run this by the Sheriff and one of our detectives. In some ways this sounds professional. By that I mean it doesn't sound like something one of our local Neanderthals would do."

"Let me think about it, Marty. I purposely haven't said anything to Steph about what's been happening. I don't want to scare her. I don't think I'm suffering from an overly active imagination."

"I don't either. It may be something simple but it could be more serious. Let's take a proactive approach. Let me talk to the Sheriff and our detective. I won't mention names. If you decide to ask us to become involved, they will have a heads up. If they think this warrants more urgent attention, I'll get back to you."

Andy agreed to that proposal. He felt a slight degree of relief after hanging up. It took him almost two hours to sand all of the bench parts. While he was working he came up with the idea to call around to some of the car rental agencies. He started with the three that had booths at the Green Bay airport. The second one he called had a charcoal gray Chevrolet Malibu with the plate number he gave them. It was being leased by a pharmaceutical company from Chicago and had been signed out four days ago to a Mr. Frank Jones. This information raised several questions, the biggest one being, 'why would a large pharmaceutical company be chasing after some little nurse in Podunk, USA and why in such a clandestine way'?

It was getting close to the noon hour. Andy and Lucy got in the truck. He drove to the job site where Rob was working. It was a large condominium complex adjacent to a golf course. Rob was on his lunch break when Andy found him. He was surprised to see Andy. Three of Rob's coworkers were present. Rob offered to show Andy around. They climbed three flights of stairs to the top floor. From there one could look out over a large portion of the golf course and could even see the Bay of Green Bay in the distance. "What's up?" Rob asked.

Andy asked about switching vehicles for a day. Rob was willing, but curious about why. "This is just between you and me." Rob agreed. "I have reason to believe that Steph is being followed. Whoever is doing it knows my truck. I need an unfamiliar vehicle to see if I can find out who it is."

"I don't know, Andy. I mean yeah, sure you can use my car, but this sounds like something for the cops. What are you going to do if you do find out who is doing this?"

"I don't know. I'll cross that bridge when I come to it."

They went to where Rob's car was parked. "This thing not only looks like a wreck, but it has several idiosyncrasies you need to know about." Rob showed him how the ignition key had to be jiggled in order to find just the right position to turn the engine on. The passenger side door could not be opened from the outside. The switch for the heater fan didn't work. Rob had replaced it with a toggle switch. The fan ran at high speed only. The windshield wiper arm on the passenger side was stripped. Thus it only had the driver's side wiper. "There's more, but since you won't be driving it at night, I won't go into those things. The wiring is kind of fucked up." He smiled apologetically.

Andy had to do some major coaxing to get Lucy to get into the car. The muffler had holes in it. She trembled all the way home and leapt over Andy to get out when he opened the door. Rob had a folded towel on the driver's side seat. Andy lifted it to see exposed springs. He found an old throw rug which he folded and placed over the towel. It took some doing but he was finally able to figure out how to open the trunk. He found the wiper arm for the passenger side. It was missing the blade. He fit the arm over the stripped post, got his drill and bored a hole through the arm into the post. He attached the arm with a sheet metal screw. He fit a spare blade for his truck into the arm and tested it. Then he called the hardware store in town, asking if they had a twelve-volt rheostat switch. The store owner checked and called Andy back a few minutes later to report that they did. Andy went to get it. Back home he replaced the toggle switch on the heater fan. The fan speed could now be regulated. He chuckled to himself that Rob wouldn't know what to do with his car when he got it back.

He called the lady who had ordered the benches. The check she had promised to send him had not yet arrived. She apologized, saying that it had slipped her mind. She would get it in the mail today. By walk time the sun had come out which helped to raise his spirits. He carried the pistol tucked into his belt under his coat. He and Lucy walked toward the woods as they had when they had spotted the trespasser. He kept scanning the woods and at the same time he kept an eye out for human footprints. There was no sign of an intruder. There were several sets of deer tracks and what he supposed were fox.

When they finished their walk he put Lucy in the house. He got in Rob's car and drove to the clinic which closed in ten minutes. He scanned the lot for any sign of a dark gray Malibu; then he parked so that he could see Stephanie's car. Fifteen minutes later she emerged from the clinic, accompanied by two of her coworkers. She got into her car and started out of the lot. He followed her. It was nearly dark. Instead of heading straight for home she drove to a mall. She got out of her car and went into a bookstore. Minutes later she came out of that store and strode over to the pharmacy. Ten minutes later she came out of the pharmacy and returned to her car. He again followed her at a distance. A part of him kept hoping to spot the Malibu. As they neared the farm, he dropped back even further not wanting to appear to be right on her heels. He drove by the driveway entrance. He saw the taillights from her car going up the driveway as he went by. He turned around at the next intersection and drove back. He remembered that he had forgotten to retrieve the mail from the box at the end of the driveway. He stopped, got out of the car and opened the box. It was empty. Getting the mail had been Andy's exclusive task. He drove up the driveway and parked next to her car. Lucy came running up to him as soon as he was out of the car. Stephanie must have let Lucy out.

When he entered the house she immediately asked where he had been. She was surprised to come home to an empty house. He smiled and said, "It wasn't empty, Luce was here."

Stephanie looked at him and said, "No, she wasn't. Didn't she go with you?" He experienced an immediate sick feeling which he tried to hide. Stephanie saw the change of expression and asked what was wrong.

"Oh, I'm just pissed with myself. I must have forgotten to put her in the house before I left." He knew that was not the case. Someone had been here in his absence. "Rob asked to borrow my truck. I ran it over to his place. I've got his car." If she thought it strange that Rob hadn't stopped by to pick it up on his way home from work, she didn't say anything.

"I'm sure that Luce was okay being out for such a short time." Stephanie turned to the dog, "You've got to stop chasing after those bunnies and squirrels and stay with Papa." She thanked him for getting her oil changed. "I was surprised that you dropped my car off at the clinic. I figured you would just keep it for the day."

"I had to run up to the lumber company. I was in the neighborhood." Something else occurred to him. "I'll be back in a few minutes. I forgot something out in the shop."

He grabbed a flashlight before leaving the house. He looked around the outside of the house for footprints in the snow. He found two or three that didn't match the prints from his work boots. Whoever had been here had made a deliberate effort to try to walk in his tracks. He found a steady trail of them that were on top of his tracks when he got away from the house and started towards the shop. He unbuttoned his coat and pulled the pistol from his belt. He entered the shop and turned on the fluorescent lights. He looked around the shop. There was some snow on the floor close to his workbench. There sitting on the bench was a stack of mail. He went to it and shuffled through several envelopes, a couple of fliers, a magazine and a catalog. He could not know if anything was missing. He viewed this discovery as a blatant message. "Gotcha Asshole. I'm the cat and you're the mouse. I'm messin' with your head, and there isn't a thing you can do about it." He hadn't felt this vulnerable and helpless since Viet Nam. 'I want this bastard's ass'. He took up the mail, stuck the gun in the inside pocket of his coat, turned out the lights and walked back to the house. Inside he put the mail on the dining room table.

Stephanie had a glass of wine. She saw the stack of mail. She looked at him, "where was the mail?" He said that he must have forgotten about getting it this afternoon. It was in the shop. "Andy, what's going on with you? You not only left here without Luce and left her outside, but you forgot that you had gotten the mail." He said nothing. "I'm serious, this isn't like you." She asked him several questions about symptoms. She had him perform some motor tasks. She had him move his hands against applied resistance. He asked her what she was looking for. At first she ignored his question. After she asked a few more questions she said, "Signs of a stroke." She frowned seriously. "You seem okay. I'm almost inclined to take you to the ER and have them do some testing. If you had a minor stroke you might be on the brink of something more serious."

"Steph, I'm okay, really I am. I just had a couple of brain farts today. I need to tighten up my act. I do dumb things like this occasionally. I've had a couple of bad nights." He was lying to her, but in a sense he wasn't. As they stood facing one another, he wondered if the enemy was out there watching what was going on right now, gloating over his psychological victory. She relaxed somewhat.

She talked about bringing home some sample muscle relaxants, "they can help you to get a good night's sleep. You know as well as anybody that stress and fatigue can cause you to become less efficient."

'The last thing I need right now is to take anything that's going to cause me to lose my edge', he thought to himself. 'I need to be on guard. This is war'. He wanted to tell her the truth about what was going on. 'Maybe I should. She might be able to shed some light on what's happening'. Before they went to bed he searched for and found the key to the deadbolt lock on the front door. He had never locked the house in all the time he had lived here. Stephanie offered to massage his back. "It might help you to relax."

He declined. She ignored him and proceeded to massage his back anyway. She had him turn over. She reached down and made him hard. She got on top of him and brought him to a climax. The relief was temporary. He still didn't sleep well that night.

Chapter 5

While Stephanie was getting herself ready for work the next morning, Andy slipped out of the house and went to his workshop. He used a broom to sweep away all the footprints that led to the shop. If anyone tried to usurp the premises they would have to make fresh tracks. He decided that he needed to do this each day until this stopped. He wondered if it would cease after Stephanie left for Florida. They had a quick breakfast together. He went out with her, ostensibly to help her scrape frost off her car's windows. It wasn't out of character for him to do that. He had surreptitiously locked the house door behind him.

As soon as he saw her brake light at the end of the driveway he got into Rob's car. He had trouble getting the key to work but moments later he found the right spot that allowed it to turn. A few miles down the road he spotted her car up ahead. He slowed down to allow plenty of room between them. As Stephanie passed a side road, he saw the headlights of a vehicle approaching the intersection. He slowed down enough to give that car time to pull out onto the main highway. He sped up again to close the distance. The vehicle turned out to be a minivan. He fell back again. No other cars appeared from side roads or driveways the rest of the trip to the clinic. He slowed down even more when he neared the clinic. As he pulled into the clinic's parking area he saw Stephanie entering the front entrance. He was about to pull into a parking space, with the intention of backing out to leave the parking area. Headlights came on near the main entrance and the car started toward the entrance/exit. Andy stopped to allow the car to move past him. It moved slowly. When it was just about along side him he could see that it was a dark colored Malibu. It stopped directly next to him. The driver's window was down. Suddenly a flashlight came on and the driver directed its powerful beam in Andy's eyes. Andy couldn't make out a thing. The driver stomped down on the accelerator and the Malibu leapt forward. Its driver made no effort to stop at the entrance, but squealed onto the highway. Andy quickly pulled into a parking space, backed out and tried to pursue the Malibu. He pushed Rob's battered old car as hard as he could. It performed amazingly well for what it was but he was unable to catch up to the Malibu.

He felt defeated once again. Whoever this was, the person seemed to always be one or more steps ahead of Andy. He was almost certain that Stephanie didn't have the slightest inkling about what was happening. A couple of miles down the road Andy pulled into a grocery store parking lot. It was light enough now that he no longer needed to have the headlights on. He sat in the car trying to sort things out. It was pretty obvious to him that his opponent was able to gather a host of information about him and Stephanie. He seemed to know their whereabouts at all times. Furthermore, he seemed amazingly familiar with the territory. He was able to make his way around with impunity. Did that mean he was local? Andy regarded him as a 'brazen and arrogant son-of-a-bitch'. It was almost like this guy had inside information except there was no insider. It was then that another possibility occurred to him. What if surveillance devices have been being planted? If they were, they wouldn't have supplied this much information, would they? A seemingly unrelated thought sprung up. Andy remembered something about how the American Indians often defeated an enemy by taking coup. They would humiliate an enemy by touching them during combat, thus destroying the enemy's confidence and sense of pride. 'This bastard's walking all over my head' he thought. Is that what this is all about? Was someone out to undermine his hard-won confidence? The only person he could think of who might bear him that much malice, was his ex-girlfriend. To his knowledge she had gone back to Illinois to live with her daughter. He didn't see her as having the resources to carry on a campaign such as this. He put the car in gear and left the parking lot. For some reason he decided to take the long way home. Andy was just on the edge of a small village that bustled with tourists during the summer. This time of the year it was almost a ghost town. He slowed down to the thirty mile per hour speed limit. As he was approaching the north edge of the village he just happened to glance over at a motel. There was one car in the parking lot. It was a charcoal gray Chevy Malibu. Andy braked and turned into the motel's far entrance. He turned Rob's car around so that it was facing toward the entrance he had come into. He got out of the car and strolled almost casually toward the Malibu. The license plate number was the same as the one he had gotten the day before. He could hear the tinkling sound of metal contracting, coming from under the Malibu's hood. He looked around before pulling out his pocket knife. He went around to all four tires forcing the sharp knife into their sidewalls. Then he went to the driver's side door and scratched a large Z into the paint.

'There asshole, I've taken coup. Gotcha'. Andy strode back to Rob's car, got in and drove off. He drove to the condominium construction site to return Rob's car and retrieve his truck. As he drove, his moment of triumph began to fade. Had he just raised the stakes? It was more than likely that what he had just done would serve to only escalate the situation to a point of possible violence? 'I've inconvenienced the asshole by my act of vandalism but it isn't going to cost him anything other than to prick his over-inflated ego. Insurance will take care of the damages'. When Andy arrived at the condominium work site, he didn't bother to locate Rob. He left a note on the front seat thanking Rob for the use of the car. He got in his truck and made straightway for home. In the event the guy would soon discover what had happened, he'd probably call the cops. Andy wanted to be hard at work in his workshop if a deputy arrived.

At home Andy let Lucy out and they went straight to the shop. He got a fire going. His plan for the day was to finish up the six benches that he and Corey had started. He was startled out of deep concentration an hour later when the phone rang. It was the sister of the lady who had ordered the benches. She wanted to know if she could come to pick the benches up tomorrow or the next day. She said that she would write him a check herself and her sister would pay her back later. He told her that he preferred the day after tomorrow and he gave her directions to his place.

Awhile later his deputy friend Marty called. "Hey Andy, guess what. We just got a call that a Chevy Malibu was vandalized in a motel parking lot this morning. It happened in broad daylight. The perpetrator slashed all four tires and scratched a big 'Z' into one of the doors. I assume the Z stands for Zorro. What's happening to our peaceful little paradise?"

"I don't know. What a shame," Andy replied. "It's almost enough to make me want to relocate. In broad daylight you say and there weren't any witnesses?"

"Not a one. Man I sure hope the victim isn't the vindictive type who's going to go looking for revenge."

"Me too," Andy said. "Some people are mean spirited. All they can think about is getting even." Marty laughed. "Yeah, I know. We have a few of those types running around up here."

Before hanging up Andy asked Marty to stop by if he was in the neighborhood. "I've got a couple of questions I'd like to ask."

An hour later Marty pulled into the driveway. Andy went out to meet him. "I'd invite you in but I have the feeling there are some ears, and maybe even some eyes in my walls." He told Marty about the most recent incidents.

Marty said, "I'm no expert on bugs, but I know a little bit. Let's go check your phones. In the house Marty unplugged the phone. He found a small disc about half the size of a dime in the phone's receiver. He left it in place. They found the same thing in the shop phone. Outside Marty said, "I think it's time you stop messing around, Andy. Bugs, all by themselves are illegal. Coupled with everything else that's been happening, I think the time has come. Who knows what other kinds of devices have been planted in your house, your vehicles and maybe even in your workshop? Our department doesn't have anyone knowledgeable about this stuff. The Sheriff will probably want to contact the State Criminal Investigation agency to see if they can be of help. I'm concerned about both of you and your safety. You've tipped your hand. Whoever's doing this knows that you're on to him and that you're not going to passively take it lying down. He might back off but I'm more inclined to think he may decide to come at you."

"I agree," Andy said. "I've done a lot of thinking about what's happening. I'm pretty decided that Stephanie is the intended target. As far as I know he hasn't done anything to threaten her but she's been acting out of sorts just in the last week or so. When I've asked her about what has been bothering her; she puts it off on her work or a visit she has planned to see her mother in Florida."

Marty agreed that it sounded like she was the target. Andy weighed saying anything more. "I'm sure there are some people out there who don't care much for me. I doubt that anyone dislikes me enough go to the kind of effort that this guy is exerting. I found out on my own that the car is being leased to a pharmaceutical company or someone from that company. Steph has been a nurse for a long time. I might be grabbing at the wrong straw but maybe she knows something that this company doesn't want anybody else to know about."

Andy had Marty's full attention. "So why don't they just snatch her and get whatever it is? Why are they messing with you?"

"Maybe I'm her Achilles heel. She might not cooperate with them or bow to their exhortations. She can be a tough nut. But she might if she knows that I'm at risk. In essence I might be kind of like a hostage."

"I take it you haven't said anything to her about what's going on."

"I haven't said a word to her about any of this. For now I want to keep it that way."

"How certain are you that she's unaware of the situation?"

"As I mentioned before, she's been acting a little different of late. I don't get the feeling that she's covering something up. If she is, she's a hell of a good actress."

"Have you got a gun?" Andy told him what he had. "I would keep it handy." He opened his coat to reveal it. "Good man. I'm going to ask the sheriff if we can arrange for an unmarked car to follow her to and from work for a couple of days. Weekends are up to you." Before leaving, he gestured to both the house and the barn. "Be careful with what you say. I would extend that to your vehicles too."

He got in his squad car and after some back and forth on the radio he said, "Detective Janet Miller will be getting in touch with you; maybe even today. Don't judge her by her appearance; she's a hell-of-a-detective."

Andy smiled. "What do you mean by that?"

"You'll see." His window slid shut. He backed up, turned around and left.

Andy went back to his shop. He spent over an hour rigging up two booby-traps just inside the shop's entrance. The first involved a box that contained blue chalk dust, the kind that carpenters use in snap lines. Because it is so fine, it clings to surfaces and is not easily removed. He rigged up a narrow shelf over the shop's entrance door. He ran string through some eye screws to connect to the door. He tested it several times to perfect it before adding the chalk. He was convinced that an intruder would be unable to avoid a dusting. The other trap involved a hinged two-by-four that would swing down. It had nails protruding two inches. They were intended to inflict injury much like the pungee stick traps used by the Viet Cong guerillas. A thin wire strung shin high triggered it. All the while he was working he was also searching for listening devices and/or miniature video cameras.

It was almost walk time when the phone rang. A woman's voice asked if she could speak with Andrew McLeod. She introduced herself as Janet Miller. A friend of hers had referred him to her. She wondered if she could arrange to see him tomorrow to discuss a project. They made an appointment for nine o'clock.

Andy set the traps before leaving the shop. He put a flimsy padlock on the door knowing that, if someone wanted to get into the shop badly enough they could easily get past the lock. He and Lucy set out for their walk. He had his gun in his coat pocket. He chose to walk along the edge of the woods rather than walking across the open meadow fully exposed. He was tense, keeping an eye on the dog in the event she picked up on anything. He thought 'what a hell-of-a-way to have to live. I'm going to end up with an ulcer if this goes on much longer'. He was looking forward to meeting Detective Miller tomorrow. He thought about driving to the clinic to surreptitiously escort Stephanie home again. He would take Lucy with him this time. She and Stephanie were his Achilles heel. He vowed that he would seek unmerciful vengeance if anything happened to either of them

When they finished their walk he tended the stoves. He had about twenty minutes before he needed to leave. He stood at the dining room window looking out on a spectacular late fall sunset. The sky was shifting from a brilliant vermillion to a vivid pink. During the six months of the year that there were leaves on the trees, it was almost impossible to view the setting sun. The forest that stood between the house and the road was too dense. The room was growing dark. He checked his watch, went to the dimmer switch and turned on the overhead light. He looked up at the light to adjust its brightness. That's when he noticed something attached to the fixture. He got a chair and set it beneath the light. On the fixture he saw a small device attached to the edge of the glass with a piece of tape. He checked all of the downstairs rooms. There was one in every room except the living room. Rather than remove them, he decided that Detective Miller needed to see them first. He looked at his watch again. He called Lucy and they left the house hurriedly. He almost forgot to lock the door as useless an effort as that was. As he drove he tried to think of a plausible explanation for locking the door. He decided that he would tell her that he only did this during the holiday season to prevent someone from stealing the Christmas presents. Never mind the fact that there weren't any presents or even a Christmas tree as yet.

He arrived at the clinic about two minutes before closing time. He parked toward the back of the lot. He had forgotten that today was Friday and the clinic was supposed to be open for another hour. He didn't recall Stephanie telling him if she would be working late this evening. She came out of the clinic on time. She was by herself and went straight to her car. As soon as she backed out of her space and began moving toward the exit he started his engine. It was dark. He decided to follow her at a closer distance. After she had gone a mile she turned on to the crossroad that she normally took to get to the highway that brought her home. After turning onto the main highway she went about a mile when her brake lights shown and she slowed. There was a vehicle ahead of her that was moving well below the speed limit. They were in a curvy no-passing area. When they got to a straight area where she could pass, she put on her directional signal and accelerated to pass. She was almost alongside the slow moving vehicle when its driver accelerated, preventing her from passing. Both of them kept gaining speed. "Slow down Steph. Get behind the bastard," Andy yelled, as if he could be heard. He had his pedal to the floor but his old truck was not able to close the distance. Suddenly the car she was trying to pass began moving to the left forcing her off the road. She slammed on her brakes and the other car veered actually banging the right front of her car. She fought to keep from losing control. The other car continued to accelerate. It soon disappeared into another curved section. Andy wanted to pursue the car, but his primary concern was Stephanie. He was sure she was shaken by what had just occurred. She drove the last four miles under the speed limit. He formulated a plan in the event they came up on the car again. 'I'll pass her and ram the son-of-a-bitch. I'm done fucking around. He could have killed her'.

When she turned into their driveway he followed her, aware that his doing so would probably add to her fear. She parked and he pulled up along side her. He got out of the truck and quickly went to her car. ""Oh god, Andy, I just had the scariest thing happen to me."

"I know I was right behind you. I saw what happened." He helped her out of the car.

"It's like that maniac was trying to kill me." He held her for several moments.

"I'm going to put Lucy in the house. Get in the truck. We're going down to the Pub."

"I have to pee."

"Okay, go pee. Then let's go."

"What's going on, Andy? You look serious."

"We need to talk and we can't do it here. I'll explain it to you."

They both went in the house. He fed Lucy. She seemed not to notice him unlock the door going in but she commented when he locked it going out."

In the truck she started to say something. He put a finger to his lips and shook his head. The Pub's real name was 'A Bit-o-Blarney'. The locals just called it the Pub. It was still early enough that it wasn't packed with the usual Friday night crowd. He steered them to a table in the back of the restaurant/bar. A waitress that they both knew didn't even bother to ask. She brought Stephanie her usual glass of wine and Andy a dark beer in an unfrosted mug. 'We'll hold off ordering for awhile Becky," Andy told her. He took Stephanie's hand and began telling her about all that had been happening over the past several days. He included his act of vandalism that morning. He told her that the house and the phones were bugged. "Our vehicles and the shop may be as well." He told her about following her in Rob's car the night before and that the reason he was right behind her when she came home tonight was that he had tried to escort her home from the clinic. He told her that he had been carrying a gun for the past three days. He purposely left out his knowledge about the rental car and who it had been charged to. He wanted to see what her reaction was before he divulged that information. When he finished telling her about everything that had happened, he asked, "Steph, do you know what this is about?"

She looked down. When she looked up she seemed to be scanning the dining room. She appeared to be weighing her response. He finished his beer. The waitress came by and asked if they were ready to order yet. "Give us another round of these Becky."

"Boy, you two must have had a rough week." She laughed and took their empty glasses.

When she was gone Stephanie reached across the table and took his hands. She was still avoiding eye contact. "Andy, I don't know what to tell you. I'm not sure I know what this is all about. If it's what I suspect, you are better off not knowing. You're going to have to trust me. I'll take care of it. I have the means to do that. I hoped that when I came here, I would be able to escape the past; apparently not."

"What are you going to do, Steph? How can you take care of this, whatever the hell THIS is?"

The waitress returned with their drinks and asked if they were ready to order yet. He turned to her and asked, "What time do you get off tonight?" She wanted to know why he was asking.

"We may need a designated driver."

"Jeez you guys, did something terrible happen or somethin'?"

"Sweetheart, you'll never know." When she returned she told them to just holler when they were ready for anything else.

"Can't you at least give me a clue as to what's going on here?" Stephanie was silent. "Look Steph, I got the license number from the car. It's a rental, charged to a large pharmaceutical company in Chicago. Don't leave me to speculate about what that means."

"Don't waste your time going down that road, Andy. It hasn't got a thing to do with what's going on. It's not the company. The company hasn't got anything to do with it. It's a person. That's all I'm going to say. Don't ask me any more questions. The subject is closed. Maybe someday I can tell you, but not now. You are simply going to have to trust me. The less you know the better."

He asked if their lives were in danger. "No, I don't think so. As a matter of fact, I think the person involved probably figures he's made his point. I suspect it's all over."

"You know who this person is." His statement was more of a question. She nodded. "What do you know? Why is this happening? What makes you think this is 'over'?" She looked down and shook her head but did not respond to his questions.

"So, what happens now? Where do we go from here?"

She continued to look down. "We don't go anywhere." She muttered almost inaudibly, "I'll take care of it."

After a long silence Andy reached across the table to take her hand again. "I'm not very good at doing nothing Steph. I want to kick somebody's ass. I feel like both of us have been violated. I feel very much the way I felt in Viet Nam. This is a goddamn guerilla war we're in. I feel just as helpless now as I did then." The restaurant was beginning to fill up with patrons. Becky came by their table to ask if they were ready to order yet. They both decided to just have sandwiches.

Stephanie squeezed Andy's hand. She finally looked up at him. "I'm very touched by your protectiveness Andy. I mean that. I have never felt so cherished. You're a good man."

"Yeah, well I feel like a character in some Greek tragedy. I feel like goddamn Sisyphus."

She smiled meekly. "That's the one thing about you that drives me nuts, Andy. You can't take a compliment."

When the food came neither of them were all that hungry. They ended up taking half of it home with them. As they walked to the house, Andy noticed the house was completely dark. "Steph, maybe you better go sit in the car for a few minutes." She asked what was wrong. "The house is dark. I had the dining room light on low." He pulled the forty-five out of his coat pocket and cocked it. She insisted on coming with him. He could hear Lucy barking frantically inside. At the door he turned the handle. The door opened. Since there was only one key for the lock, and he had it, he quickly deduced that the lock had been picked. He muttered, "The bastard, Lucy had better be okay." His heart was pounding so hard he could feel it. He threw the door open and charged inside with the pistol raised. "It's okay Luce." She whined and barked and scratched. The intruder had put her in the bathroom and closed the door. It was the only room in the house with a door. He moved into the dining room area.

Stephanie was two or three steps behind him. "I'm going to turn the light on," she whispered.

"No, not yet." He moved toward the bathroom door. He debated opening it. 'If the son-of-a- bitch is still in the house and Lucy goes after him, she's going to get hurt'. "Steph, try to get into the bathroom without letting Lucy out." She did. His eyes were adjusted to the dark enough that he was sure he could catch any movement. Andy went from room to room. When he was sure no one was in the house he turned the living room lamp on. He went to the stair well. Andy had a foam insulation barrier at the top of the stairs that was like the one in the barn/workshop. He saw that it was in place. He went back into the dining room, closed the outside door, and flipped on the ceiling light. "You can come out now." He placed a chair under the dining room light fixture. He got up on it to find that the listening device had been removed. The two of them checked each room. The comforter on the bed was askew. "Whoever came in here, stood on the bed to get this one," Andy reported. He unplugged the phone and took it apart as he had seen Marty do that morning. The disc was gone. "It looks like he's methodically removed all the bugs." He asked for Stephanie's opinion.

"I don't know. Maybe it's a sign that he's decided to back off."

I need to go out to the shop to check on something. He took a flashlight with him. Stephanie followed close behind. The padlock on the shop door was undisturbed. He shined the light in the window of the door. The booby traps had not been triggered. He decided to not enter the shop. They started back toward the house. "The thing that bothers me the most is that whoever is doing this comes and goes however he damn well pleases. He seems to know our every move. As pissed as I am about all that's been happening, I have to give him some credit. He's clever. He's right up there with Charlie." Stephanie asked who Charlie was? "The VC, the Viet Cong. They were wily. They always seemed to be one step ahead of us. This guy is too. However, he's got something Charlie didn't have. He's got technology. He must have spent a lot of money on this operation. Whatever he's after must be pretty damn important to him." He studied Stephanie for her response. She said nothing. "This is almost like a special forces operation." She still showed no visible reaction.

"It's not a cleverness to be admired, Andy," Stephanie said. As cold as it was, they stopped to look up. The stars seemed to shimmer. A faint display of northern lights was beginning to develop. Broad shafts of white light flashed dimly to the northeast, then to the north. She asked what was happening. He told her. "I've never seen the northern lights before. Will this go on all night?"

"Sometimes they do," He told her. "Sometimes they even display greens and purples."

Come on, let's go in the house. It's too cold to stand out here. We can watch them from the upstairs window." After tending the stoves, Andy poured a glass of Romana Sambuca a liqueur he normally saved for very special occasions. They watched the display as it developed in intensity. As it began to fade they undressed and crawled into the upstairs guest bed. They made slow, reuniting love before falling asleep in one another's arms.

Chapter 6

A little before nine the next morning, a light blue sedan came up the driveway. Andy was in his workshop. Lucy alerted him by barking. He went outside and walked toward the car. A short lady with dyed, highly teased, long platinum-blond hair got out of the car. She wore a heavy eye make up and dark red lipstick. She had on a black leather hip-length coat and chartreuse stirrup pants. She spotted Andy and started walking toward him. Lucy ran up to her and she leaned over to pet the dog. She straightened up and extended her hand. "I'm Janet Miller." He noticed a slight accent. 'South-side Chicago' he decided. She had just enough of a smile that he could see she was missing at least one of her upper right molars. After shaking hands he invited her into the workshop. Inside she looked around; then asked if they needed to go to her car to talk.

"I'm not sure. We went out for dinner last night. When we got back, we discovered that someone broke into the house while we were gone. The visitor appears to have removed most, if not all, of the surveillance stuff." Andy invited Detective Miller to follow him to his workshop. He went to the shop phone and unplugged it. He took it apart to discover the disk was still in place. "He took the one from the house, but not this one." He showed her the booby traps that he had set up two days before. "I've got to tell you detective, whoever it is, he's one clever hombre. He's always at least one step ahead of me. I'm sure he's figured out that I'm on to him. I don't know if he figured out that I set up these traps or not. For whatever reason, he didn't come in here last night."

Detective Miller reached into her huge purse and withdrew a camera. She photographed the bugged telephone. She asked if he had something she could stand on. He had an old wooden kitchen chair. She had him set it below one of the fluorescent shop lights. He helped her to get up onto it, but she was too short to see the top of the fixture. Andy got on the chair and found a small cylinder atop two of the fixtures. She had him photograph them; then place them into separate bags. They didn't find anything else.

She decided to set all three devices outside. "Do you mind if I smoke?" Andy had never been a smoker. He disliked the smell of cigarette smoke intensely. Nonetheless, he granted her permission. He found a coffee can and gave it to her to use as an ash tray. She pulled out a pack and lit a cigarette. She unbuttoned her coat. She was wearing a pink sweater that was tight enough to reveal she had ample bosoms. Now he completely understood Marty's remark about not judging her by her appearance. Her garishness reminded him of some of the schizophrenic women that used to come into the mental health clinic he worked at. They would come in every other week for an injection of a prolonged acting antipsychotic medication.

Andy and Detective Miller talked for almost two hours. Detective Miller went through several more cigarettes. She took sparse notes. Mostly she wrote down times and dates and catch-words that would serve as reminders. After gathering the sequential facts, she asked several questions that seemed aimed at identifying patterns. The most glaring consistency was that the intruder knew so much about their every movement. At one point she came right out and asked. "How much do you trust your lady friend?"

Andy reacted defensively. He sighted several things that had happened that Stephanie couldn't possibly have known about. Detective Miller stuck another cigarette in her mouth. She didn't light this one. "Okay, so am I to assume that you walk around talking to yourself, announcing all your plans and intentions for each day? That's the only way the bugs can be tipping this guy off." He didn't do that." She lit the cigarette. "You're not whacko are you? You don't look like a nut case. You're not making this entire thing up are you?" She was not smiling. He assured her that he may be what some people would regard as eccentric, but he was reasonably sane. She asked, "What makes you think it's a guy? If it is a guy, what makes you think he's operating all by himself?" He didn't know the answers to either of those questions. She came back to questioning Stephanie's veracity.

"Look, Detective, I find it impossible to believe that Stephanie is in cahoots with anyone. Not only have things happened that she couldn't have known about, but she'd have to be able to share information with an accomplice on a daily basis. When would she have the opportunity to do that? Besides, what would be the point? I mean what's in it for her. It's not like I'm a millionaire. She doesn't stand to gain a fortune from me. I'm this poor schlemiel wood carver. I barely make a living. Look at my house." He risked telling her about the way he lived. She was in a position of authority. If she reported just his non-conforming waste water system, he'd be faced with having to correct that at great expense.

Detective Miller looked at him with an undaunted expression. "Speaking of your house, let's go have a look at it." Inside she asked if he had a bathroom. He pointed to it. To his surprise she went in the bathroom, closed the door and made use of it. When she re-emerged she said, "I see what you mean. This isn't exactly five star accommodations. How the hell do you flush the toilet?" He explained that it was a self-composting toilet and how it worked. "Interesting," was her only comment. She wanted to search the downstairs for any more bugs. "They forgot this one." She plucked a device held to the dining room wood stove by an attached magnet. "We'll check your truck before I leave." She looked around the room. "Marty says you've got a weapon." He nodded. "Let me see it." He opened his coat and produced the pistol. She took out the clip and removed two of the bullets. She examined them and put them back into the clip. She expertly ejected the one from the chamber and studied that also. "When's the last time you fired this thing?"

"I don't know. Maybe two or three years ago, maybe longer," Andy told her.

"Come on, let's go outside." She led the way. A few steps out the door she spotted his stacks of firewood. She led them to a position about twenty feet from the neatly stacked cords. "Shoot at the wood pile," she pointed. He wondered what this was about. He raised the forty-five, clicked off the safety, pulled back the hammer and squeezed. Nothing happened. "Eject the round and try it again." He did it two more times. None of the bullets fired. "You'd have been better off throwing the gun at him. You got any other ammunition?" He reached into his coat pocket and produced a hand full of cartridges. "Here, I'll hold those for you. Empty the clip. When it was empty she handed him one bullet at a time as he reloaded the clip. He took aim and the pistol fired. "Jesus, I forgot how much noise a forty-five makes. Try another round." This time she covered her ears. Again it fired.

"Do you think someone tampered with the bullets that were in the gun?" he asked.

She shrugged, "Maybe. Could be the primers got oil soaked. Who knows? The point is; if you're going to keep a gun around, you need to shoot it from time to time, not once every two or three years. I'll take the bullets that were in the gun and have one of our guys check them over. Maybe they were tampered with."

They went back inside so she could retrieve her purse. He walked with her to her car. "So where do we go from here?"

She handed him her card. "Your lady seems to think it's over with. I hope so for your sake. We'll see. If anything else happens, let me know. I'm going to send the stuff we've collected to the crime lab in Madison. With the holidays almost upon us, I don't expect quick results. When did you say your lady is leaving for Florida?" He reminded her that it wasn't for another three weeks. "I'll arrange to have a squad escort her to and from work for the next few days. Let's see what happens." He thanked her. Before she got in her car she said, "I have to agree with Marty, whoever's involved knows what they're doing. There are some things about this that don't add up. This one's going to be a challenge." She pulled out another cigarette and lit it before starting the engine. She rolled down her window. "I forgot we were going to check your truck for bugs." They went through the truck's cab together. She told him what to be looking for. He said that he would go over Stephanie's car when she got home.

The phone was ringing when Andy returned to his workshop. It was the lady who had called him before about picking up the benches for her sister. Andy had forgotten all about it with all that had been going on. The lady apologized profusely for not having come to get the benches as promised. She said that she would like to come and pick them up on Monday, probably late in the morning. Andy made a note of it and put the note on his workbench. The fact is, he didn't have all of the benches completely finished. He was relieved that things had worked out that way.

When Stephanie got home that evening she asked, "So, how was your meeting with Detective Miller this morning?" He started by describing her physical appearance. "What do you think of her? From what you describe, she sounds kind of weird."

"There is no question that she is weird from an appearance standpoint," Andy said. "But the more we talked, the more I was impressed that she knows what she's doing." He chose not to try to substantiate his opinion with specific examples. He was ashamed to admit that he was beginning to have some doubts about Stephanie. Detective Janet Miller had not planted seeds of doubt. They were already there. However, she had certainly helped some of them to germinate. He hoped they would fail to grow. For now he would wait to see what happened next. He wanted to know the truth, whatever that proved to be. They spent a quiet evening. Stephanie worked on her knitting, Andy tried to read, and the flies rebounded off the lamp shades.

The next day was Saturday. As usual Stephanie went grocery shopping and did whatever other errands she needed to do. She arrived home early that afternoon. He helped her unload groceries. She told him to go back to the workshop. "I've got a couple of things to unload that I don't want you to see." She came out to the workshop awhile later and sat down on a stool. She seemed to be in a more pleasant mood than she had been over the past two weeks. They chatted amiably for awhile. To Andy's surprise she suggested that they take a walk even though it wasn't the time that he and Lucy usually went for one.

Stephanie suggested heading out across the meadow and going up through the woods. She took his arm as they walked. "Last night was perfect Andy. Between the light display and our lovemaking, it served to lessen the trauma of what happened earlier in the evening." He agreed. This felt like the way things had been before but he maintained a cautious skepticism. She changed the subject by asking if Brian was coming up for sure to spend Christmas.

"He'll be here unless we get socked with a blizzard. I invited him to bring his girlfriend and her daughter. From what he's told me, he seems to really like that little girl. She sounds like a sweetheart." From there the discussion changed to the subject of children.

Stephanie reiterated what she had said before, with a slight twist. "I know I've said this before. I'm glad now that I didn't have any kids. The other side of it is; I think things may have turned out a lot differently for me if I'd had a couple of kids."

He looked at her. "Are you ever going to tell me what happened to bring this all about?"

"Andy, look; let's try to get past this. I know we can't pretend that it hasn't happened, but let's try not to let it ruin our lives. I'm almost positive that it's over with, and we won't be bothered any more."

"Steph, if the shoe was on the other foot, could you do what you're asking me to do?" She did not respond. "I'm sorry, but I'm angry. Our lives have been turned upside down. I feel like we're in real jeopardy; especially after what happened last night on your way home. I think it would be stupid of me to let my guard down in light of all that has happened. I'm at a point right now that if I encounter the bastard, I'll shoot first and ask questions later." She remained silent. "Steph, my kids and you are the most precious people in my life. I'll include Lucy. I'll hunt down anyone who threatens any of your lives. That's a promise."

"I understand what you're saying. I understand why you feel the way you do." She gave a slight smile. "Lucy is now a person?" She continued, "Look, I understand that it's going to take some time for you to trust that this is behind us; that it's over with. In the meantime, go ahead and carry your gun, look over your shoulder. All I'm asking is that we don't let this completely ruin our lives." They walked in silence for awhile. She finally squeezed his arm. "What are the chances of seeing the Aurora Borealis again tonight?"

He looked up at the sky. "See those high, thin clouds that are moving in," he pointed upward. "They usually precede a change in weather. There's a slim chance of seeing the Aurora tonight but they might pass on over." It somehow seemed analogous to what was happening in their lives. At least he hoped so.

Around two in the morning he awoke to the sound of strong, gusting winds. He got up to tend the stoves and pee. Back in bed he heard what sounded like the crack of a rifle. It was not close by but he got up and got his pistol nonetheless. He lay awake for the next two hours. He thought back to Viet Nam. He remembered the fatigue, the oppressive heat and the never being dry, never being able to relax his guard. He remembered how those things had combined to erode everyone's ability to cope and make rational judgments. It wasn't just the stress of combat and being in constant, imminent danger. It was the place. Even if there had not been a war going on there, Viet Nam was a different world. Most of the men who served in Viet Nam were truly strangers in a strange land. They were ill-suited aliens. Andy never made a secret of his primary reason for choosing to come here, to this place. He had come here to escape from having to witness constant human suffering. He had come here to escape from the stress that often triggered memories. This was a haven as well as a sanctuary. He was able to experience a sense of peace and safety being here. He rolled to his right side and reached over the side of the bed to touch Lucy. He stroked her a few times. She gave his hand a lick.

When they got up in the morning there were wind driven flurries. There was additional snow on the ground. He fixed a breakfast of sausages and eggs with hash browns. Stephanie asked why he was going to so much effort for breakfast. "We never have time for a big breakfast during the week. I was just in the mood for something special."

By eight-thirty the flurries had turned into a blizzard. Later in the morning she came out to the workshop and watched him assembling the last of some step-stools he had designed. "You keep coming up with all these new ideas Andy. Where do they come from?"

"Three o'clock in the morning." He smiled, "I wish they'd pick a more convenient time." They talked about her upcoming trip, about Brian bringing his girl friend for Christmas. They avoided discussing the events of the past several days, not out of denial, but because they had reached an impasse. There was nothing more to say for the time being. It was now a matter of waiting to see whether it was over or not. It seemed to Andy that there was an undercurrent of weary sadness about Stephanie that he had not seen before. He wondered if this secret she kept was like some kind of cancer that had lain dormant and was active again. It seemed to be draining the joy out of her.

When it was this cold and windy, he had to feed the stove frequently. The barn was not insulated, except for one inch Styrofoam panels that he had lined the insides of the walls with. The wind dissipated the heat quickly. "I'm just wasting firewood trying to heat this place on a day like today. I'm going to pack it in for today." They left the shop and trudged across the yard to the house. Inside he said, "I think we're going to forego taking our usual walk. This is miserable. I'll get plenty of exercise clearing the driveway once the storm passes." He sat down to read. She took up her knitting project. After awhile he nodded off. She awakened him. "Andy, let's go lie down and take a nap. I think we're both exhausted."

When they awoke it was almost dark. The wind was still strong, but it had diminished from a scream to a moan. He turned on the outside light. The snow had almost stopped entirely. He decided to go out and begin blowing snow. She bundled up and went out with him to shovel a path to the cars and to the wood shed. It had snowed about eight inches but there were two foot drifts in places. Other areas were completely bare. It took nearly two hours to clear the entire driveway. He knew that by morning he would need to redo parts of it again because of drifting. The passing snowplows would surely bury the end of the driveway.

They ate some of Andy's homemade chili for supper. "You know I planted all those trees on the south side of the driveway with the hopes that they would someday serve as a wind break. I didn't realize that it would take so long for them to take hold and start growing." She asked when he started planting. "I started the first year I moved here. I planted a thousand to fifteen hundred trees each year, for eight years. Those were the first ones I planted. They're just now starting to shoot up."

"So that means you've planted close to ten thousand trees over the years."

"Twelve thousand," he told her. "I haven't decided whether to plant anymore or not." He laughed. "One year I went to see the state forester about putting in walnuts and oaks. He asked me why on earth I would plant those species here. I couldn't believe a forester was asking such a question. He explained that they were slow growing and I wouldn't see them mature in my life time. "I told him that I regarded that as a short sighted point of view. I went on to say that I saw myself as being a steward of my little piece of the planet." He apologized and explained that his reason for not recommending those species was the soil conditions. He was right about that. It's mostly limestone bedrock up here. They have a tough time putting down tap roots. Amazingly though, most of the trees I planted that year have made it. It's taking them forever but they're getting there."

"You know Andy, whenever I look back to when I first knew you, I never would have guessed any of this about you. I always thought you liked what you were doing. It was no secret that the director of the agency was grooming you to become his eventual successor. I was almost shocked to learn that you had just up and quit and run off to 'do your own thing'. What happened that caused you to make such a dramatic change in your life?"

"My glib answer is 'attrition'. I just got worn out." He pondered what to say. "I remember looking around me and seeing a lot of my colleagues coming to work each day and putting in their time. I don't know if they just didn't give a damn anymore, or if it was their way of not letting the daily tragedies and frustrations grind them down any further. One of the things I liked and admired about you was that you cared; you gave a damn. You were dealing mostly with institutionalized schizophrenics. Those poor people didn't have a clue about how to function in the outside world. They'd spent the majority of their lives on the back wards of mental hospitals. With the advent of antipsychotic drugs, as soon as they were made symptom free, they were dumped out into the community. It was your job to shoot them up and keep them symptom free, so the hospital didn't have to take them back. In reality it turned out to be a revolving door. I don't know what kept you going. Looking back on it, I view it as mass cruelty. How did you keep from burning out?"

"I did later on. When we worked together that was only my second job out of nurses training. I was gung ho. I think a lot of the doubtfulness about what I was doing developed later on. It had more to do with my own personal unhappiness. It was easier to blame my depressed attitude on 'the screwed-up system', than to face my own unhappiness."

"So, when did you finally turn around and face yourself?"

"About eight months ago." Tears began to brim up. He beckoned her to sit in his lap. She got up and came over to him. The tears ran down her cheeks. He rubbed her back. "Andy, I've made a lot of really stupid mistakes over the years. I didn't know what I would find when I came up here. I felt good about you and about this place from the very start, but I was reluctant. I decided to give it a try; to see what would happen. Over the past several months I've come to trust you completely. More importantly, I've develop a sense of trust and confidence in myself. I've never been happier in my life; not ever. We're best friends. We're partners and great lovers. You've been an inspiration to me in trying to start a whole new way of life. You've encouraged me every step of the way." He gave her his bandana to dry her tears. They held one another as the wind moaned outside.

They got up early on Monday morning. The sun had not risen yet. It was five degrees outside. The wind had died entirely. After feeding stoves and dressing warmly, Andy went to the barn. He started the snow blower and set about clearing the driveway. The worst part was the bottom ten or twelve feet. The county snowplows had thrown heaps of snow across the entrance, compacting it more and more with each pass. He, like most people, praised the plows for doing such an efficient job of clearing the roads. There was no solution to their refilling peoples' driveways in the process.

After a quick breakfast they both went out to the vehicles to clear the snow from them and warm them up. When Stephanie got into her car to start it, nothing happened. She got Andy's attention. He was starting his truck. "Something must be wrong with my battery Andy. It doesn't even turn over. There's no sound."

"It's probably just a bad connection. The terminals may be corroded," although he doubted it as she had such a new vehicle. Andy lifted the hood of her car to discover the battery was missing. Someone had stolen it. "Son-of-a-bitch," he said out loud. She asked what the problem was. "It looks like jerk-ass paid us another visit last night. Who the hell would be out in that kind of weather?" She got out of the car to see for herself. "So much for the assumption that it's all over with. Come on, get in the truck. I'll take you to work." She asked what he was going to do about her car. "I'll pick up a new battery and put it in." She was apologetic. "Hey Steph, it's not your fault."

"If it weren't for me none of this would be happening. I was wrong. I thought for sure that it was over and done with."

Andy went to get Lucy. As he was driving out of the driveway, he remembered, "Detective Miller said they were going to assign a deputy to escort you to and from work. They must be busy with accidents from this storm. This always happens with the first few storms. The damn fool people haven't got sense enough to slow down. I'll call her later just to make sure someone didn't screw up and forget." He drove well below the speed limit as there were several places in the open areas where the road had drifted back over. She asked if he was still carrying his gun. "Yep; it looks like I'm going to need to for awhile." She asked if it wasn't illegal for him to be carrying a concealed weapon. "Maybe, but both of the cops I've talked to know I'm carrying and haven't told me not to. As a matter of fact, they've encouraged me to do so. Besides, what am I supposed to do; strap a holster on every day and carry it in plain view?"

There was little traffic out on the road. When he approached the intersection where he needed to make a left turn he slowed so as not to apply too much pressure to the brakes. He didn't want to lose control. He did the same thing at the next intersection turning right. At the clinic he let her out. "I'll see you at five." They kissed and she apologized again.

As Andy was about to leave the clinic parking lot he saw a car approaching from the right. As it drew closer, he saw that it was the charcoal gray Chevy Malibu. When he saw the Z he had etched into the driver's side door he knew it was his nemesis. He stepped down hard on the gas pedal, hoping to broadside it, but he couldn't gain enough traction because of the slippery pavement. Once on the road he floored the truck in pursuit. He was gaining on the Malibu when it made an abrupt left turn onto a side road. Andy braked hard almost losing control. On the side road he pulled the pistol from his inside coat pocket and set it on the seat beside him. At the next intersection the Malibu blew off the stop sign and made a right turn onto the main highway. Andy braked hard again glancing to the left for any oncoming vehicles. A car was approaching from the left but it was still some distance away. Suddenly the brake pedal went to the floor. He pumped the pedal to no avail. It took him three or four seconds to respond by hitting the emergency brake pedal. The rear brakes immediately locked up and he lost control. The truck began to spin as he slid into, and across, the intersection. He spun about a hundred and twenty degrees before the truck plowed almost broadside into the snow bank on the opposite side of the road. The oncoming car came to a halt. The driver put on his emergency blinkers and got out of his car. Andy got out of the truck.

"Hey buddy didn't you see the stop sign?" The guy sounded critical.

"My brakes failed. I hit the emergency brake and lost control."

"Well I saw you and that asshole ahead of you. Both of you were going too fast for conditions."

"I'm sorry," Andy said. "I was chasing that 'asshole' ahead of me. He drove two people off the road back on the other highway." He gestured to the west. "I was trying to get a license number so I could report him to the cops."

The other man apologized. "Hey man, I'm sorry. You look like you're stuck pretty bad. Let's see if we can dig out the other side, maybe I can pull you out. If you take it easy maybe you can drive to a nearby garage. Man, it takes all kinds. I hope the prick ends up in a ditch on some secluded road." Both of them had shovels in their vehicles. Three or four cars came by as they were digging.

They were about to try pulling the truck out of the ditch, when a farmer came along in a four wheel drive pick up. He had a huge German Shepherd sitting on the seat next to him. "You need a tow?" Andy said that he did. "Yer the third one I've pulled outta the ditch so far this mornin'." He got out of his truck. He was a big, burly man with a lush, red beard. He had a tow chain in the bed of his truck. Andy took one end of it and hooked it to the frame of his truck. As he was about to get into his truck the Chevy Malibu came by heading north and moving slowly. The car's windows were so heavily tinted he could not make out the driver. He was sorely tempted to grab the pistol. It was on the floor of the truck. He wanted to empty it at the Malibu with the hope of hitting the driver or at least disabling the vehicle. He called to the first driver. "I think that's him. I think that's the guy who ran those people off the road." The guy asked if he was sure. "If his car has a 'Z' scratched into the driver's side door, that's him."

"I'm tempted to chase after him," the other driver said, but Andy waved off the idea.

When Andy's truck was back on the road he discovered that his emergency brakes were locked up and wouldn't disengage. The farmer said, "The brake cables are probably corroded and frozen up." He threw a burlap seed sack down next to Andy's truck. He lay down on the sack and told Andy to apply the emergency brakes and release them. The farmer pulled on the cables to free them. After doing that six or seven times, the brakes released on their own without having to be freed manually. Andy offered both of the men some money for their help. Both of them refused. The first driver was heading in the same direction that Andy was going. He offered to follow behind to make sure Andy got to the next town safely. There was a service station there. Andy knew and trusted the mechanic that owned the station.

Vern, the mechanic had several cars waiting to be worked on, but he took a few moments to check the truck. He found that both front brake hoses had been cut. "They weren't cut all the way through or you would have lost your brakes immediately," Vern told him. "They were cut so that they would burst under pressure. You could have driven an hour or a day or a week before they went. If I were you I'd report this. It could have been serious." Vern wouldn't be able to get replacement hoses until early afternoon. He had his apprentice mechanic take Andy home.

When he got home, Andy and Lucy went to the shop. He got a fire going, then called Detective Janet Miller. She was unaware that an officer had not shown up to escort Stephanie to work. He told her about the missing battery and his brake lines having been cut. "Are you at home?" she asked. "I'll be up to your place in about an hour. Make sure your mechanic saves those brake hoses." She asked if he had replaced the battery on Stephanie's car yet. "It sounds like a setup. Maybe he was hoping to get two birds." It took Andy awhile to figure out her meaning.

He called to the service station. "Vern, I was so shook up when I was there awhile ago I forgot. Someone stole the battery out of Stephanie's car. When you bring my truck back, can you bring a battery for the car too?"

"Man, Andy, somebody's got it in for you. Have you called the cops?"

"I just got off the phone with Detective Miller."

Vern laughed, "Now there's a piece of work. I hear she's supposed to be good but you'd never know that by looking at her."

Detective Miller drove up the driveway exactly to the minute that she said she would arrive. Today she had on bright yellow stirrup pants. She had on what looked like Santa boots. They were shiny black patent leather with a wide faux fur collar around the tops of them. She had on the same black leather coat. She had one side of her hair drawn back and held in place with a tortoise shell comb. Andy stepped out of his workshop and waved to her. She had parked behind Stephanie's car. She motioned for him to come there. He got his coat. He and Lucy went to where Detective Miller was standing with the hood raised. She again greeted Lucy and this time gave her a treat. "It looks like the battery fairy paid you a visit while you were away this morning." She pointed to the engine compartment. Andy looked to see that Stephanie's battery had been replaced. "I'm going to dust it for prints, not that I expect to find anything, but you never know." No prints showed up. Andy got in Stephanie's car and it started right up. "When your mechanic gets here with your truck, I want him to check Stephanie's car to make sure nothing else has been tampered with." He wondered how she knew that Vern would be delivering his truck. As if reading his thoughts she said. "I stopped on the way. I've got the cut brake lines. He told me that he was going to bring your truck here as soon as he had it back together."

Andy didn't bother to lower the hood. "You want some coffee? I've got a thermos in the shop." The two of them walked toward the barn.

"How long have you been living this way?"

Andy laughed, "that's an interesting way of putting it." She asked him how he would put it. "I hope to put up a livable house next spring." She reminded him that he hadn't answered her question." He told her that it had been over ten years. "And how long has Ms.

Brandt been living here?" He wondered what she was driving at. He said that Stephanie had moved here at the beginning of July. "And everything was copasetic until recently?"

In the workshop he poured both of them some coffee. He called Vern to tell him that the battery had mysteriously reappeared. He wouldn't need to bring a new battery. Detective Miller unbuttoned her coat. She was wearing a lavender, V-neck sweater. He noticed a scar across the front of her neck just above her collar bone. He wondered if the scar was the result of surgery or an injury. Today she was wearing a hot pink shade of lipstick. She got out a cigarette and her note book. She lit the cigarette and sat on the stool. Andy supplied her with the same coffee can ashtray. She had him tell her the events of the morning in detail. When he told her that he was almost certain that the perpetrator had casually driven by just as he was about to be towed out of the snow bank she said, "he's a ballsy son-of-a-bitch. You know, of course, he's upped the ante. We can charge him with attempted reckless homicide, that is, if we ever catch him. I'm surprised he hasn't changed vehicles." Detective Miller went on to tell Andy that someone had called the Sheriff's Department on Sunday afternoon. "He told the dispatcher that you wouldn't need an escort for Ms. Brandt as had been arranged. How the hell do you suppose someone was privy to that information?" Detective Miller asked. "I raised holy hell. I made it clear that either the sheriff or I were the only two people who could cancel an escort or surveillance. As for what happened this morning; this was a set up. These people knew that a deputy wouldn't be here. They stole Stephanie's battery to force you into the situation of driving her to work. Either you let her use your truck to get to work, or you take her to work yourself. Option one, Stephanie is put in harm's way. Option two, both of you are in jeopardy." She looked at Andy. She waited for him to respond. She took a deep drag from her cigarette and said, "what I find puzzling and troubling is that these people are getting so much information. I've made a special request to get a surveillance expert up here. We need to sanitize this place."

Andy asked a direct question. "You keep using the words 'they' and 'them'. Apparently you think there is more than one person involved with what's going on."

"Don't you?" She asked. "Even if it's just this one guy who's implementing the plan; there have to be several others operating behind the scene." She lit a new cigarette off the one she had been smoking. She squashed the previous one out in the can. "Let's get back to what we were discussing. The way things were set up this morning, my guess is that both of you were targeted. That could have two or three meanings." Andy asked her what she meant by that. She ignored his question as she took a long drag from her new cigarette. She delivered a volley of questions. "Are you going to be here for Christmas? If so, is anybody coming to visit you in her absence? When is Ms. Brandt supposed to be returning from Florida?" He told her the plans. "When is your son planning to leave here?" He told her the day after Christmas. "So you'll be here by yourself for a few days after that." He nodded. She wrote something down on a blank piece of paper from the back of her note pad. It said that she was having a deputy stop by at least once during each of the three daily shifts. She wanted him to turn on an outside light during the hours of darkness if something was amiss. That would serve to alert the deputy. If Andy didn't come to the door, the deputy would first have the dispatcher try calling him. The deputy would enter the house only if no one responded to the call. When he had read the note, she asked him if he understood. He did. She had him initial it. She took it from him, folded it, and put it in a coat pocket.

Just as Detective Miller was about to leave, Vern drove in with Andy's truck. At Detective Miller's request he made a visual check of the engine in Stephanie's car, including the belts. Andy started the engine. Before he left he said, "I sure hope you catch up with who ever did this to Andy. He could have ended up being hurt badly or even killed."

Vern needed someone to take him back to his station. Detective Miller said she would as she was going that way. She turned to Andy. "I'm going to have a deputy pick Ms. Brandt up and bring her home this evening. I think it would be prudent for us to do that until she leaves." Vern had gotten into the unmarked car. She got right in front of Andy. "If you do get a chance to use your cannon, don't go for a body shot. Go for the groin or the legs. Heads are a risky shot and, besides, we need to be able to question him." He asked why not the body. "He undoubtedly knows you're armed. He's probably wearing a vest. I would also recommend you get in a little target practice." She went to her car and got a carton of ammo. "Here are a hundred rounds of forty-five cartridges. They're compliments of a drug bust awhile back. Nobody in the department carries forty-fives any more."

"Hey, it's a good weapon. Lot's of stopping power."

She shook out another cigarette. "Apparently you haven't heard the expression 'user-friendly'. Nine millimeters have almost as much stopping power with the right ammo. They're not as loud, nor do they have as much recoil. In short, they're easier to shoot."

Back in the workshop, he called Stephanie at work. He told her that a deputy would pick her up from work this evening. She want-

ed to know what that was about. "I'll tell you when you get home."
She objected saying that having a deputy pick her up was going to
arouse all sorts of questions from her colleagues. Andy hadn't
thought of that. He said he would pick her up himself and ask that
the deputy escort them home. After hanging up he called and left a
message for Detective Miller, asking that she please call him back. He
took a piece of cardboard and drew out the frontal outline of a
human, using a marking pen. He was about to go outside for some
target practice when the phone rang. It was Detective Miller. "Yeah,
what now, McLeod?" He explained how having a deputy pick
Stephanie up from work was going to prove awkward. He asked if
the deputy could escort them instead. "Yeah sure, what vehicle are
you going to be driving?" He told her he would use his truck. She
wanted the license plate number. He had to go outside to get it for
her. After he gave it to her she said, "memorize it. Check it every time
you go to use the truck to make sure it hasn't been switched. I'm sure
you understand the need for such precaution." He did. She hung up.

The lady that was to pick up the benches arrived close to noon.
Andy got his homemade target and set it up to practice. All the
while he wondered if he was being observed. It had upset him to
even think that he may have reason to not trust Stephanie. This
morning had changed that. Whoever it was, had methodically set the
whole thing up. First, he had cancelled the police escort. Secondly he
removed Stephanie's battery, expecting that Andy would take her to
work. Thirdly, he had sabotaged Andy's truck with the hopes of getting both of them. He now understood what Detective Miller had
meant by saying, 'the guy was hoping to get two birds'. He took
careful aim and groin-shot the target. It gave him pleasure in knowing that a forty-five would obliterate the genitals on a live human
being.

The lady that was to pick up the benches arrived close to noon.
"I thought I was going to have to postpone coming up here again
because of yesterday's storm. I was surprised. The roads were in
good driving condition all the way from Green Bay." She was also
surprised at how compact the disassembled benches were. She had
borrowed a friend's minivan expecting to need the extra space it
afforded. "Golly, if I had known they would take up so little space, I
could have gotten them into my car." Andy loaded the benches into
the van for her. She handed him a check. It was for twenty-five dollars more than the cost. He thanked her.

Chapter 7

By the time Stephanie and Andy arrived home at 5:30, the temperature was barely above zero. The sky was clear. The weather forecast was predicting over-night temperatures below zero. Andy had burned down one of the stoves during the day in order to clean out a week's accumulation of ashes. He had just started a fire in that stove and the house was cold. Stephanie said, "I was hoping to take a hot bath when I got home, but I think I'll wait until the house warms up." She poured some wine, changed out of her uniform and put on her jeans, a turtle neck and one of Andy's heavy flannel shirts. They sat in the warmest place in the house, the dining room.

Andy had given a lot of consideration to what he was going to tell her the next morning. Part of his decision making was based on his concern that the house may still be bugged. He had prepared himself for their conversation with a pad of paper and a pen in case he needed to write messages to her. She asked if he had replaced her battery. She had her check book handy to reimburse him for a new battery. When he told her the car's battery had been returned during his absence from the house, she looked incredulous. "Do you mean somebody brought it back and left it for you to find?"

"No, it was re-installed in the car."

"But you couldn't have been gone long enough for anyone to have done that."

He explained what else had happened; about how his truck had been deliberately sabotaged. "The bastard baited me to get me to chase after him. I'm sure he did that to ensure that the hoses would burst." He told how the guy had brazenly driven right by the entrance to the clinic as Andy was on his way out of the parking lot.

"Do you think he intended to try and get both of us by stealing my battery?"

"That's a possibility. If I hadn't been driving so cautiously on the way to the clinic, that could have happened. However, there's another possibility. I could have let you take the truck by yourself." He was scrutinizing her as he spoke. He went on to tell her about the call someone had made to the sheriff's department to cancel the escort. She shook her head with disbelief. "Steph, what's so baffling is how this person knows so much about our daily activities." She had a worried expression. "Apparently we're still under surveillance." He asked her if she had said anything about what was happening to anyone at work. She hadn't.

"Andy, I know this sounds far-fetched, but how much do you trust this Detective Miller?"

"I trust her implicitly. It's true, I've given her a lot of information, but remember; she wasn't brought into the situation until very recently. It wasn't until after the house and the workshop were broken into that I realized we were being bugged. Besides, the only information I've given her, are about things that have already happened." He went on to say, because of what happened this morning, the perpetrator could be charged with attempted homicide. "Steph, look, two days ago you were sure that this was all over with. It's not only not over with, but it's getting worse. It's gone from mischievous to life-threatening. What happened this morning could have ended up with one or both of us injured or dead. Up until now he's just been messing with our heads."

She agreed. "I don't know what to say. I really was convinced that it would be over with the other day." Andy got up to tend the stoves. He and Lucy had not taken a walk this evening because of the severe cold. He mixed a martini for himself. Stephanie didn't want anything. When he sat back down she said, "maybe I need to leave here, Andy. What's happening is because of me. If I'm gone it will stop. I don't want anything to happen to you because of me."

"That's not an option, Steph. I don't want you to leave. Besides, no matter where you go, whoever this is will find you and it will be the same thing all over again. I think you need to tell the cops who's behind this and what it's about. Everybody's hands are tied. We've got to put an end to this. We can't unless you fess up."

She said nothing. She was looking down at her hands folded in her lap. Finally, in almost a whisper she said. "If I do that, I'm as good as dead."

He wrote on the pad of paper. "If you don't, both of us may die. It may be our only chance."

She wrote back, "I'll take care of it."

He wrote, "How?"

"I don't know for sure."

They decided to make supper. She heated some tomato soup while he made some grilled cheese sandwiches. He stood behind her at the stove and put his arms around her. "Steph, promise me that you're not going to leave. Let's see what happens. Maybe today was the last hurrah, the parting shot." She turned around and the two of them held one another. She said nothing. She did not promise anything. After dinner she took a hot bath. They went to bed at eight-thirty. They both were asleep within minutes.

He was awakened at close to one o'clock in the morning by Lucy's low growl. He reached for the gun on the night stand. It was close to a half moon and with the snow cover it was almost like daytime outside. He got out of bed and looked out the bedroom window. He saw nothing unusual. He went to the living room window. He searched the yard area that stood between the house and the barn. He was about to go into the dining room when her heard the eerie screaming sound of a pack of coyotes. They sounded like they were on the move and getting closer. It was cold in the house. The only thing he was wearing was a sweatshirt. He went back into the bedroom and put on his jeans and a worn pair of slippers. When he returned to the living room window, the coyotes sounded even closer. Moments later a group of six of them came across the yard, close to the barn. He had heard them numerous times before, but this was the first time he had actually seen them. They didn't stop. Half howling and half screaming, they soon vanished from view, heading north toward the woods. After peeing and adding wood to the stoves he returned to bed. He put the gun back within easy reach. Stephanie reached over to touch him. He took her hand. In a sleepy voice she asked if everything was alright. "Yeah, a pack of coyotes just passed through. The moon is bright enough I was able to see them." She snuggled close to him. Soon her breathing deepened with sleep. He lay next to her hoping that it was too cold for the phantom to be out tonight. He considered the word phantom and decided it was too nice a term to be wasted on the likes of him. On the other hand he did seem to possess some truly uncanny abilities. He remembered having felt the same way about the Viet Cong. Charlie was a cunning enemy. Somewhere along the way, he had begun to develop a kind of admiration or respect for Charlie's resourcefulness, ingenuity and tenacity. Long before his tour was over, he was convinced that Charlie would prevail. For him, his mission had gone from trying to beat the enemy, to surviving and getting the hell out of there in one piece. It was an attitude he shared with most of his comrades.

In the morning they had a quick breakfast. He went out and started Stephanie's car to let it warm up. His truck groaned but it eventually started. He didn't have to go anywhere today but he let both vehicles run. There had been a heavy frost that night and he was still working to clear her windows when she came out of the house. Moments later a sheriff's deputy drove in the driveway. It turned out to be Marty. He rolled down the squad car window. "Cold enough for you?"

"Let's hope it was too cold for our guy to be up to any of his merry pranks last night."

"I heard about what happened yesterday. Things have turned nasty. We're all on the lookout for a Malibu with an engraved 'Z' on the door. I'm surprised he's still running around in that thing. Maybe he wants to get caught." Stephanie appeared. Andy introduced Marty to her. She got in her car. "Have a good day." Marty waved. His window slid shut and he backed down the driveway.

Stephanie rolled her window down. He gave her a kiss goodbye. She thanked him for starting her car and cleaning the windows. "Call me when you get to work," he said. She backed up and turned to head down the driveway. He waited until her car disappeared before going back into the house. On the way he checked his outdoor thermometer. It said sixteen below. On his way to the workshop with Lucy he stopped to examine the coyote tracks. They were more defined where the snow wasn't so deep. He noticed some drops of blood in the tracks. He wondered if one of them was injured.

The phone rang just as he had finished disarming his traps. It was Stephanie. She had gotten to work without incident. She thanked him again for having taken care of her car. "Andy, I don't always tell you, but it's all the little things you do that mean so much to me. I really appreciate your thoughtfulness. I love you. I'm really sorry about what's happening."

"Steph, I have a question. How far back does this go, I mean with the stuff that's going on? I assume it has happened before."

There were a few moments of silence. "Nothing like this has ever happened before."

"Was it a relationship that didn't work out?"

"I have to go Andy." She hung up.

He found it impossible to quell his imagination. A realization developed. 'If this 'stuff' stopped right now it was probably going to take a long time for the two of them to put this experience behind them. If it continued, he wasn't sure how much more he was willing or able to tolerate. It was taking too much of a toll on him and their relationship. He knew that at some point it would reach a breaking point. He tried to consider his alternatives. The two most obvious ones were to either end the relationship or to leave this place that he loved so much. So far he had refused to entertain either of those ideas. He found himself beginning to harbor a growing resentment toward Stephanie for refusing to let anybody in on what any of this was about. He picked up the phone and called Detective Janet Miller. He had her number memorized. She was not available. He left a message. He had just finished getting a fire started in the workshop when the phone rang. "McLeod, this is Miller. What's up?" He asked if she was busy. "Yeah, I just discovered one of Santa's elves is a drug dealer and another's a pimp. I'm trying to gather evidence." He was amused by her endless flow of sarcastic humor. "Sorry, a little detective humor, what's happening?"

"Are you going to be in the neighborhood today?"

"I can be. How about one o'clock?" That was fine.

Detective Janet Miller came up the driveway at precisely one o'clock. She parked in Stephanie's space. Today she had on black stirrup pants and her Santa boots. Both sides of her hair were drawn back and held in place with what looked like imitation mother of pearl combs. She was chewing gum aggressively. After a few minutes in the shop she unbuttoned her coat. She was wearing a black jersey turtleneck with an aqua and yellow crocheted sweater vest over that. He wondered where she found such bizarre clothing. In the shop Andy offered her the coffee can ashtray. "Naw, I've decided to quit smoking. I do that about once a month. It usually lasts until I get so bitchy everyone begs me to start back again. That usually takes about two days. So, what happened today?"

"Nothing, I'm happy to report."

"Oh I get it, you asked me to drive all the way over here because you missed my scintillating self."

"Are you always this sarcastic or does not smoking bring it out in you?"

"Buddy boy, you ain't seen me at my rapier best yet. Miller, call me Miller. I reserve Jan for my lovers."

"Miller, I really wish you'd kick the habit. You give up too easily. I can't stand the smell of cigarette smoke. I'm not going to tolerate your smoking in my workshop anymore."

In the time he had known her he had not seen the slightest hint of a smile until this moment. She smiled so broadly that he could see that she was missing three of her top molars; two on one side. "Good McLeod, I was beginning to wonder if you were one of those classic martyr types. You know, the kind that never says anything, and puts up with all sorts of bullshit." She reached into her purse and withdrew an unopened pack of cigarettes. "The freaking tobacco companies; they're every bit as bad as drug dealers." She pulled a piece of paper out of her pocket and took the wad of gum out of her mouth. She wrapped the gum in the paper and put it in her pocket. She opened up another stick of gum and stuck it in her mouth. Andy wondered what Miller's house must look like. She handed Andy the pack of cigarettes. "Toss them in your stove." Andy set the pack on his workbench instead.

"Since I'm uncertain about my privacy, can I suggest meeting elsewhere."

She looked around the shop, then motioned for him to follow. They went to her car. He began the conversation. "I've had a few thoughts I would like to bounce off you." She motioned for him to continue. "Here's what we know. We know the car he's driving is probably registered to an alias." She nodded. "We know that it has been charged to a pharmaceutical company. What little I've been able to glean from Steph, is that the person behind what's happening is probably pretty rich and powerful."

"Does this mean she knows, or is pretty sure she knows, who it is?" It was his turn to nod. "Hmm, and she's refusing to say?" He nodded. "I had considered that possibility and I've compiled a list of names of the honchos of that company." She thought for a few moments. "Have you got any other ideas banging around in your head?"

"I'm just happy to come up with one bright idea a day."

"That one has some possibilities, McLeod. Has she said why she's not able to give us any hints as to who her antagonist is?"

"I've pressed her about that a few times. I tried again last night. She seems to think that if she points a finger, she's a dead woman walking."

"That could be a smokescreen," Miller said skeptically.

"Maybe, but she sounded genuine when she said it."

"I know you don't like my insinuating that Ms. Brandt may be involved with what's going on, but I'm having trouble with the fact that this creep knows so much about your routines. I'll let you know what I find out, unless I don't."

"Thanks Miller. If I don't see you before, have a good Christmas. I'm taking Steph to the airport next week. We'll see what happens after she leaves."

"In your case, no news will be good news. You have a good one too McLeod."

Andy got out of the car. He stood and waited until she started to pull away. They waved to one another. He walked back to the workshop thinking about Detective Miller. He wondered if she was married. If she was single, what was she going to be doing for the holidays? He was sorry he hadn't thought to give her something he'd made as a way of thanking her. He found nothing physically attractive about her. She was an abrasive, crude, bizarre, apparently undisciplined, profane individual. On the other hand she was intelligent, perceptive, street-wise and unaffected. She was an enigma but he liked the lady.

Even though it was below zero, when walk time approached there was very little wind. Andy decided to take an abbreviated walk. The drifted snow was so deep in places it would have been difficult managing to carry his usual late afternoon libation. Lucy seemed less than enthused about the jaunt. After they had gone a quarter of a mile he decided that it just wasn't worth it. He turned around and retraced his steps. As he entered the house the phone was ringing. He answered it to hear Brian's voice. "Hey Pops, I was just about to hang up. You weren't out for a walk in this cold, were you?"

"Unfortunately, yes. Judging from what you've just said, it's miserably cold there too."

"It's terrible. Are you managing to keep the house warm?"

"It's not bad when the wind isn't screaming. It's another story when it is. So, what's up?"

"Nothing much. School is out a week from today. I'll have ten days off for Christmas break. I just thought I'd call to see how things are, and to see if you needed me to pick anything up for you. We're planning to leave early that next Saturday morning. Amanda has to be back to work on Wednesday. So we'll need to leave sometime on Tuesday."

They chatted for a few more minutes after which Andy mixed a drink, tended the stoves and went into the living room. He noted, not for the first time, that he had become a real creature of habit. Almost everything about his life fell into some kind of routine. He sat down in his swivel rocker without turning on a lamp. Stephanie would be leaving a week from now. She would fly to Chicago, changing planes at O'Hare to complete the trip to Orlando. She had written her itinerary down for him and he had it posted on the refrigerator. She was scheduled to return late in the afternoon the following Thursday. She had included her mother's address and phone number in Melbourne, Florida.

It seemed odd to him that, to his knowledge, Stephanie's mother had never called once in the almost six months since Steph had come here. Nor did the phone bill reflect any long distance calls made by Stephanie to Florida, or to any other place for that matter. It was as if she had deliberately left everything about her previous life behind. He wondered whether the roommate in Chicago even knew where she had gone. Had her coming here been a disappearing act? If so, it was rife with defects. It wouldn't be difficult to determine her whereabouts. There was her social security number, her nursing license, her driver's license and vehicle registration, and on and on. A dull witted boy scout could find her—unless. He hadn't considered the 'unless' prior to this moment; 'unless she's got more than one identity'. His train of thought was interrupted by the sound of a car crunching up the snow packed driveway. Lucy got up and went to the front door wagging her tail. Andy got up and went to turn on the yard light and to let Lucy out. When Stephanie and the dog came in, she gave him a quick kiss. She asked if he had checked the outside temperature. "I'm afraid to. Luce and I started to take a walk this evening and had to abandon it. I'm sure it's already in the minus teens." She had a shopping bag that was folded over. It looked like it contained books. She set it on the table. As soon as she had her scarf, coat, and hat off, he noticed she was wearing an attractive pair of gold hoop earrings. "I didn't know you had pierced ears. Those look good on you."

She laughed, "their a gift from John and his wife. He pierced my ears this afternoon so I could wear them. He said that he was opening up a whole new door of gift giving for you."

He remembered that his previous girlfriend, Josie, had pierced ears and she'd had an impressive collection of earrings. Her ears had been sensitive to most metals. She claimed she was only able to wear solid gold or silver ones. Anything else caused her ear lobes to swell and turn red. He had learned that the hard way, after buying her two sets of earrings for her birthday and having to return them. "Their very nice. A lot of women can't wear the dangly kind but those look downright sexy on you."

"I'm going to go get comfortable. Would you pour me a glass of wine?" He checked the outdoor thermometer through the kitchen window and reported that it was already eighteen below. She was coming out of the bedroom when he came into the living room. He started to turn on a lamp. She asked him not to and instead she lit one of the kerosene lamps and a couple of candles.

He gave a slight laugh. "The first couple of years I lived here I had a pretty inefficient stove. I used to light two or three kerosene lamps at night, as much for the added heat, as for the light and the ambiance. It was commonplace for the electricity to go out whenever there were storms. I half-jokingly used to say, "if a fly farted in Tierra del Fuego the power went out. The kerosene lamps were a necessity. The electric company has gotten its act together in the last few years. Power outages don't happen much anymore."

Stephanie was sitting on the couch. He went to sit next to her. "I'm going to miss you. In some ways I wish I was coming with you."

He asked her what she would like for dinner. "I'm really not very hungry. Everybody brought stuff in today and I've been nibbling all sorts of goodies. I can heat up something for you if you'd like." He decided to just have some cheese and venison sausage on crackers. She tried a piece of the sausage. "This is really very good, Andy.

Would you mind if I took some of this to my mother." Then she said, "I know that Christmas is over a week away but I'd like you open one of your presents tonight." She got up and retrieved a big package from upstairs. "This is actually for both of us." He opened it to discover a mattress pad heater. "If we remember to turn this on before we go to bed, the bed will be nice and warm when we crawl into it."

"I didn't know that such a thing even existed. I don't like electric blankets, but this is brilliant." They went into the bedroom and installed it. They went to bed early that night partly to get warm. He told her about Brian's plans to come up the following weekend. He didn't tell her about his conference with Detective Miller. They had gone almost two full days without any further incidence from the tormentor. He attributed the reprieve to the extreme cold. He still kept the gun within easy reach at all times. Stephanie went to sleep quickly. He lay wide awake next to her for close to two hours. He found himself thinking about the house that they were planning to build this coming spring. If this harassment was going to continue, he decided it would be silly for them to invest in putting up a new home. It would only serve to tie them to this place even more. He came back to the option of leaving here and trying to make a fresh start. If it came to that, they would have to be smart about it. He found himself going through numerous scenarios and picking each one of them apart. At some point he became aware of the mattress pad heater. It was working beautifully. He turned it to the lowest setting. 'There may have been a day when a person could disappear and get away with it fairly easily. It was nearly impossible in today's world unless a person had some help'. This led him through another door he hadn't considered before. 'A person couldn't simply disappear by themselves anymore. People who 'disappear' today are only able to do it if they were able to receive help in assuming a whole different identity. That's what the whole witness protection program is about'. He played with that idea. 'Is she someone who might be eligible for protection? If she is, and she were to tell the authorities whatever her secret is; it might be a way to save her life'. The more he thought about that idea the less he liked it. He wondered what had been keeping her alive before she came here. He wondered if something like this had happened to her before. Is she out here on her own? He finally gave up, deciding that it wasn't getting him anywhere. He drifted off into sleep in the early morning hours.

While Stephanie was getting ready to go to work, Andy again went out to start both vehicles. Clouds had moved in during the night and the temperature had actually risen to three below. It looked like it could very well snow. Marty arrived to escort Stephanie to the clinic. She hadn't come out of the house yet. Marty invited him sit in the squad until she showed up. He asked, "have the powers that be said anything about resuming these escorts when Steph gets back." Andy didn't know. He thought that they were going to wait to see what happened after she left. "I probably ought to keep my mouth shut but I can't help but think that whoever this is, knows Steph is leaving and where she's going."

"I've thought about that too, Marty. To be honest with you, I'm half expecting them to make a move on our way to the airport. It's been more than two days since anything has occurred. I'm even more concerned that something might happen to Steph while she's in Florida."

Marty frowned, "Christ, Andy, it's been too freaking cold the past two days for anybody to try to pull anything. Let me talk this over with Miller. Maybe we can set something up to get her to the airport safely." Andy liked the idea. "If Miller and the Sheriff go for it, she'll call you." Stephanie came out and got in her car. Andy waved to her as she drove off followed by Marty.

When he got to the workshop a few minutes later, he opened the door just enough to disarm the first of his booby traps. He discovered the string had been cut. The box with the chalk sat on the floor in the middle of the shop. The thin wire that was to trigger the hinged pungee board had also been cut. Andy stood just inside the door. He studied the situation. He opened the door and let Lucy in. Suddenly the hinged boards swung down. The trip wire had been rerouted and she had triggered the trap with her tail. It startled her and she scampered several feet away. Because of her size the boards missed her by several inches. He examined what had been done. It would have missed him too. He would have been past the line of trajectory before he triggered their release. The famous line from Butch Cassidy and the Sundance Kid flashed through his mind. In the movie Butch Cassidy kept asking "Who is this guy?" Andy asked the same question. He added, 'I can't believe this son-of-a- bitch. How did he know'?

He had no sooner gotten a fire going in the stove, when the phone rang. "McLeod? Miller. See you in half-an-hour." She hung up.

He had just finished carving a mirror frame and had put the final finish coat on it the day before. He had it wrapped as a present for Detective Miller. She drove in right on time. She honked. He knew that was her signal for him to come to her car. He brought the package along with him. When he got in the car she was chewing gum. "I see that we have managed to stay on the wagon since last we met."

"No smart ass, WE ran out of cigarettes." She backed up and

started out the driveway. "WE are going to go buy some right now. What have you got there?"

"A Christmas present for you," he told her.

"Department regs prohibit us from accepting presents. Conflict-of-interest or some bullshit to that effect."

"How about your buying it? The price is one dollar. I can lend you a dollar."

"Open it. Let's see if it's worth a dollar."

"Nope, not until you've had at least six drags."

Minutes later, she was about to pull into the local gas station. Instead she made a U turn. "Screw it. You're right McLeod, I give up too easily." He noticed she had on turquoise stirrup pants today. She was wearing her Santa boots and she was back to her single tortoise comb, this time holding her hair back on the opposite side from before. He wondered what kind of garish sweater she had on today. He suggested that she drive up the street to a local coffee shop. "So open it, the suspense is killing me." She pointed to the wrapped present.

"Nope it's yours to open." She pulled up across the street from the coffee shop. She was hesitant about opening the wrapping paper. When she did, he saw for the first time a show of softness to her expression. "You did this? You made this yourself, McLeod? This is the kind of stuff you do?" He nodded. "This is beautiful. Really, I mean that. You've got real talent. I've got just the place for it." She handed him a five dollar bill. He tried to give it back. She refused. "I didn't get you anything. Have a beer or two on me." They sat parked across from the restaurant and talked. "I like Marty's idea. One of our sharp shooters and I are going to follow you to the airport next week."

He told her about his just having discovered his booby traps had been foiled. She asked several questions. "I gotta tell you, McLeod, this guy's shrewd. I'm beginning to think that we're dealing with a former Special Ops. He's too damn sophisticated to be some ordinary hired gun. Plus, he's got access to stuff that the boys in the crime lab aren't even familiar with. Somebody has set him up with the very latest in technology. It wouldn't surprise me if he's not only been listening but he's probably been watching most of your moves."

"The thing that's pissing me off the most is that it's not over," Andy said. "After a two day hiatus he's right back to giving us the finger again." She agreed. "Remember what you told me the other day about not aiming for the body if I get a shot at him." She nodded. "Well, I've thought about it and decided I'll take anything I can get. If he's wearing a jacket, the impact of a forty-five, even at a distance, is going to knock him on his ass and probably break something."

She smiled, "frankly, I don't think he's going to give you that opportunity."

They decided to forgo the coffee. She took him home. She thanked him again for the mirror. Before he got out of the car he asked, "what kind of top have you got on today Miller?"

She smiled broadly, unbuttoned the two top buttons of her coat, and showed him a loud orange sweater with a crocheted collar. "I'm looking forward to escorting you to Green Bay next week. The only stuff the resale shops around here have is boring, conservative, old lady stuff. I'm going to check out St.Vinny's and Goodwill while I'm down there."

Chapter 8

It started snowing shortly after Detective Miller left Andy off at his place. He mulled over the things she had said to him as he worked on carving more frames. He recalled a few of the experiences he had had with Navy SEALS when he was in Viet Nam. He was surprised the first time he encountered a team of them. He had expected them to be huge, muscular, Schwarzenegger types. Instead most of them were wiry average looking guys. A couple of them even had a bit of a gut. He remembered that they kept to themselves for the most part and were all business when it was time to rock and roll. One of them had tried to teach Andy how to go into what he called an Alpha state. It was a way of what he referred to as 'being able to zone out'. One could put himself into a semi-conscious state, able to gain full consciousness when the situation required it. Andy didn't get it at the time. It wasn't until later that he found himself doing it automatically. It was a way of tuning out the miserable conditions and yet being able to react if something happened. It became a tool of defense; a way of surviving mentally.

'Assuming that I'm up against a highly trained operative', he thought, 'a part of me wishes I could meet this guy under different circumstances'. He doubted that his opponent would feel the same toward him. 'He's walked all over my head for the past two weeks. He probably regards me as a buffoon'.

The phone rang. It was Detective Miller. "We're all set for the little trip we talked about. The sheriff has given the plan his blessing. Incidentally, I showed my present to a couple of my colleagues. They were quite impressed. Thought you'd like to know. Thanks again."

It snowed lightly off and on the rest of the day. It was nearing walk time when Rob drove in. He pulled up as close as he could to the workshop entrance. He came into the shop. "How about a beer?" Andy offered.

Rob looked at his watch. "It's a little early, but sure what the hell."

"How come you're off work so early? I thought you worked until four."

"I do, but I had a doctor's appointment. I knocked off a little early today. I saw Steph when I was at the clinic. They're going to miss her there." Andy wasn't sure what Rob meant by that. He decided that Rob was referring to her planned trip to Florida.

"What did you need to see John about?"

"Oh, I slipped and fell down one of the unfinished stair cases yesterday. I banged my elbow up. It hurt like hell. It was still so sore I could hardly use my arm today. They x-rayed it and found that I had a spur on my elbow. It broke off. I've got a lot of fluid in my elbow. I asked John about draining off the fluid. He says they used to do that but not anymore. The body absorbs the fluid. He gave me a shot of cortisone right into the elbow and some pain pills. It still hurts but at least I can use my arm."

Andy asked, "what are you going to do for Christmas?" Rob said he didn't have any plans. He'd probably spend the day working on his house. "Why don't you come over for dinner on Christmas day? My oldest son will be here with his girlfriend. You haven't met Brian. He's the school teacher." Rob accepted the invitation. "We'll probably eat around four. Come on over earlier for some libations."

"You know, I been trying to tell myself for years that Christmas is just another day," Rob said. "The truth is, I dread it." He asked if he could bring anything. Andy didn't think so. "My main reason for coming by today is that I have a bunch of beautiful red oak scraps that they were just going to pitch. It's all cut offs but I thought you might find a use for it. I've got it in the back of the wreck." As Andy put on his coat Rob said, "incidentally, I was pleasantly surprised to discover you had fixed my wiper and put in a rheostat switch on my heater. I owe you."

"Rob, you don't owe me a thing. I appreciate you letting me use your car." While they unloaded the wood from the car he told Rob about finding the culprit's car in a motel parking lot and about his act of vandalism.

"That must have pissed the hell out of him. Has he tried to get even?" Andy told him about the brake hoses being cut on his truck. "Jesus Andy, that's freaking serious; things are escalating."

"It remains to be seen what will happen after Stephanie leaves for Florida." He changed the subject. "I can't believe they were just going to throw this wood out, Rob. It's beautiful. I appreciate you thinking of me and saving all of this."

Rob promised to bring him at least this much again. "I'm glad you can use it." He laughed. "I made my kitchen counter using a bunch of it. I figure if you don't use it for anything else, it's decent kindling." After he left, Andy and Lucy took their daily hike.

When Stephanie arrived home she mentioned she had seen Rob at the clinic today. "He just left here awhile ago. He brought me a bunch a scrap wood from the construction project he's working on. It's beautiful red oak. I invited him to join us for Christmas dinner. The poor guy was going to be by himself and spend the day working on his house."

Before going to the bedroom to change clothes, Stephanie said, "the staff all went together to get me a nice travel toiletry kit as a Christmas present. It's on the dining room table."

He examined it, "I think they all appreciate you, Steph. As much of a micro-manager as John is, he's turned a lot of things over to you. That's a real compliment to you."

There was barely any wind tonight and the house was warmer. Stephanie insisted on leaving the lamps off. Andy heated up some chili for supper and they ate in the living room, enjoying the relative absence of flies.

Stephanie routinely took a bath before going to bed at night. While she was doing that, Andy let Lucy out. In bed he told her, "if anyone were to ask me what man's greatest invention is, I'd have to say 'hot running water', but this mattress pad heater is a close second." They made love. Afterwards he held her. "You know, our love making has improved despite all the stuff that's been going on. I felt like I was losing you. You seemed to be withdrawing from me. He was unaware until she reached for some tissues to blow her nose that she was crying." He snuggled to her back and held her.

She told him she loved him. "Maybe someday I can explain all of this to you."

The next several days were incident-free. Andy wondered what was going on. 'Why the lull' if that is what it was? It raised new and different questions. Detective Miller called him a couple of days before Stephanie was to leave, to check and see if they still wanted an escort to the airport. They agreed that it would be the prudent thing to do.

The evening before Stephanie was to leave, she suggested they open their Christmas presents to one another. When he gave her the robe she laughed saying that there seemed to be a theme emerging. "We're preoccupied with warmth." She gave him a book of poetry and Gibran's book, The Prophet. He went upstairs and brought down the cross country ski package. She had never done that kind of skiing. He explained the difference between downhill and cross-county skiing.

"What I like about cross-country skiing is that it's a way of getting out and getting fresh air and exercise. It's also a way of exploring places that you can't see any other time of the year."

She gave him two extra-heavy flannel shirts, "Since I've more or less confiscated your favorite one and your other one is thread bare."

Finally he produced the wedding ring. "I debated whether to give this to you now or wait until you got back home. She knew what it was from the size and shape of the package. She was visibly shaken and held the box for what seemed like a long time before opening it. After lifting the lid she put her fingers to her lips and began to cry. He sat down next to her. "It's beautiful, Andy. I love the simplicity of the design. I wasn't expecting this at all." She tried it on. It seemed a little big on her. "It will probably fit just perfectly when the weather warms up. Rings tend to be loose when it's cold like this."

She dried her tears with his bandana. "I'm not going to wear it until we get married. I'll leave it here. I don't want anything to happen to it. I have another present for you Andy, but it hasn't arrived yet. When you get it, go ahead and open it without me." They chatted for awhile before retiring for the night.

They arose early the next morning. Stephanie was traveling light. She had one suit case and a carry-on bag. She wore a nice pair of slacks, a turtleneck jersey and a tweed jacket that Andy had never seen before. "You look outstanding my love," he complimented. "I really do like those earrings." Detective Miller arrived as he was loading Stephanie's luggage into the back of the truck. She had the other officer with her. Stephanie and she had never met before. When Stephanie came out of the house, introductions were made. Andy, Stephanie and Lucy got in the truck and the two vehicles departed. Neither Andy, nor Stephanie, said much during the first part of the trip to the airport. It wasn't until they were almost half way to Green Bay before Stephanie said, "Andy, I know I've said this before but I want you to know how very sorry I am about all of this. I really appreciate how you've stood up for me. Thank you for everything. I've never felt more loved by anyone. You're a very precious man. I will always love you." She turned her attention to Lucy. "I'm leaving you in charge. You take good care of this man. You have my permission to sleep on my side of the bed." Lucy gave her a lick.

In the terminal just before she was about to board the plane Andy blurted out. "Steph, am I ever going to see you again?" She asked him what made him ask that. "I just have a feeling. What you said a little while ago sounded like a farewell."

She kissed and hugged him. "I'll see you in a week. You have a nice Christmas. Say hi to Rob. Tell Brian I hope to meet him soon. I'll call you tomorrow. I won't get to Melbourne until late tonight."

Detective Miller approached him as soon as Stephanie had disappeared. She had on lime green stirrup pants today with running shoes. "Do you want us to follow you home?"

"I'll be okay. Why don't you go check out the resale shops?" He touched her arm. "Thanks Jan, for everything."

"My pleasure, McLeod. Have a nice Christmas." Walking back to his truck Andy felt an overpowering sense sadness overtake him. The background music in the terminal was," Have Yourself a Merry Little Christmas." He felt a profound sense of sadness.

Back in the truck he petted Lucy. He sat for a long while. When he started the truck he said to her. "Well old dog, it's just you and me against the world; onward and downward." He was almost at the end of the parking section and about to make the turn toward the exit gate when he spotted the charcoal gray Malibu with the etched 'Z'. It was parked at the far end of the section. It stood by itself with no other cars surrounding it. "Oh shit," he hit the steering wheel. "Is that bastard on the same plane with her?" He was immediately sorry that he had dismissed Detective Miller. He paid the parking fee and drove around to return to the terminal building. He parked the truck in a ten minute parking zone and ran into the building. He asked two different airport personnel before he was able to get directions to airport security. It took him several minutes before he was finally admitted to the office of the man in charge of security. The man was far beyond imposing. He must have weighed close to three-hundred-and-fifty pounds. Andy introduced himself and explained that he had reason to believe a dangerous man was on the same flight as his fiancée. He gave the man a brief description of what had been happening over the past two weeks and that sheriff's deputies had even escorted them to the airport.

The man finally interrupted him to say, "I'm sorry, didn't you notice the sign on the door when you came in here? It says airport security. I am in charge of airport security. The second an airplane's wheels leave the ground, I am no longer responsible for who or what is on that airplane. The best I can do is to have the tower alert the airplane's crew members. Can you give me a description of this individual?" He could not. "Do you have the passenger's name?"

Andy asked the man if he meant Stephanie's name. The man said he meant the name of the man who he suspected of stalking her. "How the hell would I know his name?" Andy practically yelled at the man. "If I knew his goddamn name, he'd be behind bars right now."

The man seemed unperturbed. "I'm very sorry Mr. McLeod, but without more concrete information to go on, I don't see how we can even begin to help you."

Andy thought, 'you passive-aggressive son-of-a-bitch'. He tried to compose himself. He asked, "what about at the other end? Could you call O'Hare's security and have them meet her plane?" He was willing to do that much. Andy gave the man Stephanie's name, a complete description of her, and what her connecting flight was. The man placed a call and relayed the information. Andy knew that the plane from Green Bay would land in Chicago before he would arrive back home. He debated what to do. If he waited here at the airport, the house would be close to freezing by the time he got home. If he left immediately, Stephanie would already have changed planes and be on the second leg of her journey to Orlando. He wouldn't be able to find out anything until later. He decided to stay at the airport. The security man told him that he would keep him informed. After moving his truck to the short term parking a staff member showed Andy to the VIP lounge.

A little over an hour later Andy was summoned back to the security office. "Mr. McLeod, there appears to be some confusion. A Ms. Stephanie Brandt was booked on a plane leaving here for Chicago. However, O'Hare's security informs me that there is no such person by that name booked on any flights from Chicago to Orlando or for that matter any other destination. Would she have perhaps used another name?" The only other names he could think of was her former married name of Fitzpatrick or her mother's alleged name, O'Hara. The security man placed another call to O'Hare's security. A few minutes passed. Neither name turned up anything. Finally the security man said. "If she is aware that she's in some danger from this individual, perhaps she booked herself under a fictitious name. The best I can do is contact Orlando and give them her description. Security there may be able to spot her. She may have even booked with a different airline or perhaps taken a circuitous route. I can request that they be on the lookout for anyone meeting her description on all incoming flights for the next forty-eight hours. Frankly Mr. McLeod, I think we're trying to find a needle in a haystack."

He thanked the security man for all of his effort and gave him his home phone number. The security man apologized and expressed his hope that everything turned out for the best. Andy left the main terminal building. He had covered Lucy with a blanket, but when he got to the truck she was shivering. "I'm sorry Luce. Let's go home." As he drove out of the parking lot he saw that the Malibu was missing from where it had been parked. He wondered if his foe had turned the car back into the rental agency or if he was still around to cause trouble. ' It was late enough in the afternoon that it would be dark before Andy would be half way home. As he drove he kept checking to see if he was being followed. Before long it was too dark to be able to tell. As the miles passed, he deliberated what had happened. He felt almost certain that Stephanie was gone for good. He began to replay several of the scenarios he had considered before. He did not want to bother Detective Miller again but he felt an overwhelming need to talk to her. He had no one else to turn to who could be of any possible help. Lucy was curled up beside him. He put a hand on her back.

When he got home the temperature in the house was forty degrees. There were very few embers left in either stove. He got a strong fire going in the stove that he had cleaned yesterday. He cleaned out the other one before starting a fire in that stove. He fed Lucy. Still in his coat, he called the home number that Detective Miller had written on her card. She answered on the third ring. "Miller, its McLeod." She told him to hold on for a second.

A minute later she was back. He heard a tinkling that sounded like ice cubes in a glass. "What's up?" She asked. He told her about what had happened after she left him at the airport. She listened without comment. He could hear the occasional tinkling sound. Finally she asked, "so what do you think?"

"I haven't got the slightest fucking idea."

There were a few moments of silence. "Andy," It was the first time she had ever used his first name. "I think you have a pretty good idea about what's happening."

He matched her silence. He finally said, "I'm afraid to admit it but I think she's gone." She said nothing. He struggled to hold back tears. "I think she's left for good."

There was another long period of silence. "If that's the case; then she's gone up several notches in my book. All of this stuff that's been going on is because of her. She knows why and who's behind it. She's refused to level with you. If she has, in fact, gone back underground; then she's made a very painful and courageous decision. I respect her for that."

"What do you mean when you say 'back underground'? Do you think she was underground before?"

"I'll be up tomorrow. I'll see you at nine. I'm treating you to breakfast compliments of the department." After they hung up he found himself feeling a sad sense of relief that he had called her. She had confirmed some things for him but in the process she had raised some questions he wasn't sure he wanted the answers to. He tended the stoves again. The house was slowly warming up. He still had his coat on. He mixed another martini, lit the two kerosene lamps and went to sit in his chair. The reality of the situation brought a mixture of sadness and relief. He felt heart sick. In all probability he would never see her again. He felt angry at whomever or whatever it was that had forced her to make this decision. 'When did she decide this? Was visiting her mother in Florida a ruse?' He could find out the answer to that question right now. He got the phone number Stephanie had left for him. He dialed it only to get a recording telling him that the number was no longer in service. He dialed it again just in case he had dialed it incorrectly the first time. He hadn't. He called information. There was no one by her mother's name in the entire code area. There wasn't even such an address. He thanked the operator and hung up. He took off his coat, put more wood in the stoves and put on his old cardigan sweater. He went back to the living room and sat down.

Andy thought about Stephanie's withdrawal from him weeks ago. She must have known then that she'd been discovered? She must have been struggling with the decision to leave. He decided that her most recent behavior was the result of her having made that decision. In the past several days she had seemed more at peace with herself. The struggle had been resolved. It was like the depressed person wrestling with the decision to end his life. Many times there is a sense of relief once the decision to give up has been made. He doubted that she had either a confidant or a cohort. He felt almost certain that there had been no one who was there to help her reach the decision or to help orchestrate her disappearance. Once she got to O'Hare she could go anywhere in the world from there. She would be smart enough to take on a completely new appearance and identity. His thoughts took off in a different direction. Andy asked himself what he really knew about her. 'We've lived together for the last six months. It appears that she's deceived me about almost everything either by outright lies or what she didn't say'. He wondered if she had run out on her former husband, Michael, for the same reasons or was all of this post-Michael.

Another thought occurred to him. He got up and went into the bedroom. He turned on the overhead light. Sitting on top of his dresser was the box with the wedding ring. Underneath the box was a sealed legal size envelope. He opened it to find the signed title to her car and a life insurance policy for fifty-thousand dollars that had been taken out on December 2nd. It named him as the beneficiary. There was a cashier's check from a bank in Chicago made payable to him for twenty-five thousand dollars. A note was clipped to the check. 'Please put this toward the new house'. He went to her dresser. The only things left in it were his flannel shirt, that she wore much of the time when she was home and two pair of her long underwear. He went upstairs to the back bedroom which he used exclusively for storage and closet space. There were a few things of hers hanging neatly grouped together. A note was pinned to a winter coat; 'Please donate all of these clothes'.

He went back downstairs to the living room and sat down again. All doubts were erased. 'She's gone for good. She knew she wasn't coming back. He recalled their conversation at the airport just before she had boarded the plane. His instincts had been accurate when he had asked her straight out if he would ever see her again. Thinking about it now, he asked himself, 'what could she have possibly said? Have a good life. Hey, it was fun while it lasted. Hope you find somebody new. I'll never forget you'. He was becoming maudlin. He finished his drink and got up to check the stoves and mix another. It had been years since he had gotten drunk. He hadn't eaten anything since breakfast. He wasn't particularly hungry now. He went to the refrigerator. Nothing appealed to him. He went back into the bedroom and turned the mattress pad heater on just on his side. He let Lucy out and took off his work boots. The inside temperature was at forty-five degrees now. When Lucy came back in, the two of them went into the bedroom. He was exhausted. He lay down on the bed not bothering to undress. He took a few sips of his drink before falling sound asleep.

He awoke at close to one o'clock in the morning. The moon had risen and it was light enough that he could make his way around the house without turning on a lamp. After brushing his teeth and checking the stoves, he got undressed and crawled under the covers. He remembered Stephanie once asking him if he ever felt lonely. His answer had been, 'very seldom'. He felt an overwhelming loneliness now, 'oh Steph, I miss you so. I don't know if I want to stay here without you'? He wondered, if he had known about her planned disappearance, would he have decided to join her? Would she have allowed him to come along? He thought back. In retrospect he could see that there had been numerous signs about what had happened. He criticized himself for being too dense or stupid or in denial to recognize any of them. I just kept hoping that the crap would cease, and things would go back to normal. She even led me to believe that was what would happen. I was gullible enough to buy what she said more than once. Was that an effort on her part to buy more time'? It still seemed so unreal. He wanted to believe that she would call him in the morning as she had promised. He wanted to believe that she was going to return next Thursday as planned.

Lucy made a low growl. He had not thought to bring the gun into the bedroom. He got up and retrieved it. He checked to make sure the door was locked. As he started through the living room he heard the haunting screams of the coyote pack. He relaxed slightly hoping that was what had aroused Lucy. He set the gun on the night stand. The bed was almost too warm from the heater. He turned it to low. He patted the bed and tried to coax Lucy to jump up next him. She refused. He wondered if it was because she was unsure about where Stephanie was. As much of a one man dog as Lucy was, she had formed an attachment to Stephanie. Lucy always greeted Stephanie upon her arrival home from work. She would often curl up close to Stephanie on the couch in the evening.

He could hear the coyotes getting closer. He did not feel like getting back out of bed to see if he could spot them again. He thought about how suddenly and dramatically his life had been turned upside down. When he had come to this place a few years ago it had been a new beginning by choice. This time he was forced into having to start over. For the first time since coming here he felt like just letting go of everything and maybe leaving here. He thought back to an encounter he had had with some retired people at his shop. They had sold everything and bought a pickup truck and a twenty-six foot travel trailer. They were traveling around the country going where they wanted, when they wanted, seemingly carefree. 'Luce and I don't need a big trailer to just wander around the country'. He entertained that fantasy for awhile before falling back to sleep.

Chapter 9

He had been at work in his workshop an hour before Detective Miller arrived. He walked to her car and got in. He noticed that she was not wearing her usual garish amount of makeup this morning. Instead of stirrup pants she had on a pair of stylish looking, brown slacks, and navy blue, wool coat with a hood. Her hair was un-teased. Nor was it thick with hair spray. She told him she was taking them to a Swedish restaurant. "They have pancakes that are to die for."

He debated whether or not to say anything about her appearance. He decided to go ahead and risk it. "I like your new look detective."

She showed a bit of a smile. "I know how people in these small towns are. I didn't want anybody seeing us together, thinking you're with some bimbo." He started to say something. She beat him to it by asking, "so you've had some time to digest what happened yesterday. Did you get drunk last night? What have you come up with?"

He told her about trying to call Stephanie's mother's number. He told her about the envelope with the check, the life insurance policy and the signed car title. "I don't think there's much question that she left for good. I haven't been able to bring myself to call the clinic to find out if and when she resigned. I guess I don't want to go through the embarrassment of revealing that I didn't know anything about it."

"I already took care of that." Miller said. "I called John first thing this morning. He said she gave him a two week notice. She told him that her mother has been diagnosed with cancer and she was going to Florida to be with her. She didn't know when she would be back. He tried to offer her an extended leave of absence. He said that she was a hell of a nurse and he hoped he could hire her back when she returned. She told him that she wanted him to feel free to hire someone else if the right person came along. So what else have you come up with?"

"I don't know. I guess I want to believe that somebody is helping her, maybe someone like the FBI."

She nodded, "maybe, although I kinda doubt it, go on."

He looked out the side window. "This is the hard part." He was struggling to maintain a steady voice.

"A big chunk of you wants to try and find her and, if not, to bring her back, or at least go to join her."

"Yeah," was all he said. He pulled out his bandana and blew his nose. "Two things about that: I know the chances of my finding her are slim to none. The second thing is: I'm beginning to wonder whether she might have been looking for a way out. Maybe she doesn't want to be tied down or at least not to me."

"Look Andy, you're not going to like hearing this but in some ways it would be easier on you if she were dead. It's tough knowing that she's out there somewhere and maybe in some sort of danger. I have no doubt that she was very special to you. It sounds like you're beginning to doubt whether it was mutual." She glanced over at him. "I can't answer that but I'm inclined to think she cared about you a great deal. Like I said last night, I think her decision to leave was difficult and painful. It remains to be seen if that decision is going to change the situation for you."

"I have to admit I'm mad as hell. I would like to find out who's behind all of this and what it's all about. Depending on what I found out, I might be tempted to do some serious ass kicking."

"What do you figure the chances of that are?"

"About minus one million."

"You've done a lot of processing over the past several hours; anything else?"

"I don't know Jan. I'm going back and forth. One minute I feel like some chump who's been deceived; maybe from the very beginning. The next minute, I'm wanting to believe that she started out with the best of intentions and things just didn't work out." He paused for several moments. "You know about our plans to put up a decent house this spring. We were both working toward trying to save enough money so we wouldn't have to borrow any more than necessary. We came up with a design to our liking and we have contracted with a builder. Steph had even gotten loan approval. I'm wondering where she came up with the twenty-five grand she gave me toward the new house. I'm almost certain that she didn't borrow it." He lapsed into another brief silence. "I don't know. I'm at a point of wanting to put my place on the market and just take off. The dream died yesterday. I don't know if I want to stay here anymore. I don't care about much of anything right now. I don't know what I want. I don't give a rat's ass about much of anything."

They pulled into the restaurant parking lot. "Andy, you will be going through a lot of ups and downs for awhile. Advice is cheap and people seldom take it anyway. That is, unless it's what they want to hear. I'm going to toss some at you anyhow. I think you need to hang on to that place. Don't ask me how I know that. There's something almost magical about it. I felt it the first time I came there. I think

Stephanie did too. It may be one of the reasons she risked herself the way she did. She may have figured that she could get away with trying to have a normal life. What the hell, this place is a different world. It's way off the beaten track. She probably thought she could hook up with this easy-going, low-profile guy. She could take a job in this small town clinic and she could have this quiet, serene life away from everything. God only knows how whoever was looking for her found out where she was. From what you've told me and what I've been able to put together on my own, she did a real disappearing act when she left Chicago. Her roommate there thought she was moving to Galena, Illinois. She told no one where she was actually going. She collected her last paycheck on a Friday, cashed it and closed out her checking account which incidentally was in another name. If someone was following her, all of this would have started a lot sooner, like last summer."

"It sounds like you've done some investigating beyond just here."

"I was a Chicago cop for several years before I came here. I've got friends in the city who I can call on." He noticed that she had not had one cigarette thus far. "One other thing I'm going to share with you. Ms. Brandt has a list of aliases. I've uncovered four. I suspect there are others. She's only used the first name of Stephanie twice: once when she was married to Fitzpatrick and now with you under the name of Brandt. She went under the names of Elizabeth Slocum and Patricia Barber at other times. Stephanie may be for real."

When detective Miller took off her coat in the restaurant she was wearing a cream colored blouse with a brown and white sweater vest. Andy commented, "I've got to tell you, I feel like a real slob dressed this way. You look downright spiffy."

She laughed. "Now there's a word I haven't heard in a long time. My grandfather used it occasionally." They had Swedish pancakes filled with lingonberries and topped with whipped cream. Neither of them could eat more than half of their portions. They took the leftovers for later. When they came out of the restaurant, Detective Miller asked, "are you in a hurry to get back?" He said that he wasn't. "Come on, there's a nice bookstore up the street, let's go browse for a little while." She took his arm as they walked. "I gotta tell you Andy, if it had been me that this had happened to, I'd have gotten major shit-faced last night."

"I started to but I figured I had suffered enough damage for one day."

They spent an hour in the book store. Jan bought three mystery novels. "You would think doing what I do, this would be the last kind of book I'd be interested in reading. I love good mystery novels.

Maybe it's because the good guys almost always win."

He bought two children's books. "My son is coming up for Christmas. He's bringing his girlfriend and her little girl. I just realized that I haven't gotten anything for her for Christmas. I'm glad you suggested coming here." On the way back to the car he asked her, "do you have any plans for Christmas dinner?"

"A few of us cops are volunteering to serve a noon meal for the needy at one of the churches."

"How about coming to have dinner with us afterwards? A friend of mine is coming over. It will just be the six of us. I've got a turkey and all of the trimmings." She was hesitant. "Come on, it's not like this is a conflict of interest kind of thing." She tentatively accepted with the stipulation that it would depend on the weather. "Fair enough, the bar opens at three and dinner will be sometime around four. Incidentally, what do you drink?"

"I normally drink brandy Manhattans but since I'll be on the road beer or wine will work."

On the way back to his place, Andy said, "during my ruminating last night I came to the realization that there are a whole lot of things I didn't know about Steph. Now I'm beginning to wonder how much of what she told me was true."

"McLeod, are you aware that you're already starting to talk about her in the past tense?"

"Miller, have you noticed that you haven't had one cigarette in close to two-and-a-half hours?"

"I went to the doctor. He prescribed this patch thing that's supposed to reduce the craving for nicotine. We'll see. So far, so good. You know how I feel about cigarettes. I hate the goddamn things. I figure I could save myself close to a grand a year if I kicked the habit. Not to mention the health benefits. Christ, I cough up both lungs when I get up in the morning."

When she left him off, he thanked her. "You've gone way beyond the call of duty. I appreciate everything you've done."

"McLeod, I know that right now you're feeling like a real loser. You're not."

He went to the house before returning to his workshop. He added wood to the stoves and made sure nothing had been disturbed. He did the same thing when he got to the shop. Nothing seemed out of place. He needed a couple things from the hardware store in town. He and Lucy got in the truck. He stopped at the branch office of the bank to deposit the cashier's check Stephanie had left for him. After finding what he needed at the hardware store he looked around for a small present for Rob and for Detective Miller. He found a photo calendar that featured pictures taken of various scenic spots around Door County. He bought four of them. He would give one to Brian, one to Rob, one to Jan and one for himself. He left there and drove down the street to the gas station to fill up the truck. On the way he passed a small Scandinavian apparel shop. He stopped at the shop on his way back through town. After looking around he decided on a hand woven scarf. The shop owner knew him and gave him a twenty-five percent discount. "I was half thinking about giving this scarf to myself," she said. "It's hand woven wool you know. It's so soft and I love the colors and design. Stephanie is going to be very pleased." He didn't tell her that it wasn't for Stephanie. He thanked the woman and wished her a merry Christmas. He was sure that if Stephanie were here, she would be very pleased with it. 'She loves handmade things and this really is elegant'. He felt a twinge of betrayal about buying something this nice for someone else.

When he got back home, Andy located the Christmas-tree stand upstairs in the barn. He got his bow saw. Accompanied by Lucy, he trudged out to find and cut a tree. Space was limited in the living room. Thus, he needed to find a fairly small tree. He found a five-foot scotch pine that had a nice shape. An hour later he had the tree installed in the living room. He would decorate it that evening.

It occurred to him as he was working that afternoon that maybe Rob would be interested in buying Stephanie's car. He thought about how much the car was probably worth. He decided to offer it to Rob for a ridiculously low price. He knew he couldn't just give it to him. He was sure Rob would refuse it as an outright gift. He smiled, 'Hell, he won't know what to do with a decent set of wheels. I'll bet he'll hang onto the wreck though, just to have something to go back and forth to work in'.

Andy was in the process of making a doll cradle for Brian's girl-friend's daughter. As he worked, he thought about whether there had been any clues earlier on that Stephanie was on the run from some-body. He recalled the noticeable change in her mood right around Thanksgiving. Other than that, he could not identify anything else. He was still surprised by the discovery of her having taken out a life insurance policy. Did she think she was in imminent danger? He recalled how certain she appeared to be that the threat would be over. He remembered that it was the night the guy had tried to run her off the road. She had sounded so sure when they were at the Pub. He had disclosed all the things that had been going on. Maybe what she was so sure of was what she needed to do. The threat wasn't over. It wasn't going to go away by itself. From what he could recall of their conversation, he had gotten the impression that she was going to take care of it, as if she could bring an immediate halt to all of it.

Finally, the question he had been unable to ask broke through. 'Why had she not been killed? It wasn't for lack of opportunity. Did she know something or was she holding on to something that was keeping her alive? Was whoever this was, hoping that she would lead him/them to it? How confident can these people be that she didn't share her secret? How can they know that whatever it is, isn't here? Am I still in jeopardy? I've got to stop raising these impossible questions and speculating about everything. I'm driving myself nuts. I'm just going to have to wait and see. In the meantime I'm going to keep watching my back'. He still hoped he would hear from her, even if it was indirectly. He wanted to know that she was okay.

By walk time he had the doll cradle finished except for painting it. He would do that first thing in the morning. As he and Lucy trudged through the snow, he found himself looking forward to the next couple of days. Brian and company would be here tomorrow. He would be sharing Christmas. The pain of losing Stephanie was acute but maybe Christmas would help ease the misery. 'It's after Christmas, when I'll be by myself entirely, that's going to be the real challenge. It's going to be one damn long winter'.

The sun was just about to set as their walk ended. He stood in the lee of the house watching the sky change colors. He wondered where in this world Stephanie was and if she was able to see the sun setting. In the house he remembered to get the turkey out of the freezer to thaw. After pouring a drink, he set about wrapping the calendars and the scarf. It seemed strange to not see Stephanie's coat hanging on the rack near the door or her boots next to the dining room stove. He went searching for and found his bartenders guide to look up the ingredients for a brandy Manhattan. He had some brandy in the cabinet but no sweet vermouth or bitters. He put them on his last minute grocery list.

He thought about Jan. She had made a real effort to make herself look presentable this morning. She had used less makeup and she really was dressed tastefully. As the saying goes 'the girl had cleaned up nicely'. He had grown to like her. He sensed the feeling was mutual. He could see them being friends and maybe even getting together socially from time to time. He could not see the two of them ever ending up as lovers or partners. He hoped she would be successful in kicking her cigarette habit. It was a thing that he found to be almost repulsive. He didn't know why but he found it especially obnoxious in women. He had been impressed with her perceptiveness from the very beginning. He thought she had a wisdom about her that could only come from lots of life experience and an uncommon sensitivity.

He wondered how she saw him. It had made him feel good this morning when she had assured him that he was not a loser. That was how he had come to look at people during his career as a social worker. There were the winners and the losers. He didn't think it was because of his cynicism that he had come to see the losers as outnumbering the winners. In his opinion it was the other way around. It was because there were so many losers or people who were afraid to risk themselves at anything, that he had become so cynical. He sensed that Detective Miller had a large core of that too, but for whatever reason, she had not directed much of it toward him. He imagined that she was capable of being unmercifully caustic under certain circumstances. He suspected one of those circumstances had to do with intimacy. She avoided closeness. She disclosed very little about herself to anyone. Unlike Stephanie, who had misled him with untruths, Miller revealed little or nothing.

Andy scrounged up some cheese and crackers. He found a venison sausage that he had set aside for Stephanie to take with her in one of the refrigerator drawers. He sliced a few pieces. He had just started decorating the tree when the phone rang. It was Brian. "Hi Pops, I'm just calling to see if you needed anything before we head out in the morning?" He thought about it as they chatted.

"Yeah I just thought of something. Pick me up a small bottle of sweet vermouth and some bitters." Brian asked if he had changed from drinking martinis. "No, it's for a friend of mine who may join us for Christmas dinner. She drinks Manhattans. I've got another friend who's going to join us as well. I hate to think of anyone having to spend Christmas alone." Brian asked, "if he had heard from Stephanie? Had she arrived in Orlando safely?" "Yeah, she's doing just fine. She was smart to leave Thursday rather than Friday. I imagine O'Hare was a madhouse today."

"In my opinion O'Hare is a madhouse every day." Brian commented.

Andy chuckled, "spoken like a true McLeod." After they hung up, he realized that this was the first time he had even come close to laughing in days.

When he went to bed at 10:00, the temperature had fallen to three degrees. He lay in bed appreciating the warmth of the mattress pad heater. He made a mental list of things he needed to do tomorrow morning which included bringing in firewood, vacuuming and dusting. He needed to make up the bed upstairs. He assumed that Brian and his girlfriend slept together. He would get out sleeping bags and a pillow to make a bed for little Allison. He couldn't think of anything else. He went to sleep easily.

Andy got up the next morning as it was just beginning to become light out. The temperature was eight below. He went upstairs after a breakfast of vegetable juice and tuna salad that he ate while standing at the kitchen sink. He hadn't noticed before, but Stephanie had already made up the guest bed. She had also gotten out the sleeping bags for the little girl. He thought to himself, 'she was like that; she saw things that needed to be done, and she did them'. He felt melancholy returning. It increased when he found the cross-country ski package he had gotten for her in a far corner of the room. He ran the vacuum and did some minor dusting, mainly in the living room. He filled up the wood bins for both of the stoves. He was at work in the shop by nine o'clock. He didn't expect Brian to arrive before the middle of afternoon. 'I'll try calling Corey this evening to wish him a Merry Christmas'. He hoped the package he had sent over a week ago had arrived. Among other things, it contained some cookies that Stephanie had baked which was another of her thoughtful gestures. While he was waiting for the shop to warm enough to paint the doll cradle, he carved Allison's name into it. More than once during the day he wondered if he was still under surveillance. He considered doing a search to see if he could uncover any devices. In the end he decided, 'Fuck-em, I've got nothing to hide. If someone wants to sit around listening to or watching me, they'll end up dying of boredom'. He thought about whether to tell Brian anything about the situation with Stephanie. He decided not to, 'why spread gloom? This is going to be a pleasant Christmas. I'll need to tell him later rather than sooner'.

Brian and company arrived a little before three o'clock. "We'd have been here sooner Pops but we drove through about forty miles of heavy snowfall that started just north of Sheboygan. That must be what they mean when they call lake-effect snow." It had only gotten up to twelve degrees. The clouds were thickening.

"Luce and I usually go for a walk this time of the day but it's too cold and windy. We'll skip it," Andy told them. He helped carry luggage and Christmas presents into the house. He warned the little girl, Allison, not to get too close to the stoves. "Their very hot sweetheart. It's how I make my house warm."

Allison was drawn to Lucy. She talked to Lucy telling her what a nice dog she was. Lucy was her most gentle self with the girl. "Lucy really likes you," Andy told her. "Put your face close to hers and she will give you a kiss." Throughout the next hour Allison sought and received several Lucy kisses which were always a single lick.

"Pops, I brought you a special present. I want you to open it now." Brian handed his father a package. He opened it to discover a large bottle of expensive imported gin. Brian asked if he had ever had this particular gin.

"Not ever. I've probably had a few quality martinis in my life at the officer's club, but I was too young and stupid to know it or appreciate them." He opened the bottle. He invited Brian to join him.

Brian declined, saying that he and Amanda were strictly wine drinkers. He opened a bottle of wine they had brought with them. Andy mixed a martini. "Christ, I'm going to be so spoiled I won't be able to go back to that panther urine I'm used to."

They all sat down in the living room. Amanda said, "this place is quite charming. It's not at all what I expected. The way Brian described it, I was expecting something really run down."

"It's run down," Andy told her. "The house is circa a hundred-and-thirty-six years old. I've managed to make a few improvements but it's not worth trying to save. I'm hoping to put up a decent place possibly this spring." He showed her around so she could see how he lived. She modified her description from charming to quaint. "It's beyond quaint. Primitive is probably a more apt description," Andy corrected. Moments after he turned on the lamps, the flies began to buzz and careening off the lamp shades. He was sure that Amanda was now searching for a word that superseded primitive like backward, primordial or Stone Age. 'This was probably why Steph had not wanted him to turn on the lamps the last two nights she was here? Was she sick and tired of this place?' He apologized for the flies and explained that was only one of the reasons he was planning to build something livable. "This poor old house is infested with them." She asked if he had ever sought the services of an exterminator. "I had a guy come in the first year I lived here. After three visits and vacuuming up literally gallons of dead flies, I gave up. It wasn't making any difference. The guy said that I needed to tear off all the exterior siding and put up a barrier. To do it right I also needed to raise the house up and pour a concrete slab underneath. He couldn't guarantee that those efforts would solve the problem. The house isn't worth going to that kind of expense. Since then, my goal has been to save up enough money to build anew."

That night he lay in bed thinking that he probably shouldn't have told her about all of the things wrong with this place. She impressed him as being a fastidious person. He could see that she was becoming increasingly uncomfortable with being here. In some ways, she reminded him of his ex-girlfriend Josie. It was going on three years since Josie had left here. She'd written him a few times after leaving. It had been months since he had last heard from her. He seldom thought of her. He wondered if Josie had heard that he was with someone else. He soon dozed off. He was awakened at two o'clock by Lucy's growl. He picked up the gun and made the rounds of the house. It had started snowing. Looking out the dining room window he guessed that there was already an inch of fresh snow on the ground. He heard the coyotes. From their increasing loudness, he could tell they were getting closer. He went to the front room window, just in time to see a pack of eight of them come into the yard. Four of them stopped briefly to sniff around. They yipped and howled; then vanished quickly.

He heard voices upstairs. Moments later Brian descended the stairs partway. He saw his father and asked, "What's that terrible screaming sound, Pops?"

"It's alright," Andy assured his son. "It's coyotes. There's a pack of them that pass through here every once in awhile. They sound scary, but there's nothing to worry about. They try to avoid humans."

"You're right, they do sound scary. I thought it was just wolves that formed packs."

Brian said goodnight again and went back up stairs. Andy fed the stoves. He could hear Brian and Amanda talking. When he returned to bed, he petted Lucy. "I have a feeling that we won't be seeing that young lady again."

Andy got up early the next morning to get things organized in preparation for Christmas dinner. When he heard people stirring up stairs, he called up the stairs, "do you want to open presents before or after breakfast? I'm planning on making pancakes."

"I think Allison wants to open them before." Brian called down.

They came downstairs a few minutes later, fully dressed. "If anyone wants to take a bath after breakfast, feel welcome. Brian knows the drill for running the hot water." Amanda looked cross and haggard. Andy surmised it was from not having gotten much sleep.

"It looks like we got quite a bit of snow, Pops."

Andy glanced out the kitchen window, "we got maybe four or five inches. There's not much wind so it's not drifting. It's cold. It will be light and easy to blow. I'll wait until it slows down before I get the blower out." He poured coffee for Brian and Amanda and a glass of orange juice for Allison. They went into the living room and Brian began distributing presents. Allison liked her doll cradle. He had made a jewelry/music box for Amanda. He could see that she was struggling to be gracious. He had built a table top dictionary stand for Brian that could also be used as a portable lectern. He had made several folk toys as stocking stuffers for Allison. Brian gave his father two books on chip carving along with knives and a sharpening stone. "How thoughtful," Andy commented I've read a couple of articles about this type of carving. It looks like a perfect way to embellish wood working projects." Amanda and Allison gave him some leather mittens that had wool liners. He was sure Brian had influenced that purchase.

After breakfast, Brian helped clean up the kitchen. Amanda took Allison into the bathroom to give her a bath. "Pops, I hope you won't be offended. Amanda is a city girl. She's really uncomfortable being here. I tried to explain this place to her. I think between the flies and the coyotes early this morning, she's gone beyond her limit. If you don't mind, I think I'll see if I can find a motel for us to stay in for tonight. She's willing to do that. I think she would like for us to leave today but with it snowing like this, I don't think we should risk it. I'm really sorry."

"You don't need to apologize. This place is an embarrassment. I don't blame her. Hell, I don't know how Stephanie was able put up with it for as long as she did; Josie either, for that matter."

Brian studied his father; then asked "why did you just refer to Stephanie in the past tense? Has she left?"

Andy looked away. Reality finally came crashing down. Tears welled up, "yeah, she's not coming back."

"Oh Jesus, Pops, I am so sorry." He put his arms around his father. They held one another. When Andy was finally able to regain some composure, Brian asked why she had left.

"It wasn't this place. It's a long story. I can't tell you about it right now for several reasons."

"Did you know she was leaving for good on Thursday when you took her to the airport?"

"Maybe some part of me saw what was coming. I just didn't want to face it. It's something that just had to be."

"Is she sick or something?"

"No she's not sick. I'm sorry to be sounding so secretive. He touched Brian's arm. "To be honest with you, I don't really know what it's all about myself. I have practically driven myself crazy over the past couple of days speculating. I'm trying not to do that. The fact is I may never know the real reason. It's just something that had to be."

"You loved her didn't you, Pops?"

"Besides you and Corey, I've never loved anyone more."

Amanda came out of the bathroom with Allison. Andy turned his attention to Allison. "Hey, sweetheart that's a nice outfit you've got on. It that your special Christmas sweater?"

She came over to him and he picked her up. She touched his beard, "can I call you grandpa?"

He smiled at her. "Well, you know, I'm not really your grandpa.

You already have two grandpas. Why don't we just stick with Andy?" He let her down and she went to get a kiss from Lucy. "I need to take care of a couple of things out in the workshop. I'll be back in awhile to put the turkey in the oven."

He put on his coat. He and Lucy went to the barn. He started a fire. He sat down on the stool and watched the snow coming down. He felt pretty certain that Jan was not going to be able to make it for dinner. He tried not to let himself get discouraged. He went upstairs in the barn to find some basswood that he could use to practice chip carving on. He found two boards that were suitable.

Brian came into the shop a few minutes later. "I found a motel that's fairly close by and has a room for tonight. The lady said that all their rooms are booked between Christmas and New Year's. I guess a lot of people come up to go snowmobiling and cross-country skiing for the week." Brian apologized again. "What are you going to do with Stephanie gone, Pops? It's going be a hell of a long winter here by yourself. Have you thought about going somewhere else?"

"I've decided not to decide anything for right now. Everything is set for construction to start on the new house in April." He reminded Brian, "besides, it's not the first winter I've been here by myself."

"Can you afford to go ahead with the house on your own, Pops?" Andy explained that Stephanie had left him some money to help out. He didn't tell Brian how much. "I don't understand, Pops. She left you but gave you money towards a new house. Does that mean she's planning to come back sometime in the future?" Andy told him that he seriously doubted he'd ever see her again.

Andy apologized again. "I'll tell you about it someday but I can't right now. He went to his work bench and wrote a note to Brian telling him that he suspected that the workshop and house were bugged. After Brian read it, Andy crumpled the note and threw it in the stove. He added more logs. Brian wrote a note back asking if that was why he couldn't say anything about what had happened. Andy nodded. "Jesus, Pops, maybe you ought to think about getting out of here."

"I've thought about it. I might. We'll see."

"Are you in any kind of danger?" Brian asked.

"A lot of things have happened in the past few weeks. I'm hoping things will settle down now that she's gone."

"You haven't answered my question, Pops. Have you gone to the authorities?" He nodded. "I don't suppose they can do much. I mean they're probably not equipped to deal with a situation like this."

"Actually they have done an outstanding job. They've bent over backwards to be of help. Look, I'm sorry that I slipped and let the cat out of the bag. That was dumb of me. Most people wouldn't have picked up on it. I appreciate your concern but for now it's best that we change the subject." Brian understood. "Let's go stick that turkey in the oven."

Brian said that he could do it. He asked what temperature he needed to set the oven at and how long it needed to be in. Before leaving the shop he said, "I was hoping I could show Amanda around. She's never been up here before. The weather isn't cooperating."

The phone rang shortly after Brian left the shop. It was Janet Miller. "Andy, I'm sorry. I don't think I'm going to be able to make it for dinner. The roads are treacherous." He agreed. He wished her a Merry Christmas and told her he would call her early next week.

After hanging up with Detective Miller, the phone rang again. It was Rob. "Andy, the wreck died. I think it threw a rod. I'm not going to be able to make it for dinner. I'm trying to figure out what I can do for transportation. This couldn't come at a worse time."

"Relax my friend. I have a solution to your problem. You can use Stephanie's car. I'll clear my drive way right now and come get you. It might take me awhile. I'll call you before I leave here." The snow was diminishing. He got out the snow blower and wearing his new lined mittens, he blew the driveway clear. Brian helped by shoveling paths to the cars and cleaning snow off the vehicles. He asked to go with to pick up Rob. On the way Andy asked that Brian not say anything to Rob about Stephanie. "His car went south on him. I'm going to let him use her car. Actually, I'm going to offer to sell it to him at a price he can't refuse, but that can wait until later."

The turkey took longer to cook than Andy has anticipated. They didn't eat until after five. Rob left at seven-thirty in Stephanie's car. Brian and company left for the motel at eight. "I think we'll leave right from the motel in the morning, Pops. I'll call you when we get home. Thanks for everything." Amanda gave him a token hug. He sensed that she couldn't wait to get out of his varmint infested abode. Allison hugged Lucy and then him. After they were gone he turned on the mattress pad heater, mixed a drink and lay down on the bed. He was almost asleep when the phone rang. "How did it go McLeod?" He spent half an hour talking with Detective Miller. Before hanging up he thanked her for calling. He told her that he was disappointed she hadn't been able to come for dinner. "I'll be up your way the day after tomorrow. I'll buy you a cup of coffee. I'll see you at 8:30."

Chapter 10

It was cold but there was very little wind when Andy got up the next morning. He worked the entire day finishing up a half dozen benches that he would add to his inventory for the next season. He noted that it had now been almost four full days without anything happening. He was still carrying his pistol and he kept it handy all of the time.

Rob drove in just as Andy and Lucy were entering the house. He was almost giddy. "Jesus Andy, you don't know how good it feels to drive something this nice. I really appreciate you letting me borrow it. I hope it's alright with Steph."

"I talked to her last night after you left. She's happy to have you using it." Rob asked if he needed to have it back by Thursday. "No, you can hang onto it. It turns out her mother is very sick. She has cancer. Steph has decided to stay in Florida to help her mother out. I'll let you know when she thinks she'll be coming back. I don't expect it will be anytime soon."

Rob promised to take good care of it. He stayed for some leftover turkey, "I probably shouldn't say this but Brian's lady friend seemed kind of uncomfortable yesterday. Is that just the way she is?"

"She was very uncomfortable," Andy told him. "Brian says that he tried to prepare her for what to expect about this place. She was enamored with it for the first ten minutes they were here. The flies and the bathroom facilities got the best of her. The final straw was a pack of coyotes that came screaming through here at two o'clock Christmas morning."

Rob smiled, "well, you have to admit Andy, this place is pretty primitive. It's barely a step above tent camping." Andy agreed. Rob went on, "frankly my friend, I don't know how you've managed to live this way for so long." When Rob left, he thanked Andy again for the use of the car. "Say 'Hi' to Steph when you talk to her."

That night Lucy got up on the bed with him for the first time since Stephanie had come to live there. She stayed the entire night. The next morning Detective Miller was her usual punctual self. She was also back to her absurd clothing. Her hair was teased. She had on dark brown lipstick, violet stirrup pants and a green and white knit sweater. She took the two of them to a coffee shop that had homemade pastries. She was talkative on the way and seemed in a good mood. "I was really disappointed that the weather turned so shitty for Christmas. I was looking forward to meeting your son. I brought some of the leftovers from the church dinner home with me. People are so brain washed about the holidays. It's almost impossible for them to face spending them alone." He asked her if she had family back in Chicago. She completely ignored his question.

At the coffee shop Detective Miller ordered a large latte and a gigantic cinnamon roll. Andy just had a cup of coffee. After they were seated, she asked, "have there been any more incidents since our girl left?"

"No, nothing has happened. I don't know if I'm still being watched or not. I trust there's some way that can be checked?" She said that was one of the reasons she was here. With his permission, the sheriff was going to request 'techies' from Madison go over his place including the vehicles. He responded by saying, "I've given the matter some thought. I'm inclined to leave well enough alone for the time being. If I'm still bugged, it's because they, whoever the hell 'they' are, think that I know something about where Steph went. Let's let them waste their time, energy, and money watching me. They'll eventually give up on their own accord out of sheer boredom. It doesn't matter to me that they're doing something illegal. We'll probably never find out who they are anyhow." She asked why he was so willing to sacrifice his privacy. "Miller, my life is about as exciting as watching a species evolve. Boring their asses off may be the only vengeance I'll ever extract." When she dropped him off, she told him to call her if anything came up. He told her to hang on for a minute. "I've got a couple of small Christmas presents for you." She objected saying that he had already given her a present. He went in the house and got the two presents and brought them to her car. She liked the calendar. She especially liked the scarf.

She asked, "I've seen your workshop but I haven't seen the rest of your house, just the dining room and the toilet. Would you mind showing me around especially after what you told me about your son's girl friend?"

He explained the house to her as he showed her around. She said nothing. He told her about the house that he had plans to put up in the spring. She asked if he had the plans for it. He located them and showed them to her. "I like the design, McLeod. I really think you ought to go ahead with it. You can't leave here. If you let go of this place you'll be kicking yourself for the rest of your life. Most people would give an arm and a leg to have a place like this." She turned to face him. "You'll get over this. You'll find someone else to share the dream with." After she left he went back to his workshop.

The week went by quickly. On Sunday afternoon, the day before New Year's Eve, he called Detective Miller. "Yo, Miller, it's your favorite victim." She sounded glad to hear from him. He asked her, "what are you doing for New Year's Eve?"

"I'm staying home and getting drunk all by myself and, no, I'm not coming up to your place. I'm not risking my life driving anywhere on that night in particular."

"How about we meet half way in between for an early dinner?" He told her the name of the restaurant he had in mind. She knew of it. "I'll buy. I promise not to whine, speculate or ask questions."

"McLeod, you don't whine much, but you don't know how not to speculate, or ask questions."

"May I take that as a 'yes'?" He suggested they meet there at six o'clock.

He arrived at the restaurant a few minutes early and ordered a dark beer on draft. She showed up punctually dressed nicely in a pants suit. She took the initiative and gave him a friendly but slight hug. "What do you do, Miller? Do you sit somewhere and wait so you can arrive at the exact time?" She did not answer. She ordered a glass of wine. "I take it that I've just asked a question you've decided not to answer."

She sat down on one of the bar stools. She set her purse on the bar and looked straight at him. "Andy, in the course of the past several weeks we've got to be kind of friends. That threatens to muddy the waters. I think we need to back off and resume the professional relationship we started out with." He asked what she meant by that. She looked down and shook her head. "I think I'd better go home. Being here is against my better judgment." She picked up her purse and started to get off the bar stool.

"Jan, look I don't know what has happened in your life but we've both been around the block more than once. Let's have dinner. You're right, we do have a kind of friendship. You've seen me through a bunch of crap and you've shown great sensitivity to the situation." She hesitated. "Come on, let's go have dinner."

The hostess seated them asking if they were going to stay for the New Year's celebration. "No, we're just here for dinner, thank you," he told her. They splurged and had barbequed ribs, which, it turned out, was a favorite for both of them. Over dinner they talked about their previous professional lives in Illinois. After dinner he walked her to her car. They gave one another a terse hug. He watched her drive off, then got in his truck and went home.

It was a few minutes before midnight when Andy was awakened by the phone ringing. He answered it groggily. It was Detective

Miller. "McLeod, Happy New Year."

Not long into the conversation he said, "Jan, I don't know what to make of you." He recounted their previous lengthy conversations and how formal and abrupt she might be the next time they talked.

"I know. I'm sorry." There was a long silence. He could hear the tinkling of ice cubes. "Andy, I'm kind of, I have a bit of a problem. Sometimes I drink too much. I'm sorry, I shouldn't have called you." Click.

He had to search for her home number. He was angry with himself that he still hadn't memorized it. He let the phone ring numerous times without an answer. He hung up and repeated the same process. She still refused to answer. The third time he tried, she answered on the tenth ring. "Piss off, McLeod, leave me the hell alone."

"I'm not going to do that. Talk to me." Her voice sounded congested. He wondered if she had been crying.

"Andy, I'm a goddamn mess. I'm a ridiculous human being. Who in the hell in their right mind would...?" She stopped herself. "I'm drunk. I'm going to sleep."

"Don't hang up," He almost begged. He waited to see if she had anything more to say. She didn't. "You know, women in general are an enigma to me. You, more than most. One minute you're outgoing and friendly and the next you act like I'm a total stranger. We've spent a couple of very nice times together. Tonight was one of them." She did not respond. "Is it just me or are you like this with everybody?"

"I wish I wasn't so goddamn drunk. I'm in no condition to carry on a sensible conversation." After a shorter delay she said, "I'll call you next week." Before he could say anything, she hung up.

He lay back in bed. Lucy jumped up beside him. He put a hand on her back. "Jesus, Luce, the longer I live, the less I know."

In mid-January Andy received a letter addressed to him from the American Consulate in Mexico City. The letter expressed regret and sympathy about having to inform him that Ms. Stephanie Brandt had died in an automobile accident near the city of Guadalajara on December 27th. All attempts to locate her next of kin have been unsuccessful. His name was the only one found among her personal belongings. Could he be of any assistance in locating any of her relatives? He immediately called Detective Miller. She was not available. An hour later she called. She apologized for not getting back to him sooner. He asked where she was calling him from. "I'm in my office."

"Can I meet you somewhere? Something has come up that I need to discuss with you."

She sounded tired. "Can this wait until tomorrow, McLeod?" He said that it could. "I'll meet you at the coffee shop at nine."

The rest of the day and a good part of that night, he pondered the validity of the letter. Was Stephanie really dead or was this a part of the disappearing act or was it some kind of trap? He had no idea as to whether she had any living relatives. He couldn't refer the consulate to anyone. He was willing to offer to take care of her remains. From one of their early-on discussions, he knew that she wanted to be cremated. It wasn't until this moment that he realized some part of him had been clinging to some thread of hope that he might see her again. He was certain that he didn't want to ever go through what he had been through the previous two months. He had managed to convince himself that, if she showed up in the future, he would refuse to resume the relationship. 'It would be sheer stupidity to risk myself like that again. I don't blame her for what happened before, at least not entirely. She took a chance and it failed. I would have only myself to blame, if I allowed it to happen all over again; first time, shame on you; second time, shame on me'. That was the reasonable side of him. That night in bed, the loneliness and the longing took its turn. 'If whoever is after her is convinced that she's dead, maybe in time we might find a way to get back together. It can't be here. He did miss her. He didn't want to go on living alone. 'We had something few people ever experience. Having experienced that, I don't want to live out the rest of my life alone'.

He met Detective Miller the next morning. She had on medium gray stirrup pants, a lemon yellow satiny blouse and a lavender vest. Her hair was freshly dyed and was platinum-colored. He thought it made her look older. "How's the patch thing doing? Are you still nicotine free?"

She gave a sarcastic laugh. "I don't know what's in those patches. I had a cigarette the other day and within minutes, I was so sick I was afraid I was going to live. Talk about aversion therapy. Yeah, I'm hanging in there. The craving's not quite so strong. It's the worst when I get up in the morning. I love a cigarette with my first cup of coffee. So, what's up?" He showed her the letter from the consulate. After reading it she said, "Christ, I could use a cigarette right now." She looked at him, "what do you think, McLeod? Do you think this is for real?"

"I've got a quarter. Do you want to flip for the best two out of three?"

"Yeah, those are my exact sentiments." She went back over the letter; then looked at him again. "Did this open up wounds?"

"A little," he shrugged. "I think the way I need to handle this is to leave the letter lying around. I've decided to write the consulate and tell them that I have no knowledge of any living relatives. That's the truth. I'll tell them she and I were partners up until recently, and I'm that willing to assume responsibility for taking care of her remains."

"What's the point of involving yourself at all?"

"Maybe she is dead. If so I might have an opportunity to verify her remains." Detective Miller doubted it. "Okay, but if what appears to be her remains are sent to me, then maybe whoever has been out to get her, will give up for once and for all." She doubted that too. "Well, what would you do?"

"I'm not you. You're still determined to try to find out what this is all about aren't you?" She softened her tone a little. "Look Andy, if this is going to put an end to what has been happening; then fine. Go for it. It's a crap shoot. Maybe it will work. I doubt it but I've been wrong before." She took a couple of swallows of coffee. "Just don't pin too many hopes on this bringing you relief. It sure as hell ain't going to bring you any closer to the truth. If I've learned nothing else over the years, it's that the 'truth' is seldom what it appears to be." She gave him a weak smile. Before getting up to leave the coffee shop she said, "If you'd like, I'm willing to look over your response letter before you send it." He tried to pay the bill. "Hey, this is your tax dollars at work. I'm on official business. I'll pay."

She called him the next day. "Have you written the letter yet McLeod?" He had. "Is it typed?" It was not. "I'm in the neighborhood. I'll be by in fifteen minutes. I'll get it typed for you and bring it by tomorrow for you to sign." When she arrived she had on the same gray pants. He couldn't see what she had on under her coat. She read through the letter. "This is good, McLeod. It's very businesslike. I think you should insist that they send the body. Leave out any mention of cremation." She pursed her lips then positioned herself in front of him. "McLeod, I'm sorry about the way I treated you the other night. I got drunk on my ass after I got home from dinner. I have trouble with the holidays. That's just the way it is. No, I don't want to talk about it. I was touched by your effort to reach out to me. I'm sure I sounded like an absolute bitch. It's my way of trying to protect you from me. Am I forgiven?"

He nodded. "What happened?"

"It's none of your damn business. Believe me, you don't want to know. Besides, talking about things doesn't do jack shit. It just keeps old wounds from healing. I'll tell you something else. Time is not the healer it's cracked up to be."

"What does heal?"

"There are things that can't be healed, not ever."

She started to turn to leave. He leaned back against his work bench. "Jan, what keeps you going?"

She glanced back at him. "I don't know. I could ask you the same question. Maybe for me, it's trying to put as many bad guys away as possible. See you tomorrow McLeod."

By walk time it had started snowing again and the wind was increasing. Andy waited until they were back from their walk before he mixed his drink. He had made up a pot of chili a couple of days before. There was too much of it for one person. He had frozen half of it. He was about to heat up a bowl of it when Rob showed up. He invited Rob to join him for supper. "Andy, I just noticed yesterday that there's a ding in the front right fender of Steph's car. I don't know if someone banged into it at work or not."

"No, that happened shortly before she left. We just didn't get around to having it repaired. Don't worry about it." Andy chose to avoid telling Rob about how it had happened the night Stephanie had almost been run off the road. Rob asked how Stephanie's mother was doing. "Her mom has terminal cancer. She's refusing to go through any kind of treatment for it. This could go on for awhile. You're welcome to hang on to her car for the foreseeable future." Rob asked about maintenance and specifically when it needed to have the oil changed. "I just had that done about three weeks ago. You're good for the next three or four months."

As he was about to leave Rob complimented Andy on his outstanding chili. "You're going to make Stephanie a hell of a wife."

Detective Miller called at eight o'clock the next morning. "McLeod, I'll meet you at the coffee shop in twenty minutes." Click. He went out to the workshop and started a fire, then drove to the coffee shop. He was two minutes late. Detective Miller was already seated at one of the small tables. She had on the lime green stirrup pants today. She had her usual latte and large cinnamon roll. She also had a cup of coffee and a roll for him. "If I'm going to be decadent, you might as well join me." She announced that she had signed up at the local YMCA yesterday. "I was up at six this morning. I worked out and went for a swim. Man, am I out of shape. You wouldn't know it to look at me now but I used to be svelte. I have a brown belt in karate. I haven't practiced it in so long, I don't know if I can remember even half of the moves." She looked at him. "So say something."

He shook his head and smiled. "Miller, you're a piece of work. I never know what to expect from you."

She ignored his comment. "About your letter, the more I thought about it I decided to make a couple of revisions. I have you requesting her body as opposed to her cremated remains. You are requesting that her body be transported at U.S. government expense, since there are no living relatives that we are aware of. Let's see what happens."

"What do you think will happen?" She shrugged as she handed him the letter. He noticed that it was on official Sheriff's Department stationary. "What's this about?" She said he might get better results if the consulate thought they were dealing with someone in law enforcement. He read it through and signed it.

"I'll mail it for you. It's official business."

"How's your day? I mean are you busy for the next couple of hours?" Andy asked.

"I'm always busy. So what are you asking?"

"I want to take you on a hike." She looked at him skeptically. "I'm serious. There's a special place not very far from here that I think you'll enjoy seeing. It's probably a mile hike one way."

She looked at the last bite of her cinnamon roll. "What the hell, I need to burn off some of these calories, why not?" They took his truck. The road into the point was snow covered. Because it was sheltered by the surrounding forest, the snow was not drifted or deep. They parked and Lucy jumped out of the truck to immediately begin exploring. After hiking a quarter of a mile, detective Miller asked, "what is this place? I didn't know this road even existed."

"I've never been out here in the winter. I think it is probably one of the most magical places on the planet." It was starting to snow lightly.

She took his arm, "Andy, I'm sorry that I'm such a bitch at times. I've had some bad experiences with men. Sometimes I let those get in the way. You're a nice guy. I end up kicking myself when I treat people badly. I didn't say what I meant to say what I meant to say other night when we went out for dinner. I mean the part about 'resuming a professional relationship'. We're friends. There's no reason why we can't have it both ways."

"I really don't know what to make of you at times, Miller. Maybe I'm just too sensitive. I get to feeling like you're pissed with me about something when you're so curt. The next time I talk to you, you're back to being sensitive and friendly and intuitive. Maybe that's just the way you are with everybody. I have a tendency to take things too seriously."

"You're a sensitive soul, Andy. I'll try not to be so 'curt', as you put it." They arrived at the point. The more she saw of it, the more she was awestruck. "Honest to god Andy, this really is an unbelievable place. I didn't know it even existed." They came to the very edge of the promontory looking out over the lake. They were standing side by side. Andy put a hand on her shoulder. He could feel her tense up. He withdrew it and apologized. They stood in silence for several long moments. She said, "let's go." She seemed angry. They began trudging through the snow in silence. About half way back she stopped. "Alright goddamn it, I'm going to tell you what happened. Do not, I repeat, do not show me even the slightest pity." She took a deep breath. She glared at him. She started, "when I was twelve years old an uncle who lived with us started molesting me. After the second or third time, I tried to tell my mother. She called me a liar. She accused me of trying to ruin his reputation and fuck up our whole family. It continued. By the time I was thirteen I started running away and I ended up in juvenile detention. I was placed in a series of foster homes. None of those worked out. I ended up back in juvey and was labeled incorrigible. I was damaged goods. I got pregnant at sixteen. I gave the baby up for adoption. I got pregnant again at seventeen and married the father. The bastard beat me up so bad, I lost the baby. Guess what? I was so screwed up, I had so little sense of self-worth, I refused to press charges and I went back to the son-of-a-bitch. One night he came home with a bunch of his buddies to watch Monday night football. The next thing I knew they were gang banging me. They all took turns doing me." She unbuttoned the top three buttons of her coat and pulled down the front of her sweater. "See this scar? One of the mother-fuckers cut my throat afterwards and they left me to die. I managed to pull a pillow case off and use it to put pressure on my throat and call 911. When I got out of the hospital a month later, I bought a gun. I learned how to shoot. I started taking karate lessons. I swore I would never let anything like that happen to me ever again. I was done being a victim. I caught up with a couple of the bastards who had raped me. I had them arrested. I'm sorry now that I didn't just shoot their goddamn brains out instead of trying to rely on the criminal justice system. They both got off with light sentences. End of story." They stood in silence. The snow was coming down heavier.

"Come on lady, we're both freezing. Let's go back to my place. I'll make some coffee and teach you how to chip carve."

She looked at him incredulously. "What? You're going to teach me how to do what?" She started to laugh. "McLeod, are you fucking nuts, or what? I warned you not to treat me with pity. Instead you offer to teach me how to carve a stupid piece of wood." He shrugged and they began walking briskly. Neither of them said anything further until they reached the truck, "I can't come up to your place. I've got a bunch of things to do today. I'll take a rain check." He drove her back to the coffee shop to retrieve her car. Before she got out of his truck she said. "What I just told you about me. It's just between you and me. Nobody up here but Sheriff Cummings knows anything about my past. He doesn't know as much as what I've told you. Don't make me sorry for having let you in on my past." Andy agreed. She looked right at him. "One other thing, given what I just told you about me, you might prefer to have someone else assigned to this investigation. If so, I understand."

"Miller that is the schmaltziest thing I have ever heard anyone say. I can't believe you just said that. How am I supposed to respond?" He softened his tone. "I do have to say, it's one of the saddest stories I've ever heard. No, I don't want anyone else assigned to 'this investigation'. Back in the beginning Marty told me you were one of the best. You've proven that many times over. I still want to be friends with you." They shook hands. "Hey, thanks for redoing the letter and typing it for me."

She called him that evening. "Thanks for taking me to that place today, Andy. What's it called? Has it got a name?"

He told her it was called Thorsen Point named after the family that settled there in the 1850s. "There's a book written about the history of the place. I've got a copy of it. I'll let you borrow it. The last of the original family members died about ten years ago. She lived here in this town the last few years of her life. I saw her around but I didn't know who she was or about the Point until after she was gone." They talked for over an hour. He asked her about her becoming a cop, about her decision to leave the city and why she chose to come here. He asked her where she stood with herself at this point in her life.

"I still struggle with my past. I probably always will. I have my good days." She coughed and gave a slight laugh. "Hell, I have my good and bad hours every day. Your comment today about my running hot and cold; I know I do that. I'm impossible to live with. It seldom has anything to do with the other person. It's me. When I'm down on myself about something, I just want to be left alone. I push people away from me when I'm in a negative space. You're one of the few who refuses to be scared off completely. I figure it's just a matter of time before you join the ranks. You're a glutton for punishment, McLeod." He said nothing. There was a long silence. She started to hang up.

"Jan, have you ever considered seeing a shrink and trying medication?"

"I'm taking my medication of choice as we speak. It's called a Manhattan."

"I'm talking about antidepressants."

"Are you saying that you think I'm depressed?" He thought so. "Look, the way I see it is, I've got every reason in the world to be depressed. No goddamn happy pill is going to change what has happened to me or my back and forth Gemini personality."

"Jan, there's no question you've been through some heavy stuff but it might give you a leg up in dealing with it. What have you got to lose? If it works, great. If you're willing to consider at least giving it a try, I'll shop around for a good psychiatrist. I'll even go with you to the first visit." He told her about his years of experience as a clinician working in a community mental health center. He planted the seed; he did not push her for an immediate decision. He changed the subject. "What sex was the child you gave up for adoption?" She said it was a girl. "Have you ever thought about how you would handle it if she came looking for you?"

"I hope that day never comes," she said flatly. He asked her what she would do if it did. "I'll cross that abyss when I come to it."

"In other words, end of subject."

"You know, sometimes your persistence can be a downright pain in the ass, McLeod." He apologized.

"I'm proud of you Jan. How many weeks has it been since you gave up smoking?" She told him that she was going on five weeks. "Do you still get the craving?"

"They're not as intense or as often. What bothers me now is all the stuff I'm hacking up. The doc says now that I've stopped abusing my lungs, their trying to clean themselves out. I've gotta tell you, I'm at a point where I don't think I'll ever go back to it. I don't want to have to go through this kind of misery all over again. Besides, I just found out that after I've been smoke free for a year, my health insurance premiums will be reduced. The county pays part of the cost, and we have to pay the rest." Before they hung up she thanked him for his encouragement. "I'll think about seeing a shrink. You're right, what have I got to lose? Maybe it will help to improve my disposition. I know I can be a real ball-buster at times."

After hanging up with her, the phone rang again. "Jeez, Pops, have you got a new girlfriend? I've been trying to get a hold of you all evening?" Andy sidestepped the question and asked Brian what was up. "Well, Amanda and I have decided to go our separate ways. Its okay, I'm actually kind of relieved. Things have been headed in that direction for awhile. I don't know why it took this long to finally make the decision."

"You're too much like your old man, that's why. Besides, you really like little Allison. She's a sweetheart. The two of you adore one another." Brian agreed with the part about Allison. Andy recounted how it had taken him so long to give up on the relationship with Brian's mother, and with Josie. "A friend of mine told me not long ago that I was a glutton for punishment. I don't know if that's so true. I think both of us just have a tough time giving up on people that we're involved with. I think we keep hoping that, somehow things will get better." They talked about what was going on with Stephanie. He told Brian about the letter from the consulate informing him of her alleged death. It was almost eleven o'clock when they hung up.

Chapter 11

It became a ritual that Miller and McLeod met at the coffee shop on Wednesday mornings. Two weeks after writing the American consulate he received a letter requesting identifying information and evidence that he had been involved in a relationship with Ms. Stephanie Brandt. Detective Miller discouraged him from sending a copy of the life insurance policy. A copy of her car title was fine. She presented him with two letters of affidavit suggesting that he get one signed by his friend Rob and the other from Stephanie's employer. "All they need to do is sign them and have them notarized. In essence the letters said that they are familiar with both of you and that they were aware that the two of you resided together until recently."

Ten days later he received a letter saying that Ms. Brandt's remains would be released to him. It advised that it would be cheaper and easier to cremate her body and have the ashes sent to him. If he insisted on having her body transported, it would have to be transferred directly to a licensed mortuary. "It's your call Andy. You know you won't to be able to identify her body if it's cremated." He decided that he needed to be able to identify her remains.

At the end of another three weeks he received a notice that he had a parcel at the post office that required his signature. It was her ashes along with three copies of her death certificate and a letter apologizing for the misunderstanding. The Mexican authorities ordered her cremation in accordance with their laws, which forbid maintaining a corpse beyond sixty days without either a burial or cremation. "It's bullshit, McLeod," Jan said while they sat in her car. "Someone didn't want you to see her actual body, if there really was one. For all you know, that box of ashes may not even be human remains. I'm sorry, this smells of some sort of conspiracy. The only good news is, if you even want to label it as such, is that you have a death certificate. Now you can claim the life insurance money. You can go ahead and build that house the two of you planned." It was into March and he knew that he had to make that decision post haste.

"I've decided to go ahead with it. If I decide to leave, I'll have enhanced the value of the property. In the meantime, it will be nice to return to civilized living again. I admit that I'm not feeling particularly enthused. It was a dream we shared together. I guess it's also the money thing. It's not earned money."

"Jesus Christ, McLeod," She challenged him. "It's not a 'shared dream' anymore, and who gives a flying-fuck where the money came from. It's something you'd been hoping to do for years; long before she came on the scene. I remember you telling me that the bank refused to lend you the money you needed because you didn't earn enough. Screw the bank. Now you've got it. Loan it to yourself and pay it back to yourself, if it's that damn important to you."

He gave a slight laugh. "You do have a way with words Miller. Thanks, I mean that." He changed the subject to the proposal about her seeing a psychiatrist. "I found someone that's well respected. He's an older man. He's in Green Bay." He gave her the psychiatrist's name, address, and phone number. "I promised to go with you and I will if you want me to."

"My life sucks, McLeod. The only two things I look forward to are my job, some of which sucks big-time and our little weekly coffee-klatches. I don't have any friends. I don't go anywhere. I've been out on one, quotes 'date' in the three years I've lived here. That was with you on New Year's Eve. If you recall, I almost blew that off. The only positive thing I've done for myself has been to quit smoking. I started going to the YMCA to get myself back in some kind of shape. That lasted a week. I'm going through a 1.75 liter bottle of brandy every two or three days." There was a long lapse before she said, "I know I need help Andy. I've been thinking a lot about a couple of things you've said to me. One of them was about the kid I gave up for adoption. What if she does show up someday? It could happen. What she'd find is this miserable, burned-out, old sot; not someone she can admire and respect." He asked her what the second thing was. "Well, it's not anything in particular that you've said. It's been much more subtle. You've challenged me to look at myself. You've shown me that each of us carries around our own self-definition. We live by those definitions. They become our reality; our self-fulfilling prophecies. We cling to them even though they may be killing us. I watched you get the rug pulled out from underneath you this winter more than once. Somehow you got up and started over. I know Stephanie was special to you and that you still miss her." Jan looked like she was close to tears. "Andy, you've been a good friend. I keep waiting for you to fail me and turn out to be just like all the rest. I have a real problem being able to trust anyone; men especially. For whatever its worth, I trust you more than anyone else I know." She gave him a slight smile. "Don't let it go to your head, McLeod. I trust you about as far as I can throw you."

He smiled at her. "One of my favorite sayings is: 'you can't keep a good person down'. I don't know many people who could do what you did just now." She looked at him quizzically and asked what he meant. "You're aware of yourself Jan. That's important. An awful lot of people have their noses imbedded in their navels. They either can't or won't look at themselves. You see yourself pretty clearly. A person can't change anything about themselves unless they're willing to face what needs changing." He paused for effect. "Another one of my favorite sayings is: 'the only thing insight ever cured was ignorance'. You've got the insight. Now it's time to make the changes; to take the action."

"Okay McLeod, anything to get you off my burro. I'll call the shrink this afternoon. And yeah, I'd like you to go with me."

He spent a little time explaining to her that typically, antidepressants needed time to build up their effect. "It might be two or three weeks before she would notice any kind of results. I'm sure the doc will explain all of this to you. It might take some time to find the right medication and dosage level. Hang in there. Don't give up. If I'm right about what's going on, you're going to discover what it feels like to be normal, maybe for the first time in your life."

"I've always regarded 'normal' as being pretty boring, McLeod." She scoffed. "Maybe I need to give this shrink-thing some further consideration."

"Just do it." Andy shot back. "Let me know when the appointment is so I can make room in my hectic schedule. She called him that evening to say that she had an appointment for the following Monday at two in the afternoon. "Good, I'll meet you at the Justice Center at noon. That should give us plenty of time to get to Green Bay and find his office." She told him specifically where to meet her. She didn't want half the department knowing she was going anywhere with some strange man.

When he met her that Monday he almost didn't recognize her. She had had her hair cut much shorter into a page-boy style. She had the color changed to a streaked light brown. She wore only a modest amount of makeup and a fresh smelling cologne. She was dressed in the same outfit that she had worn for their 'night out' on New Year's Eve. He complimented her on how nice she looked. On the way, he chided her, "the doctor is going to wonder what the hell is wrong with this lady when he sees you looking this good." She directed most of the conversation en route to everything but herself. They talked a lot about his sons. When they got to the clinic address, she said, "Andy, I want you to come in with me. I mean into the doctor's office. I don't want to go in there by myself." He agreed that he would if it was alright with the doctor. "No, if he won't let you come in with me, we're out of there."

Doctor Jordan was running a few minutes late. He came to the reception room himself. Andy judged him to be in his late sixties. He was kind of paunchy and balding. He wore a dark, charcoal suit, with a vest and a red bow tie. With a disarmingly friendly smile and wire rim glasses, Andy thought he looked grandfatherly. After introducing himself, Doctor Jordan asked Jan if she wanted Andy to accompany them. She most certainly did. In his office Dr. Jordan asked her what had brought her to him. She wanted Andy to explain it. She looked like she was ready to bolt at any second. The doctor turned to Andy, who gave him a concise explanation of why he thought Jan might be suffering with a chronic neurochemical depression. Jordan turned back to her and asked her a number of specific questions. He asked her about suicidal ideation, "I think about it a lot." She turned to Andy, "I'm sorry, but it's true." Andy nodded.

In the end he gave her a two week supply of sample medication. He urged her to eliminate drinking if she could. "Try to limit yourself to no more than a glass of wine in the evening." He explained essentially the same things that Andy had said to her about how antidepressants worked. "I want to see you in two weeks to see what effects, if any, this is having. We have a repertoire of medications available. If we're lucky we'll come up with the one that works best for you right away. The one I'm starting you out on is usually effective with the type of symptoms you and Andy are describing. If it doesn't seem to be doing the job, please don't get discouraged. We'll find the right one. Once we do, we still might have to play around with the dosage. "He told her about possible side-effects, insisting that she call his answering service if any of them were severe. When they stood to leave, Doctor Jordan took Jan's hand in both of his. "Janet, you've been this way for a very long time. When you start to feel better, you're going to experience what a lot of long term prison inmates go through when they return to the outside world. The world is going to feel a bit alien. Hopefully, the analogy will break down positively and you'll begin to enjoy life. Unfortunately, some people give up and opt for the familiar, as miserable as that may be. Medication can help to overcome the neurochemical aspects of depression. I would urge you to also seek some talk-therapy. You're going to need help in adjusting to your new found freedom. Maybe Andy can help you find someone you can feel comfortable talking to."

Back in the car, Jan was reserved. She agreed with Andy that Doctor Jordan seemed like a nice man. No, she wasn't sorry that she had done this. Andy asked her, "so why are you looking so glum?"

Jan looked out the side window avoiding eye contact. Andy pressed her. He asked her if she was going to be able to limit her drinking. "I don't know. It's going to be hard. It's gotten to be a habit. The first thing I do when I get home at night is mix a drink. Sometimes I don't even bother with eating; I drink supper." After a few miles she said. "I've probably got a stash of three or four bottles of brandy. I'll quit drinking when I've finished them off."

Andy challenged her, "What's going to prevent you from going out and buying some more?"

"I don't get paid until Friday. I haven't got enough money to buy any until then." He asked her what else was bothering her. "What makes you think something else is bothering me?" She sounded irritated. "

You're upset about some of the stuff Jordan had to say about chronic depression aren't you?"

"Well wouldn't you be?" She barked. "He's comparing me to being like some goddamn prison inmate." Andy asked her if that was all she'd heard. "I don't need to spill my guts to some asshole stranger, McLeod. It doesn't do any good. If anything it makes things worse. It won't change a freaking thing. What happened to me in the past needs to stay in the past. That's precisely why I'm here and not living in Chicago. I came here to make a fresh start. I came here to get away from that whole miserable scene." They drove in silence for several miles. "I'm sorry, Andy. Look, if it will make you feel better, you can follow me home and I'll give you my stash of booze." He agreed to do so. They lapsed into another period of silence. Jan broke it, this time speaking almost apologetically. "I've talked to all kinds of shrinks over the years, Andy. At juvey, at some of the schools I attended, at Family Services and Catholic Social Service; you name it. It's not like I haven't ever been exposed to what Jordan calls 'talk-therapy'. None of it helped. I never felt like any of those so-called professionals had a clue as to what my life was like." She finally looked at Andy, "You were in Viet Nam?" He nodded. "Do you ever talk about it?" He shook his head. "Why not?"

"I know where you're going with this Jan. To some extent you're right. I don't talk about it because I don't want to open old wounds. I don't talk about it because a person had to have been there to understand what it was like. Hell, I don't even talk about it with fellow Nam vets."

"So, you understand where I'm coming from when I object to this talk-therapy bullshit."

"There is one fairly big difference, Jan. You've never known the joy of being loved and being able to love. I did. I grew up in a nurturing, loving family. When I went to Viet Nam, I was taken out of one world, and thrown into another completely alien one. When I came back to this world, I admit I had trouble adjusting. I was pretty screwed up for awhile. I still regard a lot of what's going on in this world as stupid, absurd, and asinine. Despite the idiocy of this world, I'm able to enjoy life and the people around me. He glanced over at her. "I understand your trepidation about talking to a counselor. It's not something you have to decide in the next ten minutes. Doc Jordan merely made a suggestion. He's not making his help contingent on whether you seek counseling or not. It's up to you, Jan. For my part, I want you to know how pleased I am that you took this step today. Let's see what the medication does. I completely agree with Jordan about the alcohol thing. I hope you're going to be able to cut back on the amount you drink. If you don't, you're negating whatever benefit the medication may provide."

"Thanks, Andy. Sometimes my Irish temper gets the best of me." Andy was surprised by that statement. "My maiden name was Brady, my married name was Ruiz. I changed my name to Miller when I came up here. Part of the fresh start thing."

When they arrived back in Sturgeon Bay they stopped at the Justice Center for Jan to get her car. Andy followed Jan to her apartment complex. She invited him to come in. Her apartment wasn't at all what he had expected. It was immaculate and orderly. It was Spartan. There was one painting on the living room wall. She located three bottles of brandy and put them in a shopping bag.

He smiled at her and said, "Where's the other one?"

She glared at him for a moment. Finally she went to a closet and got a fourth bottle. "I suppose you're going to insist on searching the whole apartment." He said nothing. "That's it, I don't have any more." She was almost irate. He put the fourth bottle in the bag and turned to leave. "Andy?" He stopped at the door. "I'm sorry."

"Call me if you need to. I haven't got a whole lot of answers but I'm a good listener."

"You are that, McLeod."

She didn't call him on Tuesday. He decided to chance it and go to the coffee shop Wednesday morning. She had arrived before him and was half way through a cup of coffee rather than her usual latte. She looked haggard but she was nicely dressed and didn't have on a garish amount of makeup. He got himself a cup of coffee and refilled hers. He sat down and looked at her. She almost whispered, "Andy this is a bitch. I think I'm going through D.T.'s. I'm a fucking alcoholic. I don't know if I can make it until Friday. I can't function. I don't know how I even made it here." He held his hand out across the table. She took it and held it tightly. "I'm a goddamn mess." She could not hold back the tears. He handed her a napkin and waited. After a few minutes she was able to speak. "I think I need to be in a hospital. I've never felt this desperate in my whole life. I don't think I can wait until my next appointment with Jordan."

"Okay, I hear you. Can you follow me home? I'll put in a call to Jordan. If I can get through to him I'll tell him what's happening. I'm with you." She agreed to follow him. At the house he called Doctor Jordan. He was with a patient. Andy stressed that it was important that the doctor call back as soon as possible. "Jan, why don't you go lie down and try to sleep? It's a way to escape." He showed her to the bedroom and helped her off with her boots. He covered her with the top quilt and touched her head."

"Andy, please don't go away?" He told her that he wouldn't, and that he'd stay in the house to wait for Jordan's call.

"Just try to sleep. Lucy will snuggle up with you. She's a great snuggler." He called to Lucy and patted the bed. The dog jumped up and instantly curled up next to Jan. "I'll be in the dining room. I won't be far away." He stayed with her until she closed her eyes and began to relax.

Almost two hours later Doctor Jordan called. Andy explained the situation. "What do you think, Andy? Do you think she's a serious threat to herself?"

He was surprised and somewhat taken aback that a very experienced psychiatrist was asking his opinion. "Doc, I have very mixed feelings. A part of me thinks that she needs to be hospitalized. Another part of me feels like, if she can get through the next couple or three days, the medication might start to kick in."

Doctor Jordan surprised him again. "I have an idea. I'll call in a prescription for a stimulant medication. As you are probably aware, stimulants take effect within an hour. It's a fairly recent approach that has been very successful in treating a number of depressed patients. We'll try this along with the antidepressant. We'll know within the next few hours whether we're on the right track or not. If not, then the next step will need to be hospitalization." Andy thanked him. "No, I thank you. Janet is lucky to have you as a friend. Let's hope this will work. She impresses me as being a lady with a lot of spunk who's been through a lot."

He gave the doctor the name of the closest pharmacy to call with the prescription. After hanging up, Andy checked on Jan. She was sound asleep with Lucy still curled up next to her. He left and drove to the pharmacy. When he got back she had just awakened. She was a bit groggy. "I need to call the office and find out what's happening."

He explained his conversation with Doctor Jordan and had her take one of the pills. She put on her boots. "Jan, would you consider staying here for the next couple of nights? One or the other of us can sleep upstairs. I know this is the pits but it's better than you being in that apartment by yourself."

She said nothing as she put on her coat. He repeated the appeal. "I'll be alright, McLeod. I get paid on Friday. I'll pay you for the prescription then." She left.

As soon as she was gone he went out to the workshop. He started a fire in the stove, debating what to do. "What an enigma. Two hours ago she was desperately crying out for help and admitting that she's got an alcohol problem. Now she's back to 'bugger off, I can handle it by myself'.

After he and Lucy went for their walk he decided to call her. She did not answer. He tried calling her repeatedly. By eight o'clock that night he decided that he should drive to her apartment to see if she was there and okay. His phone rang, "McLeod, it's me." She sounded slightly out of breath. "Did you just try calling?" He said that he had tried calling her several times. "I'm sober. The new med seems to be working. I'm feeling much less shaky." He asked her where she had gone after she left him.

She avoided his question. "Andy, I'm sorry. I was such a bitch. I didn't mean to treat you that way by just walking out on you."

After a long silence he asked, "Are you going to be okay by yourself? Do you even remember my offer?"

"I remember your offer. I can't do that. It's either the medication or the hospital. I really am feeling a lot better with the uppers. I really do appreciate everything that you've done for me."

"Jan, you're not going to do something stupid are you?"

There were several moments of silence, "what do you mean?"

"You know exactly what I mean. I think I need to come down there and get you. You need to either come home with me or go to the hospital." He hung up on her. When he and Lucy went to get in the truck he discovered her service revolver on the seat. He debated what to do. He went back and called her. "I just discovered your gun. Is this the only one you have?" She said that it was. "So, you knew when you left here this afternoon that you were that desperate."

"Andy, I've been that desperate most of my life. There's seldom a day that goes by that I don't think about quitting." He asked her how she was right now. "I was serious when I told you before that this new med seems to be working. I admit I'm scared. If this doesn't work, I don't know what I'll do. I know I can't go on this way."

"Jan, I don't want to lose you."

"I'll be okay." She changed the subject. "Do you want to go out for a fish fry Friday night? We can go Dutch treat."

"Goddamnit Jan, you do this constantly. You change subjects whenever you want to avoid an issue you're uncomfortable with."

After a long pause she said, "Fair enough, Andy. I promise you that I'll call you if I find that I can't handle the situation. For right now, I'm feeling a whole lot better. I'm scared, too. I want this to last. I truly appreciate what you just said about not wanting to lose me. No one has ever said anything like that to me ever before." There was another pause in the conversation. "So, what about the fish fry?"

Andy gave a weary sigh. "Sure, a fish fry would be nice." He paused. "If it's alright with you, I'll call my friend Rob and see if he can join us. You missed meeting him at Christmas. He's a very nice man. I think you'll like him. He's an adventurous soul." They decided on a time and place. After hanging up with her, Andy still felt apprehensive. He wanted to trust her but knew he would never be able to forgive himself if she ended her life. He didn't believe for a second that she only owned one gun. The weapon she left with him was probably the only one she had with her at the time. All the cops he was familiar with owned several guns.

His phone rang again. It was Jan. "I went to the place you took me to the other day, that abandoned resort. There was a bitter cold east wind off the lake. I didn't stay long. I needed to see if it had the same effect on me. For want of a better way to describe it, that place has good karma. Do you know what I mean?"

"I do, but I don't think everyone that goes there experiences it."

"Probably not," she agreed. "I'm okay, Andy, really I am. I went back to the office and worked on the mountain of paper work that has accumulated. I don't know if it's just my imagination but I found myself able to focus my attention and concentrate. Do you think this new medication can have that kind of effect?"

He told her that it could well be that it did. "It's often used to treat hyperactive kids and people who have ADD, Attention Deficit Disorder."

They talked about that. Looking back Jan was almost certain that she had been dyslexic as a kid. She had come to think of herself as stupid and she had learned to hate school. "Getting through the academic parts of the police academy was a major struggle for me. To this day I hate writing reports. It takes me forever to read anything. It's a freaking chore. It wasn't until I moved here that I started reading for pleasure. What the hell else is there to do? " When they finally ended the conversation, Andy felt a genuine sense of relief about her.

He was up early the next morning. He waited until seven o'clock before calling her. She answered on the fifth ring. "McLeod here," he said in a formal voice. "I wish I had some clever excuse for calling. I just wanted to see how you were doing."

"You interrupted my Tai Chi. Christ, I haven't done it in so long, and I'm having trouble remembering the moves." He apologized. "You know, this new med I'm on is a stimulant, but I'm not feeling jacked up by it at all. As near as I can tell, it's making me feel like what a normal person must feel like."

He explained that if she had 'normal' brain chemistry she would feel jacked up and hyper. What the medication was doing was actually normalizing the way her brain worked. "I'll explain it to you one of these days." He decided that he would call Dr. Jordan later in the morning to let him know that the stimulant medication seemed to be working.

On Friday night, she met him and Rob at the Pub. She was dressed casually in jeans, a turtle neck, and a gray pull-over sweater. She had on a modest amount of makeup. He introduced the two of them. She opted for a diet cola. He hadn't told Rob that she was in law enforcement. It wasn't until midway through dinner that he asked her what she did. When she told him, Rob asked "are you the one that's been involved with Andy with the stuff he and Stephanie have been going through?" She told him that she was. "Ahhh, it all makes sense to me now. Andy has said a lot of good things about you. You're not at all like how I had pictured you."

She smiled self-consciously. "I've made several changes in the past few months. His description of me was probably accurate." She shifted things away from herself. "Andy admires you, Rob. He regards you as 'an adventurous soul'." Over dinner she asked Rob several questions, drawing stories out of him about some of the things he'd done in the past, especially his Alaskan adventures.

When they left the Pub, they all went their separate ways. Andy decided to go to bed early. He was almost asleep when the phone rang. "McLeod, it's me. I just wanted to let you know that I really enjoyed this evening. Your friend Rob really is a nice guy. I'm glad I got a chance to meet him." They chatted for awhile.

Before they hung up he invited her to go cross-country skiing with him the next day. "We can go to the state park. The park grooms miles of cross-country trails." He saw no point in telling her that he was going to outfit her with the ski set he had purchased for Stephanie for Christmas. He suggested that she dress in layers so she could shed clothing if she got too warm. Jan arrived promptly at nine the next morning. She wore no makeup. He had never seen her that way before. He studied her as he showed her some of the basics about skiing. She finally asked him why he was looking at her that way. "I've never seen you without make up. I like that you've taken to using a whole lot less of it. Now I'm trying to decide about your natural look."

She smiled at him. "You know, between giving up smoking, drinking and not spending a small fortune on makeup, I'm saving a lot of money. If I keep this up, I might be able to eventually afford a down payment on a small house. I've never even thought about having a place of my own before."

They loaded the equipment into the back of Andy's truck and with Lucy, they drove to the park. After they had skied a distance of about two miles, they stopped at the edge of a large meadow area. There were several deer out in the meadow browsing saplings. "The deer are so used to people here in the park they hardly pay any attention to us. The does will be giving birth to their fawns in another few weeks." He got a plastic bottle of water out of the day pack he was wearing. He handed it to her. They took turns drinking. He asked how she was feeling. "Are you game to go on or do you want to head back?" She said she was feeling good and wanted to continue on. "You're doing great, Jan; you've really caught on quickly. It's too bad I didn't think to invite you earlier in the winter. The season is nearly over. We might lose most of our snow in the next week or two, if it warms up much more."

"What do you do in the early spring?", she asked. "Late March and early April are the pits up here."

He agreed. "A couple of years ago I made a delivery trip that took me down through Iowa and into southern Missouri. I ended up going down to north central Arkansas. It was beautiful. Spring was in full bloom. I wouldn't mind doing that again and maybe staying there for a few days."

"Why don't you? I think it would be good for you to get away."

"Not this year. Too much going on with the house. I've got a few deliveries to make in the twin cities area and in the Milwaukee and Chicago area. I'll make two separate trips and be gone for a couple of days when I go to Illinois. My older son lives out west of Chicago. I'll visit him." They skied for almost four hours that day.

When they got back to the house he invited her to join him and Lucy for a walk. "I should probably head for home. You've had enough of my face in yours for one day."

"Come on, Brady. I'll let you know when I'm tired of your face. You've never seen my property." It had warmed up during the day and the snow was almost slushy. He decided to forego his martini in deference to her effort to stop drinking

They walked in silence for awhile. He asked her how she was feeling. "I'm doing good. I really had a nice time today. You were very patient with me."

"You're a quick study, Jan. You picked up on the skiing quickly." He invited her to stay for supper.

"I think I better go home."

He asked her why. "You're just going to sit in your apartment by yourself. You probably aren't even going to have anything to eat."

She hesitated, "Andy, I think you're still being bugged. I might be wrong but my instincts tell me something isn't right. I wish you would consent to having a technician come in and scan your place. You don't have to consent to having anything removed but at least you'll know for sure."

"I'm taking the 'let sleeping dogs lie' approach." He argued. "I figure, if they're able to monitor me unobstructed; maybe they'll eventually quit and leave me the hell alone. It seems to be working thus far."

Jan conceded. "Okay, let's go out for a hamburger; then I'm going home." she said firmly.

They drove separately to the Pub so she could leave from there. The waitress remembered them and automatically brought him a dark beer. Jan had a glass of ginger ale. After dinner he walked her to her car. She was looking down. He asked her if she was okay. "I'm okay. I'm kind of worn out. It's been a long day and I'm not in the best of shape." She got in her car and drove off.

On the short way home, Andy went from feeling comfortable about her to beginning to worry again. He remembered that he had forgotten to get the mail. He stopped at the end of the driveway to check the mailbox. The temperature was dropping. The stars were out. He stopped to breathe in the aroma of the smoke from his wood stoves. Back in the house he went through the mail. There were two seed catalogs, a utility bill, and a small envelope with his address printed and no return address. He opened it first. Inside he found a single piece of paper with a neatly printed message: "Make the dream come true. Build the house." It was neither signed nor dated. Andy immediately concluded that it had to be from Stephanie. Even using a magnifying glass, the postmark was hard to decipher. It looked like Truckee, California. 'Where the hell is Truckee?' Aware that he might well be under surveillance he went on to open the rest of his mail. He put the note in his shirt pocket and went outside to pee. 'Goddamn, what a stupid thing for her to do. I need to talk to Jan'.

He decided to drive back to the Pub to call her for the sake of certain privacy. He waited half an hour before he made the call to ensure she had time to get to her back to her apartment. She answered on the second ring. He tried to sound casual. "I'm fine, Andy, really. Today was exhausting but it was a lot of fun."

After a few moments of small talk he told her about the note he had received, possibly from Stephanie. Jan's response was immediate and angry. "That stupid, fucking woman. I'm serious, Andy. That is just plain moronic. She's put both of you at risk all over again. It's bullshit, Andy. I'm going to request a scan of your place. This has got to stop. If it's her, then she's an idiot. I don't care whose behind all of this, it has to stop. No more of the passive game plan. You need to get proactive. If we find bugs we'll remove them and we'll keep removing them for however long it takes. They've got a lot of expensive equipment. If they want to piss away their money, then we'll provide them with the urinal."

They talked for a brief while. After hanging up he admonished himself for having relaxed his vigilance. He began looking for his forty-five. He couldn't find it. He discovered that his twelve gauge shotgun, his 30-30 lever action deer rifle, even his twenty-two rifle were also missing. He went into an immediate tirade. He was angry at the thief. He was angrier at himself for having dropped his guard. He checked where he had kept the ammunition for all three guns. All of it was gone as well. He took Lucy and drove back to the Pub. They were in the process of closing. He told the bartender that his phone was out of service and asked if he could use theirs. He called Jan again. She answered on the fifth ring. "Jan, all of my guns and all of my ammunition are missing."

"I'll see if a deputy is nearby. I'll call you back." She hung up before he could tell her that he was not at home. He thanked the bartender and raced back to his place.

The deputy arrived a few minutes later. Andy met him outside. The deputy asked several questions. Andy told him that he didn't know when the weapons had gone missing. He hadn't carried the pistol for the last several days. The theft could have happened anytime during the past two or three days. He took the deputy inside to show him where he had kept the guns and the ammunition. He had a record of the missing guns' serial numbers. While the deputy was copying them the phone rang. It was Jan. She said she had tried calling him a couple of times. He explained that he had been outside. She asked to talk to the deputy. When the deputy turned the phone back over to Andy she explained. "I've asked Dan to leave his assault shotgun with you for tonight. I'll be up to your place in the morning. He's reluctant about letting you have it. I told him I couldn't go into detail with him over the phone. Maybe you can explain it to him.

Outside Andy gave the deputy an abridged version of what had been going on. The deputy was still reluctant to cooperate after hearing the story. "I'd like to Mr. McLeod. It's against department policy for me to turn over a firearm to a civilian. I could end up being fired if anybody found out." Andy understood. "I'll swing by here a couple of times before I go off duty and I'll ask the deputy on the eleven to seven shift to check on you as well." The deputy offered.

Sleep did not come easily for Andy that night. The note from Stephanie reopened the door of speculation. The postmark date was barely readable, but he was fairly certain that it had been mailed within the past week, meaning what? The theft of his weapons destroyed whatever hopes he may have had that the siege was over. He tried to force himself into thinking that the theft may have been someone else entirely. Not likely. Did they know that she was alive? Did they think that he knew where she was? What would happen next?

As usual, Jan arrived punctually the next morning. She commented that he looked like he hadn't gotten much sleep. She handed him a nine millimeter Smith and Wesson semi-automatic pistol. "It's loaded with hollow point rounds." She handed him two boxes of ammunition plus another full clip. "This will have almost the same close range impact as your forty-five with a third more fire power. Each clip holds thirteen rounds. All you need to know for now is to flip off the safety and start squeezing the trigger. It's got double action, unlike your Colt. It doesn't have nearly the recoil that cannon of yours has. I suggest you spend some time shooting so you get the feel of it. Andy, I'm pissed. That stupid bitch not only tore open wounds, but you're back to being in jeopardy again. On top of it, she's put her own safety at risk. I'm still baffled by how these people are able to keep track of everything you do. The good news is we can rule her out as an insider. For awhile I was convinced that it was her."

He reminded her that the letter might not have come from Stephanie. He asked her where the pistol had come from.

"It's mine. I carried it when I was a uniformed officer in Chicago. It's been reworked so you barely have to squeeze the trigger. It's got night vision combat sights. It's a sweet gun. Keep it with you from now on." He asked what she carried now. "A Beretta nine millimeter. It's okay. It's lighter and more compact. But I love that S&W." She started to leave. She stopped and asked, "Incidentally, did you have your forty-five registered?"

"No, I carried it in Nam. I was supposed to turn it in. I reported it missing in combat and brought it home with me. It was my companion even after I returned home."

"You never know, your guns might just show up one of these days." Before leaving she gave Andy an assault shotgun. She also gave him a letter signed by the sheriff deputizing him. "I assured him that you're a reasonably stable human being who will not abuse the authority he's investing in you. I couldn't vouch for your intelligence or your taste in women."

Chapter 12

It began snowing during the night and it was still coming down in huge wet heavy flakes when Andy awoke. He judged that there was six inches on the ground already. Late winter snow storms were always more difficult to deal with. His snow blower was useless. It wasn't powerful enough to handle wet snow. It clogged up frequently and could barely throw the snow at all. The other side of the coin was that snow this time of the year usually melted off in a few days. He recalled his trip to northern Arkansas. He thought how pleasant it would be to make a similar trip this year just to get away from this.

When he started to leave the house to go to the workshop Andy could barely get the front door open because of the snow. He spent close to two hours shoveling a vehicle wide passage up his driveway so he could get in and out. Later in the morning he was at work in his shop when the phone rang. It was Jan. She was checking to see that everything was okay. It stopped snowing by noon and the sun came out, melting off much of what had fallen. Andy was in the process of assembling some quilt racks when Rob stopped by briefly that afternoon. He came by to report that he was keeping his eye out for an affordable car but hadn't had much luck in finding one thus far.

"I don't think Steph is going to be returning anytime soon. Her mother isn't getting any better." He asked when Rob was planning to make his annual buying trip to Bali. "I'm leaving this Sunday. That's the other reason I came by. Can you take care of my cat again? Also, I have two plants: a Norfolk pine and a cactus. I got both of them at a rummage sale last fall." Andy told him he would be happy to.

That evening Andy sat down to read but fell asleep after only a few pages. He was awakened at eight-thirty by Lucy growling. He had the gun on the table next to him. He picked it up and turned the lamp off. He listened, thinking that maybe it was the coyotes coming through early. He moved through the house. The house had no windows on the south side which was where he parked his truck. He thought he heard an engine running but couldn't see anything out either the east or west windows. He thought about turning on the outside yard light. Lucy was on the verge of barking. He put her in the bathroom and closed the door. He slipped his coat on, and let himself out the door. The temperature had dropped noticeably. There was definitely an engine running. He stepped carefully, taking the safety off the pistol. Just as he reached the south corner he saw a figure moving toward a sedan that was parked just behind his truck facing the road. The person opened the passenger door. Andy decided not to yell out a warning. He squeezed off four rounds shattering the rear window glass; then he moved as quickly as he could on the icy surface of the snow. The car's wheels spun as the driver tried to get away. Andy fired six more rounds into the back of the car, hoping to puncture the gas tank. At the end of the driveway the car turned south onto the road. It's headlights were still off. Andy went back into the house and dialed 911. He told the dispatcher what had just happened. She asked if he had gotten either a plate number or a description of the car. "It's a dark late model sedan, that's all I can tell you. It was heading south from my place. It should be easy enough to spot. It's missing its rear windows and there are some bullet holes in the trunk."

She asked him, "Wasn't there a theft reported at this same address last night? There were weapons stolen." He confirmed that. "Do you think anyone was wounded?" He told her that if they were, it was most likely from flying glass. "We have a deputy about ten miles from you. I'll put out an APB on the vehicle matching your description."

'An APB', Andy almost laughed. 'There are two deputies on night patrol in the whole county this time of the year. There wasn't much chance that these guys would be caught'. It was then that he consciously realized that there were two of them. The one he had seen outside the car got in on the passenger side. In his mind this marked more than a resumption of harassment.

Next he called Jan at home. Lucy barked. While he was waiting for Jan to answer. He let Lucy out of the bathroom. "Don't go near your truck Andy. Alert the deputy that it may have been tampered with." She asked if he was okay.

"I'm okay, but I can't vouch for whoever was in that car."

"Well, one thing is for sure. They know that you're armed again." She repeated her warning to stay away from his truck. "I'm concerned about what they may have done to it." I'm bringing some technicians up there in the morning." He could almost hear a smile in her voice. "Isn't that S&W a sweet weapon?"

"It is. Not nearly the recoil of my forty-five." He thanked her.

It took the deputy longer to get there than had been anticipated. "The roads are treacherous. All that melted snow today is freezing over. I just got a message via our dispatcher to be cautious about going near your truck. I was even careful coming up your driveway not to drive over the exiting tire tracks."

"That was smart of you deputy. I never would have thought of that." The deputy got out a camera and his powerful flashlight. He took numerous pictures of foot prints and tire tracks. He pointed out that the foot prints led up to the front of the truck and then to the left side of the hood area. He was guessing that the intruder had done something under the hood. He photographed the spent cartridges, noting that there were fourteen of them. He asked if Andy had loaded a second clip. "No, this one holds thirteen rounds plus one in the chamber." He showed him the empty clip. He had already put the other clip in the pistol. A message came over the deputy's handheld radio that a car had just been reported stolen from a tavern parking lot. It was described as a white Chevy Impala. Another car had been found in the back of the same parking lot. Its rear window was shattered and it had what appeared to be bullet holes in the trunk. It was obvious what had transpired. "Would you like some coffee deputy?" He declined, not wanting Andy to go to the effort of making a fresh pot.

It was after ten o'clock when he and Lucy got into bed. He stroked her back. "You did good tonight old dog." At one o'clock she awakened him again with her low growl. He grabbed the pistol and got out of bed quickly. After a few steps he felt an overwhelming dizziness and nausea. He dropped to his knees and felt like he was about to lose consciousness. He was sweating profusely. He tried to fight it off leaning against the bedroom door jam, "this is not the time for this to be happening." In three or four minutes whatever was happening to him began to subside. He managed to get to his feet. He heard the coyotes. They were not close enough to be seen. He remembered having experienced a similar dizzy spell one night in Viet Nam. His unit had come under attack and he jumped up quickly. He remembered experiencing the same symptoms and the same helpless feeling that he was about to pass out." Before going back to bed he changed his t-shirt. The other one was damp with perspiration. He decided that he would schedule an appointment to see John at the clinic to find out what this was about.

In the morning Jan drove into his place at ten o'clock, followed by a big white van. Two men got out of the van. They introduced themselves to him. They were technicians from the state police criminal investigation unit. They explained that they were going to go over everything in his house and workshop. "We'll start with your truck in light of what happened last night. One of them got inside the cab and disconnected wiring from the ignition switch. One of them put on protective garb. They moved everything a safe distance from the truck. Using a tripod device they raised the hood.

Andy asked what that was about. One of them said, "We're concerned about a booby trap or a bomb. What they found was that the line from the brake's master cylinder had been almost entirely severed. All the fluid would have bled out when you applied your brakes." He told them about the incident last fall when his brake lines had been tampered with. They found a high-tech listening device in the cab. It took them the rest of the day to go through the house and workshop, where they found several strategically located cameras and microphone devices. "This is extremely sophisticated and expensive equipment." He showed Andy where several of them had been hidden. Some of the audio devices were about the size of pill capsules. "We'll leave a scanner with Detective Miller. She can go over your place a couple of times a week to see if the premises have been re-infected. Whoever is behind this is out a bunch of money. They were probably aware as soon as we started, that the place is being sanitized." Andy asked about how information from such devices was monitored. "It's probably being bounced off satellites. For all we know the information is being monitored hundreds of miles from here. We have no way to trace where it's going. Maybe the military does, but we can't. Pretty scary isn't it? So much for privacy in the modern world."

Detective Miller made a statement intended as a question to the man in charge. "Whoever's behind this is pretty serious. They wouldn't be going to this much effort for a cookie recipe."

"That would be my guess." He turned to Andy. "I try not to speculate about things like this but it appears this guy is very serious and rich. I doubt that the FBI goes to this much trouble unless it's someone big and important. I'll discuss this with my superiors. If the feds aren't already involved, they probably ought to be."

The technician turned to Jan, "before we leave we'll go over your car, your apartment and your office to make sure you're clean." He addressed Andy, "I suspect last night's visitors got a big surprise. Between you shooting at them and us de-bugging your place today, it will be interesting to see what happens next." He turned to his colleague. "Jeff, do we have any motion detector alarms with us?" They did. "Let's set up three or four of them." He turned to Jan and Andy. "What we'll do is set these alarms. The monitor can receive messages from up to six locations. We'll give you a diagram of where each of the sensors have been placed. It works like this: when number three light goes on it will tell you that the number three location is detecting an intruder. It will only take a few minutes to set the system up. I'll show you how it operates. Hopefully, it will give you more of a heads up than just your dog."

Jan stayed behind after the team left. "Are you going to be okay here by yourself?"

He shrugged. "Let's see what happens." She told him that she would call him later. After she was gone, he and Lucy went for their walk. Andy carried the shotgun and the pistol. It was a pleasant evening but the temperature was falling quickly as the sun dropped behind the trees. 'Perfect maple syrup making weather, warm days and below freezing nights'. The stroll was not relaxing. He was exhausted by the events of the last eighteen hours. In the house he fed Lucy and sat down to watch the evening news. A few minutes passed when the alarm device went off. It was signaling that someone was coming in the driveway. He picked up the pistol and moved quickly to see who it was. When he saw that it was Rob he placed the gun on top of the refrigerator. Rob approached the house carrying his Norfolk Pine tree and cactus. Andy held the door open for him. "Jesus, Rob, I forgot all about you leaving." Andy went to get the cat. Rob brought in Mel's litter box and an ample supply of food and litter. "I forgot to ask you, how are you getting to the airport?"

Rob smiled, "What are you doing tomorrow? I know its short notice. The girl who was supposed to take me has to work. I'll pay your gas if you can take me." Rob asked if he had eaten yet. "I'll treat you to a burger at the Pub," he offered. Before they left, Andy slipped the gun into his coat pocket. They were gone for over an hour. Back at the house, Andy invited Rob in for a beer. When they got to the house, the door was standing wide open. Inside they discovered the plants strewn on the floor. Neither Mel nor Lucy were in the house. The alarm receiver was laying on the floor smashed to pieces. Andy went to the phone. It was dead.

"Rob, go back to the Pub, call 911, and tell them about a break in at this address, then call Janet Miller." He wrote down her number. "Tell her about what has just happened." Rob asked if he was going to be alright here by himself. "I'll be okay. Just go do it. I'm going to see if I can find the critters." Rob left immediately. Andy went directly to the workshop. As soon as he opened the door he could hear Mel's vociferous meowing. The cat came to him and he picked him up. There was no sign of Lucy. In the event the intruders had replanted listening devices, Andy said in a loud voice, "If you bastards hurt so much as a hair on my dog, I will kill you."

He walked around the house with a flashlight looking for foot prints. He found nothing. The shotgun and the ammunition that Jan had left with him were missing. He was on the floor cleaning up and trying to repot the plants when Rob returned. "Did you find Lucy and Mel?"

"Mel was in the workshop. There's no sign of Lucy." He told Rob about what had happened last night. "I'm just sorry that I didn't try to take the bastards out when I had the chance. I'm done fucking with them. This is war."

"Jesus, Andy, what's going on here? You don't think they might have done anything to hurt Luce do you? What's with the gun?"

"Rob, I honestly don't know what's going on, but it's turned downright mean." Rob got down on the floor to help clean up. He said that it was a good thing that Stephanie wasn't here. Andy sat back on his haunches. "Rob, I might as well tell you. Stephanie is gone. She's not coming back. When she left here before Christmas, I honestly thought she was going to Florida to visit her mother." He proceeded to tell Rob the entire story.

"Sweet Jesus, this is something you read about in novels. It's not something that happens in real life. What do you think happened to her?"

"I have no idea. I'm sure I'll never see her again, even if she's still alive. Whoever is after her believes that I know where she is. That's what all of this crap is about. I don't know what it will take to convince them that I know nothing."

"How much more of this can you take, Andy?"

"I don't know. My biggest fear right now is what they may have done to Luce. I feel totally helpless. I'd give anything to get my hands on them. The problem is that I have no idea who the hell they are. I'm pretty sure they're pros who are working for someone or some organization." Rob asked why he hadn't told him any of this before. "I kept hoping it would all go away. I naively figured they would leave me alone once they realized Steph was gone for good."

"Andy, if this goes on much longer, you're going to end up bonkers. You need to get out of here. This place isn't worth what it's costing you." They went back to cleaning up. "Why don't you consider moving into my place until I get back? I'll be gone for three weeks. Maybe that will throw them off track."

He thanked Rob for the offer and said he would consider it. Before Rob left it was decided that they would leave for the airport at 9:00 the next morning using Stephanie's car. As soon as Rob was gone, Andy went back outside with a flashlight to see if he could find Lucy. He went back out to the workshop and searched upstairs. He was just leaving the workshop when headlights entered the driveway. He quickly took cover with the pistol at ready. The car pulled up next to his truck and the lights went off. When the interior light went on he could see that it was Jan. As she started toward the house he called to her. "I'm coming from the workshop."

They went into the house. He showed her what had happened. She told him, "I called the phone company and explained that this was a police emergency. They'll have a repairman here ASAP." He told her about Lucy being missing. She grimaced. "You should have shot the bastards last night." She waved her hands. "I know that was a stupid thing for me to say." He told her the shotgun she had given him was missing. He showed her around, she asked several questions including how much he trusted his friend Rob.

"I trust him completely but it occurs to me that the one thing that was overlooked in the surveillance scanning was Stephanie's car." He told her about his plans to take Rob to the airport in the morning using that car. "I don't have the scanner with me. I'll be here first thing tomorrow to check out her car." She looked at him with an expression of sorrow. "Andy, I know that Lucy means more to you than just about anything. I want to believe she's okay and that she'll be found. I'm not one to try to give false hopes, you know that." They stood without speaking. "I've got another shotgun and shells in the car. I suggest you take it with you wherever you go."

"Jan, I just can't understand how they knew I was away from the house. Rob just showed up here impromptu. We didn't have any arrangements as to when he was going to bring his cat or his plants. We decided on the spur of the moment to go out for something to eat. We were gone maybe an hour. Even if the technicians that were here today missed one or two bugs, these guys have to be close by in order to move in so quickly." He showed her the smashed motion sensor. "And how would they have known about this? It's like they're parked on my back forty."

"That's a point I hadn't considered, Andy. Maybe we should bring in a canine unit and see if dogs can pick up a scent. If they've got Lucy, or if they left their own scent, maybe we can track them."

A phone service man arrived a few minutes later. "I checked out your line down at the road. It's okay there." Jan asked to see some identification before allowing him to proceed. He found the wire from the pole to the house had been severed in the middle. He had to run a new wire. Afterwards he checked the phones in both the house and the shop to make sure they were operating. "This is a first for me," the repairman said. "I've never seen where the line to the house has been deliberately cut in the middle like this. Whoever did it, had to be a hell-of-a-shot, or maybe he had one of those pole-type limb pruners." They both thanked him and he left.

They walked down the driveway. She shined her flashlight up to locate the electric line. "They spent a few minutes scanning the immediate area to see if there were any foot prints. "Look Andy, you've lost all means of warning. You haven't got Luce or the sensor device. Maybe you ought to call Rob and see if you can spend the night over there."

He assured her that he would be alright. "There was a time in my life that I learned how to sleep with one eye open. I can do that again." It was almost ten o'clock when she left. After she was gone the impact of Lucy's absence hit him. He went outside to search for her again. He called her name several times to no avail. The sky was clear. He was sure that the temperature was in the teens. He decided to set up a couple of simple alarms. Back in the house he stacked three pots in front of the door with the intent that an intruder would knock them over and the noise would awaken him. Mel followed him around meowing. He turned off the living room lamp. He positioned pillows under the blanket in his bed to give the appearance of someone occupying it. He went upstairs. He had just gotten into bed when the phone rang. He took the pistol and almost tripped going down the stairs. When he got to the phone it was Jan. She breathed a sigh of relief. "I was just about to hang up and dispatch a squad to your place. I was just calling to make sure your phone is working and that you're okay. I'll call you at six sharp." He thanked her for her concern. It took Mel awhile to settle down.

At midnight he was awakened by a clattering sound. He quickly realized it was the pots he had set in front of the door. He grabbed the pistol and listened for any movement downstairs. He was afraid to get out of bed, lest he make some sound himself. He heard Mel's meow coming from downstairs. His pounding heart subsided slowly. He got up and cautiously made his way to the stairwell. He descended the stairs, careful to stay to the inside of the stairs which were less likely to creak. He moved throughout the downstairs. He discovered nothing other than the toppled pans and concluded Mel must have knocked them over. He reassembled the stack. Before returning to the upstairs he checked the phone for a dial tone. There was less than a half moon. He looked out the bedroom window. He heard a dog barking off in the distance. He had no fires and the house was cold. He decided to build a fire in the living room stove. Back in bed he waited for his body heat to re-warm the bed. He was tempted to just get back up and go do something, sure that he was too wide awake to get back to sleep. Within minutes, however, he dozed off. He dreamt about a particular night in Viet Nam. Parts of it were real. A siren went off and the perimeter of the base-camp lit up like a football stadium. At first there was just the sound of small arms fire. Then there was the loud thudding boom of in-coming mortars. He pulled on his fatigue pants and grabbed his rifle and ammo. He didn't bother with his boots. He started for the tent opening.

A mortar round went off close by. He thought 'fucking' Charlie is zeroed in already'. Outside he heard another incoming round. He didn't know which way to go. Instinct made him dive to the ground. It struck in between two tents about fifty feet to his left. He got up and began running toward the tent to see if there were any survivors. The tents were engulfed in flames. He heard another incoming round. He hit the deck again just as it exploded. It landed directly on the tent he had been sleeping in. Some flaming debris landed on him. He rolled over several times in the damp soil to smother the hot embers that were landing on him. He heard American artillery beginning to fire. There were maybe two more in-coming mortar rounds and that was it. The attack was over. There were the remains of three dead soldiers. Then he saw himself in bright orange monk's robes. His hair was shoulder length and he had a beard. He looked Christ-like. He was carrying a broom and a dust pan and was sweeping a tile floor. He heard what sounded like someone dribbling a basketball and the floor was now wood. He dropped the broom and started toward the dribbling sound to discover three Viet Cong playing basketball. The ball was an American soldier's head. He woke up after seeing that the head had Stephanie's face. He was shaken by the dream and he lay awake trying to cipher its meaning. He didn't have a clock in the upstairs bedroom.

After awhile, Andy got up, gathered his clothes, and went downstairs. It was close to four-thirty. He started coffee in the dark. He turned on the pump and took a hot bath. Mel strutted back and forth on the rim of the tub and then on the closed lid of the self-composting toilet and then back to the tub rim. "I'll feed you in a few minutes Mel." The cat meowed the whole time. After he was dressed, Andy fed the cat. The sky was growing light as he poured his first cup of coffee. He went to the dining room window just in time to see the lights of a passing vehicle headed north on the road. 'Who the hell is out there at this time of the morning going in that direction'? He shook his head thinking, 'nice way to drive yourself nuts McLeod.

He read until six when he called Jan. She answered on the first ring. She sounded like she had been up for a while. He asked if she had been. "I just finished doing my Tai Chi exercises and I'm about to do my Tai kwon do. Did you get any sleep last night?" They talked for a few minutes. "I'll be at your place at eight. Do you make decent coffee or do I need to pick some up for us at the shop?"

"I make very good coffee. I'm reasonably competent in the kitchen. I've never burned Jell-O." Before hanging up she asked if there was any sign of Lucy. "No, she's either dead or they've got her. Rob's cat is a miserable substitute."

Andy had just finished doing a load of laundry when Jan arrived.

He was in the process of hanging it up to dry. "Jesus, McLeod, I haven't seen one of these old wringer washers since I was a kid. Do they still make these things?"

"This is déjà vu." Andy said. "That is the exact same thing Stephanie said to me the first time she came here." Jan showed little interest. "To answer your question, I have no idea. I got this at an estate sale. I think I paid ten dollars for it." He looked at it, "I kind of like doing laundry this way except that you can't just throw in a load of wash and walk away. You have to be there for each step of the process." She asked him if he was going to miss living this way once his new house was up. "I've thought about it. Living this way eats up a lot of time that I could use for other things."

Jan went through his house, the workshop, and his truck with the scanner. "I don't know, Andy unless I'm not using this thing properly, I don't find a thing. She showed it to him. There was a dial switch that put the device into different frequency ranges. He asked her if she had fiddled with that at all. She said that the technician that showed her how to use it had set it and said that should pick up everything operating in the normal range. Andy dialed it to a higher range and scanned his dining room. Nothing showed up. He dialed it to a lower range and the needle moved. As he moved toward the stove the needle kept rising. Underneath the spark guard on the front of the stove they found a magnetic audio device. He pulled it off the stove and dropped it into a kettle of water on top of the stove. They found four more such devices all in the downstairs of the house. Rob arrived just as they were about to go to the workshop. They went over Stephanie's car. It was clean. Rob and he needed to leave for the airport. Jan told him she would finish up the scanning on her own. Andy told her, "I'll leave the key in the deadbolt. Go ahead and lock it when you leave. I've got a spare." He unlocked the padlock on the workshop door. "I'll call you when I get back."

Enroute to the airport Rob asked several questions that had occurred to him starting with Lucy. Was there any sign of her yet? He asked about the relationship Andy had with Detective Miller. "I guess you'd say we're good friends. We've gone out to eat a couple of times. No, we're not sleeping together. She's seen me through a lot over the past few months." He left out the things he had seen her through except to say, "She's really gotten her act together since I first met her. In the beginning it was the deaf leading the blind. Rob asked what he meant by that. Andy thought about how to answer that question. "Let's just say that she was kind of a fish out of water. She grew up in the city. She'd been a Chicago cop. She was going through some culture shock. I, on the other hand, was this bumpkin who was caught up in a web of intrigue." Rob seemed satisfied with that answer. He said, "I'm worried about you amigo. Do you think you're in any real danger? I mean, if they think you know Steph's whereabouts, what's to prevent them from trying to make you tell them? Never mind that you don't know where she is. If they think you do, they might resort to torture."

"I know, after Stephanie left, things seemed to quiet down for awhile. It wasn't until a few days ago that it started up again. They've probably been watching me the whole time."

"Do you think she's still alive and hiding out somewhere?"

"I honestly don't know. I have a box that supposedly contains her ashes. For all I know they may be the ashes of a donkey. There's no way to verify them one way or another."

"If she's still alive, do you think you'll ever see her again?" Andy looked irritated and shrugged. "I'm sorry. That was a stupid question," Rob said.

"It's not a stupid question, Rob. I wonder the same thing. It's just a question that I have no answer for. I've somehow ended up in a game that I can't win and I can't get out of. It's entirely up to whoever is behind this whole thing as to when, or if, it's ever going to end." Andy thought, but did not say, 'I wonder what will happen if they ever become convinced that I'm of no use to them. Are they going to grease me'? Instead he said, "I thought about trying to take off but I doubt that would work. I'm convinced that they'd find me no matter where I went."

At the airport Andy accompanied Rob to the security check point. "Don't worry about Mel. You have a good trip. I'll see you in three weeks." They hugged and Rob departed. It hadn't been until their conversation that Andy was finally able to admit to himself how dire his situation was. On the drive home he began mentally composing his last will and testament. There was no question that he would bequeath the farm to his sons. He would give Rob his truck and his tools. He wanted to give Jan something of value. He realized that, other than Rob, she was his only other close friend. He had several fairly good acquaintances, but he felt the closest to the two of them. He couldn't think of anything he could give to her. He turned to the decision about the new house. He decided that he needed to go ahead with having it constructed. His thoughts turned to Lucy. He felt such a terrible void. Not knowing if she was dead or alive was more than he could manage. His emotions caught up with him and tears began running down his cheeks. He reached under the seat and retrieved the pistol Jan had given him, thinking, 'Goddamn them. I'm going make them pay for what they've done'. He wondered if these people had ruined other people's lives.

It was early afternoon when he arrived home. It was a beautiful day. A nice breeze had come up and the temperature was in the low fifties. The remaining piles of snow were shrinking fast. He let Mel out. There was a note on the dining room table from Jan. She was taking the devices they had found to send to Madison. She asked him to call her when he got home. There was a P.S. 'You do make good coffee, McLeod'. He noticed that she had even run the vacuum to clean up from last night's mess. He called the sheriff's department non-emergency number. Detective Miller was in a meeting. He left a message for her. He opened a couple of windows to let in fresh air, and then he went out to take down his laundry which was completely dry. He folded each article as he took it down from the line. He had just come in with the laundry basket when Jan called. "The Sheriff and I are coming to your place. We're bringing some other people along." She asked if there was any sign of Lucy yet. He told her he was just about to go out looking for her. "Wait until we get there. See you in an hour." As an after-thought she asked, "I trust your trip to the airport was uneventful." He told her it was.

Less than an hour later two squad cars, Jan's car, and a large van came up his driveway. The sheriff and Detective Miller were in the first car. There were two deputies each in the squads. The van had a dog handler and his daughter. There were four cages in the back of the van. Two of them contained German shepherd's, a third had what looked like a Beagle/hound mix, and the fourth looked like a coon dog. The dog handler was an older, grizzly-looking man. He had on baggy, wool trousers, suspenders, a faded chambray shirt, and a beat up looking dress hat. His daughter looked to be in her early thirties. She was medium height and wiry with exceptionally long hair that she had tied back. She had on jeans and a faded flannel shirt. Jan introduced Andy to all of them. A plan had been devised. The sheriff and one of the deputies were going to accompany the handler. They were taking the beagle mix and one of the German shepherd's. They would be attempting to follow the scent of the intruders. The daughter and two deputies were going to follow Lucy's scent. Her scent would be the most prominent. They anticipated that both scents would be commingled. Jan and the last deputy were going to be in the patrol cars and would be in radio contact with the men on foot. Andy asked what he was supposed to do. The sheriff told him to just stay here. Because it was a potentially dangerous situation, the Sheriff didn't want Andy directly involved. Jan gave him a handheld radio. "You can keep track of what's going on with this. The handler and his daughter were led to where the dogs could be introduced to the scents. Lucy's was easy. It took the other two dogs several

minutes before the handler seemed fairly certain that they had the inter-
lopers' scent. The two teams of people, led by the dogs, got underway
and headed in a northeasterly direction out across the meadow. Jan said
to the deputy, "judging from the direction they're moving in, it looks
like they're headed toward those woods." She pointed. "There's a road
that runs parallel to the road that runs past here. It's probably a quarter
mile over. It connects with the highway south of here." The deputy was
not familiar with this part of the county as he patrolled the southern end
of the county almost exclusively. She spread a map out on her car hood
and showed him what she was talking about. "Come on, follow me.
We'll set up a blockade on this other road before it reaches the highway." They quickly went to their cars and left. Andy went to
Stephanie's car and got the shotgun and shells out of the cargo area. He
made sure the shot gun was loaded and put it on the seat of his truck.
He waited a few minutes, listening to the radio the whole time. There
were no transmissions for several minutes. One of the deputies sounding a bit out of breath, broke the silence to report that they had spotted
a pickup camper parked up ahead in the woods. The dogs could be
heard barking over the radio. He next reported that the pickup's engine
had just started. Now it appeared to be moving. He reported that it was
now on the road and was moving south. The Sheriff asked Jan if she
copied. She said that she did and that she and the other deputy were
setting up a blockade on that road. Andy quickly got into his truck. He
drove out of his driveway hoping not to get behind some geezer doing
twenty miles per hour. He got to the parallel road. A few hundred yards
up the road he made a U-turn and parked on the side of the road. Jan
reported that the camper had come to a halt maybe a hundred yards
north of her position. The Sheriff was panting. He asked what seemed
to be happening. "I don't know. I think they're trying to decide."

The sheriff said they were too far away to be of help. "We're
going to get to the road in case they decided to try to turn around and
back-track. If they start toward you." Jan interrupted, "it looks like
they're going to try to run our blockade." Her radio went silent.
Andy heard shots being fired, then heard a crashing sound. Thirty
seconds later he saw the camper in his rear view mirror as it came
around a curve in the road. The front end of the vehicle looked damaged. The camper swerved and almost went out of control. He
stepped out of his truck and took aim at the oncoming camper. When
the camper was less than forty yards from him he opened fire, aiming at the driver's side of the windshield. He emptied all five rounds
of the shotgun, blowing out the entire windshield. The camper
swerved to the left running off the road and crashing into a clump of
small trees. He heard the siren from the squad car that had accompa-

nied Jan coming up rapidly. If it was damaged he couldn't see it. The deputy slammed on his brakes, stopping short of where the camper sat. He threw his door open and immediately trained his shot gun on the camper. He was crouched behind the car door. 'Where's Jan? Is she okay?' Andy started his engine. He drove close enough to the camper that it would be impossible for it to back up. He started to get out of his truck when an explosion inside the camper blew its door completely off. The interior was immediately consumed in flames. If Lucy or anyone was inside, they had to be dead. Andy quickly slammed his truck into reverse and backed up a safe distance. Jan drove up. She jumped out of her car. She and the other deputy ran to the passenger side of the camper. She trained her gun on the door and the deputy jerked it open. The limp arm of a man dropped out. Andy approached holding the shotgun at ready. Inside the cab of the truck there was the bloody body of what must have been the passenger. Whoever else had been in the truck had exited from the driver's side.

She said to the deputy. "The other one's probably gone into the woods. Stay behind the camper." She checked the man pulse. "This one's still alive, but barely. His throat's been slit. We've got to get him out of this thing before it blows up." She reached over the man and freed his seat belt.

While Jan provided cover, the deputy and Andy dragged the man away from the truck. The man's head fell back and blood streamed out. They got him to the other side of the road, fearing the camper was going to explode at any moment. The man was dead. The deputy and Andy took up defensive positions while Jan radioed a request that fire trucks be dispatched to the scene. She gave the location. She changed channels to apprise the Sheriff of the situation.

Watchful for the escapee, she asked Andy in a loud whisper, "McLeod, did you shoot at the truck?" He told her he had. "Did you use the shot gun?" He nodded. "Give it to me." She holstered her pistol and took it. She handed him her shotgun. "You didn't shoot at anyone. Have you got that?" He nodded. She asked if there had been any sign of Lucy. He told her there hadn't. "Maybe she's back where they were parked." In a low voice she said, "They must have had an incendiary device rigged to destroy the interior of the camper just in case they got caught. I wonder if the delay was purposely set to take out an intruder. Don't say a word to anyone about firing the shot gun," she repeated. "Get out of here right now. Go on back to your place. Wash your face and hands several times to get any cordite off. Change your clothes and put the ones you're wearing in the wash. I'll see you later."

"Am I in trouble?" he asked.

"Go on and do as I say. Get back home before the Sheriff shows up here."

The deputy that was with her had his assault shotgun. He was already searching the edge of the woods. He called to Jan to tell her that he had found some blood. He was pretty sure he had located where the escapee had entered the woods. Andy went to his truck. He was debating driving to where the camper had been parked to see if Lucy was there. Jan anticipated his actions. "McLeod, someone will let you know if Luce has been found. Go home."

Andy pulled into his place a few minutes before the sheriff and the others appeared from the woods to the east. He went to meet them. He held up the radio Jan had given him. "I heard what happened. Was there any sign of my dog?"

The sheriff said, "I think it would be best if you stayed here. We'll call you if we find her." The sheriff and the two deputies got into the squad car and left. The dog handler and his daughter returned a few minutes later and began putting their dogs into their cages. He asked them if they had seen any sign of his dog. They looked at one another. The daughter said that they couldn't say for sure.

He confronted them. "Something has happened to her hasn't it? She's dead isn't she?" They said nothing. Andy went to his truck and got the pistol. He started jogging across the meadow.

The daughter ran to try to catch up with him. "Mister McLeod, I don't think you want to see your dog." He ignored her and increased his pace to a run. She yelled to him. "She's still alive, but just barely."

When he got to the area where the camper had been parked, he found a wooden crate. It had already been opened. He saw Lucy. She was in a comatose state, lying in her own waste, barely breathing. He gently lifted her out of the crate, talking to her softly. "I'm here babe. I'm here. I'm going to take care of you. You're going to be okay. Hang in there baby, please. Don't give up. Jan's car came roaring into sight. She was by herself. "Jan, can you take us to the vet. Call the dispatcher and ask her to call Doc Bitner. Tell him McLeod is coming with Lucy. It's an emergency." Without hesitation she did as he requested. Andy got in the back seat of her car holding Lucy. Jan backed up, asking where the vet was. He gave her directions. "His clinic is about seven miles from here." Jan drove right by the camper. There were three squads and two fire trucks at the camper scene. One of the squads was a state trooper's car. The sheriff motioned for her to stop. She lowered the window. "We're on the way to the vets." He waved her by. Whatever he wanted to say to her could wait.

Ten minutes later they arrived at the clinic. Doctor Bitner came out the front door. He opened the rear door of Jan's car. "Oh my," he whispered. He led the way into the clinic. There were people waiting for appointments. He said to his receptionist. "Try to reschedule as many of these folks as you can. This is bad." He led them into a surgical room. He had Andy lay her on a stainless steel table.

"Can I stay here with her doc?"

"Absolutely." The vet immediately examined her with his stethoscope. "She's barely breathing. I'm going to start an intravenous. She's severely dehydrated which also means her electrolytes are likely way out of whack. Andy, there's a very slim chance of her making it. What happened to her?"

"Someone took her a couple of days ago. They had her in a wooden crate. I don't think she was let out of it or given any food or water." Doc Bitner shook his head. He was too busy to ask how Andy had been able to recover her. Andy stroked her gently, speaking to her softly. "Come on babe, you can make it. You just have to. We're going to put up our new house. No more pioneer living."

After Doc Bitner had done everything he could, he said to Andy. "Two things may happen. She might go into cardiac arrest, and/or her kidneys might shut down if they haven't already. I won't be able to tell about the latter for awhile. If she can't pass fluids, then I'll try catheterizing her, but if she can't void on her own within twenty-four hours; then we'll have to call it quits. I'll keep you posted." He asked Andy if he knew who did this to her.

"No, not really." It was the truth.

"You know Andy, she's not conscious, but she knows you came for her." Tears began streaming down Andy's face. Jan met him in the reception room. She asked what was happening. Doctor Bitner went outside with them and explained the situation. When they left the clinic the two of them drove in silence back to his place. She radioed the sheriff. "We're back. What's happening?"

"There are twelve of us out here in the swamp, including the dog handlers. This guy knows his way around the woods. It looks like we've got some Rambo-type on our hands. It appears that he slit his partner's throat. He must have decided the guy was a liability who would only get in the way, and maybe spill some beans if he was interrogated. Is McLeod there?" She said that he was. "Is his dog going to make it?"

"We don't know."

"Tell him I'm sorry. We've got a goddamn, mean-assed, psychopath on our hands. I want you to stay there with McLeod. I have a sneaking suspicion this bastard might try to circle his way back there. Make sure McLeod is armed. Tell him I'm deputizing him again. Don't mess with this monster. If he shows up, dispatch him."

Chapter 13

Andy had heard the entire conversation between Jan and the Sheriff. He commented, "The sheriff's biggest concern right now ought to be for the people living in the surrounding area. My guess is that Rambo is looking for either a place to hide or transportation and hostages. I don't think he should waste time combing the swamps. They're not going to find him there. I would call everybody in and start sending teams to each house."

Jan agreed. "If he's wounded and he dies out there in the woods, good riddance." She got back on the radio with her boss. "Sheriff, Andy just came up with an idea that makes better sense than chasing around out there in the woods." She told him Andy's proposal. The Sheriff said that he would get back to her.

A few minutes later he called back. "I discussed the idea with Mark and Marty. They agree. I'm going to call in all the search personnel. I'm requesting all available personnel to join in the search. I want everyone to meet me ASAP at the town fire station. Call Vern and ask if he will tow the camper to the impound garage. The techs can finish going over it there. If anything comes up call me. It's going to get cold out here as soon as the sun goes down. Maybe that'll finish this guy off. Incidentally, tell McLeod that I appreciate his suggestion. That was good thinking on his part."

After she finished talking to the sheriff she turned to Andy. "What do you think the chances are that this guy is going to try to circle around to get back here?" Andy said nothing. He looked out across the meadow. "You're hoping he will, aren't you?"

Jan noticed that the front door to the house was open. Andy thought that maybe he had left it that way since it was such a pleasant day. Nonetheless she insisted they have a look. As soon as they got inside Mel came bounding down from upstairs meowing. It startled both of them. Andy picked Mel up and petted him. Then he set him back down and poured food into a bowl for him. Before they went back outside Jan said, "Maybe we ought to check the barn too. Keep a distance between us. There isn't any cover from here to the barn."

After checking the barn Jan asked if he was going to be okay without her here. She wanted to be at the fire station when the sheriff briefed the search team. He thought that he would. Andy called the vet's office as soon as she left. Doc Bitner talked to him. "There isn't any change Andy. I know this sounds a bit unorthodox, but it might help if you came up here to be with her. Even though she's not conscious, my personal feeling is that having you near may help to lessen her stress. She may be aware of your presence at some unconscious level."

"I'll be there in a few minutes. Thanks, Doc." He disabled Stephanie's car, by taking off the coil wire to prevent it from being stolen. He put the pistol under his truck seat. After trying unsuccessfully to reach Jan on the radio, he called the dispatcher and asked her to relay a message to Detective Miller about where he'd be.

At the veterinary clinic Doc Bitner escorted him to a room where he had placed Lucy. She was lying on a blanket in a stainless steel cage. One of the vet's assistants had cleaned her up the best that could be done. Andy fought back tears. "Here's a stool for you to sit on Andy. Talk to her and pet her. Let her know that she's safe now. You can stay for however long. I'll get you some coffee." Doc left and came back a few minutes later with the coffee. He examined her with the stethoscope. "Her heart rate is rapid and shallow." He let Andy listen. He lifted an eye lid, "notice the pupil isn't dilating, and the eye isn't tracking movement. She's comatose. I tend to think that short term comas are a survival mechanism; their an autonomic reaction to severe stress or trauma. We don't know if creatures have any awareness about what's happening in their surrounding world when they're unconscious. As I said before, my personal opinion is that she may be aware of you being here."

Doc Bitner checked in on them every once in awhile. Three hours passed. Andy was asleep with his head on his arms on the table. When Doc came in again Andy awakened. Doc Bitner checked Lucy and groaned. Andy could tell from his tone. "Andy, I'm so sorry. She's gone." He seemed almost as upset as Andy. After a few minutes, he suggested that Andy pull around to the back door of the clinic. After putting Lucy's body in a double layer of thick plastic bags, he helped Andy load the body into the back of the truck.

Andy thanked him. "I'll come by in the morning to pay you. I didn't bring my check book." Doc Bitner told him not to worry about it. When Andy got home he drove to the area behind the barn where he had buried Buck.

He was on his way to get a shovel when Jan drove in. She could tell from his expression that Lucy had died. He got the shovel. "Andy, I'm so sorry." She stood by as he began digging. He dug as deep a hole as he could before hitting bedrock. She helped him put Lucy into the hole. He placed several flat rocks over her before filling the grave back up. He said it was to prevent critters from digging her up. It was almost five o'clock. "Mix yourself a drink McLeod. Let's take a walk." Half way across the meadow he began sobbing. She put her hand on his arm. "Were you with her when she died?" He nodded. "Good, I'm sure she knew you were there." After awhile they resumed walking. She took his arm. "There's been no sign of Rambo. Personally, I hope the bastard dies out there in the swamp. It's still too early for the summer people to be returning. He may have broken into one of the vacant cottages. The sheriff has contacted two of the surrounding sheriff's departments. They're sending three, two-man squads first thing in the morning. There's going to be a house-to-house search. There are about a hundred and fifty homes in about a ten mile radius." When they got back to the house they stood outside. "Andy, I don't want to leave you here by yourself tonight."

He spoke for the first time, "I'll be okay. Thanks."

"No, I don't think you should be alone tonight. I need to go back to my place to get my medications, shower, and change my clothes. I'll be back in a couple of hours. I can sleep upstairs. Besides, what if Rambo shows up here during the night? We need to take turns keeping watch." He started to say something. She told him that she would see him in awhile and left.

It was a beautiful spring evening. He felt lost. He didn't know what he wanted or needed. Mostly he ached with grief. He went to the barn and found a couple lawn chairs upstairs. He brought them to the fire pit. Within a few minutes he had a campfire going. Sunset was approaching and it was getting chilly. He went inside and put on one of his old flannel shirts, remembering it was the one that Stephanie had commandeered from him. He toyed with mixing another drink. He decided not to. He would maybe have a glass of wine when Jan returned. The sun had set and he was sitting by the fire in the afterglow when she returned. "Perfect McLeod; I was thinking on the way back here what a beautiful evening it was. Did you catch that sunset? It was exquisite." He hadn't paid any attention to it. She already had a jacket on. "I brought you a bottle of wine. I don't know if you're a wine drinker or not."

Andy asked Jan if she thought she could handle having a glass of wine. "I'd better not. I'd love to, but no. One of the medications I'm on warns against alcohol consumption. It's right on the label." She followed him into the house. In the kitchen she asked, "How are you doing?"

He leaned back against the small kitchen counter and shrugged. Mel jumped up on the counter and meowed while marching back and forth, rubbing himself against Andy. He picked the cat up and scratched its neck. "I've decided that loving is a bitch. The pain is just too terrible." She looked down. He leaned over and set Mel down on the floor. "Come on Brady, let's go sit by the fire." She nodded. "How about some cheese and crackers? I'm not really hungry but we should eat something." Andy got some cheese out of the refrigerator and sliced it. He opened some crackers and spread them out on a plate.

They sat by the fire, mostly in silence. As it grew dark the spring peepers began their monotonous chirping choir. He went inside and got an old sleeping bag. He had Jan stand up and he put it in her chair. After she sat back down she brought it around her. After awhile the chalky smear of the Milky Way became visible. They had no idea of what time it was when they decided to go in. The temperature had dropped into the forties and they were both getting cold despite the fire. Inside they took turns using the bathroom. "Jan, I've got a mattress pad heater on my bed. You can sleep there. I'll go upstairs." She reluctantly accepted his offer. As he started for the stairs she said to him, "I'm sorry for the way things turned out, Andy."

He nodded, "I appreciate everything you've done for me, Jan." He hesitated. "You know, I just can't understand how anyone could do what those bastards did. How can anyone treat an animal that way? The suffering she must have endured."

As he climbed the stairs, Mel bounded by him and met him at the top. He undressed in the dark and crawled into a sleeping bag. Mel curled up next to him purring loudly. He thought about Lucy. He berated himself for not having kept her with him. He was consumed with vengeful feelings toward not only those two men, but whoever had hired them. He thought about Jan. He had come to appreciate her even more. For the first time since they had met, he allowed himself to think about reaching out to her physically. Not sexually, but to hold her and lie next to her. His knowledge of her past made him wonder if she would be able to risk herself with any man, ever. He found himself feeling angry with Stephanie. If it weren't for her, none of this would have happened. 'She had to have known what was at stake the day she walked into my shop. She took a chance knowing full well that, if it failed, it was going to bring disaster down on me, too. Goddamn you Steph. You have no idea how much misery you've caused'.

He eventually fell asleep, only to awaken a little after midnight to the sound of movement downstairs. He slipped out of the sleeping bag and carefully put on his jeans. He picked up the pistol and crept toward the stairs. He listened. He heard the bathroom door creak open and downstairs movement. He half whispered. "Is that you Jan?"

She apologized. "I had to pee. I'm sorry; I didn't mean to wake you." He said that he had been dozing off and on. "I guess neither of us is getting much sleep tonight. Maybe we ought to take two hour shifts."

He said, "I'm going to set up an alarm system." He slipped on his sweatshirt and went downstairs. She was wearing a long flannel night shirt that came down to her knees. She watched him as he stacked some pots in front of the door. "I did this one other time but Mel knocked them over, scaring the bejesus out of me."

"It's cold in here. I'm freezing. I'm going back to bed." She said goodnight as she left for the bedroom. Andy debated starting a fire, but decided not to. In the living room he called out to her to ask if she needed another blanket. She said that she was fine. He went back upstairs. He looked out the bedroom window. There was just a sliver of a moon. The sky was cloudless. He could see that frost was starting to form on the grass. He wondered about the guy who everyone was now calling Rambo. He couldn't imagine anyone being able to survive the night out there in the woods with the night this cold. He had no empathy for the man.

They were both up before six the next morning. There had been a hard frost that night. He asked her if she wanted to take a hot bath. She said that she'd shower at home. He offered her some breakfast before leaving. He had already started coffee. She seemed to be in a bad mood. He wanted to think it was because she had not slept well. "I'm going to take off McLeod. I'll call you if there's any news about Rambo." She went to the door and bent over to pick up the pots he had stacked last night.

He moved to take them from her. He looked at her and asked, "Are you alright?" She looked away and said she was fine. "You seem pissed about something."

"We'll talk later. Now is not the time." She turned and left.

He heard her car start up. He took the pots into the kitchen and returned them to the lower cabinet next to the sink. The coffee was done brewing and he poured a cup. He fed Mel; then put on a jacket. He stuck the gun in his belt. Outside he heard an engine running. He pulled out his gun and moved cautiously toward the corner of the house. It was Jan's car. She was sitting behind the wheel. He went over to the car and opened the door. She looked ashen. She had an almost desperate expression. "What's the matter Jan? Are you alright?"

"Andy, something's wrong." She was sweating profusely." He reached across her and turned off the engine; then he undid her seat belt and reclined the seat as far back as it would go.

"I'll be right back." He ran into the house and called 911. When the dispatcher answered he identified himself, gave his address, and said that there was a woman having an apparent heart attack. Please send an ambulance immediately. He identified Jan. Moments later the dispatcher said that help was on the way. There was an ambulance less than five minutes away. He ran back out. She looked even paler than before. He told her an ambulance would be here in a few minutes. It was close by. He pulled out his bandana and wiped the sweat from her face.

"Andy, I can hardly breathe. I feel like my stomach is about to explode." He heard a siren in the distance. He touched her cheek. "I hear the ambulance." Something told him that she was about to get sick. He ran back to the house and grabbed a plastic waste basket. He got back to her just in time. She threw up just as the ambulance came into the driveway. She apologized. "The key to my apartment is the one next to my car key. Take care of my plants will you?" He wiped her face again. Moments later two paramedics emerged from the ambulance and ran to where Andy stood next to her car. He stepped back to get out of their way. One of them asked him what her symptoms were. The other was applying a blood pressure cuff. The first one, who seemed to be the one in charge, asked Andy to help him retrieve a wheeled stretcher from the ambulance. Once it was in place the three of them lifted her out of the car and onto it. As soon as she was in the ambulance the first paramedic began attaching the electrodes for an EKG.

"I'll follow the ambulance Jan." Andy told her. The second medic closed the back of the ambulance then got behind the wheel, backed up, and drove off.

Andy went back in the house and called 911 and again identified himself. "The ambulance just left my address with Detective Miller. Would you please inform Sheriff Cummings that Detective Miller is on her way to the hospital? She appears to be having a heart attack." He hung up, checked to see that Mel had enough water for the day, got the shotgun, and locked the door to the house on his way out. He put the shotgun in the back of his truck and locked the cap covering the bed of the pick up truck. When he got to the hospital Jan was still in the ER. He was only able to spend a few moments with her as she was about to be transferred to the intensive care unit.

She held out her hand to him when he approached. "I'm sorry I was so bitchy this morning." He touched her cheek. "I didn't mean to treat you that way." Two attendants appeared. One of them drew the curtains back.

"I'll see you once you get settled in ICU." He told her. The attendants wheeled her away.

The ER doctor was making some notations. He looked up. "Are you the one that called in the emergency?" He said that he was. "Are you aware that your friend had a heart attack?" Andy told the doctor that he had thought so, but wasn't sure. "We're going to run some more tests on her. It may be that she's going to require surgery." The doctor told him, "We'll be transferring her to Green Bay if it's what I think it is. We're not set up to do anything major here." Andy asked what kind of surgery. The doctor explained what might be involved, angioplasty, which was a less invasive procedure. He warned that she might require bypass surgery. He asked Andy a number of questions before explaining, "heart attacks in women are often quite different than in men. They're much more subtle and the symptoms can be quite different than they are with men. This could have started days ago. Ms. Miller may have been suffering an ongoing attack. The symptoms sometimes even subside temporarily." Andy told the doctor that Jan was a detective with the Sheriff's department. He told him that Jan had been involved in a criminal pursuit the day before. "That may be what triggered a full blown attack, but..." The doctor interrupted him and went on to explain some of the accumulative effects of heart disease and how it had finally caught up with her.

By early afternoon it was determined that Jan would need to undergo bypass surgery and arrangements were made for her to be transferred by ambulance to Green Bay. Surgery would be performed that evening. Andy was allowed to see her briefly. "I'm scared Andy. I guess I'm paying the price for all those years of abusing myself. If something happens and I don't make it; take whatever you want of my stuff. Either burn all of those ridiculous clothes or re-donate them. Maybe a bag lady could use them. Pitch everything else." Andy took her hand and she allowed it. "Are you afraid of dying?" she asked him.

"I'd like to put it off for awhile," he told her.

"Yeah, I guess I would too. Most people are afraid. It's the great unknown. I never thought I was," she said. "But I was scared today. I knew something was wrong. By the time I got to my car I knew I couldn't go any further. I came close to hitting the panic button, Andy. I guess it wasn't my time."

"It was paranoia that saved you Jan," Andy told her smiling weakly. She asked what he meant by that. "If I weren't so damn paranoid about all that's been happening, I wouldn't have come outside and found you when I did. It might have been too late if I had come out ten or fifteen minutes later."

She showed a slight frown. "I guess I have Stephanie to thank for that."

Andy changed the subject. "Construction starts on the new house next week. The builder thinks that it should be ready to move into by the end of July. I'm planning on having a house warming party when it's finished. I want you there for it."

She squeezed his hand. "I'll try." She placed her other hand on his. "McLeod, you know that I've had mostly bad experiences with men over the years. I just want you to know that I regard you as a standup guy. I appreciate what you've done for me." She smiled weakly. "Last night when you got that sleeping bag and wrapped me up in it, that was really nice of you." The orderlies arrived to take Jan to the ambulance. He kissed her forehead before they wheeled her away.

Andy drove back home to check on Mel and make sure everything was okay. He locked up before leaving for the hospital in Green Bay. Locking doors seemed like such a futile, ridiculous thing to do. Jan was already in surgery when he arrived at the hospital early that evening. It was late that night when she was brought to her room. One of the nurses told Andy that she would be pretty much out of it for the next several hours. One of doctors who had performed the surgery met with Andy to explain what had been done. He told Andy, "She's one lucky woman to have survived. She's probably been suffering with mild symptoms for awhile and either didn't recognize what was happening or she was ignoring them. When she's fully recovered she's probably going to feel better than she has in years."

Jan went back and forth between sleep and half wakeful. Andy doubted that she even knew he was there by the time he left the hospital at midnight. He stopped at a twenty-four hour grocery store on the way home to pick up a few groceries and some gin and vermouth. It took close to two hours to get home. He felt especially lonely without Lucy beside him. Mel greeted him when he came in the house. He fed the cat before bringing in the rest of the groceries. He went out to the workshop to check on things. Nothing seemed to be out of order. Back in the house he locked the door and set up the pot alarm. He mixed a drink. The house was chilly.

He was awakened at six in the morning by the telephone ringing. He almost went into a panic fearing that something had happened to Jan. "McLeod, its Sheriff Cummings." Andy was breathing hard. He told the sheriff that he had just returned from an early morning run. Sheriff Cummings asked about Jan's surgery and how she was doing. Andy told him what he could. "She's one of my favorite people," the sheriff commented. He had nothing to report about the fugitive. "That was a good idea you had yesterday, McLeod about searching the houses in the vicinity. He would have had a tough time surviving last night's temperatures out there in the woods without a fire. If he's still out there I'm hoping he's holed up in one of the vacant houses. I'd hate to think he found one that was occupied and taken anybody hostage."

They talked for awhile longer. Sheriff Cummings said that he had given instructions for the deputies on patrol to check on him and his place. "So don't be alarmed if a patrol car comes up your driveway in the middle of the night." Andy thanked him, wondering how a deputy would be able to tell if he was okay without awakening him to find out. Before ending the call the sheriff told Andy that the three guns that had been stolen from him had been found in the debris of the camper. "One of the deputies found your 1911 under the driver's-side seat. It's in good shape. The ammo was in a metal box behind the seat. The rifle and shotgun were in the camper. They look to me to be ruined. I'll send you a report. Maybe you can file an insurance claim and get some money to replace them."

Andy left for Green Bay before seven. Jan was asleep when he got to her room. He had his thermos of coffee. He poured some and sat down beside the bed. A nurse came in to check on Jan, awakening her. In a weak voice she said, "Andy? You weren't here all night were you?" He told her that he had gone home and just returned a few minutes ago. She seemed relieved. She wiggled her fingers, beckoning him to move closer. He did. She coughed weakly which caused her to grimace with pain. "I broke several ribs a few years ago. This feels the same. It hurts to even breathe."

"I know the feeling," he told her. The nurse brought her some fresh water. Andy held the glass so she could drink.

"Have they found Rambo yet?"

"Sheriff Cummings called just before I left the house to see how you were doing. They hadn't caught him as of then." She nodded.

Andy stayed with her most of the day. She drifted in and out of sleep. He waited until seven when the evening traffic would be less. As he got up to leave Jan said, "Andy, I appreciate you going to all the trouble to come down here. You don't need to. You've got lots to do. Stay home tomorrow."

He leaned over and touched her hair. He kissed her forehead. "Sleep well."

She was much more alert and lively when he arrived the next morning bearing a small bouquet of daffodils that he had picked from his property. She seemed happy to see him. "I know you told me that you weren't much of a reader but I brought you a couple of books that I thought you might like." One was the Gibran book that Stephanie had given him at Christmas. She began to fade after an hour. "I've got a few errands to run," he told her. "I'll come back to see you later."

When he returned early that afternoon she was dozing. Two large bouquets had been delivered to her room. One was from Sheriff Cummings and the other was from several of her colleagues. He had just sat down when she awakened. They talked for awhile. At one point in the conversation she said, "Andy, if anything happens to me I want to be cremated. I want you to spread my ashes out there at Thorsen Point. I wrote that down and had it witnessed. I also don't want to be kept alive if I become a turnip. I wrote that in there as well.

I'm giving you power of attorney. I hope we can go back out there again before the tourists arrive and it gets crowded." He smiled telling her to plan on it. She gave him a serious look. "I think you need to get another dog, Andy. You're really lost without Lucy."

"What kind of a dog?"

"I've never had a dog before. I suppose just a mutt. I've always heard that their the best; better than most purebreds. I always wanted a dog when I was a kid. It was probably just as well that it never happened." She asked, "Do you think people can make up for having a shitty youth when they grow up?"

"I think so but a lot of people just keep repeating the misery of their past. I've watched you over these past few months, Jan. You're not the same person I first met. You've come a long, long way in a short time. You're one of my heroes."

"Yeah," she said. "I had pretty much given up on myself." She was running out of energy.

It was late afternoon. Andy told her he was going to take off to beat the evening traffic. "I'll see you in the morning. Sleep well." She thanked him for coming. When he leaned over to kiss her forehead she put a hand on his cheek.

Andy was up at 5:00 the next morning. It promised to be another nice day. He went for a three mile run. He left the house before seven and arrived at the hospital a little before nine. He brought her a small tape player and a couple of recorded books, explaining that he listened to books a lot while he was in his studio. It was now Thursday. She told him that the doctor said she could possibly go home by Saturday. However, he was concerned that she not be alone for the next week or two. "The hospital social worker is in the process of contacting local nursing homes to see about transferring me to one of those," she told him. "I'm not keen on going to a nursing home but it's less expensive than being here in the hospital." Andy hesitated before proposing that she could come and stay at his place. She flatly refused his offer.

"Think about it Jan. You don't have to decide right this second. I'm around all the time to keep an eye on you. Your being there wouldn't be an imposition. You can have as much privacy as you want or need. I know that it's not even a two-star accommodation, but the price is right. I'm a pretty good cook. Besides, I'm lonesome." No decision was made by the time he left that afternoon.

That evening Sheriff Cummings called Andy, ostensibly to see how Jan was doing. The news everyone dreaded hearing was that Rambo had indeed found a place to stay. "The bastard spent the last three days holed up in an elderly couple's house. They live there year around. He took off this morning with the old man in their car. Every law enforcement agency in the state is looking for him. He's apparently wounded but not seriously. He's armed and he robbed them of close to a thousand dollars.

Andy commented, "Christ, I don't know which of those two old people I feel the most sorry for. I guess her. She has no idea if she will ever see her husband alive again or not."

"Exactly," Sheriff Cummings said. He didn't offer any further comment, except to say that he had notified the FBI. He was scheduled to meet with agents first thing tomorrow. "They may want to interview you, Andy. Jan's reports are thorough. Nonetheless, you've been the target of whatever this is about." Andy was willing to do so. He told Sheriff Cumming about Jan possibly being released from the hospital on Saturday and the doctor not wanting her to be staying by herself. The sheriff didn't know of anyone in his department that she could stay with. He was aware that she had no family or close friends. Andy told him of his offer for her to stay at his place and her refusal. The sheriff applauded Andy's intentions. He tried to tactfully say something about the house being a bit primitive. Andy thought, 'you have no idea just how primitive Sheriff'.

After hanging up, Andy mixed a drink and was starting out the door for a walk when the phone rang again. It was Doc Bitner. "Andy, I don't know if you are even willing to consider getting another dog so soon after losing Lucy. I just learned about a young Border Collie whose owner died a couple of days ago. It's a neutered male. The daughter wants to give it to a good home. I immediately thought of you. I know the dog. It's not Lucy, but he's a nice animal. He's well mannered, smart as hell. His name is Cassidy. If you're interested I'll give you the name and number to call." Andy hesitated. "Andy, conventional wisdom says people should wait for awhile after losing a pet. I tend to agree with that in most instances. In your case, I think you need to fill the void and this is not like starting from scratch with a puppy."

"Give me the number Doc. I'll go take a look at it. You're right; I'm feeling a terrible void." Doc Bitner gave him the number. Andy decided to take his walk before calling. By the time he was back he had all but decided that he would take the dog unless it proved to be a mismatch. He called and was invited to come to see Cassidy that evening if he wanted.

He drove to the address given him. It was still light out. It was an old farmstead. He was met at the door by the dog owner's daughter. She was a stout woman perhaps in her thirties. She was not unfriendly but she was anything but refined. She led him out to a dilapidated barn where she had Cassidy tethered. "My mother kept the dog in the house.

He's house broken, but he won't leave my cat alone so I put him out here. I don't know if you know anything about Border Collies, Mister, but they're not happy unless they're busy. They're working dogs."

Cassidy was a bit bigger than Lucy. He had one black eye and one white. He stood wagging his tail. Andy knelt down in the straw bedding and petted him. "Cassidy, I have a nice place. I think you'll like it there. There's lot's of room for you to run." The dog gave a bark. He turned to the daughter. "What do you want for the dog?"

"Are you kidding, Mister? All I want is to find a half-way descent home for him. If you want him he's yours for the taking. You can have his food and bowls too. He's a purebred. I'll get you the papers on him. There is no way I can keep him, but I hate the idea of having him put down. I thought my mother was crazy when she got him. An old lady getting a puppy; I mean what was she thinking?" Andy assured the woman that Cassidy was going to have a wonderful home. He got the impression she didn't care about that one way on another. "Are you going to take him with you now?"

"Absolutely, have you got something I can use as a leash?" The lady got Cassidy's retractable leash, along with everything else that belonged to him. Before Andy left, she made it clear that, if things didn't work out, the dog was now his responsibility. "Don't worry; things will work out. I'm sorry about your mom. Cassidy will have a very good home. He may be the perfect therapist for a friend of mine who just had heart surgery."

On the way home Cassidy sat next to him looking eagerly ahead. Andy talked to the dog knowing that it was his tone that mattered. He decided that he would take the dog with him to Green Bay the next day, even if it meant having to go back out to the truck several times. It was dark when they arrived home. Andy put Cassidy on the leash and walked around with him for awhile letting him get familiar with his new surroundings. Cassidy sniffed everything he could reach. In the house Mel and Cassidy cautiously sized one another up. Mel seemed to approve of this newcomer. Before going to bed Andy called the hospital. The nurse reported that Jan was resting comfortably and seemed to be doing quite well.

Cassidy reluctantly accepted an invitation to sleep in the bedroom that night. Andy wondered if the old lady had allowed the dog that privilege. Before he fell off to sleep he thought about what had happened to Lucy. He felt good about this dog. He reached down and petted him. Cassidy licked his hand, sighed, and curled up on what had been Lucy's bed. Mel decided to stay upstairs. Andy remembered that he had to pick Rob up at the airport on Sunday.

Chapter 14

The next day Jan ate her first full breakfast and was allowed to shower and wash her hair. She seemed rejuvenated. She was glad to see Andy when he arrived. "Have I got a surprise for you." He told her about Doc Bitner's call last evening and his adoption of Cassidy.

Jan reacted like a little girl on Christmas Eve, she was so excited. "I can't wait to see him. I thought after losing Lucy you would never risk getting another dog again." He told her that Sheriff Cummings had called him last night to ask about her. He brought up the subject of Rambo abducting an old man. "I know; I saw the report on TV this morning. God I hope he doesn't hurt that old man." She asked if Andy knew who the people were.

"Not by name, even though it's a small community. I may have seen them around town and just never learned their names."

He broached the subject of Jan coming to stay with him in a round-about way. "Construction starts on the new house Monday. I'll be around most of the time. I want to be as much a part of the process as Dan will allow, without my getting in the way. Maybe with my helping it will cut down on the costs. If you decide to take me up on my offer to stay at my place, I can look in on you regularly."

"I can't do that Andy. It's nice of you to offer, but I just can't. The social worker came by yesterday. She's found an assisted living place that I can go to that's not far from where I live."

He didn't argue his point any further. He assured her that if she changed her mind his offer still stood. There was a knock on the door. It was Sheriff Cummings. He entered the room and shook hands with both of them. For whatever reason, Andy hadn't realized until now what a large, imposing man the Sheriff was. The Sheriff seemed a bit awkward not knowing quite what to say. Jan told him some of the details of her surgery and recovery. "The doctor tells me that I'm going to have a lot more stamina when I get back on my feet. He says that this was something that was building up over a period of time." The Sheriff only stayed for a few minutes. Before leaving Jan asked if Rambo had been caught yet.

"Not yet. We've had reports that he may have been spotted in western Wisconsin late last night. If he crosses into another state, then he's facing federal charges. There's no word on the old man he abducted." The Sheriff stopped at the door. "You take care of yourself, Jan. Let me know if there's anything I can do. I'll call you know, if and when, he's caught."

Later, when the nurse came in, Jan asked her if Andy could bring his new dog in to see her. Andy assured her that the dog was well behaved. The nurse said that wasn't possible, but she suggested that Andy could take Jan down to the ground level atrium. He could bring the dog into that area as long as he was on a leash. She helped Jan into a wheel chair. Jan was still on an intravenous drip. When she was ready to go, a volunteer pushed the wheel chair and Andy wheeled the drip-bag. He left her briefly to get Cassidy. The dog seemed accustomed to being on a leash. He kept glancing back at Andy as if he were checking to make sure he was doing the right thing. When they got to where Jan was, Cassidy immediately sat down close enough that she could touch him. "My Cassidy, what a handsome fellow you are." She reached out to pet him, asking what kind of dog Cassidy was. Andy told her that he was a purebred Border Collie. "Aren't they working dogs?" Andy nodded. "They're supposed to be very smart and easy to train." Looking at Cassidy she said, "you're a very special fellow, Cassidy, I can just tell. You're going to have a wonderful new home to live in pretty soon." After a short time Jan looked like she was becoming tired. Andy left her to take Cassidy back to the truck. He and another volunteer took her back to her room. A nurse helped her get back into bed. "Andy, I've given your offer to stay at your place a lot of thought. You looked downright disappointed when I refused. I've decided that I'll give it a try with one stipulation." She had a determined look. "If either of us decides that this isn't working out, for whatever reason, then we'll go back to plan 'A' which is the assisted living place." He agreed. Her expression softened slightly. "You know me well enough to know that I won't hesitate to let you know if I think it's not working. I'm not sure that I trust you to do the same. You damn social workers have a penchant for suffering."

He held his hands out; palms up. "Look, no nail holes. I abandoned martyrdom awhile back."

"Cute, McLeod, I'm serious."

He sat down on the bed next to her. "I know you are, Jan. I'm pleased. I'm also curious as to what made you change your mind."

She looked down. "Several things, I'm excited about the new house. I want to see it happening. There's something about your place that's healing. With Rambo gone, maybe things will settle down." She made eye contact. "Most importantly, I think I can trust you, Andy." They were both silent for several moments.

Andy cleared his throat. "That's a compliment Jan." A tear started trickling down her left cheek. He reached for a box of tissues. She took a couple of them and wiped her eyes. He changed the subject. "Do you want me to stop by your apartment and get a few things on my way home today?" She said they could stop tomorrow. He reminded her that he had to come back to Green Bay on Sunday to pick Rob up at the airport. She asked if he had heard from Rob. "No, but I never do unless he encounters some delays. That's only happened once."

In the hospital parking lot, Andy transferred Cassidy from the enclosed bed of the truck to the cab. He stopped at a wayside north of Green Bay to allow both of them to pee. Most of the way home he thought about Jan. He went back and forth between the pragmatic and the emotional. He needed to set a few things up for her, to facilitate her being there. He would put a drape up on the bedroom door to give her complete privacy. He would put an electric heater in the bedroom in case it got cold at night. His biggest concern was the toilet and bathing facilities. That was not only the most embarrassing aspect about the way he lived, but it posed some physical challenges. It might be difficult for her to get in and out of the bath tub and to step up to the elevated seat on the self-composting toilet.

Andy considered their relationship. Their friendship had grown gradually. It wasn't nearly as fragile as it had been back in the beginning. He doubted that she would ever be capable of trusting anyone entirely. That was just the way it was with her. He could accept that. It seemed to him that they had an honest relationship. It was probably the most honest relationship he had ever experienced with a woman. Neither of them seemed to have any need for pretenses with each other. He regarded her admitting that she trusted him as a supreme compliment. He cautioned himself that, for her, trusting anyone was tenuous. It was probably one of the things that made her such a good cop. She had an intuitive sensibility when it came to deceit. If he had any reservations about her, it was knowing that a large part of her was always on guard for any kind of deceit. That, by itself, could end up ruining a relationship if it continued adinfinitum. Having her there was going to require an investment of energy. He'd have to tread lightly and be tuned into her moods. He knew that constant mistrust and moodiness could wear thin pretty quickly. Perhaps he was exaggerating this concern. 'Hell both of us are pretty gun shy. We need to give this a try. It's an opportunity for both of us to slay some of our dragons'.

Jan was scheduled to be released after the doctor had made his rounds the next morning. Andy wanted them to meet with the doctor together. He was sure that they both had questions. When Andy got to the hospital, the door to Jan's room was closed. A nurse told him Jan was having her dressings changed. The doctor had weekend plans; thus he had already been in to see her. When Andy was allowed into the room, Jan had just finished dressing into her street clothes. It was beginning to cloud over. The forecast was for rain later in the day. She seemed a bit on edge. He smiled at her. "Are you having buyer's remorse?" She admitted that she was feeling somewhat dubious about her decision. "Yeah, me too. I had to tell myself, it's not like we're getting married."

She told him she had to change her bandages every day and that she couldn't dress herself completely. "I can't bend down enough to get a hold of my panties or my slacks to pull them up. I think I should see if I can stay here until Monday. Then I can go to the clinic to have the bandages changed. Maybe by then I'll be able to dress myself."

Andy pursed his lips and weighed what to say. "Can we get a list of the stuff you'll need? We can stop on the way home to get them. Do you think you can change the bandages yourself? If not, I can run you down to the emergency room tomorrow? We can go to the clinic up north after that." She supposed she could. "We'll figure out some way for you to get yourself dressed."

They were both silent for several moments. "Look, Andy, I'm not so sure this is such a great idea. I just feel like this is asking too much. I didn't think I would be this dependent. Maybe a couple more days will make a difference."

A nurse knocked on the door and entered the room. "I've got your discharge instructions that we need to go over. After that you're set to go."

Andy and Jan looked at one another. She turned to the nurse, "Sure, I want Andy to hear them too. I'll be staying at his place for the next few days." She reached out a hand to him. They turned to give the nurse their attention.

Cassidy sat between them on the way home. Andy told Jan that he had a plan. He would lay out her slacks and panties on the floor. He would attach clothes pins that had strings on them. "All you have to do is step into them and pull them up with the strings to where you can reach them." She told him that she wasn't able to wear a bra because of the healing incision on her chest. She said the incision was starting to itch like crazy. "I should have asked if they had something to relieve the itching."

"I'll ask the pharmacist what he can recommend for the itching when we stop for the other stuff." Andy said.

"I've got a couple of prescriptions that I need to pick up on

Monday." She told him." They gave me enough pills to last for two days." He asked her if she had been off her psych drugs during the time she was in the hospital. She had and she was aware that it would take a few days for the antidepressant to build up in her system again. Before they were even half-way home, Jan said she needed to lie down. Andy put Cassidy in the back of the truck and she curled up on the seat next to him. He gave her his jacket to use as a pillow. It started to rain and the temperature was beginning to fall. It was early enough in April that he knew it might turn over to snow. They made a brief stop at her apartment to pick up a couple of changes of clothes and some toiletries. Jan went straight to bed when they arrived at Andy's house. He brought her things into the house and started a fire in the living room stove. He heated some soup and made sandwiches for dinner. She got up for awhile. After eating a portion of her dinner, she went back to bed. One of the times that Andy went to check on her, she asked him to come and sit down on the bed next to her. She took his hand. "Thank you, McLeod for saving my life." She held his hand in both of hers. "I missed not having coffee with you on Wednesday." He asked her if she needed anything. "I hurt like hell. Can you get me a pain pill and some water?" Within a short while she escaped back into sleep.

The next morning the temperature was in the high thirties. He stoked the fire. Jan had gone to sleep in her clothes. She decided not to change. After breakfast she embarked on the task of changing her bandages. She definitely was in no shape to be making a trip to Green Bay with him to pick up Rob. "I'll leave Cassidy here with you." He made sure the stove was burning well. If the fire gets too low you can turn on the electric heater. He made a sandwich for her if she got hungry later on.

It was mid-afternoon when Rob's plane arrived. They had a lot to talk about on the way home. Rob was appalled to hear about Lucy and that Jan had suffered a heart attack. He was surprised to learn that she was staying at Andy's house. He asked if their relationship was turning into something serious. "We're friends, Rob. She needed someplace to go. The doctor didn't want her to be by herself. She's just going be there for a week or so."

Rob's only comment was that she seemed like a nice person. He talked about his trip. He was enthused about the merchandise he had purchased in Bali. "I connected with an agent that I think I can trust. He knows how to deal with all the bureaucratic bullshit involved with customs and importing foreign goods. I'm tired of getting jerked all over the place. It's the same in most of the second world countries. Everybody's on the take. It's a way of life. Nothing gets done unless you grease the wheels. The grease is money; specifically American money." It had stopped raining before they got home. Rob came in for a quick beer and to pick up Mel and his plants. Jan was up and was sitting in Andy's rocking chair reading when they arrived. She greeted Rob warmly. He told her a few of the highlights of his trip. "I took a lot of slides. When I get them developed, I'll have you guys over for a slide show." It felt like he was treating them as a couple.

After Rob left, Jan asked Andy if he had caught any news broadcasts. He said that he hadn't. "Well, apparently Rambo killed the old man that he kidnapped. They found the old man's body and car in Missouri this afternoon. What a cruel asshole. I hope they catch up with him before he hurts anyone else."

Andy was stunned by the news. "Why the hell couldn't he have just let the old man go? He didn't need to do that." He paused, "I might go see his wife. I feel badly for her."

"Andy, I hope you don't think this was in any way your fault." He asked whose fault she thought it was. "As much as I'd like to pin some of the blame on Stephanie, the real blame is on whoever hired the bastard. A psychopath hired another psychopath to do his dirty work. I wonder if whoever hired this Rambo guy knows how dangerous a monster the guy is. Somewhere along the way the boss-guy lost control of his minion. Rambo may be as much on the run from his boss as from the law. Personally, I hope whoever hired him catches up with him first."

"It would be even nicer if Rambo caught up with the boss-man first; then got caught by the cops." Jan agreed.

The contractor, Dan Lundquist, called to let Andy know that he'd be there before eight o'clock in the morning. "The cement contractor is aiming to get the slab sight ready tomorrow and pour the concrete on Tuesday. It will need a few days to cure before we can start framing. In the meantime the well is going to be drilled and the excavation work for a waste-water system will get underway." After hanging up Andy made Jan some tea and took Cassidy for a walk. That evening, the two of them sat and visited until a little past nine. Jan seemed to be gaining some energy and her spirits were improving.

During the next week she continued to make steady progress. By the end of the week she was able to resume driving. That Friday evening Andy suggested that they go to the Pub for a fish fry. She was uncomfortable with the idea. "What are people going to think if they see the two of us together all the time? Who around here besides Rob knows that Stephanie is gone?" He admitted that his sons and Rob were the only people who knew she had left. "Look Andy, I'm going back to my place tomorrow. I can manage on my own now. I'll get out of your hair. You're busier than a one armed paper hanger with the new house. Plus, the new season is about to start. You need to get your shop in order. I'm planning on going back to work in another week. I know I'm going to have to start out slow. I'll just go into the office for a couple of hours each day for the first week or so." He said nothing. He didn't agree with her decision. "Andy, I very much appreciate everything you've done for me. Really I do. The deal was that I was going to just stay a few days until I could manage on my own. I'm at that point. It's time for me to go."

"I know." He wasn't sure if he should speak his mind. "You know Jan; there have been a couple of shifts in our relationship. I started out needing and relying on you. Then things shifted a hundred and eighty degrees. You've ended up needing me for awhile. Now it has shifted to where neither of us needs the other." He hesitated; then said, "I regard you as a good friend. I hope that can continue."

They both felt awkward. Jan finally said, "If I'm up to it, how about we take a hike out to Thorsen Point next week?"

"Sure, I haven't taken Cassidy out there yet. It was Lucy's favorite place in the world." He looked at her. "I've enjoyed having you here. I know that both of us had some trepidation about how it was going to work out. I think it went well." She nodded. "I'm going to miss you."

"Let's try to make a point of getting together once-a-week for coffee." He felt a degree of disappointment. He wanted more than just seeing her on that basis. However, he wasn't sure what he really wanted from this relationship.

The next day was Saturday. The weather forecast was for a nice weekend. Dan, the builder, asked a couple of his crew to work at least part of the day on Saturday. They showed up at eight that morning. Andy helped them by hauling lumber and cutting boards to length. When Jan was ready to leave, he helped her load her car. She only had a small suitcase and a satchel. She told him she would call him that evening. He watched her go. She waved as she started down the driveway.

The crew worked hard throughout the day. Dan decided to stop at 3:00. They had all the outside walls up and half the ceiling rafters framed. He told Andy, "my goal is to get the roof on and shingled by mid-week, weather permitting." The two crew members finished loading their tools. After they left, Andy told Dan he would clean up. He got beers for Dan and himself. They talked about the project for a few minute before Dan asked Andy, "what happened to your partner? Wasn't her name Stephanie?" Andy debated what to say. "She went to see her mother down in Florida last Christmas. She was killed in an automobile accident while she was there." The contractor was stunned by the news. "I must have missed seeing her obituary. I'm really sorry, man."

"I didn't put one in the paper. Steph wasn't from here and she hadn't lived here very long. I decided not to. She was cremated. One of these days I'll spread her ashes out at Thorsen Point. It was one of her favorite places." Andy knew the contractor was wondering who Jan was. "The lady who left here this morning is a friend of mine. She had recent heart surgery. She lives by herself. I invited her to stay here for a few days so she'd have someone to look after her. She's recovered enough to manage on her own now." Dan asked if she lived up here. "No she lives in Sturgeon. She works for the county.

Jan called him that evening. He told her about the progress they had made with the framing. He asked how she was feeling. "I'm pooped. I stopped to pick up some groceries. By the time I got home I barely had the energy to bring them in and put them away. I took a long nap this afternoon. That's something I never do. I just got up a little while ago." After awhile they ran out of things to say. Andy was tired himself from having worked so hard all day. He went to bed shortly after hanging up with her.

To his surprise Jan showed up at his place close to quitting time on Wednesday. The weather had been almost perfect the past few days. The roof was complete. The forecast was calling for rain for the next two days. She was surprised at how much progress had been made. While the men put tools away and covered materials with tarps she looked around the construction site. She was wearing a faded pair of jeans, a sweatshirt, and tennies. Andy commented that he had never seen her in jeans before. "I found these at a resale shop. This is the first time I've ever worn jeans. I like them. They're comfortable. I can see why you like them." He commented that she looked like she had lost quite a bit of weight. She told him that she had lost just under twenty pounds. "I hope I can keep it off. I feel a lot better."

Dan and the crew left. Andy asked her if she wanted to join him and Cassidy for a walk. She accepted with the understanding it would have to be a brief one. She wasn't up to going long distances yet. They went in the house to get sweaters. Andy asked if she wanted anything. "I have a bottle of water in the car," she told him. In addition to the sweater he also got her a light jacket to put on. They began walking north toward the woods.

They discovered that the trillium were just starting to come into bloom. "In another week or so the woods will be carpeted with them," he told her. He warned her not to pick them. "Picking them kills them. They won't come back." Cassidy was running all over exploring the many scents. She took his arm as they walked. She asked him the names of various trees and plants. He knew most of them but he confessed that he hardly knew any of the names when he had first come to live here.

"You really did start from scratch, didn't you?" A little further on she said, "I have to say I've never felt so alive. Doc Jordan was right. I've been depressed most of my life. I think this heart thing was contributing to my lack of energy and feeling so down. I've felt worn out a lot of the time over the past year or so. I have a lot more energy now. I couldn't have cared less about the world around me before. It's like my life has been given a jump-start. I have a new awareness about the things around me. I'm going to get some books and start learning about the native plants and wildlife."

When they finished the walk, Jan offered to treat them to a hamburger at the Pub. Andy reluctantly asked her, "how come you're willing for us to be seen together now and not the other night?"

"I'm exercising my feminine prerogative to change my mind."

On the way to the restaurant she asked if there had been any more incidents. "Nope, but I'm afraid to let my guard down. I still keep the pistol handy." She asked where it was now. "It's in the rucksack that I take back and forth to the shop with me. I keep the shotgun locked in the back of my truck during the day. I bring it in with me at night. Incidentally, I forgot to tell you. I got my 1911 back. One of your deputies found it in the pickup truck that blew up. It hasn't got a scratch on it."

In the restaurant she was more talkative than usual. "Better safe than sorry as long as Rambo is still on the loose," she advised. "I seriously doubt he'll come back here. If it starts up again it will probably be a different crew. I hope he's on the run from his boss too. He screwed up. Both sides want his ass. He compounded his mistakes by killing that old man. He's facing murder one for both of his killings." During dinner she commented, "I know that losing Lucy was devastating for you, Andy, especially the way it happened. I'm glad that you decided to get another dog so soon. Cassidy is terrific. He seems to have adapted quickly. He couldn't be more your dog if you had raised him as a puppy."

"He's very fond of you too, Jan." He brought up a subject that he had been giving some thought to of late. "Jan, if something happens to me, will you try to find a good home for him?"

"Nothing's going to happen to you, McLeod." On the way back to his place she thanked him again for having watched over her the past couple of weeks. For the first time they hugged before parting. "How about we get back to our Wednesday morning coffee routine next week?" she suggested.

"We can do that, but it'll have to be earlier so that I can open the shop." She agreed.

As her car disappeared down the driveway, Andy felt a pang of loneliness. There was some lingering daylight. He thought about taking another stroll. He headed toward the house to get a glass of wine. He discovered an envelope taped to the front door. In it was a printed note, 'You can end this. Where is she? Leave the information in your mail box'. The author called himself 'The Panther'. Andy's initial reaction was one of disappointment, "Oh shit, here we go again." His next response was anger. 'What an arrogant asshole. Who does he think he is? After this much time, if he hasn't figured out that I don't know where she is, he's stupid'. Andy fumed. He waited to assure himself that Jan had sufficient time to arrive back home. He called her. She answered on the second ring. He told her about his discovery.

She groaned in disappointment. There was an edge of anger to her tone as well. "I guess the only thing that surprises me is that it took the weenie this long to resume the bullshit." They discussed the situation not caring if their conversation was being monitored. "Obviously he's convinced that you know her whereabouts. What does she have that makes her so goddamn important to him? He's gone to extreme lengths to find her. I suppose its good news that whoever this Panther guy is, he's got balls enough to finally approach you directly."

"I have to admit that there have been times when I've been mad as hell at Steph for what has happened. I've been mad enough that I would have cheerfully turned her over to them. She may have come here thinking that she could pull off starting anew. I'm sure she left here feeling regretful. I hope, for her sake, she can succeed in eluding the weenie. I just wish I could find some way of getting him off my burro."

Jan stopped him. "Why, do you suppose, she didn't go to the authorities and give them whatever information she had. If it's all that important, she could have ended this a long time ago."

"I've considered that. The fact is, we don't know if she tried to contact anyone or not. It may be that she did and they just didn't acted on it for whatever reasons."

"I'm sorry, Andy. I know you cared for her, but I can't help thinking that there's another scenario we've overlooked. It may be that she's done something illegal herself, in which case she can't go to the authorities. Their conversation ended with both of them admitting that they were getting nowhere through conjecture. After Andy hung up with her, he sat down to compose a letter to 'the Panther'. Andy thought that title was much too elegant and over-the-top-arrogant.

He started out his letter by saying, 'I'm sorry, but I find your choice of titles degrading to Panthers'. He went on, 'when your harassment stopped for a brief while, I concluded that you found whatever it was you were looking for. Apparently not. I honestly don't know where Stephanie is. For awhile I surmised that you had caught up with her, apparently not. You seem to think she's still alive. Maybe she is. I don't know. She sure didn't do me any favors by bringing you down on my head. I have to admit that I am curious about what she's done to you. You've gone to extreme lengths to find her. It has cost at least two people their lives. I am extremely pissed by what your minions did to my dog Lucy. I won't forgive that, not ever'. He signed it, McLeod. He wrote out a copy of the letter, put the original in an envelope, and walked down to the mail box with it. His mail was usually delivered by mid-afternoon. He would check the box before then to see if his unaddressed letter had been picked up.

He slept fitfully that night. He got up early, dressed and went down to his mailbox. He found the envelope had been taken over night. It had stopped raining, but it was overcast. Despite it being cold and damp outside he went for a run with Cassidy. Afterwards he did a load of laundry. He had just finished when the construction crew showed up. Dan commented that he hadn't seen a wringer washer in years. He remembered helping his mother doing laundry with one. They were to begin sheathing the exterior walls today. Andy planned to spend the next two days at his shop downtown getting it ready to reopen for a new season.

Jan came into the shop late in the morning. She said that she was on other business but wanted to stop by to see how he was doing. He showed her the copy of the letter he had written. "You're right Andy; he does think she's alive and that you know where she is. At least he's giving you an opportunity for some kind of dialogue. We'll see if it leads anywhere. Your not-so-veiled threat about Lucy is a nice touch. It will be interesting to see what his next move is. I hope you've contacted your insurance agent and put coverage on the new house."

Andy hadn't even thought about doing that. As soon as she left he called his agent. The agent commented, "I don't know how you've managed to live in that old farm house this many years, Andy. My father, who's in his late eighties, says he remembers that place. He says it was an old house when he was a boy." Andy laughed.

When he got home that evening there was another note from the Panther in his mailbox. It asked about what was done to his dog, Lucy? Andy was incredulous. 'The jerk-ass doesn't know what Rambo and his associate did to Lucy? He really hasn't been in control of what's been going on. Either that or he doesn't give a shit and he's turned them loose to do as they pleased. He wondered what else the Panther didn't know. After inspecting the day's progress on his new house, he and Cassidy went for their walk. Along the way he thought about what he wanted to say next. He hit upon the name Draco rather than 'the Panther'. He would use that name henceforth in addressing future letters, assuming there would be any future correspondence. Cassidy ran all over the meadow but kept returning to Andy. At one point Andy leaned over and hugged the dog. "Cassidy, you're a great puppy, I won't let anything happen to you."

That evening he wrote another letter, again making a copy of it. It started out, 'Draco'; He went into a detailed description about what had happened to Lucy. "Since you are unaware of what was done to her, you may be unaware of what else has happened over the past six months." He gave an accounting. He listed every incident that he could recall which took up three full pages. In the end he made an appeal. "Your people have inflicted barbaric, Draconian suffering over a prolonged period of time. I would think that by now you would have reached the conclusion that I don't know where Stephanie is or if she is even alive. You have wasted a tremendous amount of time and resources and you have caused great pain to several people. The irony is you are apparently even more vulnerable and helpless than me. If Stephanie is alive, she apparently has you by the gonads, assuming you have any. That gives me great solace. Sincerely, McLeod." He put the letter in an envelope and put it in his mailbox.

He called Jan. After reading it to her, she cited two things he had forgotten to include. Her other comment was, "If your letter gets to Draco, I doubt that he gives a rat's ass. I really like your ending. It hadn't occurred to me that she's the one who's really in command. God, I'd love to know what she's got that gives her so much power." She asked, "incidentally, who's Draco?"

"It's the name of an Athenian Legislator." Andy told her. "He was known for his extremely harsh, cruel legislation. If he was alive today he'd probably be the head of the Republican party."

Jan laughed. "So, tell me how you really feel about conservatives."

Andy ignored her comment. "I played with calling him Viper. In the end I decided not to demean poisonous snakes. Mosquito has too many syllables. I considered Slug, Hitler, and Stalin. Draco ended up a fitting title."

She chuckled. "At least your sarcastic wit is still alive and well."

By Friday the house was completely enclosed, sided and the windows and doors were installed. Dan stopped at the shop to tell Andy that they would be starting on the interior on Monday. "Mother Nature has cooperated. We've had a near perfect spring. The farmers are probably complaining but it's been ideal for us. If anything we're ahead of schedule, Andy. You may be able to start moving in by early July." Dan had a few questions about cabinets and trim work. As he was leaving he said, "the guys have all commented about the old house. They're amazed that you lived that way for so long. They're a good bunch. I can depend on every one of them to do quality work. I think you're going to be very pleased when we're finished." It was close to quitting time. Rob showed up. Andy suggested that the three of them go over to the Pub for a beer. The owner of the Pub allowed Andy to bring Cassidy into the bar. Cassidy curled up right next to him at a table. After Dan left, Rob and Andy stayed for a fish fry. Rob was all excited. He had a new girlfriend with whom he seemed smitten.

It was almost dark when Andy got home that evening. He took the pistol out of his rucksack and stuck it in his belt. He got the shotgun out of the back of the truck. He went to the house where he discovered a large, bulky envelope taped to the door. When he got inside he turned on the light and opened it. He discovered cash and a letter which read: 'I am truly sorry about the loss of your dog. The enclosed money is intended to compensate you for her loss, as well as the many indignities you have been subjected to. That was not a part of the plan. The man you have dubbed Rambo has been decommissioned. Harassment of you will cease. You are correct. I am preoccupied with finding Ms. Brandt. You are still considered as a possible link to her. Enjoy your new house. The Panther'.

After reading the letter he counted the cash. There were ten packs of ten crisp new one hundred dollar bills, ten thousand dollars. It was almost nine o'clock. He decided to call Jan but there was no answer. He started to leave a message when she picked up the phone. "I'm sorry for bothering you this late in the evening." She sounded out of breath. She said that she had just come in from a brisk walk and commented on what a beautiful evening it was. He read her Draco's latest note and told her about the enclosed cash.

There was a long pause; then she said, "that son of a bitch, he thinks he can buy his way out of everything. Don't touch the money.

I'll be up in the morning. There's a slight chance that it can be traced. Don't worry, you'll get it back. Personally, I'd donate it to charity. I wouldn't accept anything from that creep."

When he didn't make any comment, she asked if he was still on the line. "Yeah, I'm here, but you just shot down my plans to buy a new truck." She said nothing. "I'm just kidding. What do you think he means by Rambo being 'decommissioned'?"

She paused, "I'll try not to be too sarcastic. What, pray-tell, do you think he means?"

"I doubt that it means he's simply given Rambo a pink slip."

"Good, McLeod; that would be my guess." Jan replied. She went on to say, "I find it hard to believe that he's actually sorry for the grief he's caused. A part of me thinks he's just trying to seduce you into thinking he's an honorable person; a regular nice guy. You hit the nail on the head when you pointed out that he's vulnerable. I'm surprised he admitted it. I don't trust him any further than I can throw the state of Wisconsin. Watch your back, Andy. I think you may have struck a nerve or two."

"Oh, that's comforting."

"I'll be up in the morning to pick up the money. Put it in a plastic bag and hide it. Is Cassidy a good watch dog?" He told her he didn't know yet.

After they hung up, he bagged the money. It was well after dark. He did not turn on any lights. He put the bag in the waste tray underneath his self-composting toilet. He couldn't think of a less likely or more unappealing place for a would-be searcher to look. Rather than just let Cassidy out to pee, he turned on the outside flood light and went out with the dog. It really was a pleasant evening. He looked up at the stars. He was wavering about what Jan said about the money. 'I know she's right'. His truck was over ten years old. It would be nice to replace it with something newer. He thought about what charities he would donate the money to if he decided to go that route. He'd give a large chunk of it to the Humane Society animal shelter in honor of Lucy. He and Cassidy went to bed. He lay awake for awhile thinking. He should probably do regular searches of the new house for surveillance devices. He had been lax about doing that. It was almost six months since Stephanie had left. In some ways it seemed like years. It hadn't occurred to him until now that he didn't have a single photograph of the two of them together. He had a couple he had taken of her. The only other reminder he had of her were the perennial flowers she had planted last summer. He had returned the wedding ring and gotten a refund. He had given the cross-country skis to Jan.

He was awakened in the very early morning hours to the distant rumble of thunder. Awhile later it began to rain gently. He reached over and petted Cassidy who didn't seem bothered by the approaching storm. Lucy had always been anxious about thunderstorms. He thought to himself that he was becoming comfortable living by himself again. He was missing Stephanie less and less. He thought about Jan. He had no idea of how long she had been by herself but she seemed to prefer living that way. He wondered if she would ever be able to live with anyone after what she had been through with her ex-husband. They had a loyalty to one another. He wondered how she would react if he were to meet someone and begin dating again, not that he had anyone in mind. 'What a pair we are, the monk and the nun'.

He got up at five-thirty the next morning. It had stopped raining but looked like it could start again at any time. He and Cassidy went for a run. The construction crew showed up a few minutes before eight. Dan told him they would spend the day framing the interior walls. "One of the guys is a skilled electrician, whose going to start installing the wiring. He'll give you plenty of outlets. He's going to put external outlets on each side of the house and two of them in the crawl space."

After going to the post office, Andy went to the coffee shop to meet Jan to give her the package of money. She was already there when he arrived. Cassidy greeted her before going to fetch a dog biscuit treat the shop owner gave him whenever Andy brought him in. Cassidy brought it back to his place beside Andy before eating it. "You know, McLeod that dog is almost too polite. It's spooky." He gave her the package of money. "We'll check for finger prints and run the serial numbers. I don't expect to find anything. Draco is too smart for that. He must feel very confident in his anonymity to be risking correspondence with you." Andy asked her what she thought about the idea of asking the builder to be on the lookout for surveillance devices. She thought about it. She asked how much he trusted the man to keep his mouth shut.

"Implicitly," he told her.

"I don't know. If you ask him to be on the lookout for bugs, you have to tell him something. I don't know what you can say that isn't going to make him feel paranoid. If it were me, I'd keep it to myself and hope that your own efforts will suffice." She added "It's also a matter of protecting Dan. No matter what you tell him you're going to implicate him and put him at risk." Andy hadn't thought of that. "I've still got that detection device that the boys from the State gave me in my car. You can run your own scans. If you find anything,

Draco will know what's happening but screw him. All's fair in war. I'll come by after the crew leaves today and we'll go over the new house. If I were you, I'd do it on a daily basis after hours."

The day turned sunny by early afternoon. Andy had several sales that day. Over the years he had cultivated a number of repeat customers. He always enjoyed visiting with them. As the pace of the season began to accelerate more of them began to show up. It had taken a long time to become established and to develop a base of loyal customers. During a lull in traffic that afternoon he decided to clean off his counter and organize things. He had cleared everything off and sprayed furniture polish. He buffed the wood top and began putting things back in place. He picked up the old cash register and by chance happened to feel something underneath. He discovered a listening device attached to the underside. "Goddamn it," he muttered. It was held in place by what looked like putty. He decided not to touch it. He would show it to Jan. He spent the rest of the afternoon searching the shop under the pretense of cleaning and dusting. He discovered two micro-cameras attached to cross-beams. One was aimed at the counter area and the other at the entrance.

Near closing time Andy was working outside the shop. He saw Jan approaching. He went to meet her and told her of his discoveries. "That should come as no surprise, McLeod." She went back to her car and got the scanner. She reviewed how to use it with him and the two of them went back over the shop. Another camera was found outside looking down on the work bench he had there. "It's your call. Do you want to remove them or leave things be for now." He decided to leave them. She told him, "I'll leave the scanner with you. I need to take off. I'll call you later this evening to find out if anything turned up at the new house." She touched his arm, "I know you're pissed. I am too." She smiled and waved her hands. "I know, I know, your mantra is that you're out to bore the hell out of them. You need to get a life Andy. You're all work and no play." He refrained from making the same accusation about her.

The construction crew was gone when he got home. He and Cassidy went to the new house. It appeared that all of the downstairs interior walls were framed and maybe half of the wiring was roughed in. He used the scanner but found nothing. He got out his riding mower and cut the grass. It took him over an hour during which time he thought about Jan's comment about getting a life. He had seen very little of Rob since the new season had begun. That was typical. Now that Rob was involved with his new girlfriend he saw even less of him than usual. As twilight approached, he thought about starting a fire in the fire pit and sitting outside but the mosquitoes were horrendous. He and Cassidy retreated into the stuffy house. Because of the dampness from the rain, the house smelled of bat guano. 'God, I'll be glad to get out of this place'. The phone rang. He thought it was Jan calling. Instead it was his ex-girlfriend Josie. He hadn't heard from her in almost two years. He was surprised to hear her voice. She asked how he was doing. They made small talk about one another's kids and what she was doing now. He finally asked her why she was calling after all of this time. She hesitated. "I was just thinking about you and wondering how you were doing. I have some vacation time. I was thinking about coming up to Door County in early August. I would like to visit a couple of my friends that I've stayed in contact with. I thought maybe we could go out to dinner one evening. You know, for old time's sake."

"I know I'm being blunt and tactless but I'm going to ask you anyway; what do you want?" She asked him what he meant. "You know what I mean, Josie."

After a period of silence she asked him, "Are you involved with someone, Andy? I mean if you are that's fine. I certainly don't want to interfere. It's been a long time since we've seen one another." He told her that he wasn't seeing anyone and he repeated his question about what she wanted. "Are you annoyed that I called you?"

"I'm curious about, why now? It's been several years since you left here." She reiterated that she had just been thinking about him. He deliberately tried to sound skeptical. "Uh huh," After a moment of silence he heard a click and then the dial tone. He looked at the receiver. 'I'll bet one of your friends told you that I was putting up a new house. You're curious as hell about it and how I've been able to afford to do it. Maybe you're even hoping to be invited back'.

He had no sooner hung the phone up and it rang again. He braced himself for a possible tirade from her. It was Jan who picked up on his cautious tone. "You sound like you're expecting a call from a bill collector. What's up?" He told her. "You didn't exactly finesse her, McLeod. It sounds like she's on an expedition. Correct me if I'm mistaken but I seem to detect some residual bitterness."

"I wouldn't call it bitterness. I guess I've developed a zero tolerance for bullshit. I don't dislike her. I just don't want her back in my life. I suspect she's heard that I'm putting up a new house and she's curious. Hell, if she wants to see this place, she can do that anytime she wants without my ever knowing. I'm not trying to hide anything from her." Jan changed the subject to his scan of the new house. He told her that it appeared to be clean. Before hanging up he asked her if she was going to be up this way tomorrow.

She playfully asked, "What are you really asking, McLeod?"

"Tomorrow's Friday; I'm asking if you would like to go out for a fish fry. You know me, I don't go out by myself."

"Sure, that sounds good. Let's douse ourselves with bug spray and hike out to the point after you close up." He commented on how bad the mosquitoes were. "I know. I tried to sit outside on my patio this evening. It's impossible."

After hanging up with her, the phone rang again. It was Brian. They talked for close to an hour. Brian asked about coming up for a visit over the Fourth of July. He asked if the house would be close to complete by then. "They're making terrific progress but I don't know if it will be ready to move into by then or not. We'll see."

Brian offered to help him move when it was finished. "I'm really glad for you, Pops. You've paid a lot of dues living the way you have these past few years. It's going to be a huge relief for you to have the modern conveniences back again, especially in the winter. God, you spend half your time heating the house and your studio. I hope you can afford to put up a decent studio one of these days. Who knows what kind of creative energy that will free up?" He asked if his father was dating anyone.

"Nope, Detective Miller and I go out for dinner occasionally and we have coffee together every Wednesday morning."

"What the hell are you doing for sex, Pops?"

"What kind of question is that for a kid to be asking his father?" Brian laughed and apologized. He told Brian about the conversation he had earlier with Josie.

"She's playing games, Pops. I ran into her at the grocery store a couple of months ago. I told her you were about to start construction on a new house. I got the impression that she hasn't been very successful in her quest for male companionship or in the job market. It doesn't surprise me that she's making a play for you. I'm willing to bet she calls you again after she gets her nose back in joint."

Andy brushed his teeth and had just gotten into bed when the phone rang again. It was Josie. She sounded like she'd had too much to drink. "Who were you on the phone with all night?"

He told her it was none of her business, that she sounded sloshed and it was close to midnight. "Good night, Josie." He hung up. Cassidy jumped up on the bed and curled up next to him. "Jesus, Cassidy, she'd be giving birth to a concrete block if she saw you on the bed." He petted the dog.

Chapter 15

It was overcast and somewhat foggy when Andy got up at 6:00. After working out he went out to his workshop to rout a sign. The construction crew showed up at their regular time. Dan told him the plumbing would be completely roughed in by tomorrow. He hoped to start hanging the dry walling on Wednesday or Thursday. "The painters will be here early next week. After that we'll do the finish carpentry. We're getting there. You've been easy to deal with, Andy. You'd be surprised at how many people insist on making changes each step of the way, especially when we get toward the final stages."

"It's shaping up to be even nicer than I had envisioned when we planned this out last fall," Andy told him. "I'm pleased with the work you're doing, Dan."

The sky brightened somewhat as the day progressed. Jan arrived at the shop an hour before closing time. She browsed and ended up buying two items as presents. She refused to accept any discount. "Andy, in my opinion your work is under priced." He asked her how come she called him by his last name sometimes and other times Andy. "I don't know, I guess some of it depends on my mood." He asked her what that meant. She didn't know.

"It seems to me that I'm Andy when you're feeling friendlier toward me and McLeod when you want more distance." She needed to think about it. Some people came into the shop. After browsing briefly, they left and he closed up. He drove to where they had to park in order to hike to Thorsen Point. Cassidy stayed close by as they started walking. Andy thought that was odd. He asked her if she had her gun. She did. He went back to the truck to get his. She asked what that was about. "I don't know. It's just that Cassidy is usually running all over the place when we come here. He's acting kind of strange this evening. He even stayed here with you rather than following me back to the truck." Besides the gun, Andy had also retrieved a can of insect repellent. They took turns spraying one another. He sprayed Cassidy too.

They didn't talk much on the way to the point. They were both vigilant. When they got to the shore, Cassidy waded out into the water, but he didn't go for his usual swim. Andy dipped his hand into the water. "The water is still really cold. I guess we just haven't had enough hot days yet." As he stood up he spotted some movement at the edge of the woods behind them. Cassidy came bolting out of the water. He was barking furiously and the hair on his back standing up. Andy caught sight of a man with a gun. He shoved Jan hard as he pulled his gun out from the back of his belt. There was the crack of a shot being fired. Andy yelled for Cassidy to come back. The dog had advanced a few yards and was barking wildly. Andy fired five quick rounds where he had spotted the figure. Jan had her gun drawn. "We need to get back to the truck." She began running. He followed, starting to feel a burning sensation on his right shoulder. He realized that he must have been grazed by the assailant's bullet. Cassidy ran a bit ahead of them. At the truck Jan was panting hard. They discovered that both front tires had been slashed. "Have you got the shotgun in the back?" she gasped. He did. He unlocked the cap, and got it out. He had a box of cartridges in the rucksack. "Here, give me those." She took the box of cartridges. "Go on, I'll follow. The bastard has to be parked out on the road. See if you can beat him there." Andy told Cassidy to stay with Jan. He began running the potholed, gravel driveway until he reached the paved road. He was worried that her running was going to hurt her. At the road he turned east and slowed to a jog. As he came around the first curve he saw a black car parked half off the road. He slowed to a cautious walk. He was less than thirty yards from the car when a man emerged from the woods. The man didn't see him. He probably hadn't expected him to make it to road this soon. He looked Hispanic. He was short and somewhat overweight. He was wearing a tank top and his arms were adorned with tattoos. When he got to the car he turned spotted Andy. Instead of shooting, he jumped into the car and started the engine. Andy stopped twenty-five feet from the car. As it started to move forward, he fired all five rounds of the shotgun at the windshield and the front of the car. The car leapt forward but veered sharply and ran into the ditch on the opposite side of the road. Andy pulled out his pistol and knelt down on one knee, training the weapon on the driver-side door. Several moments later Jan came around the curve. She crouched down gasping for breath. He asked if she was alright. She nodded and handed Andy the box of shotgun shells. She aimed her gun at the car while Andy quickly reloaded the shotgun. He half-whispered that it looked like it was just one person. "Cover me," she said in a strained, half whisper. He didn't have a target. He just aimed at the car, ready to shoot anything that moved. She approached it cautiously. Jan ordered whoever was in the car to throw out his weapon, then get out of the car slowly with his hands raised. The car's engine was still running. Finally an arm emerged from the driver's side window. The occupant dropped a pistol, yelling "I'm hurt. I can't get out." Andy moved closer to the car. He could hear another vehicle approaching from behind. Jan moved quickly to the side of the car. She was stooped down so that she was below the car's windows. She rose up quickly with her gun ready. The occupant was indeed wounded. She could not tell how seriously. The approaching vehicle slowed down as it approached. Andy waved the car on by but when it reached him the driver stopped to ask what was going on. Andy told the driver that he was a police officer. He asked the man to leave immediately and call 911. The driver looked confused and fearful but obeyed. Cassidy remained on the other side of the road further back and in a crouched position. After the passerby's car was out of sight, Andy approached. Jan had the driver's side door open. She had already cuffed the driver's hands to the steering wheel and was checking for any other weapons. The man's face had several cuts, probably from broken glass and some buckshot. He didn't appear to be seriously injured.

Andy pointed to the gun that the would-be assassin had dropped out the window of the car. Jan squatted down. She had Andy find her a stick. She inserted it into the trigger guard and lifted it up. "Jesus, this is bigger than that forty-five cannon of yours. This is a forty-four magnum."

Andy noted that it had a long barrel and was equipped with a scope. He had never seen a scope mounted on a pistol before. "It looks like he meant business."

"He would have succeeded if you hadn't moved so quickly and shoved me."

"He would have succeeded if it hadn't been for Cassidy's warning us," Andy amended.

They heard the sound of a siren in the distance. She got the man's wallet and checked his driver's license asking him if this was his license. He said that it was. She tried to compare the license photo with the man. A few moments later a sheriff's deputy drove up. Another siren could be heard. The deputy recognized Jan and told her that an ambulance was on the way. He asked if the guy in the car was dead. She told him he was injured. She gave the deputy a quick explanation of what had happened. The ambulance arrived. After the paramedics extracted the man from the car and got him into the ambulance, Jan had them look at Andy's shoulder. The paramedic in charge reported that it was just a minor flesh wound. He bandaged it and recommended that Andy see his doctor. "A doc will probably want you on some antibiotics."

Jan asked the deputy to summon a tow truck. The deputy went to his squad to do so. Moments later the ambulance departed. Jan turned to Andy. "You saved my ass again, McLeod. That was intended for me." He looked puzzled. "I'll explain later." Then she commented, "you might not agree but that," she pointed to his wound, "is a good thing. It will serve to support a claim that you acted in self-defense."

The deputy asked if Jan was going to file a report about what happened. She said that she would. She asked the deputy to take several photographs and make diagrams in the likelihood that the matter ended up in court. She helped him take measurements of the scene and she directed what photographs to take. Awhile later Vern, the mechanic from town, arrived with his tow truck. He asked where the car should be taken. "Store it behind your place for tonight Vern." Jan told him. "The Sheriff will likely order it impounded." The deputy asked where their car was. She told him that Andy's truck was parked at the entrance to Thorsen Point. He offered to drive them. She explained that the perpetrator had slashed both of the front tires of Andy's vehicle. Vern offered to tow Andy's truck first and come back later to get the disabled car. The deputy was almost done with the task of diagramming the scene.

She, Andy and Cassidy climbed into Vern's tow truck. It turned out to be a tricky process of getting Andy's truck moved into a position so that it could be towed. The area was bound in tightly by large trees. It took half an hour of maneuvering and the rest of the bug spray before they were on their way. After dropping Andy's truck at his garage, Vern drove them home. Jan suggested that they take a stroll. She invited Andy to mix a stiff drink for himself before they departed. She showed concern for Andy. "Are you alright, McLeod?" He asked what she meant. "I mean, are you alright about having shot that guy?"

Andy shrugged. "He shot first. Yeah, I'm okay with it." He looked at her. "Jan, it's not the first time. I shot at and probably killed several people in Nam." He paused. "What I'm not okay with, is that I find myself here, in this place, in a combat situation."

They stopped walking. Jan positioned herself directly in front of him. "Andy, what just happened out there had nothing to do with either you or Stephanie. That was my ex-brother-in-law, Ramon. I recognized him mostly by his tattoos. I'll explain it to you later. I'm sorry you had to be involved. I'm sure he was after me but he probably would have wasted all of us. He's a bad hombre." They resumed walking in silence. Finally Jan said, "Andy, I want to stay here tonight." She stepped in front of him again. "Andy, hold me." She put her arms around his waist and he put his arms loosely around her shoulders. She avoided looking at him. "This relationship scares me. It's not you. You've been a gentleman in the truest sense of the word." She lightened up a little. "I've been thinking about a question you posed. I guess I call you Andy when I'm feeling less afraid. I thought I was getting better at that." He patted her back. "What just happened this evening has set me back several giant steps. Some very nasty people have found out where I'm at. I'm feeling very much like a Stephanie at this point." After a period of silence she said, "like Stephanie, I know who's after me and I know what they want. My first inclination is to run. I don't want anything to happen to you or to Cassidy or anybody else. You both mean too much to me."

Andy interrupted her. "Come on let's head on back to the house. The mosquitoes are taking over and I need to take something for pain. My shoulder is really starting to burn." They retreated to the house. Jan got the shotgun and the shells from the back of the truck. Andy went in to find some pain pills. It was light enough that they chose not to turn on any lamps. She told him to go ahead and mix himself another drink if he wanted. She chose to stick with water. Andy mixed another martini while Jan fed Cassidy. They decided to sit at the dining room table.

"It's time I told you some things about my past. It will help to explain some of what happened a little while ago." She paused as if trying to decide where to begin. "I put my ex-husband and five of his buddies behind bars six years ago. The bunch of them were into dealing drugs. They were also selling child porn. Two of my brothers-in-law were pimps. I suspected my husband and two of the others were hired guns, hit men. When I turned them in, there were several people who were pissed with me, not just the six of them. There were lots of threats of reprisal. Things got pretty intense. I realized it was just a matter of time before they toasted me. I decided that I needed to get out of Dodge. I deliberately moved around for more than a year to make sure no one was able to follow me. I decided to look for some nice quiet little backwater place to escape to. Quite by accident I stumbled upon Door County at just the right time. I thought this would be a safe place. It was off the beaten track. Sheriff Cummings was looking to hire a detective. Everything seemed to fall into place. I never let my guard down in the almost four years that I've been here. Of course, I kept hoping that the gang of them would either end up dead or stuck with life sentences. Two of them are dead. One of them is serving a ten year sentence. He's got eight years left."

Andy interrupted Jan to ask if she was warm enough. She was hugging herself. She said she was starting to feel chilled. He got his sweater for her. She thanked him. Andy urged her to continue with her story. "In light of what has just happened, it looks like I'm going to have to take off again." Andy asked if she thought this was going to continue. "I don't know, but I'm not going to take that chance."

Andy sat in silence. "Look Andy, I don't want to put you or others at risk. I care about what happens to me but you and Cassidy could have bought the farm today."

When Andy finally spoke, he said, "I don't know what we are to one another, Jan but I think we're more than just friends. We've been through a lot together. I can't imagine not having you in my life. I think I'd got nuts worrying about you if you decide to take off. There has to be some way of standing up to these people. You can't spend the rest of your life on the run. You may not realize it but you've got a family of friends who care about you. We're people you can count on. I think we have a right to be included in whatever decision you make."

"I don't want to leave here Andy. I love this place." She paused, "What you just said about a family of friends. That's a good way to put it. I feel like Sheriff Cummings and a lot of the people I work with, care about me. You and he are the only two people who know anything about my past. I don't know what I'm going to do. I just know that I don't want anything to happen to anyone because of me."

"I think you should do what you've encouraged me to do several times and that is to wait and see. Maybe nothing else will happen. The guy who came at you today was by himself. It seems to me that if these people were serious about taking you out, they would have come at you more seriously. They would have made damn good and sure they got you." Andy took a sip of his drink. He smiled at her. "You're out of shape, Brady. You were really huffing and puffing from all that running." She couldn't have agreed more.

She seemed relieved that he initiated a change of subject. She asked if he was going to miss his old house. "When I first came here I had fantasies about gutting and renovating it. Despite the fact that it has a lot of history and charm, it isn't worth pouring the money into. It's been home to a lot of families over the hundred and almost fifty years it's been here. In a way I feel like I'm turning my back on all that history and all those lives and all those great stories."

It was growing dark. The spring peepers had already begun their nightly concert. Jan mustered her courage and asked, "How would you feel about our sleeping together tonight, Andy? I'm not talking about having sex. I just want to be able to snuggle with you. I think about that from time to time."

He smiled and said, "That sounds like a stunning idea but I was afraid to ask." She reached out. They took ahold of one another's hands. "I don't know about you but I'm plumb tuckered. Let's go snuggle."

She laughed, "plumb tuckered, now there's an expression. It sounds like something Gabby Hayes would say." He wondered if she really knew who Gabby Hayes was. He asked her. "Of course I know. He was Hop-Along Cassidy's side kick." Andy made a beep sound. "Wrong answer Brady; it was Roy Rogers."

They both took turns in the bathroom. He ran hot water for her to wash up. It was after ten when they crawled into bed. Cassidy chose to sleep next to Jan on the floor. Andy gave her one of his t-shirts to wear. She lay on her side and he snuggled up to her back. She took his hand and kissed it. "Andy, that was sweet, what you just said a little while ago. I know that I'm not a beautiful woman and I know that I come across as a hard-assed bitch at times. I do regard you as a good friend. He asked her what it was he had said to her. She asked him to put his leg over her. She snuggled up to him. "The thing about you going nuts worrying about me if I took off. I've never felt like I was very important to anyone." They fell asleep holding one another.

Andy awakened at 5:30. He slipped out of bed. He and Cassidy went for a three mile run. When they got back, Jan was still sleeping. He took a bath. When he came out of the bathroom she was sitting at the dining room table petting Cassidy. She asked him how long he had been up. He told her and asked if she wanted to take a quick bath. He started the pump and turned the valves so she had hot water. "The first time you showed me what was involved, I thought, 'you have to be a freaking engineer to take a bath around here'. You're not going to know what to do when you move into your new house, Andy." He made them some breakfast while she bathed.

While eating Jan brought up the subject about what had happened yesterday. She hesitated before addressing the subject. "Andy, Ramon is one of the people I put behind bars a few years ago. I'm sure his coming after me yesterday was a personal vengeance thing. He's a psychopath and a loose cannon. He raped and killed a nursing student. He's suspected of having raped several women. He was one of the men who gang raped me. As far as I'm concerned, it's too bad he survived yesterday. If I had been able to get there before you, I would have wasted him. I'm going to put pressure on the DA to charge him with two counts of attempted murder one. If he goes down on that he'll end up behind bars until he's too old to hold a gun." Andy asked about the others. She didn't know about them. It was clear that she didn't want to discuss the matter any further.

"Jan, don't go disappearing. Please stick around. I have an uneasy feeling that you're planning to do a vanishing act."

"Andy, when I was lying there in the hospital. I knew that I wouldn't have survived if it weren't for you. You were there for me and I appreciate that. I decided a few things" She paused. "I said to myself, 'look at you, you're not pretty, you're damaged goods, you're older than him, you have no talents. You may be a half-way decent cop but that's all you've got going for yourself. You've made that your entire life." He started to say something. She hushed him. "I think that someone is going to come along that you'd like to be with. For awhile I was afraid that Stephanie would solve her problems and want to come back. Andy, we're friends. Let's leave it that way. I'm afraid that if we try to take our relationship beyond what we have, we'll screw it all up."

He asked about last night. "Yeah, well we all have needs. Nothing happened. I mean we didn't do the deed. The two of us went through a traumatic event yesterday. We needed to not be alone. I let my needs get in the way of my better judgment." He had a hurt expression. "Andy, it felt good but we can't let it happen again. It's a slippery slope. Maybe we need to back off for awhile. We're courting disaster."

He decided not to challenge her arguments for the moment. He got up and began clearing the table. It was almost time for the construction crew to arrive. "You're pissed with me aren't you?" She asked.

He shook his head. "No, I'm not pissed. I'm confused." He did not elucidate.

She looked at her watch. "I better get going. I'll call you later this afternoon. I don't know what today will bring. It's standard policy for there to be an inquiry after an officer is involved in a shooting. I may be put on temporary leave. We'll see."

"Does our spending time together put you in an awkward position with your job?"

"I don't know. I suppose it could." Before leaving she reiterated her promise to call him later. He did not accompany her to her car.

Shortly after she left, the construction crew arrived. Andy talked with Dan briefly. He called Vern's garage to see about getting his truck. Vern said he had a few good used tires. He told Andy, "your spare is like brand new. I've already put that one on. I put a used tire on the other side. I went ahead and ordered a new one. I'll put that on the other side and the used one will be your spare." Vern had a serious tone to his voice. "Jeez, Andy, someone sure has it in for you. You've sure had a string of things happen to this old truck. Is it that the guy who did all of those other things?" Andy told him he didn't know for sure. "Well, if it is, your troubles may be over," Vern said. Andy knew that Vern had a lot of questions he'd like to ask. Andy said to him, "The cops don't want me to say anything about what happened for the time being. Maybe we can sit down over a beer one of these days and I can tell you about it." Vern said he'd be up shortly to get Andy.

Andy thought about Jan throughout the day. 'What an unlikely pair the two of us are. We sure take the prize.' He thought about what she had said. She was warning him off. Maybe she was right. He had such mixed feelings about her. A part of him felt strangely connected to her. Another part of him feared that he was courting another disaster. It seemed to him that the thing Jan most wanted in life, she couldn't let herself have. 'Given my track record, I wonder if I'm not the same way'.

Jan called late in the afternoon. She reported that the Sheriff and the States Attorney had put her through almost three hours of intensive questioning. She was certain that Andy would be questioned as well. She was optimistic that, because of Ramon's long criminal history and his being wanted on five outstanding warrants in Illinois, his future didn't look too bright. She had the impression that everyone was relieved he was behind bars. She was of the opinion that priority would be given to whatever jurisdiction had the strongest and most serious case or cases against him. It would probably be Illinois. "Knowing our DA, his main concern is that our asses are completely covered. He does-n't want any uncrossed T's or undotted I's. He's going to create a paper trail to prove that everyone followed the book." She segued into saying, "I'm going to stay at my place for the time being, Andy. The fact that we were together when this happened has raised some eyebrows." He asked what that meant. "Mostly about you being an armed civilian and you shooting the guy. I'm hoping self-defense and all of the stuff hav-ing to do with 'Draco' will satisfy the D.A.'s questions."

He wasn't sure he understood her meaning. He asked, "Do I need to find myself an attorney? Am I in some kind of trouble?'" She didn't think so. He hesitated, then said, "I've thought about what you said this morning Jan. To say the least, we're an odd couple. More than once I've asked myself how we would get along living togeth-er." There was a long silence. He apologized. She asked him what he had concluded. "I haven't decided anything. I think we both like one another. We've sure as hell been through a lot together. We're both used to living alone; you more than me. I have to agree with you that we're both afraid of screwing up a good relationship."

She gave a slight sigh, "that pretty much says it, Andy. It's time that we put our cards on the table for both of us to see. I've said to myself, 'Hey Brady, you've almost bought the farm twice now'. That part of me wants to pitch caution to the wind and make the most of whatever time I've got left. I trust you, Andy. I trust you more than I do myself." There was another lengthy silence. "Andy, let's see what happens. There are times when I really do want to be with you. Then there are the other times. It hasn't got anything to do with you. It's me." She paused, then said. "You deserve someone who's capable of being a steady partner. I'm much too erratic. Christ, I even drive myself crazy." He asked if she was taking her psych drugs. There was a long pause. "I need to get back on them." She went on. "I don't feel like I need them all the time, just when I start down into one of my funks."

"Maybe we ought to go back to see Doctor Jordan. What you're describing sounds more like a bi-polar disorder than depression." He tried to explain it to her. He knew that she probably wasn't interested in anything he had to say if she was headed toward one of her highs. He knew from experience that bi-polar people were hard to diagnose and almost impossible to treat. They only sought help when they were in the depressed phase. They loved their highs. Most of them stopped taking their medications entirely when they were headed into the manic phase. It hadn't occurred to him before now that Jan might be cyclothymic. Before hanging up she told him that she'd call him later that evening.

After closing the shop that evening, Andy and Cassidy drove to the grocery store. He was expecting Brian for the Fourth of July. He splurged and bought some expensive steaks. During the hectic summer months, he made it a habit to shop ahead for two or three week's worth of groceries. Time was at a premium. It usually took twice as long to shop for groceries because of the increased summer population. The trip to and from the grocery store often took twice as long also. He didn't really know what Jan's tastes were. He hoped that she would choose to join them for at least one evening while Brian was here. He recalled their first encounters. He thought about the many changes she'd made over the past few months. She still clung to some of her ridiculous 'costumes'. Realizing now that, like Stephanie, she was 'on the run', he viewed that as part of her attempts to become incognito. In his years as a therapist, Andy had seldom seen anyone make so many dramatic changes. There was no question in his mind that getting her on psych meds had made a major difference. When she had been severely depressed last winter, they had probably saved her life. They had bolstered her mood and her level of functioning. They had helped get her through a very rough time battling her alcohol addiction. He thought about their cuddling the night before and how good it had felt being close to her. Theirs had been a gradual relationship. Over time they had developed a friendship, albeit still somewhat fragile. She seemed to like his little corner of the world. He was so engrossed in thinking about her that he almost passed Rob in one of the aisles. "Hey Amigo, long time no see." Rob greeted him.

They clasped hands. Rob asked if the new house was under construction. "Yeah, are you in a hurry to get home?"

"Not particularly, my girlfriend is working tonight."

"Why don't you follow me home and see the new place. It's

almost done. I'd like your opinion on it. We can have a couple of beers." Rob was astounded to hear that so much had been accomplished in such a short time. He was eager to see the place. He just had a few grocery items as opposed to Andy, who had close to two hundred dollars worth of purchases, which included gin, beer, and wine. Rob helped him unload his cart into the back of the pickup.

At home Rob helped him to bring stuff into the house and put it away. He asked about what had happened the other day. "It was in the paper that Detective Miller shot a fugitive out near Yacht Harbor. Your name was mentioned, too. It said that the two of you had been hiking out there and this guy had tried to ambush you. You know our local paper; they're short on facts and long on inaccurate reporting."

"I can't say much Rob. The matter is still under investigation. I'll just say that it turns out he's a very bad guy and the world will be a better place without him on its streets. He wasn't wounded seriously."

After everything was put away, they opened a couple of beers and went to see the new house. Cassidy was expecting to go for their usual evening walk. Andy reassured him. "We will. We'll go in a few minutes."

Rob was impressed both with the design of the new house as well as the quality of construction. He pointed out several things where a lot of builders would have cut corners to save on cost. "If anything, these guys are overdoing the construction. I'd like to work for this guy. He's a class act. I could learn from somebody like him." After inspecting the house, Rob joined Andy and Cassidy for their stroll. There were dark storm clouds forming and moving in from the northwest. The temperature began dropping. As they walked they could hear the growl of distant thunder. Andy asked how things were going with Rob's new relationship. "We're doing good. We're talking about the possibility of getting married this fall. I'm going away for three weeks toward the end of summer to take a crash course in log homebuilding. I'm thinking about getting into doing that. Carla and I are also thinking about leaving here and moving to Alaska. If you recall I spent six years up there working on fishing boats. It's a whole different world. It's the last American frontier."

"That's a bold step Rob. You're not going to go back to fishing are you?"

"If I decide that log home building is something I can do, we might try our hand at that," he smiled. "Why don't you come up to Alaska with us. We'd make a great team. Maybe you could escape the crap that you've been going through over Stephanie." Rob asked if that was still going on. Andy told him that for the present there seemed to be a hiatus.

"I don't know Rob. If I was a few years younger, I'd probably beat you up there. I feel like I'm getting too old to be starting all over again, at least by choice."

"I understand, but I have to tell you Andy; I think one of the things you and I have in common is that neither of us has ever been afraid to risk ourselves at trying something new and different."

Andy's response was, "there comes a time in a man's life when he decides that it's time to settle down. I like it here. I know that if I have to, I can start anew, but I'd prefer not to. It's just good to know that I can if I have to. That's a confidence that comes from risking oneself."

Rob agreed entirely. "Well Amigo, if you change your mind, you're always welcome to come join us up there." After the walk they decided to go to the Pub for a burger. It was crowded. They ended up eating at the bar.

Shortly after Andy got home, the phone rang. It was Jan. She asked where he had been. He told her that he and Rob had gone out for a burger. She told him, "I've been suspended with pay for the next week. I understand the policy and the reasoning but in the meantime I have half-a-dozen ongoing investigations that are being put on hold. Some of them are going to go down the toilet in the interim. Some bad guys just got a reprieve without knowing it."

"So, do you want to come up here since you don't have to go to work for the next week?"

She groaned, "Andy, now is not the time. You're probably going to be interviewed tomorrow since you were a participant in what happened." She paused. "This may not seem very important to you, but I want you to know. The other night was exactly what I needed."

"It's what we both needed Jan. We were both distraught by what happened. Neither of us should have been alone that night. I'm glad we had each other to turn to. It felt good."

"Thanks Andy." He asked if she would consider coming for dinner one evening next week to meet his son Brian. "I'd like that. I'd like to meet him. You've had such good things to say about both of your boys." She changed the subject six times in rapid succession. "You know, we need to take some pictures of your old house if you haven't already." She talked about his shop and the new season. She switched to talking about the state's attorney and how abrasive he could be; then onto the subject of Stephanie; then questions about the new house. She ended up the conversation by talking about Thorsen Point. She wondered if the 'ambush' would ruin it for them. Before hanging up she told him that she might stop by the shop tomorrow. "Just because I'm suspended, it doesn't mean I can't conduct some interviews. They just can't be filed."

Andy was awakened in the early morning hours by thunder and strong winds. He got up to close windows. A few minutes later it began raining hard. The downpour continued for close to an hour. He knew that his driveway was being washed out. He would have to get up early to mend it. Aside from the fact that it was such backbreaking work, it was also seemed like such a waste of precious time. Cassidy curled up next to him on the bed as the storm raged. Andy fell asleep long before the storm subsided. When he awakened at 5:30, the sun was coming up and the sky was clear. The driveway was washed out as badly as he had ever seen it. It took him close to an hour and a half with wheel barrow after wheel barrow, full of wet heavy gravel, to fill in the deep ruts. The mosquitoes made the task even worse. He ended up taking Cassidy back to the house. He doused himself with bug spray before resuming the task. When the gravel was all back in place he drove over it several times to pack it down.

Later in the morning Andy received a call from Sheriff Cummings. "Andy, the state's attorney and I need to ask you a number of questions about the shooting incident that occurred yesterday. We can come up there to interview you so you don't have to take time away from your business." They made an appointment for late in the afternoon which was typically a slow time of the day.

Jan came by the shop early in the afternoon. Traffic was sporadic. They talked about the pending interview. "I'm pretty sure Sheriff Cummings accepts the account that I gave. I'm not so sure about the D.A.. He and I have locked horns on a few occasions. He's a condescending, pompous ass in my opinion. He talks down to everybody, even Sheriff Cummings. It's like he regards all of us as idiots. I appreciate that he wants to win every case he walks into court with. Hell, we all do. We're on the same side but he treats us like we're incompetent minions who are completely ignorant of the law. I'm telling you this so you're prepared. Try not to let him get to you."

She was about to leave when he asked her, "how about we go canoeing this evening? There's a small lake nearby."

"Are you nuts McLeod? I'm not a water person. I can't swim. What if we tip over?"

"It's a shallow lake. In a lot of places the water will probably only come up to your chest. You can wear a life jacket. Come on let's do it. I think you'll enjoy the experience. It promises to be to be a nice evening." She consented reluctantly.

Sheriff Cummings and the DA, Fred Bolger, arrived at Andy's shop at four o'clock. The three of them sat down outside on benches. The D.A. immediately launched into questioning him. He persevered at length asking questions about why they had gone there and what they were doing while they were out there. He almost seemed to be suggesting that he suspected they had gone out there to have sex. Sheriff Cummings finally interrupted by asking about the shooter himself and what had transpired. Bolger took occasional notes. It was noted in three different reports that Andy had been wounded by the shooter; however the DA seemed unwilling to acknowledge that fact. Andy showed Bolger his wound. He even lifted the bandage to show him the actual wound. After almost half-an-hour of questioning they still hadn't gotten to the encounter they had with the shooter on the road. Andy held up a hand to stop. "Look, at the risk of seeming impatient, I'm going to tell you what happened as I saw it. I have to be somewhere in less than an hour." The DA started to ask another question. Andy raised his hand again. "Nope, I just want you to listen."

The DA's face turned red. "You're not in charge of this inquiry, Mr. McLeod, I am. You shot a man. You're a civilian. You were armed with a pistol and an assault shotgun. You could be charged with assault with a deadly weapon with intent to kill. You could end up spending the next several years behind bars. You'll answer every question posed to you, related to this matter. If you refuse to do so, I can and will, charge you with obstructing justice. Do I make myself clear?" Andy asked him if he was done. "No, I'm not done. I'll let you know when I'm done."

"Look, I feel like I'm being treated like the bad guy. I was shot at. I shot back in self-defense. From what I understand this guy has a long history of violent, criminal behavior, including, numerous rapes, and a murder."

Before he could go any further, the DA stopped him. He had regained some of his composure. "Mr. McLeod, your initial encounter with the shooter was well over a mile from the road. After the shooter fled the scene, did you and Ms. Miller then pursue him?" Andy nodded. "You were armed. Why were you armed? A defense attorney is going to want answers to those questions. A defense attorney might well try to prove that your actions, after the initial encounter, were predatory." He went on. "Ms. Miller has an extremely unpleasant history with this man. A defense attorney might well try to demonstrate that she was seeking vengeance for what happened in the past. He might try to convince a jury that you were in collusion with her. You could be accused of intentionally trying to lure him to a remote location in order to murder him. I assume that you are aware of that episode from her past."

Sheriff Cummings spoke to the DA, "I'm sorry Fred. I forgot all about it until now. I deputized Mr. McLeod not very long ago I have a copy of the letter given to him at the time." He reminded the DA of the threats Andy had been under. "I'm sure Mr. McLeod would agree with me. It's helpful knowing the kinds of questions a defense attorney might pose. I have to say that it was beginning to sound to me like you were pointing an accusatory finger at Andy and Jan." He turned to Andy. "He's right, Andy. Even a bad defense attorney will try to make his client out to be a choirboy. If you end up being called to testify, you'll need to demonstrate that your actions were legitimate and justifiable. Why don't you go ahead and tell us what happened once you got to the road." Andy recounted the rest of the story. The DA resumed taking notes. He interrupted Andy a few times to ask clarifying questions. In the end, Sheriff Cummings turned to the DA, "well, Fred, I haven't heard any discrepancies. Both of their stories are identical. I'm satisfied that their actions were justified."

"I want to know why you were armed Mr. McLeod. Are you in the habit of carrying fully loaded weapons with you whenever you go for a walk in the evening? That seems a little unusual, wouldn't you agree?"

Sheriff Cummings interrupted again. "Fred, we've been over this twice before; once with Detective Miller and once with me."

"I don't care. I want to hear what Mr. McLeod has to say. Humor me." Andy gave the DA a concise, but thorough accounting of the whole Stephanie story." The DA listened this time without taking notes. When Andy was finished, Bolger made a statement/question. "To this day you have no idea what any of that was about, or who was behind it."

"Nope, and I probably never will," he added. "I need to point out that you're referring to it in the past tense. While there has been a period of calm over the past few weeks, I'm not convinced that it's entirely over and done with."

The meeting had taken an hour-and-a-half. When it was concluded, Andy shook hands with the D.A. and Sheriff Cummings. After they departed he locked up his shop and headed for home to meet Jan and load the canoe.

Jan was waiting for Andy when he arrived home. After loading the canoe, they drove to the small lake. Jan was extremely uncomfortable being in the canoe at first. She was in the front with Cassidy right behind her. After awhile she began to relax and enjoy the peacefulness of the lake. They had gone close to a mile when Andy said, "try scooting yourself backwards to the center of the canoe." As she did, Cassidy deftly jumped past her to the front of the canoe. Andy continued to paddle, taking her for a leisurely ride.

Neither of them had said much. Jan finally spoke. "You'd think that when a person finally finds what they had been looking for most of their lives, they would be thrilled. I find myself almost terrified."

She said. "I'm afraid that this won't last, Andy. Do you remember how heartsick you were when you lost Lucy?" He nodded. "I don't want to go through that same kind of pain."

Cassidy turned around and made his way to her. He gave her a couple of licks before sitting down between her legs. "That's all the more reason to seize the day," Andy said. "I still miss Luce. I was devastated by her loss. I've had to remind myself many times of the joy she brought me while I had her. That was a gift. I'm glad I didn't wait to get another dog. Cassidy is a good fellow. He's not Lucy but he's helped me to get over losing her. He saved our lives yesterday."

"Do you still miss Stephanie?"

"You've asked me that several times before, Jan. No, I'm pretty much over her. Looking back on our relationship, I don't think I ever really knew her. I think she kept me at a distance on purpose. I'd like to think she did it to protect me but maybe that's just the way she was."

"I'm glad you talked me into coming out here this evening. This really is peaceful and relaxing." The sun was nearing the horizon. Loons called out from the far end of the lake. The idyllic scene was beginning to be overshadowed by the mosquitoes.

"We better head back before we need transfusions," Andy warned. Jan moved back to the front of the canoe and took up paddling again. At the landing she helped him load the canoe. He invited her to stay for dinner.

She gave no response until they arrived at his place. "I want to Andy. I just don't think I should. What if we're being watched? I don't mean by Draco. I mean the by the Sheriff or the DA." He hadn't told her about his earlier meeting with them.

"Come on let's spray some repellent on ourselves. We can take a short walk. Along the way I'll tell you about the meeting we had." They unloaded the canoe first. While walking, Andy described the meeting with Bolger and Sheriff Cummings. "You're right; Bolger can be an abrasive prick. The two of us ended up locking horns. He's very good at goading people. Even though you had warned me, he managed to get to me after awhile. I'm sure it serves him well in court." She told him that it depended upon who he was up against. She'd seen it backfire on him a few occasions. She asked Andy some specifics about what had happened. "Sheriff Cummings finally stepped in and saved the day. I'm impressed with him. He cut through the smoke and got to the core of the matter. Bolger and I were at an impasse. Cummings was able to defuse the situation. It ended up being productive. I even learned a few things in the process. He enlightened me about how defense attorneys can operate." He asked her, "you still haven't answered my question. Are you going to stay here tonight?"

"If I stay here, I'm going to want to snuggle with you again. I think I'd better head for home. Please don't be angry with me." He tried to show understanding. She got in her car and left.

There was still some lingering light after Jan left. Andy mixed a martini and he and Cassidy went to the new house. It was nearly complete. The drywall was finished. The painters had a primer coat on all the downstairs walls. The kitchen cabinets had been delivered. They were in boxes waiting to be installed once the painters were done. "Cassidy, this is going to be a dream come true. We're going to have a thermostat, flush toilets, and best of all, a shower with hot running water." Cassidy looked at him like he understood. Suddenly his ears perked up, he barked and ran out of the house. Andy followed to see what had alerted him.

He saw Jan's car parking next to his truck. He walked toward her. "I changed my mind. I stopped and bought a six-pack of NA beer."

"Come see the house. It'll be finished in just a few more days." Jan got a bottle of beer from the carton. As they strode toward the new house, she asked if he was planning any sort of celebration once the construction was complete. "I plan to. I've already mentioned it to Dan. I want him and his crew to be here for it. It goes without saying that you're invited." She asked who else. He thought about it. "Rob and his girlfriend, Doc Bitner, Brian, I don't know, that's about it." She seemed surprised that his list of people wasn't longer. "Well, there are a lot of people I could invite, but they're mostly acquaintances. I just want the people who have been directly involved with the project and those I feel closest to for the house warming."

Jan shook her head. "You know what part of my problem is?" Andy waited for her to say. "I still see myself as being a loser and you up there somewhere." He continued to listen. "I know I've made a lot of changes over the past few months, but somehow they don't feel real. I've lived most of my life feeling like I wasn't as good as most people. Maybe that's why I decided to become a cop. I knew I'd be dealing with some real scum-bag, low-lifes. It would allow me to feel that I was better than them at least. I feel like most of the changes I've made have been for the wrong reasons." He looked at her questioningly. She looked down. "Look, this isn't the real me. Maybe you're right. Maybe I'm; what did you call it, bi-polar? There are times when I'm completely unable to control myself. How can anyone feel a sense of self-confidence when they can't trust themselves? All I know is, I'm impossible to live with. At times I can't even stand living with myself. I know that if this relationship goes any further you're going to end up hating me. I think you need to find yourself some nice stable, good looking, intelligent lady who can appreciate what you have to offer."

"I thought I'd found that with Stephanie. Look what happened with that." Andy said. "I've decided that being with someone I can trust and I'm friends with is more important."

"Andy, I don't think you even know what you're looking for. I'm pretty sure it isn't me. Look, we've been over all of this before. I've lived by myself for a long time. I'm set in my ways. I'm pretty sure I don't even want to be in a full-time relationship with anyone. I like being able to come and go as I damn well please. I don't like having to answer to anyone. If I've got stuff going on, I don't have to concern myself with anyone else's needs or expectations. If I've had a rough day, I don't have to pretend to be cheerful. Most of all I don't have to exercise politeness or civility when I'm off duty. I think after two weeks of living with me you'd be miserable. Knowing you it would take months before you would muster enough courage to ask me to leave. If I saw I was making you feel that way, I'd leave much sooner. That's what would happen, and I know that you'd end up blaming yourself."

He pursed his lips. "I know your job takes a lot out of you, Jan. Being a social worker took a lot out of me. How about this; if you feel like you need to keep your apartment, that's fine. If you need downtime you can escape to it. I know that when I have shit days at the shop during the peak of the season, I can end up being an absolute bear. Usually having a drink and going for a walk helps to improve my mood. I realize that continuing this relationship carries some risks for both of us. Jan, we haven't been able to share much joy in the time we've known one another. But we've had some nice moments. This evening was one of them. We both need to squeeze as much enjoyment out of life as we can. I really do enjoy spending time with you. Most importantly..." Suddenly Cassidy began growling. The hair stood up on his back. Andy looked in the direction the dog was pointing and reached for his gun.

Jan pulled her gun out rapidly, saying in a loud whisper, "Andy, get down." Cassidy took off running toward the woods to the east. Andy called for the dog to come back. There was a crack and a bullet ripped into Andy's right side. He spun and his gun flew out of his hand. Jan emptied her gun in the direction of the shot. She crawled rapidly through the grass to him.

He was holding his side. He had already pulled out his bandana and was applying pressure to the wound. "Find my gun Jan. I think it's over there." He pointed. "I think it's just a flesh wound." She took his word for it and quickly found his gun. He asked her to try to get Cassidy back here.

She called to the dog, being cautious; not knowing if the shooter was still out there. "Cassidy, Andy needs you. Come on boy. Cassidy, come." She called him several times. Cassidy finally came bounding through the weeds, straight to Andy. He licked Andy's face, then the blood oozing between his fingers. Jan put a new clip in her gun. She gave Andy his. I'm going back to the house and call for an ambulance and backup. She had him lift his blood saturated bandana. She pulled up his t-shirt. "You're losing a lot of blood Andy." She quickly pulled off her own t-shirt and placed it on the wound. I'll be back in a minute." She took off running in a crouched position.

"Cassidy, go with her. Make sure she's all right." Cassidy looked in the direction Jan had gone; then he turned toward the direction that the shot had come from. He chose to crouch down next to Andy with his full attention focused on the woods. The wound was starting to hurt badly. Andy kept pressure on it. He lay back in the grass noticing clouds of gnats undulating in the twilight sky above him.

Jan returned to where Andy lay in the grass. She had hastily pulled on one of Andy's t-shirts. Several minutes went by before sirens could be heard. "I'm going to go get them." She left him again, running toward the house. A deputy arrived moments before the ambulance. She rode with him, directing him across the meadow to where Andy lay. It was barely light. She told the deputy that the shot had come from the woods. She pointed. The deputy got his assault shotgun and cautiously started for the woods. Jan knelt down next to Andy.

"Take care of Cassidy for me will you? He hasn't eaten yet."

"I'll see you at the hospital in awhile." She told him.

At the hospital Andy underwent emergency surgery to repair a bullet hole in his ascending colon. He was listed in stable condition. It appeared that the bullet was a small caliber, probably a 22. However it had expanded as it tore through him and barely missed hitting his right kidney. A manhunt was underway for the shooter. Sheriff Cummings arrived at the hospital. Jan told him, that to her knowledge, the threats to Andy had not resumed. She wasn't sure which of them had been the intended target.

Chapter 16

Andy was admitted to intensive care for the next twenty-four hours. Jan called Brian who drove up that night. Brian was able to get hold of Corey, who in turn was able to get an emergency leave. Brian would pick him up at the airport in Green Bay the following day. Jan was not allowed to be a part of the investigation but Sheriff Cummings called her frequently to inquire about Andy, to keep her informed and to exchange ideas with her. "Jan, either the shooter is a kid, a jockey or a petite woman. The footprints are about a size six shoe. The shooter weighs somewhere around a hundred pounds give or take. We haven't been able to find a shell casing. We're guessing that the weapon was a 22. It might have been a 223. What do you think?"

"It occurs to me that this was either staged to give the appearance that the shooter is not an experienced pro, or it really is a novice. We were both facing the woods and walking slowly. We were fairly easy targets at that range, even for an inexperienced shooter. A small caliber has a fairly flat trajectory and it doesn't expand much on impact. It's possible the shooter wasn't really out to kill, but to wound. It could have been a woman." She stopped there.

"Yeah, so what do you think? What are we talking about? You say that the shooter may not have been out to kill him, but he or she came awfully damn close."

"I don't know. My first thought was Stephanie. We both think she's alive and out there somewhere, but why would she want to kill or injure him? I can't imagine what her motive would be or that she'd take such a risk by coming back here?"

The sheriff asked. "Who else? I mean maybe the shooter is a hired gun? There are women assassins." She reminded him that she was on suspended leave, and, therefore, was not allowed to conduct an investigation. She sarcastically stated that she was a detective, not 'a goddamn wizard'. "Okay, I'm sorry. I'm reinstating you as of right now."

"No, let's maintain the status quo. It might be better if I did some free lancing. Send Marty over with everything you've got so far. I'll meet him at the fire station at seven tomorrow morning."

"Jan, you're a hell of a detective. This thing has all of us stymied.

Watch your own back. Let me know if you need anything." They hung up. Sheriff Cummings didn't understand why Jan wanted people to think she wasn't involved in the investigation. He decided he would meet with her himself sometime the next day. They needed to talk.

When she returned to the hospital the next morning, Brian was there. He had arrived from Illinois and was with his father. She introduced herself to him. Andy was on oxygen and was hooked up to an intravenous drip. He was awake but was heavily sedated. He held out his hand to her and she took it. In a somewhat strained voice Andy told Brian, "Jan was with me when this happened." Andy was in a lot of the pain. He asked her if they'd found the shooter yet.

"Not yet," She told him. "Charlie has assigned me to the investigation unofficially. Maybe I can come up with something. I'll start on it after I leave here."

After a few minutes she suggested that they let him get some rest. Out in the hall she told Brian that she was taking care of Cassidy. Neither of the boys had met the dog. Brian told her that he'd called his brother Corey to tell him what had happened to their father. "Corey is being given an emergency leave. He'll arrive in Green Bay this afternoon. I'll go pick him up."

"I've got an apartment here in town." Jan told Brian. "You're welcome to crash there if you need to rest up. The new house is almost finished. Nothing has been moved over to it yet," she told him.

On their way out to the hospital parking lot, Brian asked if he could call her Jan. She told him to please do so. "Jan, Dad trusts you more than anyone. He really likes you. He talks about you all the time." He looked down, then back at her. "I don't know why anyone would do this to him. Do you think it has anything to do with Stephanie?"

"I don't know about Stephanie. I'm not ruling that out, but I kind of doubt it." She changed the subject. "He's proud of both of you. Things have been going really well for him the past few months. This doesn't make much sense. It came out of the blue. Let me know if anything occurs to you. She told Brian to follow her to her apartment. "I have Cassidy there. I can offer you a beer and a sandwich."

At the apartment Brian was immediately taken by Cassidy. He commented that he hadn't been sure his father was doing the right thing getting another dog so soon after losing Lucy. "Cassidy, you're one neat, old puppy. Pops got lucky with you."

Jan and Brian visited for close to an hour. Much of their conversation revolved around the events associated with Stephanie. Jan was careful to find out what Brian already knew before making any comment. She didn't want to divulge anything that he had not already been told to him by his father. She definitely decided not to tell him about the shooting incident just three days before. It would be up to Andy, whether to tell his sons about that or not.

Jan told Brian she was going to take Cassidy with her to have a look around the area where Andy had been shot the night before. Brian decided he would go back to the hospital for a brief visit before heading to Green Bay to pick up his brother at the airport. On the way to Andy's, Jan talked to Cassidy. "You knew that something wasn't right didn't you?" Cassidy sighed and gave her hand a lick. "We both love that man, Cassidy. I don't know what we'd do without him." It had been a very long time since Janet Brady Miller had allowed herself to cry over anybody. She fought back tears as she drove.

To Jan's surprise, Sheriff Cumming was at Andy's place when she arrived. He'd been looking around. A couple of the guys on the construction crew knew who he was. They were more than a little curious as to why the Sheriff himself was there but they refrained from asking. When Jan and Cassidy approached Sheriff Cummings, he greeted her. She told the Sheriff how Cassidy had warned them just before Andy was shot. He asked her, "walk me through what happened last evening, Jan. I want to see if I can visualize the exact scene." As they walked together he asked her why she didn't want anyone to know that she was back on the investigation. "Do you suspect someone in the department is involved in what happened?"

"No, I don't think that. In light of what happened a couple of evenings ago, I just think I should keep a low profile." She didn't feel to the need to explain her reasoning for that. She turned back to the subject at hand. "We were ambushed. The shooter knows his way around here. He or she also knows enough about Andy's routine to be fairly sure he'd have the opportunity to get a shot at him out here in the open. Jan led the Sheriff to the place Andy had fallen. There was a lot of blood. She had Sheriff Cummings pace off the distance from there to the tree line at the edge of the meadow. She, Cassidy and the Sheriff began working their way back and forth into the woods. "I returned fire after Andy was hit," she told Sheriff Cummings. "I got off all fourteen rounds. Just maybe one of them hit the shooter. Let's see if we can find any blood."

Within a few minutes, Cummings called to her. "Over here Jan; I think I've found some." Sure enough; there were a few drops of blood on some dry leaves. It increased as they moved further into the woods. She complimented the sheriff on his find. "I hunted these woods as a boy," he told her. "I learned to track wounded deer."

They eventually came to the road that ran through the forest.

They found the place along the road where the shooter had parked a vehicle. Jan examined the spot and concluded that the vehicle had been parked half off the road. The trail of blood extended onto the pavement a couple feet. There was a small pool of it on the pavement. "It looks like he or she had a fairly serious wound," Jan observed. "I don't know how the deputies missed finding this." The sheriff made no comment. "I'll bring my car around. We need to get some samples of the blood."

Cummings said that he'd place some calls to find out if anyone had been treated for a gun shot wound."

Jan told him not to limit it to just gunshot. "If the bullet grazed the shooter, it wouldn't look like a penetrating bullet wound. It could look like a surface gash or even a burn. Before the sheriff departed to get his car, she suggested that he have a deputy interview the people who lived along the road in both directions. "Maybe somebody saw the car parked here. If we're really lucky, they may have even seen the driver." After he left, she retraced the trail of blood. She found a place where it looked like the wounded shooter had perhaps stumbled and fallen. She examined the area carefully. She surmised that the person had suffered a leg wound. As she continued her search, she found a couple of rifle butt impressions on an area of bare ground. This suggested that the person may have been using their weapon to support themselves. She went back over the entire trail of blood again. The day was becoming hot. She found herself being strafed by deer flies. One bit her. "Ouch, goddamn you." She slapped at them in vain as she made her way back to the road. The Sheriff was there. He asked her to help him collect the blood samples. If he had ever known how, he had long since forgotten the procedure. She complained to him about the flies. He got a can of bug spray from the trunk of his car and sprayed her. She took him back to show him her other discoveries. At her suggestion he brought along a camera and he shot pictures of the gun butt impression. "Those might tell us what kind of weapon was used." She told him that she was pretty sure the person had a leg wound and why.

"Good Jan. None of us spotted any of this stuff. I'll get a team going on this just as soon as I get back to headquarters." He asked her what she was going to do next.

"I'm going to hang around here and see what else I might find. I'll call you later." He gave her the can of repellant. It took her an hour but she found the exact place that the shooter had been standing when he, or she, shot Andy. It was late in the morning when she found the empty bullet casing. It was a twenty-two long rifle. Her other find was the rear lens cover for a variable, magnifying-power rifle scope. She was unfamiliar with the brand name molded into the rubber. She surmised that it was probably an inexpensive off-brand. She'd check on that later. She was still undecided as to whether the shooter had been aiming to kill or just injure. She wondered if Cassidy, having spotted the perpetrator had perhaps thrown their aim off the slightest bit causing more serious injury than intended. The biggest questions plaguing her were: 'who was the intended target, who would want to do such a thing and why'. She kept coming back to Stephanie as an improbable, but possible candidate. 'If I was the target, it could be one of several possibilities, all from my past'.

Andy ended up having to stay in the hospital for an extended period of two weeks until he was able to begin taking food. He lost nearly ten pounds. Corey only had a three-day pass before had to return to North Carolina. Brian canceled all his summer plans and stayed on. He took over running his father's gallery and stayed in the old house. He visited his father early in the evening, always with a list of questions about the house and/or the business. "A lot of people come in asking about you, Pops. I tell them that you had to have some surgery and you might be out of commission for awhile. They all seem genuinely concerned and they tell me to give you their best." Brian began making a point of getting their names.

Jan came to the hospital early in the morning and again in the evening. She stayed beyond the end of visiting hours. At the beginning of the second week she came in to announce that the new house was almost completely finished. "Dan gave me the keys this afternoon. It looks terrific, Andy."

She had a couple of beers in a bag. She opened one and gave it to him. She sat down on the bed next to him. "Sweet Jesus, this tastes good. Thank you." They held hands. "When I get home I'd like your help in picking out some drapes, Jan. I've kind of decided not to put in carpeting. Maybe just a few area rugs. I like the wood floors. What do you think?"

She laughed. "You're asking the wrong person for that kind of help. I've about as much taste in decorating as a retarded ape. You've seen my place. It's about as homey as an execution chamber." In a less mordant tone she said, "you're not going to be able to manage all by yourself for awhile Andy. Brian has to leave at the end of next week. If you want me to, I can come up for a few days when you come home. I know you're going to want to get back to running your shop. I can take you back and forth." She borrowed his bottle of beer and took a swig. "You're right, this does taste good." She handed it back to him. "I'm kind of scared about a couple of things. We haven't gotten anywhere with the investigation. I'm scared about whoever did this. I don't know if they're going to try again. We don't even know which one of us was being the targeted." Andy finished the beer. She asked if he wanted the other one.

"I do, but I'd better not. I'll be up and down having to pee the rest of the night."

She changed the subject. "I've been in the new house a couple of times Andy. It's beautiful. Dan and his crew have done an outstanding job. They're all concerned about what happened to you. Dan wants to be there when you come home. Word has gotten around that you were hurt. There are some pretty far-fetched rumors. A lot of people have expressed concern about you." In a rare moment of jocularity she said, "I don't understand that at all. Personally I think you're not a very good shot, you're an unbearable martyr. However, you do have a way with dogs."

They discussed the theory that the shooter might have been a woman. He dismissed the possibility of it being someone from his distant past. "It's been too many years since I left Illinois and shrinking heads." He had considered Stephanie but dismissed her too.

"What about your ex-girlfriend, Josie? You weren't very nice to her the last time she called you."

He explained that, "while Josie is tall and slender, I just don't see her as being capable of that kind of thing, Jan. She hated guns. Hell, she hates anything loud. She hated the chainsaw, even the lawnmower."

"I've been toying with another theory, Andy." He invited her to present it. "What if it was intended as a way of getting you out of there for awhile?" He asked her to explain. "Let's suppose Stephanie hid something somewhere on your property. Your constant presence there would preclude someone being able conduct a thorough search, in order to find it."

"I like the theory." He said. "However, it has one minor flaw. The construction crew has been there every day. Brian's been there at night. So there hasn't been much opportunity for anyone to do much searching. That wasn't very clever planning on the part of whomever, if that was the motive." He proffered another idea. "Kind of along that same line of reasoning, what if the hiding place is in the old house. The county planning department told me; back when I applied for a building permit, that I had to tear it down. I have to do that as soon as I get moved into the new place. Don't ask me what their reasoning is. Maybe they're afraid I'm going to rent it out as a vacation spa."

"It might be a wild goose chase but what if I hire movers to transfer your furniture into the new house? Then we can bring a team in to search the old place with a fine tooth comb. You're not in any shape to be moving stuff yourself anyhow. It would serve two purposes." He was willing to give it a try, cautioning, "if there's anything, it might not be in the house. It could be in the barn or buried somewhere on the property. It's like a needle in a thousand haystacks."

"I have another thought. Suppose she gave you some kind of clue before she left. You need to think back."

"I've thought back about that six dozen times. I haven't been able to come up with anything."

What did she give you for Christmas?"

"A couple of books and a couple of flannel shirts." She asked him about the books and if he had read them. "I read the book by Gibran. I haven't read the poetry book." She asked why not. "I don't know. I guess I thought it was strange that she would even give me a book of poetry. I don't dislike poetry; I just don't read much of it. I guess it's because a lot of the symbolic meaning in most poetry eludes me. I don't like working that hard when I sit down to read. I want things to be what they are."

"Where would I find those books Andy? Do you know where they are?" He told her that she had the book by Gibran that he had given her when she was in the hospital in Green Bay. He told her where to look for the other one. She asked him if he could remember the name of the poetry book.

"It's an anthology. I think it is called Some Haystacks Don't Even Have Any Needle."

"How appropriate." Jan said. "I'll see if I can find it." He asked her not to go to his place by herself. "I'll have a deputy accompany me. I promise." He insisted that she call to arrange the rendezvous before she left the room. "You don't trust me."

"Not about some things." She called to ask for a deputy to meet her at Andy's address in an hour. "If you find it, bring it back here. We need to go through it together." She protested that he would be asleep and didn't need to be disturbed. "Don't worry about that. If there's a clue in it, it's probably intended for me. Bring the Gibran book, too." Jan left a few minutes later.

It was almost nine p.m. when she returned to the hospital. He was asleep. She reluctantly awakened him. She had a Styrofoam cup of coffee. He shifted himself to one side of the bed and patted it for her to sit next to him. She kicked off her tennies and sat down next to him. Stephanie had written on the leaf page at the beginning of the poetry book, 'To Andy with love,' she had signed it. They went through the book page by page. There were no notations or underlines until they reached a poem entitled The Panther Possible. In the first line of the poem there was a reference to a tractor, which was underlined. Andy pointed to the word. "I think this is the clue we're looking for." She asked if he thought Stephanie had hidden whatever it was somewhere on his tractor. He nodded. "Don't do anything. It's been there this long. Let's just let things be until I'm out of here. Promise me." She agreed.

At ten o'clock a nurse came in to check Andy's vitals. They were sound asleep together. The nurse smiled. They both awakened. "If you would like, you can sleep in the adjoining bed Ms. Miller. There are a lot of vacant beds tonight."

Jan waited until the nurse left. "I'm going home, Andy. I'll see you in the morning."

As she started for the door he said. "Jan, please; you made a promise."

She smiled. "It's awfully tempting. You're right, it can wait. I'll take the books with me and put them in a safe place."

Andy was released from the hospital the next day. Jan had Cassidy with her when she came to pick him up. The dog whined with excitement when he saw Andy walking stiffly toward the truck. He sat next to Andy all the way home. She took him to the shop first. Brian was expecting him. "Jeez, Pops, you've really lost a lot of weight."

"Have a hole poked in your colon and be on intravenous feeding for close to a week and you'll lose weight too." The shop was having a good day. Andy checked over numerous things and asked several questions. "You're doing better at this than me, Brian. Maybe I ought to hire you to run this place for the rest of the summer."

"No sir, I've enjoyed being here and helping out but I'd go crazy doing this every day for six months. For every one person that comes in here and shows even the slightest interest, a hundred others come in and could care less. You're free entertainment, Pops. They're 'just doing the shops'. I'm sorry, but I don't know how you manage to have any ego left by the end of a season." Andy smiled. Brian went on. "I can't believe the stupid questions some people ask. I've always told my students that there's no such thing as a stupid question. I take it back. There really is such a thing. I can't figure out if some of these people are from another planet or if it's just a phenomenon that occurs to people on vacation."

Jan said, "I've heard your dad utter the same words, Brian. The sad part is that everything in here is his work. It's fantastic stuff. He's a talented man. I don't know how he does it year after year."

Jan took Andy home after a brief while. Cassidy patiently waited for Andy to gingerly get out of the truck before jumping out himself.

Jan came around to help support him. He wanted to go to the new house. Inside, there was the predominant smell of fresh paint. Andy stood in the middle of the great room. "God, Jan, this is fantastic." They toured the downstairs. Brian had moved a few pieces of furniture over from the old house.

In the master bedroom, Andy discovered there was a brand new queen-sized bed, completely made. "This is my housewarming present to you, Andy. That old bed of yours has seen better nights." He gave her a side hug and thanked her. She had also purchased a shower curtain and new towels for the master bath. She anticipated his comment. "No, this doesn't mean I'm moving in with you. This is the extent of my effort to help you decorate this place. You're on your own with the rest of it, McLeod." After they completed touring the house, she led him to the kitchen. "Corey bought you a bottle of good gin for your martini." They were just about to take a stroll out across the meadow when Brian came driving in. He got a beer and joined them. Andy had an untucked chambray shirt on. He had his gun in the back of his jeans. He was sure Jan was armed as well. Andy thought back to Viet Nam. When they were on patrol they always kept a distance between each another. If they came under attack or tripped a mine or a booby trap, the distance served to reduce the number of casualties. Andy kept an eye on Cassidy as they walked.

Brian asked, "Do think your getting shot is a continuation of the stuff that was happening last winter over Stephanie?"

Jan spoke, "We don't know, Brian. It may be, but we honestly don't know. As a matter of fact, we don't even know if your dad was the target." She was immediately sorry that she had included herself as a possible target.

Brian didn't appear to pick up on what she had just said. "So what can you do to protect yourself? Look at us. We're out here in the middle of a meadow completely exposed. We're sitting ducks. I have to be honest; I haven't had a decent night's sleep since I've been here. It's like my brain is half awake. I'm always on guard."

"I personally don't think whoever shot me wants me dead," Andy said.

"I'm sorry, Pops, but whoever shot at you a few days ago almost killed you. My question still stands. What can you do to protect yourself? Isn't there any way you can put an end to what's happening?

Jan and Andy looked at one another, then back at Brian. Andy spoke, "I had a reprieve from the harassment for almost a month. I was beginning to think it was over and I could relax. I thought that whoever was behind all of this had given up. Obviously I was wrong. I've had plenty of time to think about it during my stay in the hospital. Jan and I have come up with an idea about why I was shot. If it turns out to be right, then maybe we can bring a halt to all of this crap. For now we'll just have to wait and see."

Brian hesitated for several moments before speaking. "What happens if you can't bring a halt to it? Whoever's behind this thinks that by virtue of your relationship with Steph, you must know something. You're guilty by association."

"You're right. It doesn't make any difference that I don't know diddly squat. Whoever's behind this thinks differently. I don't think Stephanie meant for any of this to happen. She made a mistake by thinking she would go undiscovered in this out-of-the-way place. I have no idea about where she went from here or even if she's still alive."

"So in the meantime you live in constant jeopardy because of what some asshole thinks. If you knew what it is they wanted and you could give it to them, would you?"

Andy changed the subject completely. "Let's go have a pizza at the pub this evening. Let's celebrate the new house and my recovery." Jan wondered if his intestinal tract could handle pizza. He wasn't sure either but he wanted to give it a try. "The food in the hospital wasn't bad;" adding, "for hospital food."

To Andy's surprise, the entire construction crew showed up the next morning. Dan told him, "we're here to move you into your new house. With all of us working we can probably get everything moved in a couple of hours. All you need to do is direct where you want things." Andy was overwhelmed by this gesture. "It's our way of thanking you and welcoming you home. This was a fun project and you were a pleasure to work for." By noon, everything Andy wanted from the old house was moved into the new one. He promised to have a party for the crew as soon as he was up to it.

Brian stayed for two more days running the shop for his father. The weather had turned unusually hot. The three of them and Cassidy went to the lake each evening and waded up the beach for a mile. Andy had been cautioned not to go swimming to avoid infection. It would be awhile before he could resume working-out or running.

The morning Brian left, he told his father. "I'll be back in a couple of weeks for a few days. I have a bunch of stuff to take care of before I start grad school. I'm glad I was able to be of help and have the experience of being here. I'm just sorry that it happened the way it did. Being here has given me a whole new perspective. I have a real appreciation for what you've been able to accomplish. You're one of my heroes, Pops."

They hugged. Andy thanked him. "I appreciate the compliment, Brian. I'm just an ordinary guy who has bumbled along in life and has ended up having some extraordinary things happen to him. I feel sorry for all those poor boobs who are afraid to risk themselves at anything. Look at all the excitement they're missing."

Brian hugged Jan. "Thanks for everything you've done for Pops, Jan."

"Some day I'll tell you about all the things he's done for me. He has a couple of great sons. He's very proud of both of you."

It was a little after eight when Brian drove down the driveway. "Come on, McLeod, we have an hour before you need to be at the shop. Let's go down to the coffee shop. I'm in the mood for one of those decadent cinnamon rolls."

Upon returning to running the shop, Andy found he had neither the stamina, nor the desire, to be putting in twelve and fourteen hour days. He decided to only take those commission orders that people were willing to wait for. He would get to them when things were slow and he had the time. With Jan's help he threw a party for Dan and the construction crew. She would occasionally join him for a campfire and cookout in the evening. He invited Sheriff Cummings, his wife and Jan for a cookout one evening. Toward the end of August he invited Rob and his girlfriend for dinner. They planned to leave for Alaska by mid-September which was only three weeks away. Rob had put most of his inventory on sale at the very beginning of the season. There wasn't much left. He found another shop owner who offered to buy the remainder. He planned to close his shop after Labor Day; then prepare for the trip. Andy and he settled on a price of five-thousand dollars for Stephanie's car. Rob knew that it was probably worth four times that amount. Rob also knew that they were pushing their luck. They risked running into major snows crossing the Rockies.

Andy was able to resume running and working out on a limited basis. He and Jan discussed the topic of firewood. "Andy, tell me you're not going to have a semi-load of wood delivered this year. I don't think you're up to handling that much wood by yourself. Besides, this house will be much easier to heat. Why not order a few cords of cut and split firewood?" He agreed, in part, because he had a couple cords left over from the previous winter.

Cassidy was always with Andy. He never wandered off from the shop. In the evenings the two of them often walked the beach. Andy had gotten to know several of the summer residents along the way and would stop to visit as they strolled. When Jan was around they would go for occasional walks at Thorsen Point. They always carried weapons with them, as distasteful as that was.

One early unusually hot September evening Jan and he were wading along the beach. She asked, "When are we going to look over the tractor? Aren't you curious about it?"

"I've thought about it. I guess I kind of regard it as a potential Pandora's Box."

"That's what I thought you'd say. I've come up with a plan. I've already discussed it with Sheriff Cummings. How about running an ad to sell it. He's going to act like he's a buyer. He knows a guy who is what they call a jockey. He transports farm implements. He'll come to pick it up and take it to the county garage. A team from the state crime lab will go over it. By doing it this way you won't arouse any suspicions or appear to have any connection to what might be discovered."

He looked at her, "I guess there isn't any question in either of our minds that we're still under surveillance."

"Even out here?" Jan asked.

"This may be one of the few places where we aren't being listened to."

Andy had no objection to the plan. "The fact is I really don't need the tractor for much of anything, not since I've stopped logging for firewood The damn thing doesn't start when it gets below freezing anyhow. It's useless for moving snow. I've been thinking about getting the lower part of the driveway paved. That will eliminate having to repair the driveway every time it rains hard. The only reason I have for keeping the tractor is for nostalgia sake. It's vintage. Ford turned 8Ns out like popcorn after World War Two. They were so affordable, practically every farmer in America had one. One in good shape today is a collector's item."

To make things look good, Andy put an ad in the bi-weekly local newspaper the next day. He had two or three calls about it. Two days later, by arrangement with the sheriff, a truck with a trailer showed up to haul it away. Once it was off his property an unmarked sheriff's car with two deputies escorted the tractor to the county's maintenance garage. A team from the State Crime lab began going over the tractor immediately. They found nothing that day. In the early morning hours there was a large explosion at the garage. The tractor and the area it was being stored in were obliterated by the blast. Sheriff Cummings called Jan early the next morning. He told her about what had happened. They both agreed that it was not an accident. "Goddamn it, Jan, you two were probably right. It's my fault. I should have insisted on sticking with the disassembly process until we had it down to the last nut and bolt or we found whatever it was we were looking for. It means that the spotlight is back on Andy. Whoever's behind this managed to figure out that the arrangements we made were a ruse. It's time to implement plan bravo. Everything is in place." Jan signified her understanding and hung up.

She drove directly to Andy's house. He was up and had just finished exercising. She led him outside. "I'll tell you what's going on in awhile. Get your gun and ammunition, everything else is ready. We have to leave right now." She led the way back into the house and into the guest bedroom. She pulled out two loaded backpacks. "Come on Cassidy." Andy and Cassidy followed her out to her car. She said nothing as she drove toward town. She pulled into the town marina. All she said was, "We're going for a boat ride." They followed her to a large power boat. The engine was running. She introduced herself to the captain and they boarded the boat.

The Captain told her, "We'll arrive at the other side of the lake in about four hours." He asked if either of them was prone to seasickness. They both shook their heads. There was one crew member named Darrel. The captain signaled for him to cast the boat off.

As they departed the marina, Andy asked what was going on. "What about the shop and the house and?"

She interrupted him. "Andy, your tractor was blown up early this morning at the county garage. You know what that means."

Andy nodded. "Draco thinks we have what it is he's been looking for."

"Exactly, we're on our way to Michigan. We'll be met by Federal agents when we get there. I can only hope that he doesn't know we're out here, or where we're going." She asked the captain where something was. He told her. She went down below and returned with a hard shell gun case. She opened it and got out a 30-06 rifle with a scope. "If a boat or an aircraft approaches us in pursuit, we'll try to take them out?" Jan told him. "The sheriff has assigned deputies to guard your house and the shop. Right now we need to concern ourselves with keeping you alive."

Once they were out of the harbor and into open water they were in three to four foot high waves. The boat had a V-hull that cut through them but it was still a rough ride. The waves seemed to increase in size the further out from shore they got. Cassidy curled up just inside the steering compartment. He was trembling. In less than half an hour they could no longer see the Wisconsin shoreline. The visibility was becoming increasingly hazy. It took them more than two hours before they were finally able to make out the thin line of the Michigan shore. Jan asked the Captain where they were headed. He dismissively assured her that they were right on course. "That's not what I asked you," speaking loudly over the engine noise. "Turn thirty degrees to port," she told him."

"That's going to take us way off the planned course," He insisted. "Nobody has informed me of any changes."

She pulled out her pistol, "Andy, take over the steering." She told the Captain to lay down on the deck and put to put his hands behind him. He grudgingly followed her instructions. She cuffed him. The mate watched what was happening without making any kind of move. She told Darrel to get below and stay there. He moved quickly and disappeared down the companionway to the cramped cabin below deck. She leaned over the captain. "Who are you working for?" He said nothing. She backed up to where Andy stood at the helm. "I don't know where he was planning to take us, but it's not where we're supposed to go." She studied the chart and had Andy steer a new course. She pointed to where they were supposed to be going. "If we stay on the course he's got us on, we'll end up here." She pointed.

He shook his head. "How did you know what he was doing?"

"The sheriff and I set this up together. I've been keeping my eye on the compass heading ever since we left the marina. I kept waiting for him to turn more northerly. It wasn't happening. I got suspicious." She touched his back. They saw a freighter heading north a few miles ahead of them.

She went over to the Captain who was laying face down. "You might as well shoot me right now." He said. "If you don't someone else will."

She leaned down close to his ear. "It doesn't have to be that way. Tell me who hired you. We'll take care of you."

He half laughed at her. "Your offer is like some kind of cancer treatment. All that will do is extend my life for awhile."

"Captain, life is terminal. None of us gets out of this alive. Our lives are in just as much jeopardy as yours right now. You were about to deliver us to some very bad people. Did you even know that?"

"Look," he said. "Some guy came to the boat late yesterday afternoon. He flashed an ID and said he was FBI. He said that it had become necessary to change the drop off destination. He told me that he didn't know for sure but that I should be ready to depart early today, maybe even before dawn. He gave me a thousand dollars and told me not to breathe a word of this to anyone."

"All the arrangements for this were made by Sheriff Cummings. Didn't it occur to you to call the sheriff to verify the change of plans?" The captain admitted that he should have. "You're goddamn right you should have. You're not very smart, Captain. In a little while it's going to occur to the people you're supposed to deliver us to that we're not coming. All of us are going to be in danger at that point."

The course change was much less bumpy as they were headed downwind with more of a following sea. Andy opened the throttle. They passed to the west of the Manitou Islands. There were two fuel gauges. One of them was showing close to empty. Andy asked Jan about whether they had enough fuel to make their destination. "There are probably two tanks. We need to switch over to the other one. I'll ask the captain how to do that." Cassidy started barking frantically. They turned to see the Captain hoist himself to a standing position at the stern of the boat; then he lunged overboard. Andy cut the throttle immediately. He grabbed a life preserver and dove overboard swimming furiously toward the Captain, in hopes of reaching him before he disappeared beneath the waves. Jan yelled for Darrel to get up here. He scrambled up from the cabin. He looked green. She guessed that he had gotten sea sick. As soon as Darrel saw what the situation was, he made an almost instant recovery. He took over the controls. It seemed to Jan like everything was happening in slow motion. Darrel brought the boat around into the waves. It was difficult to spot the two men in the water because of the size of the waves. They were completely out of sight in the troughs. Cassidy was atop the engine compartment barking. Andy reached the Captain. He struggled to hold his head above water. Darrel maneuvered the boat just past them; then turned so that the craft would drift towards the two of them. He deftly readied two lines with loops and secured them to a cleat. Moments before they were alongside the Captain and Andy, he jumped into the water. The captain appeared drowned. With great effort he helped Andy get one of the loops around the man. Jan leaned over the port gunnel and reached out for Darrel's hand to help him back over the steep, high side of the pitching boat. It took the two of them to get Andy on board. Andy tried to offer as much assistance as he could in the effort to get the Captain back into the boat. He was a big man and it took every bit of strength the three of them could muster. After several tries, they were finally able to get the Captain out of the water and onto the deck. Jan undid the handcuffs. Andy and Darrel lifted the Captain up by his belt and water poured out of his mouth. They held him in that position for several long moments. When they let him down Jan immediately began doing compressions on his back to try and force more water out of him and get him breathing. They repeated the process three times before the Captain coughed several times and began to breathe on his own. He continued to cough up more water once he was conscious.

Even Jan was soaking wet. All of them were shivering. They

helped the Captain down below and onto the V-birth in the bow of the boat. They covered him with wool blankets. Darrel outfitted the three of them with a variety of coats and foul weather gear that was stowed in one of the boat's lockers. Before they got underway again, he turned a petcock open and turned another one into the closed position. He reported, "I just switched over to the port tank. We've got about six hours range unless we run at full bore." Andy brought the throttle three-quarters open which was the speed the Captain had maintained throughout the lake crossing. Jan showed Darrel what their destination was on the chart. "We should be able to make that easily, especially with this southwest wind." He went below to check on the Captain. When he reappeared several minutes later he carried three steaming cups of coffee. "It's instant coffee," he apologized, "but it's hot, hey." The three of them stayed in the shelter of the wheel house. They finished their coffee and Darrel went to make some more. When he returned he reported that the Captain was breathing. "He looks like he's asleep. I'll keep checking on him, hey." He said, "I had a feeling that he was getting himself inta something he might be sorry for." Jan asked him what he knew about it. "I don't know nothin'. Captain told me he'd pay me two hundred bucks ta take a run across the lake and back, hey. When I asked him what it was about, he told me that he was paying me ta take a boat ride. That's all I needed ta know, hey."

They arrived at the municipal dock in Petoskey by mid afternoon. They were met by three men who identified themselves as FBI agents. All three were dressed in similar suits. Jan filled them in on what had transpired during the lake crossing. She advised that the Captain needed to be taken to the nearest hospital. "He was nearly drowned. We were able to resuscitate him, but he's still coughing up water. There's a chance he's developing pneumonia." The head agent, Mark Kelly, said that arrangements would be made to fly Darrel back home. "No, wait a minute." Andy said. "The bad guys are going to assume Darrel knows where we are. He needs to stay with us." Kelly said that he wasn't authorized to do that. "I don't care what you're authorized to do. I'm telling you that this poor guy is in danger if you send him back. He's coming with us." Kelly placed a cell phone call. Whoever he was calling was not immediately available. Jan asked if they could use the marina's facilities to shower and change into dry clothes before they were taken anywhere.

When they rejoined the agents, Kelly told them that arrangements had been made with the sheriff's department for Darrel to be picked up at the airport by deputies. He would be protected by them. He asked whose dog it was that they had with them. Andy said it was his. "Look, this is turning into a three-ring circus. You're going to have to make some arrangements for the dog to go to a local kennel or something."

"That's not going to happen. The dog goes with us." Andy told him. Jan was frowning. Andy could see that she was uncomfortable with the whole situation.

"Look I've had all the ultimatums I'm going to put up with," Agent Kelly said, as he tried to stare Andy down.

Jan intervened, affecting a pleasant tone. "Agent Kelly, I appreciate that you were not completely informed about all the details of this operation. I deal with that all the time." She calmly gave him a quick synopsis of the past and about how Andy had come to lose his beloved Lucy. She told him how important Cassidy was to the both of them and that neither of them could, or would, abandon the dog."

"Look Detective, it's just a damn dog. Thousands of them are being put to sleep daily. He can get another one."

She maintained her composure. "Well, in that case I guess the only solution to this impasse is for you to take us back to the boat and we'll manage on our own."

He stood firm. "That's not an option. I'm told that you and Mr. McLeod's lives are in danger as a result of your involvement in a high level investigation. I have to do everything in my power to keep the two of you alive."

Jan asked, "Where are you supposed to take us from here?"

"I'm not at liberty to tell you that."

Jan paced a few steps, turned and paced back a couple of times, looking down. "Agent Kelly, how do we know that the sheriff is going to provide protection for Darrel?" Kelly told her she would just have to take his word for it. She paced some more. It was obvious he wanted to get on with the business at hand. "I think I need to talk with Sheriff Cummings. I'm just not comfortable with what's happening here." Kelly said that she could talk to him when they got to where they were going. "No, I want to talk to him right now before we go anywhere. May I borrow your cell phone?" Kelly told her that he doubted they were within range of being able to reach the Sheriff by cell phone. "Okay then, I have a long distance calling card. I'll use the land line in the marina office to call him."

Kelly responded by telling her, "Look detective, you're putting all of us, everyone involved here, at risk. We need to get this show on the road. The chances are increasing exponentially that the bad guys are going to show up. The sand is running out."

Jan looked up at him. "Well you have a decision to make right now. We're not going anywhere with you unless Darrel and Cassidy come along." Andy could sense that her instincts were on red alert. "I suggest you contact the powers that be to make those arrangements."

Kelly looked to Andy hoping for some sympathy. Andy looked just as determined as Jan. "Mr. McLeod, can you try to reason with her. All we're trying to do is provide the two of you with protection. I was led to believe that it was just going to be the two of you and the Captain. I'm just trying to do my job. I'm in no position to go beyond what I've been assigned to do. Now, all of a sudden I'm being viewed as a bad guy. We have to get going right now."

"Agent Kelly, you make it sound like the bad guys know where we are and that they're going to show up at any moment. I know Sheriff Cummings well enough to know that in planning for this 'operation' he would have provided the FBI with complete details. There seems to be some gaps in the information you were given. My experience with the bad guys, which is extensive, is this. If they wanted us dead, that could have happened anytime over the past four hours. They've had plenty of opportunity before now."

There was a long delay before his response. "Okay, we'll figure out a way to bring the dog. I don't have the authority to include transporting the crew member."

"That's not good enough." Andy said. "Darrel comes too."

"That's it. I'm done trying to reason with you people." Kelly and the other two agents exposed their weapons. "You're coming with us whether you want to or not."

Andy took Jan's arm. He whistled for Cassidy. "Come on Darrel."

"Where do you think you're going?" Kelly said incredulously.

"Shopping," Jan said. "Then back home." They began walking toward the business district.

Kelly caught up with them. "Okay, I'm going to have a lot of explaining to do over this. We'll figure something out for Darrel."

Jan insisted that the three of them and Cassidy ride in one car. The other two agents could follow in the other. Kelly drove the car they were in. Jan asked him to find a fast food restaurant. "We haven't eaten since last night. We're starved." He reluctantly pulled into a McDonalds where Jan insisted he pay for their meals. "I'm sure you have an expense account, Agent Kelly." After leaving the McDonalds Jan directed him to stop at a grocery store where Andy bought some dry dog food for Cassidy. He fed the dog in the parking lot; then walked him. It was mid-afternoon when they reached the Petoskey airport where a helicopter waited on a grassy area away from the short runways.

A piper cub was descending toward the airport from the north.

Kelly took note of it as they got out of the cars. He gestured to the other two agents who began walking quickly toward the runway area. "It may be nothing, but..." He told them he'd be back in a few minutes as he started toward what looked like a small office building a hundred yards away.

Jan whispered to Andy, "There's no one around. It's a beautiful day. Wouldn't you think there would be a fair amount of air traffic? Where's the chopper pilot?"

Andy took hold of Darrel's arm. "Are there any other towns close by?" Darrel said the town of Charlevoix was almost straight east. The town of Harbor Springs was just north of Petoskey. Darrel figured they had traveled perhaps four or five miles to get to the airport. Jan and Andy shouldered their packs. "Come on," Andy said. They started walking swiftly toward a pine forest at the south end of airfield. The trees were no more than twenty-feet in height. No one seemed to notice. When they were close to the woods, they broke into a run.

It was past sunset when they finally stopped to rest. Andy asked, "Now what? We can't go back to the boat. They'll expect us to show up there. Where do we go from here?"

"That was too easy." Jan whispered. "It's almost like they wanted us to get away."

"I like your premise, but it's going to be dark in another hour or so. The temperature is already dropping. My question still stands."

Jan turned to Darrel. "What do you think Darrel. Which way would you go from here?"

Darrel pointed to the north. "Charlevoix is too far. Harbor Springs is closer." He thought the agents had driven south and east out of Petoskey to get to the airport. He couldn't recall exactly but he thought that Little Traverse Bay extended further east before the shoreline curved to the north toward Harbor Springs. It grew dark as they made their way. Darrel asked if either of them could tell him what this was all about. Jan told him that maybe they could explain it to him later, but not right now. The less he knew the better for him. Darrel commented. "It sounds and looks to me like a cat and mouse game and we're the mice, hey." Jan told him that she and Andy didn't know for sure what it was all about either.

Andy asked Jan, "do you think this is a set up? Do you think we're being used as decoys or bait? Maybe they're hoping to catch some of the bad guys when they make a move to get us. What if the whole place is surrounded by federal agents?"

Jan said. "Too many maybes, McLeod."

Darrel asked why they had stood up for him. Andy told him, "Darrel, neither you nor the Captain knew what you were getting yourselves into, you especially. You're an innocent victim. The Captain should have suspected something wasn't right when that guy showed up with the change of plans and cash. We're both sorry that you had to get mixed up in this. We're going to do everything we can to get you home safely."

Darrel asked, "So, how come you don't trust those FBI guys?"

"We're not exactly sure that's what they are," Jan told him. "It was pretty obvious that Kelly didn't want me talking to my boss, Sheriff Cummings."

After a long silence Darrel asked, "if they're not FBI, then who they are? How are we going to get out of here?"

They heard the low throb of a helicopter approaching not far off. "Shit, if they have an infrared sensor on that thing they'll be able to detect us from our body heat," Jan said. They had just come to a barbed wire fence. A mercury vapor light illuminating a farmhouse and a barn shown at some distance, across a large, fenced-in field. "Come on," Andy said. He rolled under the fence. Darrel and Jan followed. She asked what he was doing. "Stay close to me." He began jogging in the direction of the farmhouse. They could see a searchlight on the chopper sweeping back and forth as it drew closer. They came to a steel manger fifty yards from the barn. It was half full of hay. "Get in," he instructed. Jan and Darrel clambered over its bars. "Cover yourselves with hay; a lot of hay." Andy rolled underneath holding on to Cassidy. The chopper was no more than sixty feet off the ground. It passed over slowly but continued on. It turned to the right three or four minutes later and started moving in a southwesterly direction, back toward the airport.

They left the manger and headed in a southerly direction until they had circumvented the farm house. They could hear a dog barking in the distance. The drone of the helicopter grew fainter as it continued its search further to the west. They came to a paved road. Andy said, "the airport is back that way to the west. They must think that we're heading for Charlevoix."

Chapter 17

It was three in the morning when they arrived in Harbor Springs. They had taken refuge in ditches and brush three or four times along the way when they heard oncoming vehicles. They found their way to the public marina. It took them awhile to find a boat that was not locked. It was a sailboat that had a 'For Sale' sign on it. Jan wanted to take off in it immediately. Andy argued, "That will be too obvious. There's no wind. What would a sailboat be doing out there before daylight? Besides, what if the owner shows up and finds it missing. The first thing he'll do is call the cops." They decided to wait and try to get some sleep. Darrell took the starboard quarter berth. Andy and Jan crawled into the V-birth in the bow. Cassidy curled up on the cabin floor.

Before falling asleep, Jan commented that this was a nice boat. "We ought to buy it." Andy was already asleep. When he awakened at five, it was barely light. He took Cassidy for a short walk and got him some water. He returned Cassidy to the boat; then he strolled down the street. He liked the feel of this small town with its many unique shops and galleries. He found a small restaurant that had just opened. He got three coffees to go and a half-dozen donuts. He had very little cash on him. When he returned to the boat he went about studying its details. It was fairly well equipped. It had a sail drive engine, which was a modified version of an outboard engine that was mounted through the hull of the boat rather than on the stern. It had about half a tank of gas. When Darrel and Jan woke up, he offered them coffee and pointed out to where the marina's toilet facilities were located. While they were gone he got the engine started. When Jan returned, he suggested she stay below with Cassidy.

Darrell had no experience with sailboats. "I'll show you what to do. If you steer I can manage putting up the sails." Andy judged the boat to be about twenty-five feet long. There were no charts on board. "The wind is southeasterly right now, what little there is of it." Andy asked Darrel, "If we sail due west, where will we end up on the other side of the lake?"

He wasn't sure. He thought close to Washington Island, just north of the Door Peninsula.

Darrel offered that if they followed the Michigan coastline south, they might be able to make it to the Manitou Islands by evening. "If the wind direction holds we can cross the lake from there tomorrow, hey. There's a lot of freighter traffic moving up and down the lake. We don't want to get in the way of one of those babies. From a distance you can't tell it, but they're moving at close to fifteen knots, maybe more, hey. They could run right over us and not know they'd hit a thing."

Andy decided to see what the day would bring. He thought they might attract less attention if they appeared to be out for a day's sail and stayed close to the Michigan shoreline. They took an accounting of their money. Between them they had close to fifty dollars. Darrel suggested that they could put in at the town of Charlevoix to buy gas and get some provisions.

The harbormaster had not yet arrived at the marina when they cast off a few minutes before seven. Once they were out of the harbor Andy raised the sails. The breeze was beginning to freshen out of the south and they romped along at a fair pace. The boat handled well. Jan had found a rain suit and a watch hat in one of the lockers below. Andy put them on. It was much cooler out on the lake. Around nine o'clock they heard the thumping sound of a helicopter approaching from the east. It flew low overhead but didn't slow down. It changed direction a short while later, heading south. Darrel found a small jar of instant coffee. He figured out how to light the alcohol stove and heated some water. They took turns using a measuring cup as a coffee mug. Jan was able to coax Cassidy into peeing into a plastic dish pan.

"I really like this boat, Andy. A couple of people could live aboard something like this comfortably for several days. What do you think a boat like this is worth?"

Andy smiled, "The 'for sale' sign has a phone number. Why don't you call the owner and say, 'Hi, this is one of the people who just stole the boat you have for sale. We were just wondering what you're asking for it." Darrel was napping.

Jan brought Cassidy up on deck. She sat next to Andy. "You look really tired, Andy." He admitted that he was. He showed her how to steer the boat using a compass heading. He curled up on the other side of the cockpit to take a nap and quickly fell asleep.

An hour later Jan saw a very large boat appear, as if it were emerging from the eastern shoreline. Darrell had just come on deck. She asked him about the large boat. "I think that's the ferry that runs between Charlevoix and Kewaunee."

"We're probably a couple of hours away from Charlevoix." Andy awakened and took over manning the tiller. He pointed the boat up as close as he could in a southerly direction. It took them close to four hours before they reached the municipal marina in Charlevoix. The harbor master gave them permission to tie up for a couple of hours without charge. He gave them directions to a small grocery store. Jan took Darrel with her to pick up some provisions.

Andy bought two gallons of gas. He studied a large chart that was on the wall of the harbor-master's office. He asked if he could have a piece of paper and a pencil and started to draw out a portion of the map. The man watched what he was doing. "Don't you have a chart for this part of the lake?" Andy shook his head. The harbor-master reached under the counter. He found a stack of charts and found one that pertained to northern Lake Michigan. It was very used. It had coffee stains on it and had been refolded so many times the fold lines were beginning to tear apart. "Here, you can have this." He used some tape to mend the chart's folds. Andy thanked him. "Where are you from?"

Andy lied, "We're from the upper peninsula. A little town north of Escanaba, called Gladstone."

"Never heard of it. You should have an easy trip across the lake. The wind is supposed to stay southeasterly for at least another day. Sounds like storms are moving in though. It might get rough out there by Friday afternoon. The only protected harbors on the west side of the lake are Sturgeon Bay and Baileys Harbor. He pointed to them on the large wall chart. The whole east shore of the Door Peninsula is treacherous. The bottom's all rock. No safe place to anchor." Andy thanked him for the map and the information.

When Jan and Darrell returned, they were both carrying a couple bags each. He asked how they had managed to buy that much with so little money. "I took a chance and used my credit card. One of us needs to go back. I forgot to get dog food." Darrell volunteered. Andy asked the harbor master if he could buy three towels. The man smiled. He went to a closet and got out several, somewhat ragged towels and gave them to him. "You folks didn't come very well prepared did you?"

Andy told him. "A friend of ours drove us over here to take delivery of this boat. We just bought it yesterday. You're right; we didn't think to stock up on several things. That wasn't very smart of us."

The harbor master commented, "that's one of the best sailboats made. It's made down in Holland, Michigan which is quite a ways south of here." He pointed to Holland on the wall chart. He asked Andy what he had paid for the boat. Andy asked him to take a guess. He asked how old it was. Andy took a wild guess himself and told him that it was made in the early nineteen-eighties. "Well, I'd say the owner took exceptional care of it. I'm going to guess, somewhere between twelve to fifteen thousand dollars. Is it pretty well equipped?"

Andy told him it was. It did have some basic electronics. "The man was asking twenty-thousand, but we got it for three thousand less." The harbor master thought that was a fair price.

Back at the boat, Jan pulled Andy aside. "I've been thinking. How would you feel about sending Darrel back on the ferry to Kewanee? I need to call Sheriff Cummings to let him know what's going on. He can arrange for somebody to pick Darrel up."

Andy had another suggestion. "I've been thinking about sending Darrel back to Petoskey. The Captain is probably going to need help in getting back across the lake." Jan's only objection was that they didn't know what plans had been made to protect the Captain. She decided to call Sheriff Cummings.

She used a pay phone and her long distance card. She was put right through to the Sheriff who sounded concerned, but at the same time relieved to be hearing from her. Jan gave him a brief summary of what had happened with the 'alleged FBI agents'. Sheriff Cummings was extremely dismayed by what she told him. "Goddamnit, I can't believe what's going on. I've been worried sick about you two. Kelly made it sound like all of you walked into a trap at the airport. He wasn't sure in the melee that ensued, whether you and Andy had managed to get away or were captured. He said they were continuing to search for the two of you. You're telling me that his story is bullshit." She told him that there hadn't been any melee; that they had walked away so easily, they suspected it had been intended as some sort of set up. While Sheriff Cummings was a no-nonsense kind of guy, Jan had never seen him display anger in all the time she had known him. As she told him about the experience they had in dealing with Kelly, she could sense he was growing furious. "I'm going to charter a plane as soon as we hang up. I'll be over to get the two of you in the next two or three hours. Screw the FBI; we'll take care of this ourselves. I'm going to have this Kelly guy's job. I've always been skeptical about dealing with the FBI. This goes beyond incompetence. This is criminal."

It took a few minutes for the sheriff to calm himself to where Jan could propose an alternate plan. She explained that they had the first mate Darrel with them. She made the suggestion of either putting Darrel on the next ferry leaving for Wisconsin or seeing about having him accompany the captain who had brought them to Michigan. "You're not going to like this part, Sheriff." She continued. "We kind of commandeered a sailboat without the owner's knowledge or permission. It will take us several hours to sail it back to the marina we took it from. We're hoping the owner hasn't reported it missing. It's for sale. It's a nice boat, big enough to live on. If Andy and I can work out a deal to buy it, maybe we can sail it back. No one will think to look for us in the middle of Lake Michigan." Sheriff Cummings told her to call him back in an hour. He was going to check on the captain's condition. He would try to call the chief of police in Harbor Springs to explain the situation. He was giving serious consideration to contacting Agent Kelly's superiors.

Jan discussed her conversation with Sheriff Cummings with Andy. He shook his head. "What a bald faced lie. Kelly's story goes beyond ass-covering. The man is a sociopath. If the FBI fires him today, the CIA will probably hire him by noon tomorrow." She presented the idea of sailing the boat back to Harbor Springs and contacting the owner to see about buying it. "Jan, I can't afford to buy a boat like this. Even if I could, it would be a waste of money. I haven't got time to spend sailing. Summers are just too damn busy. Last but not least, I can't afford what it would cost to store it every winter."

Jan called Sheriff Cummings back as arranged. He had calmed down. "The Captain has already been released from the hospital. He's apparently returned to his boat. I'm waiting to hear from the Petoskey police. If he hasn't left the marina and he's willing to wait for Darrel, we can go with that plan. If not, the department will pay to fly Darrel back here via a chartered plane. Call me when you get to Harbor Springs. I've already talked to the police chief there. They haven't received any reports of a stolen sailboat. I explained the circumstances. He'll take care of it if a report does come in." Jan told him they probably wouldn't get back to Harbor Springs before midnight. She'd call him in the morning. Before hanging up he asked what the price of the boat was. She didn't know. "Well, if it's not too much the department has some emergency funds I can tap into on a short-term basis. It would have to be a loan."

It was late in the afternoon when they left Charlevoix. The wind was still southerly but light. By dusk it had diminished entirely. A veil of high thin clouds was beginning to spread in from the west. It reminded Andy of autumn evenings when he was a youth. Back then, people were still allowed to burn fallen leaves. The smoke from the burning leaves cast a gauze-like haze to the evening light. When Andy turned on the running lights, the battery was so low that they were barely visible. He had to start the sail drive engine by hand. Running it however, served to recharge the battery. He lowered the sails and they motored the remainder of the way to Harbor Springs arriving close to the estimated midnight hour.

They were awakened at seven in the morning by someone knocking on one of the cabin windows. Andy got up and made his way up on deck. A short, stout, fireplug of a man dressed in a police uniform stood on the dock. "I'm Chief of Police Rowe," he introduced himself. Andy gave his name and invited him aboard. They shook hands. Jan emerged from the cabin moments later. "I trust you are aware that, Sheriff Cummings called me yesterday?" They both nodded. "Sounds like you folks have had more than a little excitement. Is everything okay? You haven't had any run-ins with anybody since yesterday?"

"So far so good," Andy told him. The chief told them that he doubted anyone had even noticed that the boat was missing. He asked if Darrel was still with them. "He's asleep down below." Andy said.

"Well his captain is still at the marina in Petoskey. I can run him over there if he wants to make the return trip with the captain. The captain wants to get going before the weather turns." Andy went to get Darrel while Jan answered some of the chief's questions about what had happened. Before Darrel left, he thanked the two of them for what they had done for him. The chief said he would stop back later on.

They showered in the marina's facilities; then went to get some breakfast. When they got back, Andy placed a call to the boat owner. He didn't get an answer. He went into the marina office and asked the harbor master about the sail boat that was for sale. "That boat's been for sale for over two years. The guy that owns it had a serious stroke about three years ago. His wife will practically give it away just to cut her losses and be rid of it. One of her kids convinced her to put it in the water this year thinking that would help to sell it. She's paid the slip fee for the whole season. I agreed to refund her whatever portion was not used, if it sold before the end of the season, but she'll probably give you the rest of the time that's left on the slip rental. I don't know for sure, but I don't think she's had any inquiries." Andy said that he tried calling the number on the sign, but no one answered. "She's probably at the nursing home. Try again in awhile." The harbor master commented, "It's a hell of a nice boat. It's made here in Michigan. I'm surprised that it hasn't sold. I guess the used boat market is just glutted." They chatted for a few more minutes.

Andy reached the owner's wife on his third try. She told him that she had lowered the price on the boat three times. She was now asking ten thousand, but she would consider taking a little less. He asked her how much less. She hesitated. She tried to get him to make an offer. Finally she said. "I refuse to go below eight thousand, but I'll let you have the slip for the remainder of the season. It's all paid for." Andy told her he would call her back shortly. He needed to consult with his partner.

When he told Jan about it he said, "I'm going to offer her nine thousand. We'll be out of here in a few days; then she can get a refund on the slip rental."

Jan smiled at him. "You truly are a bleeding-heart, McLeod. I don't know of anyone who would offer a seller more than what the seller's bottom line was. On top of it, you want to get her a refund."

She called Sheriff Cummings. He sounded almost jovial. "Half of the damn world is out there looking for you. I don't know if that includes the bad guys but the Feds claim to be frantically searching for your butts. I think they're scared the bad guys have already found you. I didn't say anything to the contrary. Screw em." Jan assured him that they were fine. She briefed him on Darrel, on meeting the Harbor Springs police chief and the pending deal on the boat. She asked him about his offer to send her some money. He asked how much. When she told him ten-thousand dollars his only response was to ask if that would be enough. He told her that he would make an electronic transfer to the First National Bank in Harbor Springs within the hour. "You two be careful. Keep me posted and let me know when and where you plan to arrive, I'll have the cavalry there to meet you."

Andy called the boat owner's wife back and told her he wanted the boat. He asked when they could meet. She said that she would come to the marina early that afternoon. He got the impression she wanted to consummate the deal quickly, before he had a change of heart. When the woman showed up, they were both surprised at how young she appeared. Jan guessed that she was in her late thirties to early forties. They had expected someone much older. They wondered if her husband was her same age. Andy introduced Jan as his wife. The three of them visited for awhile. She never asked where they were from. She told them there was a trailer for the boat. It was parked behind the garage at her house. "That was one of my husband's major considerations in buying the boat. He wanted something that could be stored at home rather than paying to store it somewhere else during the winter months." Andy asked if it would be possible for her to keep the trailer at her place for the time being. She was agreeable but wanted to know when he planned to get it. He told her that he would need to borrow a friend's vehicle. He didn't think his car was capable of pulling it. He said it might be three or four weeks. "Jesse, my husband, loved that boat. We bought it brand new and sailed it up here from Holland, which is where it was made. We hoped to be able to take some extensive cruises on it. He wanted to go up to the North Channel in Canada for a few weeks. He clung to that dream until his second stroke. Now it's doubtful that he'll even be able to walk ever again." After completing the transaction, she parted on a philosophical note. "You never know what kind of cards life is going to deal you. Jesse always said, do it before you can't." She wished them happy sailing.

After she left, Jan commented, "She seems like a nice lady. I wonder if her husband is a lot older than she. It would be even more tragic if he was crippled at a young age." She tried to shake off the gloomy thought. "I'm looking forward to us spending some time on this boat."

Andy reminded her that she had objected to going canoeing with him a few weeks before. "If I recall, your excuse was that you 'weren't a water person'."

She ignored him. "I think we should go buy a couple bottles of wine, don't you?" Andy fashioned a leash for Cassidy. They went to the grocery store and bought three bottles of wine and a twelve pack of non-alcohol beer. On the way back to the boat they talked about their situation and what they were going to do next. "I know this may sound strange, Andy, but despite everything that has happened, I feel happier and more alive than I have ever felt in my life. I think we've gotten along quite well given the circumstances. I have a feeling things are going to work out."

Andy wasn't sure what that meant. Which things was she referring to? He opted for the topic of Stephanie vs. Draco. He proffered his latest theory. "What if the bad guy or guys is not some sinister villain that the government is out to get? What if Stephanie's the real villain? What if she swiped something important and/or valuable? What if the FBI and somebody else are in a race to find the Holy Grail? The FBI let us go too easily. Maybe we're doing just what they want us to. We're running around out here trying to avoid being caught. That gets us out of the way without it costing them anything. I can't help feeling that they know exactly where we are."

"McLeod, stop it. Don't you ever get tired of these stupid 'what-ifs'? They were nearing the marina. "I think we should take our sweet time getting back. Let's go cruising for a week or two. We've got money left over from what the Sheriff sent us. We can have a nice vacation. We can enjoy ourselves for the next several days. It might even make some people happy. Maybe all this crap will be over by the time we get back home." She looked at Cassidy, "What do you think?" He barked and she petted him. "You want to go for a swim don't you?"

Andy spent much of the day going over the boat. He and Jan cleaned it. He familiarized himself with all of its systems. He commented more than once on the quality of the boat's construction and how well designed and equipped it was. They started a list of things they needed to get. By late that afternoon the weather began to change. The wind was beginning to come around to the north and it was increasing. Jan asked him what they would do if they encountered a major storm while they were out in the middle of the lake. He explained how they could reduce the sails by reefing them. "If it got to be really nasty we can drop the sails completely and use the engine." By evening the temperature had dropped fifteen degrees and it rained torrentially off and on.

They fixed a simple dinner and snuggled together under a blanket in the V-berth. "We need to get a couple of sleeping bags and pillows before we leave," Jan said. He suggested a deck of cards and a maybe a board game also.

When they arose in the morning it was a sunny, cool, clear day. They asked the harbor master where they could find the things on the list they had compiled. He gave them directions and even let them the use an old pickup truck that belonged to the town. "I'm really glad to see that boat sold. It's a nice boat. It was Jesse's pride and joy."

They spent the next several hours procuring the things on their list, and preparing to leave. Andy decided they would sail to the Manitou Islands; spend a day or two there, then sail across the lake when the weather looked favorable for a safe crossing. Leaving early the next morning and with a brisk northwest wind, they made it to the Islands by late afternoon. They anchored and swam. Along with Cassidy, they hiked the south Manitou Island for two days. Their second night, another sailboat that was passing through, anchored close to them. The skipper said the wind was supposed to turn to the southwest and freshen to twenty knots the next day. He was on his way back to Detroit. "If the weather guys are right, you'll be able to make Washington Island easily by late afternoon." He invited them aboard his boat for cocktails that evening. His boat was much larger, bordering on pretentious. He applauded Jan and Andy on their choice of boats. "You've got everything a person needs in the way of comfort, quality and convenience. I like my boat but I'm a slave to it. My next boat is going to be one like yours."

Andy and Jan left before six the next morning. He decided to reef the mainsail before getting underway, as the wind was still strong. Jan didn't understand any of what he was doing. In less than two hours they were completely out of sight of land. They spotted five or six freighters moving south. He told her that when they got closer to the west side of the lake they would probably see more of them heading north. They took turns manning the tiller. By mid-afternoon they could begin to make out the shoreline of the Door Peninsula. "God Andy, how do sailors do this if they're crossing the ocean? I'd go nuts having to sit here steering this thing for days on end." He explained that long distance ocean sailors used efficient, self-steering devices that kept the boat on course. "They need to check the compass heading occasionally to make sure they're on course." She asked him a number of questions about sailing. He was able to answer most of them. He showed her on the chart approximately where they were and where they were headed.

In the early evening he spotted Washington Island. They were headed straight for it. He opened a bottle of wine and they sat in the cockpit watching the sun descend behind the peninsula. As the light faded, the temperature began to drop. Jan went below to get a sleeping bag for herself and a hooded sweatshirt for him. He helped her to wrap herself up in it. She sat across from him. "You know, Andy, from what I've seen, most couples lose interest in one another after awhile. They may start out being attentive toward one another but as time goes by they seem to drift apart." She asked him how he felt about their relationship after being together every hour of the day these past few days.

"I think we've gotten along quite well. I've enjoyed being with you. You pitch right in and you're eager to learn. I think we work well together in lots of ways." Andy chuckled. "My initial impression of you was that you were a complete ditz that lived in utter chaos and had no control over your life."

"I was a mess when we first met. You know that," Jan said. "About all I had going for me back then was that I bathed and made my bed everyday. A lot of times I didn't do laundry for weeks. I'd often throw stuff out and just go to the resale shop and buy different stuff. I've said this to you before, Andy. You've done a lot to help me turn my self around. I'd given up on myself in a lot of ways. I can't tell you how alive I feel now. I'm glad we're friends. I confess that I'm enjoying being a fugitive. What an adventure this has turned out to be."

It was almost dark when they dropped anchor in Washington Island's Detroit Harbor. There was barely a breeze. Andy asked if she had ever been skinny dipping before. She had not. "Come on, lose your clothes." He was already stripping. He went below and got towels and soap and set up the boarding ladder.

"Are you nuts McLeod? What if people see us?" He ignored her and dove in.

"Come on. The water's nice. It's actually warmer than the air. Look, I'm standing up. It's less than five feet deep right here. Toss me the soap." Before she would undress she made him turn his back. When she was naked, she gingerly lowered herself into the water from the ladder. She agreed that the water was pleasant. Even though it was almost dark, she insisted that he keep his back turned. They took turns washing. He allowed her to get back on board the boat first. She dried herself as best she could. The night air and the lack of any breeze made it impossible to dry herself completely. He asked her if she could lift Cassidy over the side. After she did, Andy waded and Cassidy swam their way to shore. Cassidy took awhile to take care of his business. He first had to sniff out these new surroundings. When he was done, the two of them swam back out to the boat. It was much more difficult getting the wet dog back on board. Andy decided he needed to manufacture a sling and a way to lift Cassidy using a rope system. Jan averted her eyes as Andy climbed back aboard. He dried himself and wrestled his jeans and shirt back on. There were some mosquitoes, but they weren't bad. The bats were out and swooping all around them, gorging themselves on insects. Andy went below and lit a mosquito coil. There was a screen for the companionway. He inserted it to keep the cabin bug free. In the meantime, Jan fed Cassidy. There was heat lightening off to the west. They sat opposite one another in the cockpit.

Both of them were silent for quite awhile. It was Jan who broke the silence with an apology. Andy asked her for what. "I'm embarrassed. I have such a ridiculous looking body. I don't want anybody to see me naked. I hate even going to the doctor for that very reason." He asked her if her modesty was because of what had happened in her past. "Maybe some, but mostly it's how I look. I've got silly looking boobs, no hips, a flat butt, skinny legs and I'm flabby. I exercise, and I've gotten a lot better about watching what I eat. None of that seems to help. I just feel ugly." He remained silent. "Look at you. You take care of yourself and it shows. When I was in my very best physical condition, a few years ago, I still looked like a potato with sticks for legs."

Andy poured more wine for himself. Jan was nursing her last N.A. beer. He had her lean forward and he put the sleeping bag behind her, pulling it over her shoulders. He sat down next to her and pulled it up over his shoulders as well. "Is that why you used to dress the way you did when I first met you?"

He half expected her to take some degree of offense to his question. Instead she said, "I figure if God gave me a clown body, I might as well dress like one."

He gave a slight laugh. "I don't know, Jan. I've seen you several times when you've made the effort to look nice. You looked terrific in my opinion. Actually, I like you dressed the way you are right now in jeans and a sweatshirt." He pushed his luck. "What's your natural hair color?" She told him it was kind of a mouse brown. She told him she began dying it when she started running away from home in her early teens. It had been part of her attempt to disguise herself and to try to make herself look older.

"That's another thing. Look at my stupid hair. It's thin. It's frizzy. It's fucking unmanageable."

"What do you like about yourself?" She asked him if he meant physically. "Whatever," he said.

"I'm not stupid." He agreed. "I have a quick wit at times." He'd seen that from time to time. "I've learned how to make my paranoia work for me. It's one of the things that contributes to my being a fairly good detective." He was glad that she saw herself as being good at what she did. Her mood lightened to the point that she was finally able to say, "The water felt good and I feel much better having had the chance to bathe."

"You smell a lot better too," he told her. She reached over and pinched his arm.

They were up early the next morning. Andy went in the water and led Cassidy to shore again. While they were gone, Jan made them some breakfast. When they left Washington Island they sailed north along the west shore of the island. The wind was light out of the southeast and progress was slow. Andy commented that they hadn't seen any helicopters in over thirty-six hours. Her response was, "that doesn't necessarily mean they've stopped looking for us. For all we know, they've bugged the boat and are tracking us every second of the day. Incidentally, where are we heading?"

"There's a place called Fayette to the north." He answered. "It was a thriving little iron smelting town that started up shortly after the Civil War. It died out toward the end of the nineteenth century. The State of Michigan is in the process of restoring it. It has a nice, safe, little harbor with a dock. The boys and I visited it several years ago. They had just come to live with me. I want to see what it looks like now. I think you'll like it."

He was standing up close to her, manning the tiller. "A part of me doesn't want this to end, Andy." They stopped at Rock Island, just north of Washington Island, late in the morning. The three of them went for a long hike. They decided to stay there overnight and leave early the next day. There was hardly any wind when they left Rock Island. They motored nearly three hours. They encountered a huge freighter coming through the Rock Island Passage. The behemoth plowed by to their stern. Minutes later, they experienced its wake. The wind began to shift from the southeast to the southwest and increase. Andy raised the sails and for close to three hours they made steady progress northward. It was late afternoon when Andy noticed a dramatic change in the sky to the northwest. He pointed it out to Jan. "There's a frontal system approaching. It looks like it's moving pretty fast and it looks nasty." They were nearing the southern tip of the Garden peninsula. He quickly studied the charts. "I was hoping to make it to here." He showed her the small harbor at Fayette State Park to the north. "I think we better head for here." He pointed to another small bay that was much closer. "If I'm right, we're going to see some extremely strong wind. Within twenty minutes the wind shifted. Andy lowered the sails and started the engine. The wind began to increase radically from the west and then to the northwest. Jan went below to put on warmer clothes. Andy was in shorts only. She got jeans and a sweatshirt for him.

The wind was already gusting to over thirty miles per hour as they entered Sec Bay. The harbor was protected except from the south. Andy dropped anchor in the northwest corner of the bay just as it started raining. They all took refuge below, watching as a spectacular storm swept over them. The gigantic cumulus nimbus clouds looked like huge charcoal boulders. There was fierce lightening all around them. Andy could only guess but he reckoned that some of the wind gusts were in excess of fifty miles per hour. Jan admitted that she was scared. She asked what would happen if the anchor didn't hold. He told her that he was watching for that. The boat was swinging like a lassoed mustang trying to break free. "If we start to drag I'll have to start the engine, pull up the anchor, and try again. We've got another smaller anchor. I'll try setting that as a stern anchor to stop our swinging back and forth like this." She expressed fear about him being out on deck. The lightening was striking almost continuously. The anchor held. The worst of the storm passed in less than an hour. The sun reappeared, creating a vivid, double rainbow to the east of them. The tail end of one of the rainbows appeared to terminate right into the water, maybe two hundred yards to their east. Neither of them had ever seen such a sight before. Jan said that she wished she had a camera. "I doubt that a camera could capture what we're seeing right now." He told her. The sound of the thunder grew increasingly faint as the storm continued out over the north end of Lake Michigan. Andy re-anchored the boat closer into shore and he set a stern anchor; then the three of them waded ashore to take a hike. The bottom was interspersed with sand but it was mostly slippery, moss-covered rock that made it difficult to negotiate. They added old tennies or wading shoes to the list of things to have on board.

By evening the sky was completely clear. Andy told Jan that a strong, high pressure system was over them now. "It's probably going to be clear for the next two or three days. Hopefully the wind will settle down tonight."

That evening they sat in the cockpit bundled in their sleeping bags. Jan sat with her back to Andy between his legs. The stars seemed almost tangible. They saw numerous meteors and satellites. She commented on the contrast between the earlier storm and now. "How did you know that we needed to seek shelter right away? I mean we could see the storm coming but I never would have guessed that it was moving that quickly or with so much force."

He told her that he'd witnessed several such storms in the past. "They seldom last for more than an hour but it can be a terrifying hour if you're caught in it. We were lucky we were this close to a safe harbor." Because of the strong northwesterly breeze and the cool temperatures, they weren't bothered by mosquitoes. They dozed off in the cockpit. It was close to midnight when they awakened and retired to the cabin.

The next morning Andy went ashore with Cassidy. They weighed anchor and under reefed sails, they set out for Fayette again. When they arrived in the middle of the afternoon there were two or three dock spaces open. One of the other boat owners assisted them in docking their boat. The man assumed they were from Michigan because of the registration sticker on the bow of the boat. He asked where in Michigan they from were. "Actually we're from Wisconsin. We just took delivery of this boat in Michigan a few days ago. We decided to do some sight-seeing on our way home." The man commented on yesterday's storm, asking if they had gotten caught in it. Jan told him of how they had barely made it into a sheltered bay before it hit. He invited them aboard his boat which was much larger. They took Cassidy for a walk beforehand. He invited them to bring Cassidy aboard also. It turned out that he was a recently retired psychiatrist from Chicago. He and his wife had years of sailing experience. They had decided to spend the summer cruising the Great Lakes. His wife said, "we sailed across the lake and up into the North Channel of Canada. The pristine beauty can't be matched anywhere, but the mosquitoes in the evening and the black flies during the day were horrendous. After a week we decided we'd had enough. We're enjoying this area much more. It's not as primitive, but it's almost as pretty." The man and his wife offered them drinks. Andy had a Martini. Jan had a ginger-ale. The couple invited them to stay for a simple dinner, after which all of them hiked up to the bluffs over-looking Snail Shell Harbor and Big Bay De Noc.

It was after nine when Andy and Jan returned to their boat. They snuggled together in the joined sleeping bags. "Andy, let's do some-thing like what those people are doing. Let's take off next summer even if it's just for two or three weeks." She asked if he was enjoying this as much as she was. He admitted that he was, despite his con-cerns about what was or was not happening at home. "Andy, this is as close to a real vacation as I've ever come. A part of me wants to quit my job and just be a bum for a year or two." He asked her if she was tired of being a cop. She thought about his question. "Yeah, in some ways I am. There are cruel and crazy people wherever you go. I used to see my role as being a protector." She shook her head. "Maybe I became a cop because I felt so unprotected as a kid. I don't think I was on a mission to save the world; just a small part of it."

"That's pretty insightful. I notice you're using the past tense, 'you used to see your role as being a 'protector'. What do you see it as now?"

"I guess I still see it that way to some extent. I've gotten pretty cynical over the years. I see the cards stacked in favor of the bad guys too much of the time. I suppose most people in law enforcement feel that way. I know what prosecutors need to have in order to lock up bad guys. I try hard to supply them with what they need. Not all prosecutors are created equal. Some of them are incompetent or burned out. All of them are overburdened. Some of them are down-right stupid." She shifted the topic slightly. "Sheriff Cummings is a standup guy. I couldn't ask for a better boss but even he gets exas-perated by the system at times, like FBI agent Kelly." Andy asked her if she were to leave law enforcement, what she thought she'd like to do. She didn't know. "It wasn't until now that I've ever thought about doing anything else with my life. I guess I'm like the majority of peo-ple. I play it safe and stick with the familiar, even if I'm tired of it."

Chapter 18

They stayed in Fayette for three days, hiking, relaxing, and cleaning up the boat. Another boater told them of a bay to the north where they were all but guaranteed total privacy and exquisite beauty. He even gave Andy an almost full five-liter box of wine. "There isn't any place around where you can buy much of anything." The boater told them. "We'll be home by tomorrow night. Enjoy!"

They sailed to the recommended South River Bay the next morning. It was as they had been told, unspoiled, and sheltered from all directions. There were no other boats in the bay. It was completely isolated. It had a clean sand bottom. Because the day was hot Andy decided to skinny dip. To his surprise, Jan joined him without any coaxing. Cassidy barked and Jan was finally able to get him to dive in.

Having just sat in the marina in Michigan all summer, the boat had a heavy accumulation of algae on the bottom of the hull. Andy used a stiff, scrub brush to scour the underside clean.

He rigged up a sling-type of device off the end of the boom. Using the main halyard, he could lift Cassidy out of the water. Then he would swing the boom back and lower Cassidy into the cockpit. From then on, anytime Andy dove in, Cassidy followed. On the second evening, Andy reluctantly turned to the task of plotting the trip home. He calculated that it would take them at least three days depending on the wind.

Three days later they arrived at the Baileys Harbor marina. The harbor-master calculated a prorated fee for a boat slip for the remainder of the season. Jan had made arrangements with Sheriff Cummings the day before, to have a deputy meet them. The Sheriff showed up himself. On the way to Andy's place, Sheriff Cummings said, "a curious thing happened last week. I was getting regular calls from the Feds; then they stopped. I figured no news was good news. Still, I was curious, but I'm damned if I'm going to call them."

Jan told him, "they appeared to be searching for us the first couple days after we took off. After that we experienced nothing." Sheriff Cummings asked if they had any theories. "None," she told him.

They discussed the events of the past several days. When they talked about how they planned to pay back the money, he had forwarded to them, the sheriff told Jan not to worry about it, they could take up to six months to repay it. He told her he was crediting her as being on full-time duty over the past two weeks. "In a very real sense you were. The County will reimburse you a per diem expense allowance of fifty dollars for each day. According to my calculations, that comes out to about three thousand dollars." Jan asked him to credit it toward the money that had been loaned to them.

When they got home they discovered that the grass had been cut. The flowers and the tomatoes had been watered. Things were in good shape. Andy thanked the Sheriff for seeing to the place. He complimented Andy on the house. He liked both its exterior and interior design. Cassidy had a long drink of water before making an inspection tour of the immediate property. After the Sheriff left, they went to town to Andy's shop. It was late afternoon. There was a sign on the door that gave hours between ten and two. Jan was certain that Sheriff Cummings had arranged for someone to run the shop those four hours each day.

Andy unlocked the door and went in to look around. He was about to lock up and leave, when a man he recognized came up to the shop. They greeted one another. He asked if Andy was closing up for the day. If so; he could come back tomorrow. Andy asked what he needed. Half an hour later the man left with two carving tools and several blanks. Two other people came in and made small purchases. Jan sat down with Cassidy outside and waited. When he finally closed up she said, "McLeod, you're a damn institution around here. You've got a following of people who come looking for you." In the truck she scooted next to him. Cassidy took the space next to the door. I think we should go out to the point and go skinny dipping. Swimming naked ranks right up there among my very favorite things to do. They drove home first to get soap, towels and bug spray. They reluctantly brought their weapons with them.

"These won't do us much good if some bad guys show up while were out there in the water bare-assed," Andy said. There was very little wind at the point. Cassidy didn't wait for them. He plunged into the water and began swimming in circles. The late August water was almost tepid. As they wallowed and bathed, they kept a watchful eye out for hikers. They were attacked by two or three deer flies on the way back. Andy was sure that deer flies were territorial. He managed to slap and squash one on Jan's back. Cassidy snapped at them and managed to get one himself.

When they got home, Andy mixed a martini. He found a can of tomato juice and poured the juice into a glass with ice cubes for Jan. The three of them strolled out to the meadow. They found a large patch of ripe blackberries. Andy returned to the house for an ice cream bucket and they picked berries for an hour. They returned with a half-filled pail. "Andy, every day is an adventure. Did you know there were blackberries growing out there or that they were ripe now? This is paradise." There was very little in the house to eat. Jan offered to go grocery shopping in the morning. He already had a list started of things they needed. They went to the Pub for burgers.

Andy invited Jan to stay the night and she accepted. Cassidy curled up on the floor next to her. He was still damp from the swim. They fell asleep quickly.

Andy got up shortly after five in the morning and began sorting through a huge stack of accumulated mail on the counter. He separated the bills, the correspondence and the junk into piles. When Jan got up at six-thirty, he asked her if she wanted to join him for a run. She accepted the offer and after the run they went swimming and bathed in the lake. There was nothing in the house for breakfast. They decided to go to a local restaurant. They were almost finished with breakfast when Agent Kelly came into the restaurant. He was unaccompanied. Kelly walked directly to their table, half smiling as he approached.

When he got to the table, he raised his hands slightly. "I come in peace, relax." He asked if he could sit down. Jan nodded. He sat across from Andy. "I don't blame you for being a little paranoid. I would be too if I were you."

"It's not paranoia, when it's fucking reality. What do you want, Kelly?" Jan asked with a tone of contempt.

Kelly nodded. "Like I said, I've come in peace. Let me start out by laying my cards on the table. Some of it is fact, some of it is theoretical. All I'm asking is that you listen."

"I suspect a large part of it is bullshit," Jan said. "You sure fed Sheriff Cummings a load of it. That was quite a story you told him about what happened at the Petoskey airport. Who are you, Kelly?" He reached into his suit-coat pocket and produced his FBI photo identification. "We're supposed to believe this is for real? If you really are FBI, I'm surprised you still have a job."

Andy intervened. "We're listening; go ahead." The waitress came to the table. She asked if they wanted more coffee. Andy told her they would. She asked Kelly if he wanted coffee too. He declined. After she left, Kelly began by going down a chronological list of facts going back to when Stephanie first appeared on the scene. He managed to deliver a concise and mostly accurate summary. He asked if there were any details that he had overlooked or that were not accurate. Andy chose not to challenge the minor errors.

"Now for the theories," Kelly said. "I'm not sure exactly where to begin." Andy stared at him. "Okay, we know that someone very important and wealthy has been looking for Ms. Brandt. We're certain that this person, in an effort to find her, was behind much of what has happened to you."

Andy leaned forward, "we know all of that. Get to the point Kelly."

"I can't give you a lot of details. We're not sure ourselves what this is really all about," Kelly said. "We're of the opinion that Ms. Brandt is not who she appears to be. We think that she somehow managed to steal a very large sum of money from this very wealthy man who calls himself 'The Panther'. We're talking millions. Furthermore, she apparently managed to stash the majority of the money into off-shore accounts, either Swiss or Cayman Island banks. You're no doubt aware that banks in those locations provide untraceable numbered accounts to their clients. We think Ms. Brandt did everything in her power to avoid implicating you. At this point we're convinced that you didn't know anything about any of this. Furthermore, we're convinced that you don't know the whereabouts of either her or the money. Apparently the man who calls himself 'The Panther' does not share the same opinion. Everybody involved thinks she's still alive. Does that include you, Mr. McLeod?" Andy remained impassive. "For awhile we thought that she or someone she may have hired, was the person who shot you a few weeks ago." Jan asked if he no longer thought that. He side-stepped her question and went on. "We don't know if that was a screw up or not; meaning that we don't know whether it was a serious attempt to kill you or just wound you. After that incident we began making plans to take you into protective custody. We were about to move forward with a plan of our own when the tractor incident occurred. You and Detective Miller took off so unexpectedly, we were forced to improvise a secondary plan. In the course of doing that we saw that you had inadvertently provided us with an opportunity. The hope was that it would cause this Panther fellow to make a move to try to abduct you. He must have suspected that your departure was a ruse. He didn't make any such moves. We decided to let you take your sweet time getting back home hoping that he would try something. For all we know, he may have concluded that we had you in custody. We wouldn't have minded if you had taken even longer to return. Like him, we entertained the notion that a portion of the money and/or the account numbers were stashed somewhere on your property. We used the time to go over every square inch of your house, barn and property; even your retail shop with a very fine tooth comb. We haven't found a thing."

Andy sat back. "Okay, so who is this Panther guy? Do you have any notions about who he is?"

"We've narrowed the Panther's identity down to three or four candidates. The Panther may not be a single individual but rather a corporate entity or a cartel." For obvious reasons I can't comment further. This part may surprise you McLeod. We suspect Ms. Brandt was engaged by someone else to commit the actual theft. This other person was the one who master-minded the scheme. Ms. Brandt implemented it by gaining the Panther's confidence. In exchange for her part in the theft, she received substantial remuneration. We suspect that her portion of the take was approximately twenty-five percent. There's no question that she's intelligent and, if I may say so, a very attractive woman. However, we don't see her as the typical con-woman type who is capable of thinking in such grandiose terms. We don't even see her as having been knowingly complicit in the scheme. She may not have even been aware that she was being used for that purpose until it came time for the actual sting. By then it was too late. As for the person who's been dubbed Rambo; he was a highly trained, ex-Navy SEAL. He was hired by the Panther to find out what he could about Ms. Brandt's part in the scam. We're sure she's the only person who has knowledge about who the master-mind is. That person is the Panther's main interest."

"I trust your use of the past tense in talking about Rambo means he's not among the living any more," Jan commented.

"We don't know that. Since he disappeared early in the summer, he hasn't resurfaced anywhere that we're aware of. I wouldn't either if I were him."

Andy leaned forward on the table. "Here's the thing Kelly. You started out by lying to us." Agent Kelly looked like a bored teenager about to be scolded. Andy proceeded. "We feel insulted and abused. You put our lives at risk, using us as bait. We're not idiots. You didn't have either the consideration or the integrity to approach us with your plans and ask for our cooperation. I get the feeling that you view us like chopped liver used to lure the sharks? I think I can speak for both of us in telling you to piss-off." The agent shook his head as if to deny any wrong doing which only made Andy angrier. "As for your theories, we've already managed to piece most of it together on our own. We've reached some of the same theoretical conclusions. You're right. I'm surprised to hear that someone besides Stephanie was involved. You're also right to presume that she's probably not the con-woman type. She did deceive me. However, I view her deception as an effort to try to protect me." Andy paused before continuing. "Jan and I have arrived at some conclusions of our own. A few of them are different from and probably more plausible than the ones you've proposed." Kelly raised an eyebrow, showing an interest. Andy ignored his expression. "You come waltzing in here today and want to kiss and make up. Give me one good reason why we should show any willingness to cooperate with you."

Kelly apologized and said, "We underestimated you."

Andy leaned back in his chair. "Yes, you did, and NO, I refuse to accept your apology. Neither of us trust nor respect you." Andy looked at Jan and then back to Agent Kelly. "I don't know if you know this about me, Kelly. I spent almost twenty years as a psychotherapist before I came here. Over those years I saw a lot of accomplished liars. The clinical term is sociopath. I regard you as a raving goddamn sociopath. You're not sorry. You don't know the meaning of the word. The only thing you're sorry about is that you came up empty. Here's where we stand. IF, and that's a very big if, we decide to cooperate with the FBI; it's not going to be with you, comprende?"

The two of them stared at one another. Kelly finally spoke. "I think you're making a very big mistake McLeod."

"Is that a threat?"

"Not at all; at least not from me. However, if we pull out, you're going to be at the complete mercy of someone else. You already know how he operates."

"Uh huh, a lot like you."

Agent Kelly got up. Before leaving he took out one of his cards and handed it to Andy. "In case you change your mind, that's how you can reach me." Andy dropped it on the table.

"Agent Kelly," Jan said with an intonation that suggested she had a question she wished to pose. "I don't really expect a candid answer from you, but I'll go ahead and ask anyway. Have you people, meaning the FBI, had Andy under electronic surveillance for a period of time? A straight 'yes' or 'no' answer will do."

Kelly studied her for a moment. "Why do you ask? Do you suspect that someone has been spying on Andy?"

"You know damn well someone has. I'm asking if it was you; yes or no." He refused to answer the question. Instead, he simply reminded her that the FBI hadn't become officially involved in this investigation until Sheriff Cummings contacted the Bureau three weeks before. "You're a real piece of work Kelly. You want honest cooperation from us, but you you're not willing to extend that same courtesy to us. Bugger-off." Kelly turned and left.

Andy drained his coffee cup. He looked at Jan, who shook her head and smiled. "That's made for an interesting start to the day," she said. "We'll probably spend the rest of it thinking of all the things we wished we'd said." She reached over and patted Andy's hand. "Actually, I think you pretty much said it all."

On the way back home Andy said, "I'm finding myself having some serious second thoughts about who shot me. I'm almost certain it wasn't Stephanie."

"I was just thinking the same thing," Jan said. "Have you got any new candidates to consider?"

"Nope, not yet, but I wouldn't rule out Kelly and his merry band of troglodytes."

Chapter 19

After their encounter with Agent Kelly, Jan and Andy agreed that they were going to need to watch their backs. The next three weeks went by without incident. The FBI seemed to vanish from the scene entirely. Andy and Jan went sailing at least two evenings each week. As the days were growing shorter it was almost dark by the time they arrived back at the marina. They discussed plans to drive back to Michigan to pick up the trailer. Andy wanted to delay the trip until after he closed the shop for the season, at the end of October. He called the former owner's wife. She was hoping that they could come sooner. She even questioned leaving the boat in the water that late in the season. The decision was made to pick the trailer up at the beginning of the third week of October. She offered to put them up for a night since they were traveling such a long distance. She wanted her husband to meet them. "It will mean a lot to Jesse. He loved that boat. As much as he hated the idea of selling it, he's relieved. He appreciated that you paid us more than the rock-bottom price we had decided on."

Despite his two week absence, Andy was having his very best fall season ever. After being back two weeks, Jan ended up going to Sheriff Cummings to request that he consider hiring another detective. "I'm not able to keep up with the case load. A lot of cases are not getting the attention they need. I don't think it's just me. There seems to be more stuff going on that requires more thorough investigations."

During the course of their conversation Sheriff Cummings said, "Jan, I can't resist making a comment. You're not the same person you were a year ago. I don't know what's going on with you. I'd like to think it has something to do with your relationship with Andy. Whatever it is, you seem much happier."

Andy closed his shop for the season at the end of the second weekend in October. He, Jan and Cassidy left for Michigan early on Monday morning. They drove up the west side of the bay of Green Bay into the upper peninsula of Michigan and across to the Mackinaw Straits Bridge. They arrived in Harbor Springs that evening. They had made motel reservations in advance. They met with the couple who had owned the boat that evening. The husband, Jesse, was living at home again. He was paralyzed on his right side to the extent that he couldn't use a manual wheel chair. He had an electric one. His face drooped on that side. His wife kept a towel handy to wipe the drool. He spoke very deliberately but his wife still had to interpret most of what he said to them. The couple was pleased that Andy and Jan liked the boat so much. Andy presented them with a matted and framed photograph of the boat under sail, that a friend of Andy's had taken. The wife said, "it's not a big boat but it's comfortable and it's solid. We were disappointed that it took so long to sell it. We had several people look at it and give us all sorts of positive feedback, but no one came through. When you showed up out of nowhere, we were both shocked and delighted."

Andy, Jan and Cassidy left early on Tuesday morning with the trailer in tow. After crossing the Mackinaw Bridge they were on a remote stretch of road when Andy noticed that a car had pulled up close behind. There was very little traffic in either direction. The road was straight, allowing the driver of the car numerous opportunities to pass them. Andy brought it to Jan's attention as he slowed to fifty miles per hour; then to forty-five. The car still didn't pass. "The windows are so heavily tinted I can't make out the driver or if there's a passenger." She reached under the seat and got Andy's gun. She already had hers' in hand. He asked her to check the map for the next closest town. She did. Andy slowed to thirty-five. The car did too. She got Cassidy off the seat and onto the floor. She rolled down the passenger side window. Andy put his gun in his lap and rolled down his window. He slowed to twenty-five. Another vehicle that had been behind the car sped up and passed both vehicles, giving both of them the finger as he went by. "Speed up Andy," Jan told him. He brought the truck up to the speed limit. The car continued to follow close behind. "Go faster, let's hope for a cop." Andy accelerated to seventy. The car stayed right behind them. The road turned sharply south and in a few minutes they arrived at a small town. Andy slowed and pulled into a gas station. The car continued on by. Andy had a half tank of gas but he decided to fill up anyhow. Jan asked the station attendant about how she could get hold of the county sheriff without calling 911. She went to a pay phone. She asked for and was put through to the officer in charge. She explained the situation. The officer told her the closest squad was probably half an hour away. He said they were not far from the county line. He asked her to hold on. When he came back on the line he told her there was a deputy in the next county who was close to the line.

"If'n you're willing to risk it, that deputy can rendezvous with you there, eh. Otherwise you can stay where you're at till our deputy can get to where you're at. I'll arrange for the other deputy to meet you anyway, cause you'll be out of our jurisdiction pretty quick once you get back on the road, eh." Andy decided to push on. She thanked the deputy. He wished them luck.

They were no sooner out of town, than the car appeared from a side road and resumed following them again. It had no front license plate. Jan was able to identify it as a Camero. She commented, "he's got plenty of horsepower. He can easily out run most patrol cars." Andy stayed at the speed limit. In a few minutes Jan spotted a patrol car ahead, parked on the shoulder. Andy flashed his headlights. The deputy pulled out as soon as both vehicles had passed him. Jan told Andy, "Start to slow down, if he tries to pass you, block him." At forty-five, the driver suddenly started to pass. Andy moved quickly into the middle of the road. He slowed down even more. The deputy had his flashing lights on now. Jan saw an arm come out of the passenger side window of the Camero. "I think he's got a gun. I can't tell which way he's aiming." She fired six rounds aiming for the windshield. "Oh shit," she yelled. "He shot at the deputy; I think the deputy's been hit." In his side view mirror, Andy saw the patrol car veer off the road and into the ditch. He told her to shoot to kill. He braked hard. The car behind slammed into the trailer; then started to fall back. Jan emptied her gun. Andy handed her his. She fired four more rounds. The Camero looked like it was pulling off the road. Andy began to pull over and had just about come to a stop when the driver pulled back onto the road and surged forward accelerating hard. Jan told Andy to lean forward. She was kneeling on the seat and almost able to lean out the driver's side window. Just before the car was broadside of them, she emptied Andy's gun at the onrushing car. "I think I got the shooter," she said, as the car sped past. Moments later the car left the road. It rolled over two and a half times, coming to a stop upside down in the right hand ditch. Andy pulled off the road. Jan jammed fresh clips into both pistols. He asked her if he should move closer. "We need to drop the trailer. We need to go back to see about the deputy. These assholes aren't going anywhere unless it's on foot.

Jan stood watch while Andy quickly disconnected the trailer. A car approached from the west and slowed down. The driver was a well-dressed man, perhaps in his fifties. Jan flashed her badge and asked the driver to find a phone and call the sheriff. "There's an officer down back there." She pointed. The driver said that he was the local Lutheran Pastor. He would drive to the nearest farm house and call for help from there.

Jan and Andy got back in the truck and made a U-turn. Cassidy got back on the seat between the two of them. They pulled up to where the deputy's car sat in the ditch. The deputy was standing leaning against his car. His face was bloody. He was applying pressure to his forehead using a handkerchief. Jan again displayed her badge. Andy began assessing the deputy's injuries while Jan called the dispatcher, using the squad car's radio. The deputy's face was lacerated from broken glass from the windshield. It appeared that the rest of his injuries were from the impact of his squad car hitting the ditch. "It's a good thing I wasn't going any faster when I crashed." He complained that his ribs hurt. Jan retrieved a large first aid kit from the trunk of the squad. In the meantime, Andy discovered a scalp graze-wound just above the deputy's right ear. He told the deputy he was lucky to be alive.

An old pickup truck heading west drove up and came to a stop. The driver was an old man. He had his window rolled down. He spat some tobacco. "What the hell happened to ya Bradley?" He asked the injured deputy. "Did a deer run out in front of ya, eh?" The old man opened the truck door and started to step out.

"It would be best if you turned around and headed back in the opposite direction sir," Jan said to the man. "There's been an accident. There's an overturned car just up the road. Help's on the way." The old man looked ahead. He couldn't see anything on the road. He wanted to know why he couldn't just continue on in the direction he was headed. Jan walked toward him, showing her badge yet again. "There are a couple of men in that car who are armed and dangerous. They wounded the deputy here. Please sir; we don't want anything to happen to you."

The deputy called to the old man. "Amos, please do as she says." The faint sound of a siren could be heard in the distance. The old man closed his truck door and put it in gear. However, instead of turning around, he drove straight ahead. "Damn-it, Amos, turn that thing around," The deputy yelled.

Andy started for his truck knowing that there was nothing he could do to prevent harm from coming to the old man if he came under fire. By the time he got his truck turned around and started up the road, he could see a single brake light from the truck. 'Oh shit, the idiot's stopping', he said to himself. Sure enough, Amos was stopped on the road and was getting out of his truck. As Andy approached he could see the old man had what looked like a pump action shotgun. The old man started walking with a pronounced limp toward the overturned Camero. Andy slid to a stop behind the old man's truck. He already had his pistol in hand. The old man was starting down the embankment of the road. He was less than twenty feet from the car. Andy yelled for him to stop. A shot rang out and the old man dropped, screaming in pain. There was a second shot. Andy dropped to a prone position at the edge of the road. He squeezed off six rounds into the side window of the car. The old man lay motionless. Moments later a medium-sized dog jumped out the window of the old man's truck ran up to the old man, and began licking his face. Andy hadn't seen that the old man had a dog with him. He was reluctant to try and get hold of the dog. He didn't know if the shooter was still alive. He called to the dog but it lay down next to the old man refusing to move. He heard another car approaching from the west. It began to slow. He cautiously crawled toward the road. The car stopped. The driver was a lady with two young children. "There's been a bad accident. Please keep moving, Ma'am. Help is on the way."

She looked at him apprehensively, "That's old Amos's truck. Where is he? Has he been hurt?"

"If you're talking about an old man, he must have headed down there to help. I think he fell down. He's lying in the grass."

The lady told him, "we just live a mile down the road. Amos is our neighbor." The sound of the siren was getting closer. "Please Ma'am; it would be best if you left right now." She turned the car around and drove off swiftly. Andy could hear what sounded like multiple sirens. A police car was approaching from the west. Andy moved quickly to the other side of the road to flag it down. It was a state trooper. Andy quickly explained what had just happened. The trooper got out an assault shotgun. He got on his radio to the county sheriff and asked for backup from the adjoining county sheriff's department. "I don't know if the shooters are still alive or not. They've shot a deputy and a civilian. There's another civilian here who says he was shot at." After the trooper got off the radio he told Andy to take cover behind his squad car. In a crouched position, the trooper started toward the overturned car with the shotgun at ready. There was a loud report of a shot; then an explosion. The trooper dove to the ground. The overturned car was instantly engulfed in flames. The dry grass in the ditch ignited and the flames began spreading rapidly.

"Gotcha, you bastards," Old Amos yelled. He was on his knees, clinging to his shotgun to hold himself up right. The conflagration was moving toward what seemed like endless miles of tamarack swamps. The trooper hurried to his car and got on the radio again. He had a tone of urgency, bordering on panic. He gave his location and said that there had been an explosion that had triggered a fire that was spreading rapidly. Meanwhile Andy ran to old Amos. He asked Amos where he had been hit. "The sons-a-bitches got me in my bad leg fortunately, eh. He told the old man to hang onto his shotgun. He got a hold of him under both armpits and began dragging him up toward the road. The old man reeked of body odor and urine. His dog barked and jumped up and down in a frenzied state. Cassidy was in the truck barking frantically too. The trooper turned his squad around and drove fifty yards, down the road. He parked his squad in such a way as to block both lanes. As soon as Andy had moved both trucks so they were away from the dry grass, he went back and stooped beside the old man. He asked old Amos how he was doing. "I could sure use a couple snorts of brandy about now. Don't suppose you got a bottle with ya, eh."

The trooper came up to them. "Mornin' Amos; what you doing' out here so early today?" Old Amos told him it was none of his damn business. "I've busted Amos at least eight times for drunk driving," the trooper said to Andy. "Next time the judge is going to take your license away for good Amos." Suddenly, there were secondary explosions as bullets from the burning car began to go off in all directions. Andy grabbed up the old man's dog. He and the trooper ran for the ditch on the opposite side of the road. "Jesus, they must have had a case of ammo with them," The trooper yelled. Rounds kept going off. Two of them struck Amos's truck. The other emergency vehicles began to arrive on the scene. The trooper warned the emergency personnel about the exploding bullets. Amazingly, the fire didn't spread into the forest. One of the volunteer firemen later expressed the opinion, that it was because of the wet, cool summer and the lack of wind. The water in the swamps was higher than usual. He thought that was what was preventing a full blown forest fire. It took them an hour to subdue the grass fires which had spread a quarter of a mile in either direction.

The sheriffs from both counties showed up on the scene. Before leaving with the injured deputy, one of the paramedics reported that the deputy had suffered injury to his eyes from splintered glass, a broken clavicle and ribs and a graze wound to his scalp, just above the right ear. He would probably be flown by helicopter to the hospital in Marquette. Statements were taken from both Andy and Jan about what had happened. The sheriff from the county they were in asked, "If you folks don't mind, I'd appreciate you stickin' around for awhile. I'd like ta ask you some more questions, eh?" He asked the both of them, "do you reckon them fellas was out ta do you in?"

Jan addressed the question, "we don't really know. We're not sure when they started following us. They had numerous opportunities to pull up alongside and open fire. They didn't. They just stayed behind us no matter how fast or slow we went. It was only after the deputy pulled up behind them and put on his lights that they made a move. After they fired at him, they tried to pass us. They examined Andy's truck. There were three bullet holes in the side of the bed, two in the door and several places where bullets had grazed off the cab. "They got off several rounds before I opened fire. They must not have expected return fire."

The sheriff said, "we found an Uzi lying in the road about a quarter mile back and some spent cartridges. Guy musta dropped it when you hit him. Looks ta me like they wasn't professionals." He frowned, "I'd have ta say you folks are lucky ta be alive, eh."

Andy agreed. "There are some pretty remote stretches out here and the traffic is awfully light. We sure weren't expecting anything like this to happen. I was both surprised and paranoid when I realized we were being followed. I thought, 'what the hell is going on. I realized they were driving a performance car. Even without a trailer there was no way I could outrun them. I thought for awhile it was just some locals messing with us."

The sheriff commented "It's obvious that there's a bunch of stuff I don't know about. That Camero has an Illinois plate. I don't think them boys are locals. What it looks like ta me is that someone's out ta either IN-timidate you big time, or to do ya in, eh." He adjusted his hat and hiked up his gun belt. He commented as he glanced around, "Sure is a waste of a nice fall day. Why don't we head some place where we can talk instead of standin' out here? I'll treat ya to one of the best hamburgers in the whole UP, eh." He gave one of his deputies some instructions and helped Andy hook up the boat trailer. They followed the Sheriff into the nearest town, a few miles to the west. He led them to a side street where Andy could park his truck with the trailer. While Andy took Cassidy for a brief walk, the Sheriff asked Jan how her supply of ammunition was. She checked her purse and reported that she had ten rounds left, plus what was in her gun. He went to the trunk of his car and got her a box of nine-millimeter hollow points. He also gave her a twelve-gauge, pump action, shot gun with a box of shells. "We took this off some bad guys awhile back. They're doing' some time now. It's yours, eh." When Andy returned, he put the shotgun behind his truck seat. "You can bring your dog with you to the restaurant," the Sheriff told him. Jan had noticed that the Sheriff was keeping an eye on Andy and just about everything else, while at the same time he was listening to everything she said.

"Sheriff, were you in Viet Nam?" He nodded and asked how she had deduced that. "Andy does the same thing. The two of you are able to divide your attention without missing a thing. Maybe that's how you both managed to get out of there alive."

The sheriff looked at her and said, "let's not dismiss dumb luck entirely, eh."

In the restaurant the Sheriff motioned them to a booth. He talked briefly with the waitress before he joined them. Moments later the waitress arrived at the booth with a pan of water for Cassidy; then she took their orders. "Well this has been quite a mornin'. Got us two dead desperados. I don't know what keeps old Amos alive. He's livin' proof that takin' good care of yerself don't mean squat, eh. Gonna be hard to identify them two dead boys. It ain't likely they were drivin' their own vehicle." Over lunch Andy and Jan told the Sheriff the story of the past few months. He listened intently, only asking occasional questions to clarify a few points. When they were finished, he commented, "it sure is a confusin' can of worms you got yerself into. Maybe that's the point." He looked at Andy. "Thinkin' back to Nam, Charlie didn't have to try to confuse us. We already were. He just had to take advantage of our stupidity and bewilderment and maybe add to it occasionally, eh. He beat us by attrition to be sure, but we beat ourselves. Try not ta let these folks do the same."

"I've thought about that Sheriff. The one big difference is that Charlie wanted us gone; we were the invaders. I feel like the tables have been turned. I'm the one being attacked on my own turf and I don't even know why."

The Sheriff's response was, "hang in there my good man. Maybe these folks is gettin' tired." He used his thumb nail to dislodge something from between his teeth. "From what you're telling me, you getting shot, and what happened this mornin'; it sounds pretty amateur, eh. It sounds amateur and low budget ta me. These guys are probably a couple of big-city, ghetto gang bangers that someone hired ta throw a scare in ta ya, eh."

The Sheriff apologetically told them he had to leave. He stood and ran his hand through his hair before putting his wide brimmed hat back on. He paid for the lunch. On the way back to their vehicles he said, "this conversation clears up a lot of the questions about this morning, eh. Unfortunately it probably hasn't done much to clear things up for you though. I'll have a deputy follow you to the county line. I'll contact the Sheriff in the next county over to ask fer one of their deputies ta escort you, eh. I'll ask that he do the same in the next county. We'll try ta protect you the rest of the way home, eh." At Andy's truck they shook hands. "Ya know, for awhile I figured that having survived two years in country, I was home free. Nothin' worse could happen to me. I was wrong, eh. The shit never ceases. I'm sorry this is happening to you, McLeod. Welcome home."

Back on the road, neither Jan nor Andy spoke for the next hour. They were lost in thought about what had occurred. They were tired of the need to be wary. Cassidy slept on the seat next to Jan. Andy finally asked, "What was your take on the Sheriff back there, eh?"

She laughed. "I was just thinking about that. I think he was praying that we would get the hell back on the road so he didn't have to deal with any of this. I was watching his expression in the restaurant as we explained what's been going on. He went from looking almost cocky, to puzzlement, to downright worried. He's a good man but he's definitely where he belongs. He wouldn't survive ten minutes in Chicago or any other big city. I had to keep from laughing out loud when he used the term 'ghetto gang bangers'. I'll bet the closest he's ever come to dealing with gang bangers is busting half a dozen teen-age boys drinking beer out in the woods." She changed the subject. "What's with these people up here? They practically end every sentence with 'eh'."

Andy told her that was common in parts of Wisconsin also. "Darrel did it too." He reminded her.

She smiled. "It was considerate of him to set up police escorts but I couldn't help think he just wanted to make sure we got all the way out of the State of Michigan.

It was almost dark when they got home. Cassidy bounded over Andy to get out of the truck. After peeing he immediately set about scouting the premises. Both of them watched him for signs of anything out of the ordinary. Andy carried their overnight gear and the shotgun into the house. Jan had Cassidy's bowls and food in her left hand. She had her pistol in the right one. It was a clear evening. The temperature was in the low forties. Andy started a fire in the wood burning stove. After he mixed a martini they put on jackets, and went for a walk. As they began walking, Jan said, "I have to agree with what that sheriff said. I don't think those guys were professional hit men. I think they were hired. I suspect they were gang members looking to make some easy money. If they had been at all competent, we'd be dead."

Andy looked at her. "The fact that those two guys were a couple of hot-shots may be what saved us. They had the upper hand by virtue their firepower and the car they were driving. You saved us, Jan. You kept it together the entire time we were being attacked. I had some serious doubts that we were going survive; especially after they took out that deputy."

As they walked, Andy pointed off to the north. I have a feeling that there's going to be a northern light display tonight. The house was beginning to warm up from the stove when they got back. After the two of them took showers they sat on the couch and snacked on peanut butter and crackers. Andy fell asleep on the couch. Jan fell asleep in his old swivel rocker. It was one o'clock in the morning when they woke up. Andy let Cassidy out and reported that, indeed, there was a display of northern lights. They watched them for awhile from one of the upstairs, guest bedroom windows. They ended up going to bed there, out of sheer exhaustion.

The next day dawned clear. It was forecast to be a warm day without much wind. Andy decided conditions were right for him to pull the boat out and bring it home. It took him a couple hours to remove the sails and the boom and prepare everything needed to load the boat onto the trailer. His was the only sailboat left in the marina. He was able to get the boat onto the trailer and out of the water by himself. He had to enlist the help of a couple fishermen to lower the mast. It was mid-afternoon by the time he got the boat home. He had an electric pressure washer that he used to power spray as much of the hull as he could reach. The trailer's support braces prevented him from washing parts of the underside.

Jan stopped by on her way back to the office from an appointment. She helped him take cushions and the things that needed to be stored someplace warm for the winter. "If its nice tomorrow and there's not too much wind I'll cover the boat. I've got a big canvas tarp I can use," he told her. He chose a spot near the barn to park it for the winter.

After Jan got home, Andy started a campfire. There had been a couple of hard frosts the week before so there were no mosquitoes. They bundled up and sat staring into the fire, occasionally looking up to watch the stars emerge. Jan commented, "You know, as I was growing up I never saw my parents working together. There was no partnership between them. That's one of the things I liked about being a cop in the city. We were assigned to a partner. It was an unwritten rule that partners took care of one another. My first two partners were older guys. They taught me a lot and took care of me. I almost felt like I was their daughter. The third partner was younger than me. He was always trying to hit on me. I never felt like I could trust him or depend on him." Andy asked what happened with that partnership. "I filed several complaints. Nothing ever happened. I finally got promoted to detective. He ended up getting busted later on for hustling street dealers." Andy asked if she had been instrumental in his arrest. "Naw, he didn't get involved with the drug trade until after we went our separate ways."

Jan shifted the conversation. She gave a slight laugh. "Do you remember our first date? You invited me to meet you for dinner on New Years' Eve. I was so scared that I almost didn't show up. When I did, I almost got up and walked out on you before we were even seated." He asked her what that had been about. "Every red flag imaginable was going up with me. I felt like I was courting disaster. Part of it was fear. I was afraid that if you got to know the real me you'd be disgusted." He asked if she still felt that way. Jan pondered the question. After several moments she said. "There was a turning point in our relationship. It was when you went with me to see the psychiatrist, Doctor Jordan. You knew how really desperate I was." Andy poked the fire and put another log on. Jan went on, "what a mess I was. I was drinking myself to sleep nearly every night. Looking back, I realize that I was desperately lonely. My life revolved around my job and alcohol. Mostly I was apathetic. I thought that feelings just got in the way. I did everything in my power to avoid feeling. To my way of thinking a good cop was one who checked his or her feelings at the door. Apathy was a virtue. Work was all I had to look forward to. If I could have worked twenty-four hours a day, I would have. I know you were reluctant to call me when things came up. There were times when I welcomed your calls. Not that I wanted bad things to be happening to you. I'm ashamed to admit this, but for awhile, I was almost afraid that your situation would simply disappear. I felt like you and I were working together. That felt kind of good."

"There's a theory about relationships that says relationships are formed within the first five minutes of meeting."

Jan chuckled. "I'm sorry, but I think that's bullshit. I'm pretty sure your first impression of me was that I was some broken down, bimbo, bag lady. My first impression of you was that you were some dropout, hippy recluse. It took us more than five minutes to establish the relationship we have now. I feel like we're still in the process of adjusting to one another. I will admit that you've grown on me a bit."

Chapter 20

They both got up early the next morning to go for a run. After Jan left for work, Andy went out to the barn to look for the tarp he wanted to cover the boat with. It took him over two hours to spread the tarp over the boat and get it secured. When he was satisfied that it was set for the winter, he went to his workshop to resume working on commissions.

Jan called him mid-morning to tell him that the Sheriff in Michigan had called Sheriff Cummings this morning. "The Michigan authorities were able to get identification on those two guys that chased us. They were a couple of Hispanic gang members from Chicago and had mile-long rap sheets, mostly drug related. He thinks they panicked when they saw the Sheriff's deputy behind them. He told Sheriff Cummings that the deputy who was shot is probably not going to recover the vision in his right eye. He can barely see out of that eye because of the splintered glass. He'll probably end up with a desk job." She hesitated before continuing. When she did, Andy detected a change in her demeanor. "I'm certain those guys were out after me, McLeod. The facts speak for themselves."

"Maybe," Andy conceded. He likened the incident to what had happened to them at Thorsen Point. "The main difference is that these guys were hired guns. They didn't have a personal vendetta like the previous shooter." He went on to say, "what has me puzzled is how they knew that we'd be up there. They must have followed us and we just didn't notice."

"I have to go," she said, sounding somewhat impatient. There was a pause. Andy asked if she was still on the line. "Yeah, we'll talk about this later."

Andy wondered what was going on. He didn't like the abrupt change of tone. She was sounding like the old Jan. It was like she was suddenly reverting back to the erratic person she had been months ago.

After hanging up, Andy found himself going back over much of what had happened on their trip back from Michigan. He wasn't questioning her conclusion. It meant they were both under attack from two separate and distinct entities. He doubted that either of the parties knew about the other. He thought about the FBI. 'I wonder if they even knew about the attempts on Jan. They may not even be aware.' His thoughts segued to their conversation of last night. He had seen himself as having been somewhat of a loner at one time. His view of Jan was that she saw herself as being that way even more so. He felt like both of them had changed in that regard over the past few months. Their moments of partnership had increased. It had seemed to him that many of the barriers between them had dissolved during the time they had been 'on the lamb'. Now, all of a sudden, he felt a major shift occurring. He felt like Jan was stepping away from him. Was she experiencing a sense of panic, the kind of fear associated with separation anxiety? Was she trying to protect herself from some kind of anticipated rejection? Maybe it was the opposite. Maybe she was being protective toward him. Whatever the case, he found himself asking how he would react if she decided to withdraw from him entirely. He wanted to somehow get the names of the men who had hurt her years before. He engaged in some violent fantasies in which he went about systematically eliminating each of them, thereby, removing the threat they posed. 'Right McLeod, get real. You're going to march your honky ass into the big city and blow them all away'. He wondered if the word 'honky' was even used in reference to white guys anymore.

Another line of thinking emerged. "Maybe Jan was experiencing a delayed stress reaction to what had happened. Maybe it was causing her to plummet back into a serious depression. Andy returned to the subject of the two of them as a couple. 'It was the circumstances of our escape to Michigan that brought us so much closer to one another'. He knew that he had come to really care about her before then. He suspected that she had developed a fondness for him as well. Even though they had never engaged in sex, the thought had crossed his mind from time to time'. He had often wondered if she'd had any sexual thoughts about him. Given her traumatic history, he doubted that she did. For that reason he had suppressed his sexual desires. He wasn't sure what he'd do if she decided to call it quits tomorrow. 'Christ, McLeod, you'll do what you always do. You'll give her space. You'll let her go and hope that in time she'll change her mind and come back."

When Jan arrived at 5:30, she seemed in a more cheerful mood. She opened the trunk of her car announcing, "I got us some presents." She retrieved two boxes out of the trunk. "I stopped at the Yacht Harbor store on the way home. They're having a big end-of-the-season sale." Jan handed Andy one of the boxes. He opened it to discover neoprene wading shoes. "They'll save our feet when we wade back and forth to the boat. The neoprene provides some insulation too." She brought out a stainless steel collapsible handle with a stiff brush on one end. "The handle extends to eight feet. This will make cleaning the bottom of the boat easier on you." Finally she produced a large plastic bag. "It's a wetsuit top and there are some neoprene mitts in here too."

"How thoughtful of you," he remarked. He slipped one of the mitts on. "Jeez, I might even wear these when I'm blowing snow this winter, eh."

It was nearing sunset when they went for their walk. The leaves of the trees were just beyond their peak and many of them had already fallen. The setting sun accentuated the bright vermilions, scarlets and golds of the maples, birch and aspen. As they entered the meadow Cassidy bolted and ran full tilt out into the meadow. For a moment the two of them froze expecting the worst. Jan already had her gun drawn. They had completely missed seeing two deer browsing near the far edge of the meadow. The deer took off, bounding to the north and then east into the forest. Cassidy gave up the chase and returned. Three large, high-flying flocks of Canada geese passed over them, headed in a southeasterly direction toward the lake. Several smaller flocks of Sandhill Cranes made wide circles, flying in close formation. Andy told her that the cranes were congregating before they commenced their fall migration. She asked why they had chosen to do that here and not someplace else. "It's probably a combination of habit and habitat. They've got everything they need right here; food, water and a flyway that their ancestors have probably been using for centuries." The sun dropped behind the trees to the west, leaving them in an almost ethereal afterglow. Towards the end of their walk she thanked him, "that was really pleasant. There probably won't be many more days this nice before the snows fly."

When they got back to the house, Jan said, "Andy, we have to talk about a couple of things." He had half expected this to happen when she got home today. He was surprised by her almost festive mood when she first arrived. They sat down in the living room facing one another. Andy tried to keep himself from anticipating the worst. "The first thing is, Sheriff Cummings got a call from Agent Kelly today. I hope this isn't going to upset you. Somehow Kelly found out about what happened last weekend on our way home from Michigan. He also found out about the incident that happened at Thorsen Point with Ramon. He's scheduled a meeting with us tomorrow at Sheriff Cumming's office." Andy asked if the FBI was going to get involved with her situation. She didn't know. "I was up front with the Sheriff and told him that it appeared that both of those incidents had to do with me. I told him that neither of them had anything to do with Stephanie. I don't know if the FBI thinks there's a connection between the two or not." She looked down for several moments. "I ended up telling the sheriff about what happened to me; about the gang rape. I felt he needed to know what this was all about." Andy said nothing. Jan looked up. "He was extremely understanding and sympathetic. He was sorry that it had become necessary for me to have to share the details of that incident."

Andy told her, "Jan, I'm worried about your situation. One of these days your luck is going to run out. I feel badly for that Michigan deputy. His life has practically been ruined. I'm not at all sorry that those bangers got toasted." Then he asked, "what's the second thing?"

She took a deep breath. "Andy, I don't know how to say this." She paused as if to muster her courage. "I've been thinking about our relationship a lot lately." She looked at him. "Look, I had no intention of moving in here with you when we got back from Michigan." She held up her hand. "I know that I don't stay here every night but I'm here a lot of the time. This has to stop." Andy remained silent. "I want us to continue to be friends. I hope we can still go out for dinner occasionally. I hope we can go sailing every once-in-a-while next summer. I just feel like things have gone too far. I feel like I'm interfering with your life." He asked her what she meant by that. "You know what I mean," she said.

"No, I really don't. How are you interfering with my life?"

"Andy, you need someone to share your life with. You need a partner; a sexual partner. You're like a goddamn monk. It's not normal. I'm in the way of you being able to meet someone." He pursed his lips. She wanted to know what he was thinking. "You do that McLeod. You do that thing with your lips whenever you decide not to tell me what you're really thinking. I want to know."

"Frankly, I'm confused," he told her. "When you came in here a little while ago you seemed to be in a really good mood. You had the stuff you bought for the boat. Now you're saying that we need to stop spending time with one another. Not only that, but you've also decided that I should start seeing other women." Now Jan was refusing comment. "What's going on Jan?" There was a long period of silence. Cassidy hopped up on the couch and lay down next to her with his head on his paws. She reached over and petted him. Andy got up and poured himself a glass of wine. He asked her if she wanted anything. She declined. He opened a can of Coke for her anyway. "Okay, I'll tell you what I think," he said. "I think you're trying to protect me. I think you've decided that spending time together puts me at risk from whoever is out to get you." She started to say something. Andy stopped her. "I also think you're trying to protect yourself."

She took a sip from her Coke. "I agree with the first part of what you just said. Because of me you've ended up in harm's way twice now. I'm not sure what you mean about me trying to protect myself. Look Andy, I've been going back and forth about our relationship ever since I stayed here following my surgery. In many ways I prefer being on my own. I've lived by myself most of my adult life. We've talked about this before. There are times when I resent you, not because of anything you've said or done, but simply because I feel like I'm expected to be here. You can't seem to understand that. You seem completely comfortable with the relationship that has evolved between us. I see that as being kind of sad. You deserve a lot more than what I'll ever be able to provide." She took another sip. "You've talked a couple of times about how superficial the relationship was between you and Stephanie. That may be somewhat true. But, in retrospect, she had this dark secret that she needed to protect you from. The less you knew, the safer you'd be in the long run. She did that deliberately. You know that I haven't looked upon her in a very favorable light. I think the two of you loved one another. You were partners. The two of you were working toward the same goal." Jan made a sweeping gesture of the house. "You lost her Andy. I'm not sure you've completely come to terms with that. I'm not sure you ever will."

He cleared his throat. "You're right. I think we did love one another, at least for awhile. I was stuck in my anger toward her for a period of time after she left. It's easier to be pissed off with someone who you feel has abandoned you, than it is to experience the grief. The anger also served an emotional purpose." The house was getting dark. Andy reached over and turned on a lamp. He got up from his chair and found his cardigan sweater and put it on. He got a quilt for Jan.

After he sat back down, he asked, "What about us? It sounds to me like you want out or at least to back way off. I don't understand what's happening." She appeared to be pondering what to say. "Look Jan, if you recall, it was me who proposed that you keep your apartment. I've acknowledged all along that being in a fulltime relationship with me, or anybody, might not be possible for you. Do I wish you were free from those fears? Absolutely. Do I think that will ever come to pass? I don't know. I'd like nothing better than to be able to erase the scars of your past." He paused briefly. "It seems to me that you're being preemptive." She asked him what he meant by that. "I think you're afraid that the day is going to come when I'll find someone else."

"So what are you saying? It sounds like you think I'm afraid that you're eventually going to dump me and I'm trying to beat you to the punch." He told her that was one of the things he thought was going on. Jan got angry. "You know what I think? I think you flatter yourself, McLeod. I don't give a damn if you start dating other women or not. For all I care, you can spend the rest of your life whacking off."

Andy felt like he'd just been gut-punched. Jan got up from the couch. "I'm going," she said. "The meeting with Kelly is at 9:00 tomorrow morning. I'll see you there." She tossed the quilt and put her jacket on. Andy followed her out to her car. He told her he'd see her at the meeting, as she jerked the car door shut. She looked furious. He was sure she was going to cry herself all the way home. That's what women did when they were angry, wasn't it? He decided he wasn't hungry. He and Cassidy went back in the house. He got a beer out of the fridge. The house suddenly felt miserably empty. 'You really blew it, McLeod.' How had things gotten so twisted around? 'I didn't mean to come across as being what; the knight in shining armor, and her the damsel in distress? No, it's more like you were being a condescending prick'. He locked the doors, turned off the lamp and sat down in his chair. He went to sleep sitting there.

Clouds moved in that night. When Andy awoke the next morning it was raining and the wind was blowing fiercely out of the northeast. He had slept in the chair all night. His back was stiff. The house was cold. He started a fire. He hated storms like this in the fall. 'It's such a short season to begin with. Storms like this strip the remaining leaves off the trees', he groused to himself. He remembered a couple of past falls when the leaves had lasted into the second week of November. This wasn't even the end of October. They'd all be gone by this evening. He went through his morning routine, thinking all the while about Jan. Normally he would have called her to make sure she had arrived home safely. He and Cassidy got in the truck at 8:30 to leave for the appointment with Agent Kelly. On the way he thought of several things he would have liked to have said to Jan during last night's conversation. He was sure that she wouldn't have heard much, if any, of what he had to say. It probably would have only made the situation worse, if that was possible.

When he got to the Justice Center, he decided to bring Cassidy with him, if for no other reason than to add a little insult to agent Kelly. He was ushered into Sheriff Cumming office where Kelly, the Sheriff and Jan were waiting. He was more than a little surprised to see her dressed in gray stirrup pants with a peach colored satin blouse. Her hair was teased and she had on more makeup than usual. It wasn't as much as what she used to wear. Agent Kelly got up and extended his hand to Andy. Andy disliked limp half-hearted hand-shakes. That's what he offered to the agent. Kelly started out by wanting to know about the background of what had led up to the attacks targeting Jan. She braced herself and began to tell her story. Andy interrupted. "Cut the crap, Kelly. You already know the background. There's no reason for her to have to recount the past unless it's to satisfy your perverse curiosity." She gave Andy a thankful glance. Sheriff Cummings had his hands folded, surveying the inter-action that was taking place. Kelly seemed mildly perturbed. He asked her if she remembered the men's names. Andy again voiced the same objection. Kelly produced a list. Jan verified the names, pointing out that she was sure one of them was dead. Andy was debating with himself whether to get up and walk out. 'What a head fucker', he thought to himself. He knows all this stuff. There's no reason for him to be putting these questions to her'. Andy knew what Kelly was up to. He needed to stay, if for no other reason than to be a thorn in the agent's side. Besides, he might learn something he didn't know from past discussions. Jan recounted how she filed complaints against all six of the men and how she had later testified against all of them in court. All of them had been found guilty and sentenced to prison. Three of them ended up also having previous sentences extended because of parole violations. She told of having received a number of threats from the men's families and their gang affiliates. Kelly asked about specific threats, about her becoming a police officer and about subsequent encounters she had with any of them. Andy watched her as she answered the questions posed. She spoke with a composed demeanor, as if she were talking about someone else rather than herself. He thought this was probably the only way she could get through having to dredge up her past. Sheriff Cummings interrupted the meeting at one point to ask if anyone wanted some coffee. They all did. He had some brought in. Andy and Sheriff Cummings left to use the toilet. In the bathroom, Sheriff Cummings asked Andy if Kelly was trying to antagonize Jan or 'is he just a natural born prick'? It was comforting to know he wasn't alone in his dislike of Kelly.

The Sheriff commented as they were leaving the washroom. "I've always liked Jan. I was surprised to see her dressed like she used to when she came in this morning." He wondered what was going on. Andy chose to simply say that that he didn't know.

When the meeting resumed, Agent Kelly presented all three of them with the written reports detailing both of the attacks. He asked them to read them and to add any details that might be pertinent. Jan offered that it seems pretty clear that two of the attacks were aimed specifically at her. "They don't appear to have anything to do with McLeod. I also doubt that either side knows about the other." She didn't have any other comment to make.

Kelly scrutinized her. "It does appear to be that way. Furthermore, it appears that the party that's after you, Detective, is not very sophisticated or professional. We doubt that they have any awareness of the threats that have been posed to Mr. McLeod. However, I feel certain that the reverse is not true. I'd be willing to bet a large sum, that Andy's nemeses are well aware of the threats posed to the two of you. What we don't know is whether they've figured out whom as yet. My guess is that they're extremely uncomfortable right now. If I were them, the most logical conclusion I would draw, is that someone else is competing for the hidden treasure." He paused briefly. He squinted and looked briefly at the ceiling. "If that's the case; just maybe we can turn that to our advantage." He looked at Andy and Jan; then at Sheriff Cummings. He started out talking in legalese. "If the party of the first part believes they are in competition with the party of the second part, it would seem to me that the party of the first part would very much like to eliminate the party of the second part. We all know that the first party doesn't want Andy dead. The first party has a very large interest in protecting Andy and keeping him alive."

Jan interrupted, "I know where you're going with this, Kelly." Everyone in the room did. He motioned for her to continue.

"No, wait a minute," Andy intervened. "Are you wired, Kelly?" Kelly feigned surprise and asked what he meant. "You know exactly what I mean. Is this conversation being transmitted or recorded?" Kelly said that he wouldn't do such a thing without informing all of them. "Can I see those pens you have in your coat pocket?" Kelly hesitated. His face was reddening. Andy held out his hand for them. Kelly reluctantly withdrew them and handed them to him. Andy unscrewed the tops on both of them. One of them was a mechanical pencil. The other was not a pen. It looked like one of the listening devices he had seen more than once in his old house. Andy, Jan and the Sheriff stared at Kelly. Andy dropped the device into his half full coffee cup.

Kelly's face was crimson. Andy went on, "If I understand you correctly Kelly, what you're proposing is that someone provide the people who are after me with the names of the people who are after Jan. In short, you're suggesting that the one side be pitted against the other with the hope of eliminating the people who are after Jan."

The sheriff became almost irate. "Am I hearing this correctly? Is Andy right? Is that what you're suggesting, Kelly? If so, what you're proposing is something tantamount to a gang war. You want to give one side names of potential targets in order to assassinate those people."

Kelly's response was one of denial. "No one in this room heard me say anything to that effect."

Sheriff Cumming was working hard to contain his anger. "Not in so many words, Kelly, but that seems to be what you're insinuating. May I remind you, Door County is not the Mexican border. I have no intention of sanctioning this kind of crap. This flies in the face of our whole system of justice." The sheriff muttered something to himself. "Kelly, you are a dangerous human being. The FBI has the resources and the means to go after this so-called second party legally. You've got all of their names."

Kelly held up his hands. "I remind you, I haven't proposed a thing. I'm just pointing out the situation as it stands. Unfortunately it's not a situation that the FBI can become involved with, at least not for now."

Andy stood up. "So, you already knew coming in here that your agency wasn't going to take any action to protect Jan. It sounds like you don't even intend to try going after any of the people who pose a threat to her. Apparently the whole point of calling this meeting was to try to use us. I can just picture you scheming, Kelly. We'll get those hayseeds to allow us to sic one set of bad guys on another set. It will save the FBI a lot of time, effort and money."

Sheriff Cummings spoke. "I'm going to report what took place here to your superiors, Kelly. I have Detective Miller's full accounting about what transpired in Michigan, plus the previous incident that happened here in Door County. I'm going to do my very best to try to get you fired. In my opinion you're unscrupulous and therefore dangerous. I'm going to make a formal request for the Bureau to launch active investigations into both of those incidents." Sheriff Cummings decided not to waste any more time or energy on him. "Go on, get out of here, Kelly." This meeting is over."

As Kelly started for the door, Sheriff Cummings said, "Kelly, you're a snake! I can't believe the FBI is employing vermin like you." After Kelly was out of the sheriff's office, he opened the top left-hand drawer of his desk. He withdrew a recording device and turned it off. He picked up a paperweight. "This is the mike. Two can play that game. What a piece of work." Before dismissing Jan and Andy, he said. "I was serious. I have every intention of contacting his superiors about his conduct. I'm hopeful the FBI will get involved. The people going after you, Jan, have crossed state lines."

Out in the hall Jan asked Andy what he was going to do today.

He shrugged, "I thought I'd go to the Yacht Harbor store. Maybe I can find some other things on sale for the boat." He wondered why she wanted to know but she didn't say. She headed in the direction of her office. He and Cassidy took the stairs down to the first floor and exited the main entrance. At the Yacht store he found a few useful bargains.

It started raining during the drive home. Andy became lost in thoughts about Jan. He wondered what the reversion to her previous style of dress meant. Was she regressing?

He was fast reaching the conclusion that Jan was experiencing a delayed reaction to what happened on the way home from Michigan? He felt helpless. 'I've pretended to be willing to give her as much space as she wanted and needed. That's not true. That's not the way I feel at all.

As he neared home, the rain was on the brink of turning to snow. The wind buffeted the truck as he drove northward. The trees were almost naked. Realizing that Thanksgiving was three weeks away, Andy steered his thoughts to his sons. He was expecting Brian to make it home. He wasn't sure about Corey. The last he'd talked to him, Corey thought his unit would be leaving to be deployed in Afghanistan before the holidays. Corey had expected it to happen sooner. He returned to thinking about Jan. They were coming up on the anniversary of their meeting one another. He thought about inviting her for Thanksgiving, wondering if she would accept.

It was early afternoon when he got home. He went in the house to tend the stove. While washing his hands at the kitchen sink afterwards, he noticed Jan's coffee cup in the drain rack. That prompted him to make a search of the rest of the house. In the bathroom he discovered her toothbrush, hairbrush, and some of her cosmetics. In the bedroom closet there were a couple pairs of her jeans, some slacks, two or three blouses and two jackets. He also found two pair of loafers and her terry cloth robe. He had given two of the five drawers in his dresser to her. Mostly she used them to store her underwear. There were several pairs of panties and three bras in one of the drawers and three sweaters in the second one. After discovering how many of her personal belongings she had left behind, he began to wonder about her decision. His mind jumped back to how thorough Stephanie's departure had been. It had been well-executed. He wagered that even 'Draco' had been surprised by her disappearance.

He spent the rest of the day in his studio working on Christmas orders. He kept expecting the phone to ring. He anticipated that Jan would either make an appointment to pick up her things or hopefully reverse her decision to leave. The phone didn't ring.

Two weeks passed and he had still had not heard from her. He had thought about calling her a number of times. At first his excuse for not calling was that the 'ball was in her court'. It was her decision to leave. It was up to her to make the next move. Halfway through the second week he found himself vacillating. A part of him was concerned about her welfare. He hoped that she was not allowing herself to slip back to her previous self. His feelings of longing for her were beginning to diminish. Occasionally he even found himself feeling angry with her. Was their relationship that unimportant to her that she could blow him off so easily and completely? His days were spent working in the studio. After he and Cassidy came in from their walks each day he would mix a martini. He would have another after supper, if he even bothered with an evening meal. He would have a couple glasses of wine throughout the evening. He started going to bed as early as nine o'clock. He'd fall asleep quickly and easily but he would awaken in the early morning hours, between two and three. Many times after attempting unsuccessfully to get back to sleep, he would get up and read until daylight. On the mornings that he didn't go through his workout routine, he would start work in his studio as early as six o'clock.

A week before Thanksgiving he decided to try calling Jan at work. She was not in the office. He left an awkward message for her on her voice mail. He tried to sound casual and friendly in issuing an invitation. He was sure if she didn't come to his place for Thanksgiving she would most likely spend the day by herself. He wondered if she had stopped taking her psych meds and if she had gone back to drinking. He hoped she hadn't started smoking again.

She returned his call late in the afternoon. She sounded congested. He asked if she had a cold. She said that she did. His heart sank when he heard her take a long drag from a cigarette and cough. He reluctantly decided to confront her. "Jan, have you gone back to smoking?"

She made a nervous laugh, "Yeah, I've fallen off several wagons lately. Pretty stupid huh?"

"What's going on, Jan? Have you stopped the psych meds, too?"

She ignored his questions. "About your invitation, McLeod, thanks, but I've already made other plans. A bunch of us are getting together at the VFW for Thanksgiving dinner." She asked if his sons were going to join him. Before hanging up she said, "how about we get together for coffee sometime?"

When the conversation ended Andy felt a terrible sense of disappointment. It was visceral. He almost felt nauseous. He was angry with her. He was angry with himself. 'What the hell happened? What the hell is going on? She seemed like she was on top of the world three weeks ago. I should have seen this coming? I should have called her right away instead of 'giving her space'? She's probably taken my silence as a sign of my not caring, maybe even relief.' He caught hold of himself. 'Stop it, McLeod. You're not to blame for whatever is happening with her. It's got nothing to do with you. It's her life. She's the one who has decided to toss everything aside, including you'. He doubted that she was aware of, or even cared, how much pain she had caused him. A thought popped into his head. He looked up the number for the VFW. He called there and asked if they would be open for dinner on Thanksgiving Day. He was told that they would be closed that day.

Andy decided to call Sheriff Cummings. The Sheriff sounded pleased to hear from him. After a brief exchange, She sheriff asked what he could do for him. Andy started out by saying "I don't know if I should even be having this conversation with you, Sheriff." The sheriff was aware that he and Jan had been seeing a lot of one another. He knew that their relationship had progressed to something beyond casual. He had praised Andy, telling him that he was certain their relationship had been the catalyst for many of Jan's changes over the past several months. He literally groaned when Andy told him about Jan's sudden and abrupt breakup of the relationship two weeks before. "What's going on, Andy? I thought you two were getting along famously. Hell, I even had my hopes up that the two of you might even tie the knot one of these days." He admitted that he hadn't had occasion to see much of Jan lately, but he had noticed she had gone back to dressing the way she used to. "Maybe not quite as bizarre as before." He asked what, if anything, he could do to help the situation.

"I don't know that there's anything Sheriff," Andy told him. "Like I said before, I'm not sure I should be telling you any of this."

"No, no, I'm glad you did. I like Jan. She's kinda grown on most of us around here. I'm going to keep an eye on her." The Sheriff was about to end the conversation. "Feel free to call me if anything comes up that you think I ought to know about. I'll do the same, Andy."

Andy decided that he had to tell Sheriff Cummings about his real concern about Jan. "Sheriff, I talked to Jan less than an hour ago to invite her to join my son's and me for Thanksgiving dinner. She told me that she was going to the VFW for Thanksgiving dinner with friends." He told the Sheriff that he had called the VFW, only to learn that it was closed that day. "That's not good," the Sheriff said. "What do you make of it?" Andy told him he didn't know. "You don't think she's considering doing something stupid, do you?"

"She's been close to the edge before," Andy told him. He didn't know whether Sheriff Cummings was aware of that or not. "I'm scared. I don't know what to do. I don't think she'll listen to anything I have to say right now."

The sheriff responded with, "hmm, let me get back to you Andy. I need to talk to a couple of people about this." He reassuringly said, "don't worry; I won't mention your name unless I absolutely have to."

Andy told Sheriff Cummings about having taken Jan to see a psychiatrist in Green Bay last spring. The psychiatrist, Doctor Jordan, had prescribed a couple of psych meds for her. Andy expressed the opinion that the medications had been instrumental in helping her to make a number of positive changes. He enumerated two or three of them. "I'm pretty sure that she's recently stopped taking the medications all together. I have no way of knowing that for sure."

Sheriff Cummings called Andy back that evening. "It's been quite a day, Andy. I called Jan in to my office shortly after you and I talked. I laid out my concerns about her. She got pretty angry, mostly with you. She feels you broke a confidence she had with you. She feels that your only reason for calling me was to get even with her for breaking up with you. If you'd been here I think she would have tried to shoot you. Anyway, to make a long story short, in the end she agreed to sign herself into the psych unit at Bellin Hospital in Green Bay. I had that new woman assistant DA here with us the whole time. Jan understands that, if she decides to walk out of there before the hospital thinks she's ready to leave, I can and will have her committed. Two of my deputies transferred her to the hospital this afternoon. The hardest part of the whole thing was seeing her go out of here in handcuffs. It's department policy. It's my policy." He paused. "I don't know how much she was able to hear when I told her that your calling me was an act of friendship and genuine concern. I meant it. You and I have had to make some tough decisions today, Andy. I sure as hell hope they pay off. She's a good person. She's endured a lot. I hope she can pull herself back together."

"I agree, Sheriff. I regard her as a very brave lady. I can't tell you how much I appreciate what you did. Not many bosses would have risked themselves that much for one of their employees. You may have saved her life."

"You gave me the opportunity, Andy. You deserve a lot of the credit. Hey, if I don't get a chance to talk to you before, you have a good Thanksgiving. I trust you're not having it at the VFW."

"That was bad, Sheriff."

"I know. I've been at this job too long."

Chapter 21

The gun/deer hunting season traditionally starts on the Saturday before Thanksgiving in Wisconsin. Andy planned to try for one this year, having skipped hunting the previous two years. It was Wednesday, the day before Thanksgiving and there were eight inches of snow on the ground. It had snowed a couple of inches the night before. It was unusually cold for late November. He definitely didn't relish sitting outside in such cold conditions, possibly for hours on end with the hopes of MAYBE getting a shot at a deer. He didn't have the special and expensive clothing such cold conditions required. He refused to make that kind of investment on the basis of principle. "It defeats the whole purpose of hunting in my opinion, I can buy a hell-of-a-lot of meat for what all of that paraphernalia costs. Its clothing that only gets used for maybe a week, once-a-year."

In a discussion with Jan weeks before, she had pointed out that nothing was stopping him from using the insulated coat, bib pants, mittens, and boots throughout the winter, especially when he was out blowing snow. "Andy, you've paid your dues and done without for years. It's time you indulged yourself. It's not like you can't afford a few luxuries." She had smiled at him. "If it was something for the boat, you wouldn't hesitate for a second." He ended up relenting to the extent that he bought a good pair of insulated boots and mittens. She shook her head and said, "McLeod, you are the quintessential, tight-assed Scotsman."

"Aye," He replied in a brogue. "And the world's economies would naught be in the quagmire they're in if they were as frugal and prudent as we Scots."

Andy's younger son, Corey, had a week's leave before he was scheduled to be deployed to Afghanistan. Brian was in graduate school. The boys had made arrangements between themselves for Brian to pick Corey up at O'Hare that Tuesday night. They would leave early on Wednesday morning to come north.

It was still dark when Andy got up. He tended the stove and started coffee. He dressed in his hunting clothes. Cassidy wanted to go out. Andy wouldn't allow it. He didn't want the dog to scare away whatever deer might be in the vicinity. He led Cassidy back to the bedroom. Cassidy gingerly jumped up on the bed. Andy petted him.

The dog curled up in the middle of the bed.

Before leaving he added more wood to the stove. It was barely above zero. Outside he noted that the smoke from the chimney rose almost straight up. 'No wind; that's good'. His boots made a soft crunching sound as he made his way through the new fallen snow to his deer stand. The sky was just starting to lighten. The stars and a sliver of a moon were sharply visible. His stand consisted of a bench to sit on. It was at the edge of a forest of conifers he had planted years before. The trees were fifteen to twenty feet tall now. From the stand he was able to look out over the large meadow area to the north. There were several deer thoroughfares that crisscrossed the meadow. They were easily identifiable in the mixture of weeds and grasses. Andy was grateful that there was not a stiff north wind. Such a wind would make being here unbearable in this kind of cold. He had constructed a rack made from salvaged two x fours. It was designed so that he could rest his rifle stock on one of two parallel horizontal braces from either a sitting or standing position. It allowed him to take careful, deliberate aim by resting the rifle on one of the braces. He brushed snow off the bench and the rack. He carefully leaned his rifle against the rack and poured half a cup of coffee from his thermos. The light was beginning to gradually increase, as if a dimmer switch was being imperceptibly turned up. He could barely make out the stray pines, cedars and junipers that dotted the meadow. He sipped his coffee in a semi-state of reverie, recalling the first time he had seen this farmstead. He had known from the moment he set foot on the property that this was where he wanted to settle. The transaction to buy it went smoothly, reinforcing his sense of serendipity. Even though he was by nature skeptical of any notions of providence, he allowed for one exception; being here was somehow meant to be.

He was considering pouring more coffee when he noticed shadowy movement in his right periphery. He carefully set the cup down, picked up the rifle and gently laid the stock on the top cross brace of the rack. Using the scope as a telescope, he saw two large does. They were moving slowly but steadily north along the east edge of the meadow. At about a hundred-and-fifty yards out they began to angle their way across the open meadow. He clicked off the safety and took aim at the larger lead doe. To compensate for the distance and their forward motion he aimed a little high toward the top of her shoulder and forward of it almost at her neck. He held his breath and squeezed the trigger. There was a loud crack. Both deer stopped, looked up, but neither of them bolted with alarm. Instead they started walking quickly toward the west side of the meadow. Suddenly the large doe dropped to her front knees. He watched the deer through the scope.

He had neglected to eject and chamber another round. The second doe seemed to nudge the fallen one, as if to urge her to get up and continue. He stood up straight and lowered the rifle. He watched them for several, long moments. The standing doe seemed bewildered. She bent her head to her fallen companion; then raised her head to look around. She repeated this several times, as if incredulous. "I'm sorry," Andy whispered. He picked up the thermos and slid it into his coat pocket. He cradled the rifle in his left arm, picked up the coffee cup and stepped out into the open. The companion doe looked in every direction and then at him. He was certain she looked directly at him more than once as he walked toward her. He concluded that she wasn't able to detect his motion because of his direct path toward her. He angled to his right, at which point she spotted him. She took immediate flight, bounding into the nearby woods, flagging her tail in useless alarm.

As Andy approached the fallen doe she was still on her knees. She turned her head slightly in his direction. Her breathing was shallow and labored. He stood debating whether to shoot her again to end her suffering. Moments later her head lowered and her eyes glazed over. He watched the life go out of her. He squatted and touched her neck. He apologized to her, then thanked her. He found a place to lean his rifle. He tagged her before he set about field dressing her. He considered leaving her entails for scavengers to feast on; probably the coyotes. When he was done he realized that he had forgotten to bring a rope. He would need a rope in order to drag her back to the barn and to hang her carcass to cool. He pulled an old hand towel from his coat pocket and used it to wipe blood off his hands and his bare right arm. After rolling his shirt sleeve down, he put his coat back on, picked up his rifle and began trudging toward the barn. He felt a sense of sadness. It was beginning to snow again. In the workshop he located some half-inch Dacron rope. He thought to himself, 'maybe I better bring a garbage bag to put the guts in. I don't want Cassidy getting into them'. That possibility hadn't occurred to him until now. After finding a large, black, plastic bag and a shovel, he left the barn to return to the fallen deer. His thoughts drifted back in time, about several of the deer he had shot over the years. He remembered being downright thrilled about the first two or three. This one was different from all the rest. He found himself dwelling on how the second doe seemed so lost and confused. 'It was like she was stunned and in shock over suddenly losing her companion'. He realized that he was attributing human emotions to the surviving doe. 'Hell, she's probably off in the damn woods browsing cedar right this very minute, as if nothing ever happened'.

Steam was still rising off the heap of viscera when he returned to the fallen doe. He looked back toward the deer stand, thinking, 'that was a long shot, McLeod. Its two-hundred yards, maybe more and they were a moving target'. He remembered something Jan had said to him about him being a bad shot and having poor taste in women. He thought that he wasn't such a bad shot after all. He allowed that she was dead-on about his taste in women.

He knelt to tie one end of the rope above the middle joint of one hind leg. He did the same thing, using the other end of the rope on the other leg. He opened the garbage bag and used the shovel to scoop the entrails into it. The deer proved to be heavier than he had expected. After dragging her a short distance, he decided to leave the bag of viscera there for the time being. 'I'll come back for it later'. He resumed dragging the carcass. He stopped about half way across the meadow to catch his breath. He thought that he might look into getting one of those four-wheel ATV's. He rationalized that it was something he could use for lots of things around the place.

At the barn he slid the hanging door open. He used a chain hoist to lift the carcass. He got his pickup truck and backed it to the barn door. After he had the deer loaded. He got Cassidy to accompany him to Peninsula Park to register the kill. After returning home he used a heavy stick to prop the doe's hind legs apart. Using the chain hoist, he lifted the deer out of the truck bed. He would let the carcass hang for at least a day to let the meat to cool down and the rigor to dissipate. The wind was starting to pick up out of the northwest and the snow was increasing. After sliding the barn door closed, Andy and Cassidy went back to get the bag of entrails. Slogging through the snow he thought, 'Maybe animals are lucky. They live in the moment. They probably don't suffer the sense of loss and grief we humans do'. He was almost back to where he had left the plastic bag when he heard the report of a high powered rifle. He nearly panicked and dove for cover. The shooter was close by. He stayed frozen in place. His heart was pounding, he was almost panting and every muscle was tensed, ready to flee. He damned himself for having left his rifle in his workshop. He struggled to get control of his fear. His first rational thought was that if someone had shot at him, the bullet would have hit him before he even heard the shot. 'It's another hunter.' He told himself. 'He's north of me. He's close. I'm down-wind of him. Maybe he got the other doe; the one that was with the one I shot'. That notion was somehow comforting. It would spare her from grief. He took hold of the garbage bag, lifted it and started back. The bag was heavy. He guessed that it weighted close to thirty pounds. With the frigid wind to his back, the trip back to the barn was less painful. He changed hands with the garbage bag several times along the way because of its weight. He put the bag in the same area of the barn where the deer hung. 'It will be frozen solid in a few hours'. He got his rifle from the workshop and went to the house. After breakfast he took a long, hot shower.

Andy's sons arrived later than expected that afternoon. Brian reported that the traffic around O'Hare and heading north was worse than usual. He attributed it to holiday travelers. Corey got out of the car and hugged Andy. He complained, "Goddamn, Pops, it's cold up here; I'm not use to this kind of stuff anymore." Cassidy was in a dither, running back and forth between the boys as if his long lost buddies had just returned. Inside, Corey looked around the new house. "Jesus, Pops, nice digs. I mean it. This place turned out fantastic. What a monumental improvement over the old place. I'll bet you feel like you've died and gone to heaven." After a second trip out to the car to get the rest of their stuff, both boys joined their father for a tour of the new house. "Now what you need is a decent workshop," Brian said. "You need a well-insulated, well lit, heated place to work."

"That's in the works. Maybe I'll have one put up next fall. I'd like to have a shell built. I can finish the interior myself and have it ready to move into by early spring." The three of them went out to the workshop. Andy was in the midst of a project. They visited until the late afternoon walk time. Corey opted not to go. "It's too friggin' cold for my un-acclimatized buns." He was on his fourth beer. He preferred to sit close to the stove.

Before embarking on their hike Andy took Brian to show him the deer he had shot that morning. Afterwards they hiked the trails Andy had cut through the pine forest. The trees sheltered them from the wind. It was still snowing. Cassidy dashed about, disappearing in one direction and reappearing in another. Brian asked how things were going. "That's a broad question. Do you care to be more specific?" He asked about Andy's recovery from being shot last summer and about the situation concerning Stephanie. He asked about the relationship with Jan. Andy told him that things weren't very good at the present time. He told him about Jan's leaving him, her regressions and her hospitalization. Brian asked several specific questions. Eventually he asked, "what do you think caused her to fall apart like that, Pops?"

"I've asked myself the same question many times." He told Brian about the two attacks that had been made on them. "The attacks may have triggered her to go into a depression. Sometimes traumatic events do that. Hell, sometimes even not so traumatic events can have that kind of effect on people." Brian had no quarrel with the attack having been a 'traumatic event'. He wanted to know what was being done for her, how she was doing and if his father thought she would she ever recover completely. Andy couldn't answer any of those questions. He didn't know what was happening with Jan.

"She's no Miss America but I really like her, Pops. The two of you seemed to have a good relationship and you worked well together. It seemed to me you had gotten to be good friends."

"I wish you'd refrain from describing our whole relationship in the past tense," Andy said. "I still hold out some hope that we may be able to resume our friendship. I know things won't ever be the same between us but I still care about her. At this point I don't know that she feels the same way toward me." Brian apologized. He asked if he had been able to talk to anybody about her since she was hospitalized. "I've talked to her doctor and a social worker. According to the social worker, Jan goes back and forth about me. One minute she's mad as hell at me and accusing me of betraying her; the next minute she says that I'm the best thing that ever happened to her. When she's in that space, she says that it's all her fault. She says she was dragging me down and ruining my life. That's why she broke up with me. There aren't any in-betweens. Worst of all, everything is focused on me. She's either not able or she's unwilling to look at herself."

"Christ, Pops, she's really bonkers. It sounds to me like she suffering from something a lot more serious than depression. She sounds pretty schizoid if you ask me. What can anyone do for that?"

Andy showed a slight smile. "Where did you come up with that term?"

"Well, isn't she?" Brian countered.

"She's scared and she's desperate, Brian. I'm glad Sheriff Cumming got her to admit herself to the hospital. She needs to be protected from herself and from the people who are out to get her. Hopefully her doctor can get her panic under control with medication. She's not able to listen to any kind of reason the way she is right now."

"I don't know that I could extend that much understanding toward anyone, Pops."

I have to keep reminding myself that I have very little to do with what she's suffering. The past finally caught up with her. She had a dreadful childhood. Andy enumerated several of the things Jan had gone through as a teen and young adult. She's an amazing lady, Brian. She's one of those people that find ways to keep going. She managed to pull herself together and became a cop. She served on the Chicago PD several years before coming here. I have great admiration and respect for her. It's going to take an incredible amount of strength and courage for her to win the battle she's fighting now."

Brian asked his father if he loved her. "Yeah, I guess you could say that. She kind of grew on me. We got to be good friends. Back when we first met, there were a lot of things about her that I found pretty unappealing." Andy described her manner of dress and her chain-smoking as examples. "She made a lot of changes from when I first met her. I am absolutely certain that I couldn't have tolerated being with her if she hadn't. I miss the person she became."

The next morning, Thanksgiving Day, Andy and Brian were able to cajole Corey out to the barn to help skin and butcher the doe. The outside temperature had risen to the low twenties, making it easier to heat the studio area. Corey had gone through most of a case of beer since arriving and Brian had a difficult time getting him up that morning. He started drinking as soon as he got up. Brian said something to him about how much he was drinking which triggered a defensive reaction. "Hey, in two weeks I'm going to that freaking Muslim hell-hole, Afghanistan. I'll be lucky if I see another drop of beer until I get stateside again; so get off my burro, Bro." Brian started to say something more. Andy motioned for him to back off.

After they got the deer skinned, Andy cut it into two halves using a hack saw. He was about to show the boys how to butcher it when he realized he was missing something important. "I screwed up. I forgot to buy more freezer wrap and tape. I'm sure I don't have enough. I'm going to call and see if the grocery store is open." He turned to Brian. "If they're open, would you mind running up to Sister Bay to get some?" He called and found out that the store would be open until noon. Corey asked him to get him a case of beer. Brian looked to his father. Andy nodded for him go ahead and do so.

After Brian departed, Andy showed Corey how to cut roasts and steaks. He handed Corey the knife, encouraging him to give it a try. Corey began slicing, "Jesus, Pops, where did you learn to do all of this kind of stuff?"

"I learned some of it from books. I asked to watch the first couple of deer I shot being butchered. I've screwed up a few times, but you know my philosophy; mistakes are learning opportunities, if you manage to survive them." He corrected what Corey was doing two or three times by showing him. "You're pretty uptight about going to Afghanistan, aren't you?"

"Fucking 'A', Pops, wouldn't you be? I mean Americans have fucking pissed off most of the world. We're about as popular as camel shit tamales in the Muslim world. That fucking country is pre-stone age. The people I feel for the most are the fucking grunts. Man, their fucking asses are hanging out there 24/7 every fucking day they're in country. Nobody's safe over there, but those guys are the least safe. The worst part of it all, we're fucking pissing up a rope. The way we're going about this whole thing ain't going to stop, or even reduce extremists. Fuck, if anything we're just pouring gas on the fire. Just about everything we do proves to them that we're either stupid or we're bad guys or both." Corey went on venting his spleen for several more minutes. "I don't know Pops. I'm sorry I signed up for the Marine Corps. I guess the bottom line is, I am scared. I'd gladly lay my life on the line if I thought it was for something that was necessary or worthwhile, but not this. Do you know what I'm saying?"

"I know exactly what you're saying."

"You've never talked about what it was like in Viet Nam. Were you scared?"

"Every minute of every day for the year-and-a-half I spent there."

"How did you manage? I mean, how were you able to survive living that way?"

"I don't know if I have an answer to that question. I tried not to think about it. I tried not to let it get the best of me. Fear is a funny thing. When the shit hits the fan, you somehow go on automatic. You haven't got time to think about losing your ass. You just do whatever it takes to keep from buying the farm. It's the waiting for something to happen that's the worst. You know how the military works. You spend the majority of your time waiting. When things do happen, they usually happen suddenly and they're often over with just as suddenly. Then it's back to waiting again."

After Corey finished cutting off the steaks and some roast portions the two of them began to cut the tallow off the rest of the meat. "We'll grind up most of the rest for sausage." They worked together at the task. Corey asked him what he had done to manage his own fear when he was in Viet Nam. Andy pondered the question. "One of the things that helped me was to keep myself busy. It helps to have routines you can follow. If you just sit there doing nothing, you have too much time to think. Nighttime was always the worst for all of us. We needed to get a night's sleep to keep from getting fatigued. In Viet Nam we could never let our guard down enough to get a night's sleep. We were on constant alert. It wore all of us down. It affected our judgment and our moods causing tempers to flare. The slightest little thing would piss a person off. It wasn't just the fear. It was the conditions. It was the heat, the humidity, the bugs and snakes, and always being wet. I don't remember ever being dry in all the time I was in country." Andy stopped and looked at Corey. "Try to remember something. Fear generated by imagination can be your enemy. Realistic fear is an ally. It can keep you alive. I guess all I'm saying is that it's okay to be afraid. There isn't anything you can do about it anyhow. You just have to try not to let it get the best of you. It will from time to time. As long as you're alive, there's a next time."

Corey responded by changing the subject. "From what I've heard and read, the war in Viet Nam was even more unpopular than the wars in Afghanistan and Iraq. Half this country was against our being there. Did you feel that way too?"

"Yeah, it grew to be a very unpopular war. It didn't take very long for me to realize we had no business being there. There was no way we were going to win it. Even if we had, what was the point? We'd end up being stuck there for the next hundred years. The French had learned that lesson twenty years before."

"Did anyone ever call you a baby killer?"

"For a long time after I came home I was a closet veteran. I didn't want anybody to know that I'd been there. I kept my mouth shut and went about the business of trying to rebuild my life."

"Have you been able to put it behind you? Are you okay now?"

"Yeah, things are better, a lot better. I hardly have the urge to do penance anymore." Corey didn't catch the meaning of his father's gallows humor.

They could hear Brian coming up the driveway. "Thanks, Pops. I guess I need to suck it up and stop feeling sorry for myself."

"Naw, go ahead; feel sorry for yourself. Nobody else will."

Corey laughed. The two of them hugged. In the remaining few days he was there, he took control of his drinking. He limited himself to three beers each evening. Brian and Corey left late Saturday morning. It had warmed up enough that some of the snow was beginning to melt. Before leaving, Brian asked about coming to visit for a few days at Christmas. He wanted to bring his new girlfriend for Andy to meet. After the boys left, Andy went to his workshop. The phone rang early that afternoon. He didn't recognize Jan's voice at first. She sounded meek and tentative. "Andy? It's me. Can you talk?"

"Yeah, just as soon as I get over the shock of hearing your voice." He asked how she was doing.

She was not amused by his response. "I'm sorry for the way I treated you," she said with a tone of insincerity.

"I didn't mean to sound like a smart ass, Jan. I just wasn't expecting to hear from you." He apologized. "Where are you? Are you still in the hospital?"

She told him that she was. There was an awkward pause. "Did the boys make it home for Thanksgiving?" He told her that they had and that Corey was leaving for Afghanistan in a week. He told her that they had had a nice time together. He told her about getting a deer. After another lapse in the conversation, he decided to risk himself. He said, "Jan, you can't go on like this. You're at the proverbial fork in the road. It's decision time."

"I know," she said in a flat tone.

"I'm serious. "She said nothing. "Giving up is the easy way out, Jan. One of the things I've always admired about you the most is your tenacity and resilience."

"Yeah, well it looks to me like there aren't very many rewards and no guarantees to hanging in there. I've tried going that route. Look where it's gotten me."

"You're right about the guarantees. I guess what blindsided me the most was that you seemed to be enjoying life more than you ever had before. You seemed to really be reveling in the new you. Then, all of a sudden, the bottom fell out."

"Jesus fucking, Christ, McLeod. The bottom didn't just all of a sudden fucking fall out." She wasn't sounding meek and timid now. "The better things got for me, the more certain I became that it wasn't going to last. I could see the signs that my stock market was about to crash. I could feel it coming on. Don't you remember our last conversation? You as much as accused me of pulling the rug out from underneath myself." She was at the brink of yelling. "Why not, why the fuck not? It beats the hell having someone else do it to me. You're a fucking idiot, McLeod. You walk around acting like you've got all the goddamn answers. You don't know shit. You have no idea what I've been through. I'm tired of your pity and your 'poor Jan' crap. I'm sick of you acting like you're going to take care of me. Who are you trying to impress? I don't need your pitying indulgence. I don't need your protection. I'm a big girl. I can take care of myself. I don't need you for anything. Go fuck yourself, McLeod." There was the loud clank of her slamming the phone down.

Oddly, Andy didn't find himself feeling devastated or defensive. He started to feel sadness. He looked at the phone and said aloud, "Good for you Jan. Give em hell. Get in touch with all of that anger. That's step one." Cassidy looked at him with his head cocked. Andy looked back at the dog. "That was Jan, she told me to say hi to you. 'Hi'!" Cassidy wagged his tail.

In keeping with his own tradition, Andy went out the next morning to cut a Christmas tree. He had scouted out two or three candidates during his walks. He had the space for a fairly large tree in his new house. After cutting it, he dragged it back to the barn and mounted it in the stand. In order to get it through his front door he ended up having to compress the branches by binding the tree with bailing twine. He decided to wait until evening to string the lights and decorate it.

The next day he received a call from one of his long-time customers. "Andy, this is Victoria Schmidt." After the usual social niceties, Victoria explained her purpose in calling. "The priest at the church we attend has indicated that he'd like a hand-carved statue of Our Lady of Grace. I immediately thought of you." Victoria's husband was a third generation physician. She tended to speak rather formally and exude an aura of upper class. However, she had always been cordial in her dealings with Andy. "I don't know if you would have an interest in undertaking such a project. Father Byron wants it to be life-sized. I've already talked with him about you. He seems especially interested in having someone from the nearby community do it, as opposed to ordering from one of those religious supply vendors."

Andy told her that it was an honor to be considered for such a project. "I've never done anything like that before. I trust he wants a highly refined statue as opposed to something more primitive." She said that he did. A tentative appointment was scheduled to meet with the priest and three of the church's board members. The three members were in charge of raising the funds for the project. They wanted to meet with him at his studio.

By that afternoon he had gone from feeling honored to apprehensive. He was beginning to have second thoughts about the project. He asked himself, 'are you sure you really want to do this? What if it proves to be beyond your ability'? In addition to the question of his capability, there was the issue of his attitude toward organized religion. He didn't have much use for it. He felt that it would be hypocritical of him to take on this kind of a project. He ended up deciding that he should meet with the church people before making a final decision. 'If I take this on, it's really going to force me to stretch myself and it's probably going to take up most of the winter'.

He met with Father Byron, Victoria Schmidt and the three fund raising church members that Wednesday. He was shown photographs of a particular Our Lady of Grace that the church members wanted him to replicate. Fr. Byron seemed to sense Andy's hesitation. He interceded, "it's important that everyone understand that we're not asking you to produce an exact replica of this statue, Andy. It goes without saying that the final product will be a reflection of your own artistic vision. What we want is for you to carve her in this pose. The rest is up to you."

Andy breathed an emotional sigh of relief. He proposed doing the statue out of butternut wood. In his opinion butternut was one of the most beautifully grained woods in all of North America. He showed them some sample carvings he had done out of butternut. They were impressed. "I want you to understand," he explained. "Because of its beauty, it will have a natural finish. If you paint butternut, you don't even go to purgatory." The whole group laughed. He gave them an estimate for the labor, which they readily agreed to. He had no idea what the log would cost. In addition to his labor they agreed to pay for all of his material expenses.

He set to work that same day trying to locate a saw mill that had a butternut log large enough for the project. He finally found a saw mill on the west side of the bay of Green Bay that claimed to have several such logs. It was a hundred miles away. On a sunny, but cold early morning a week later, he set out for the mill. He arrived there late in the morning. By noon he was on his way home with a huge log in the back of the truck. He guessed that it weighed close to a thousand pounds. The truck rode low. When he got home it took some strategic maneuvering to finesse the log out of the truck and into an upright position. He hoped the weather would be decent enough the next day to rough the figure out using his chain saw. He had built two sturdy saw horses. Once he had the figure roughed out, the plan was to lay the large blank on the saw horses inside his workshop. He had begun taking pictures at the saw mill and unloading the log at home. He intended to photograph each step in the process.

The next day he shaped the figure as much as he felt confident in doing with his chainsaw. It took him over two hours to move the roughed out figure into his studio and position it on the saw horses. He launched into the actual carving the next day, discovering quickly that the interior of the log was so wet that water squirted out when he struck his gouges with a mallet. It had so much moisture; he had to devise a means of keeping it from freezing at night. At the end of each day he blanketed it with a sheet of plastic and put a small ceramic electric heater underneath turned on low.

He had not heard from Jan or the hospital since her call. He thought about her often throughout each day. He resisted the temptation to pick up the phone to call either her or her social worker. It helped that he was so busy with the statue. When he woke up in the middle of the night his thoughts were often occupied with technical aspects of the project. There had not been any more 'incidents' related to Stephanie. He still kept the pistol and the shotgun within reach, but he wasn't obsessed with having them right next to him at all times.

Andy got a call from the hospital social worker the second week in December. "Andy, I wanted to let you know what's happening with Jan. It's been awhile since I've talked to you." She told Andy that Jan had gone through a period of extreme agitation a couple of weeks ago. "Things were so bad with her that we had to put her in restraints for almost three days. We had to do it in order protect her from herself as well as those around her. She finally told me about her phone conversation with you right after Thanksgiving. Dr. Jordan was already pretty sure by then that she is suffering with a bi-polar disorder. She was in the midst of an extreme manic episode when she called you. It was so severe that she was even exhibiting some psychotic ideation. Doctor Jordan has since made several changes in the medications. She seems to be doing much better at the present time. For the first couple of weeks she was here, she refused to participate in therapy sessions. She appeared to be so severely depressed we were afraid that she'd made the decision to give up entirely. Then she went to the opposite extreme. Since then she's made a positive turn-around. She's begun to make an earnest effort in both her individual and group therapy sessions. My god, she's been through alot. I'm just amazed that she has been able to survive and function as well as she has, given her history." After a lengthy exchange, the social worker asked if Andy would be willing to attend a meeting with Jan, Doctor Jordan and herself. "He and I both feel that she's ready to face you now. We don't think she's trying to play the game in order to get released. She's not home free by any means but the whole staff thinks she's making progress in trying to come to terms with her past."

"Sure, I'd be happy to." Andy told her. They set an appointment for that next Monday morning.

Before they hung up the social worker said, "I can't promise you that this meeting will go smoothly. Jan has a real love/hate thing going on with you." Andy understood. "Jan's got some real issues with trust." He was impressed with this woman's clinical acumen. She was several steps above many of the social workers he had known.

Most of Andy's waking thoughts were about Jan for the next four days. When he arrived at the hospital that Monday he was met by the social worker, Anne. She was a woman close to Andy's age. Her hair was short and he noticed that she wore hearing aids in both ears. She was rather thin and what Andy regarded as 'handsome'. She was much as he had pictured her from their phone conversations. Doctor Jordan remembered Andy from their previous encounter. Jan looked nervous. She had lost a noticeable amount of weight. She was seated and didn't get up when Andy entered the room. Nonetheless he went over to her and reached out to shake her hand. In a soft voice he told her it was good to see her. She gave him a quick nervous smile. She looked like she wanted to bolt and run. He thought she must be feeling like a child who is expecting to be punished for her bad behavior. Anne conducted the meeting. Early on she asked Andy where he thought things stood between himself and Jan at this point.

He held his wool knit watch hat and he fiddled with it. "She's probably feeling like I betrayed her by talking with Sheriff Cummings. I doubt that she wants anything more to do with me." When Anne asked Jan if that was true, she just shrugged. She avoided making eye contact with Andy.

"How about you, Andy? How do you feel about the relationship?"

He cleared his throat. "Jan's my friend. She's probably my best friend. I miss her." He hesitated. "I would hate to lose that friendship."

Jan shook her head. She was looking down. Suddenly she looked up at Andy. "You're a fool, McLeod. Cut the bullshit. There isn't anything between you and me. I told you that before, you need to go out and find someone else. Someone who's not all fucked up. Just get the hell out of my life. Leave me alone."

Doctor Jordan intervened. "Excuse me, Jan. Am I mistaken? According to our records, Andy hasn't called you once in the time that you've been here. You've called him twice. Is that what's bothering you?" She asked if she could please be excused.

Anne stepped in. "I'm sorry, Jan, but I've gotten the impression that Andy means a great deal to you. It's obvious that you mean a lot to him. Do you have any idea why you're pushing him away from you?" Jan's jaw muscles flexed. "Jan, if you succeed in pushing him away from you, if you win, you're going to end up losing. The only winner will be your demons."

Jan glared at her. "I don't get you people. I feel like you're all ganging up on me. You don't get it, do you? If I succeed in pushing him away from me I'll be doing him a favor. I'll have saved his sorry ass. The goddamn demons aren't ever going to go away. They're never going to leave me alone. They won years ago. I was just too stupid to realize it."

Doctor Jordan said. "It sounds to me like you've made up your mind, Jan, and by God, that's the way it's going to be."

She softened somewhat. "It's not my decision, Doc. It's something that was decided for me a long time ago and I've finally come to accept that this is just the way it is for me."

"Jan, if I thought that was true for one minute I'd walk out of here and never come back," Doctor Jordan said. "Look at me. I'm an old geezer. I've been at this since God invented rocks. I've seen lots and lots of people mend their lives, people who were worse off than you." She again shook her head. She looked impatient like she wanted this meeting to be over with. Doctor Jordan turned to Andy. "I'm sorry, Andy. I'm sorry you drove all this distance for nothing. Janet appears to prefer wallowing in her own self-pity. Thank you so much for taking the time to come down here. May we call on you again, if she should change her mind?"

While Andy personally agreed with Doctor Jordan's assessment of Jan, he hated leaving on such a negative note. "Sure, I'll be glad to come back." He decided to play along with Jordan's apparent ploy. "The trip isn't a total loss. I've some Christmas shopping to do while I'm in the big city." Jan sat seething. He shook hands with Anne and Doctor Jordan. He didn't envy the task they had ahead of them. If Jan was making any progress toward gaining any insight, he sure couldn't see it. It seemed to him that she was stuck in a whirlpool of anger.

He did go Christmas shopping. He bought a pair of lined slippers for Jan. He had another very special present in mind for her. Before leaving Green Bay he stopped at McDonalds. He got himself an eggnog-flavored milk shake. They only have those for a limited time during the holidays. It was his favorite. He left a little in the cup for Cassidy to lap.

Anne called him the next morning to apologize for the way the meeting had gone. "No apology necessary," Andy told her. "You and the Doc said it all. I know her. She's pissed. She's at her best when she's mad as hell."

Chapter 22

Jan called Andy one evening a week before Christmas. She sounded almost cheerful. Andy found himself feeling reluctant and listening carefully for hints that this might be an act. Maybe she was just trying to put on a positive facade to get out of the hospital. She made no reference to the meeting with Doctor Jordan and Anne. She asked how things were going with him and what he was up to. He told her about the statue and Corey's departure for Afghanistan. She told him that Doctor Jordan had her on two new medications that seemed to be helping her. She chortled, "I'm in the process of pulling my nose out of my navel. I've never thought about it before but I really have spent a large part of my life feeling sorry for myself. Self-pity is insidious. It takes over without a person even realizing it. I spend a lot of energy trying to catch myself at it. I sometimes wonder if I'm ever going to get to the point that I don't have to constantly be on guard against it."

Andy made very few comments. He was making every effort to avoid sounding like a therapist. He was fearful that if he came across that way it would trigger a strong negative reaction from Jan.

Before hanging up Andy asked if he could call her some evening. "I'd like that, Andy. I understand now why you stayed away from me. I was hurt at first. I took it as proof that I meant nothing to you. I won't go into the whole gamut of emotions I've been through about you in the past four weeks. Suffice it to say that I've gotten things into much better perspective. I'm glad we're still friends."

Andy felt much relieved when they hung up. He poured out the remaining half of his second drink. When he went to bed, he slept soundly for the first time in almost a month. Unfortunately that meant that he failed to get up to add wood to the stove during the night. The house was cold the next morning.

Brian called the next evening to ask if it would be alright for him to bring his new girlfriend with him for Christmas. Brian told his father that she was a graduate student, pursuing a master's degree in fine arts. She was attending the same university as Brian. Her main interest was in sculpture but she was also a very talented potter. Their plans were to come up on the Sunday before Christmas to spend a week. Christmas was on the following Tuesday.

Andy called Jan on Thursday evening. She was in a group thera-py session when he called. When she returned his call she sounded happy to hear his voice. She asked about the house in terms of com-fort during the cold spell. She asked about his progress on the statue. She asked about Cassidy and jokingly told him that she missed the dog more than him. She asked about Corey and about Brian and what he had planned for Christmas. She kept away from saying anything about herself. Andy finally said. "Its hard work not comparing every-thing and everybody to yourself, isn't it?"

She gave a relieved laugh. "It's a bitch," she was almost whisper-ing. "I never realized how ego-centric I'd gotten to be. I'm spending an unbelievable amount of energy every day just trying to catch myself at thinking that way. Are there any secret shortcuts to getting past this thing?"

Andy smiled. "Hang in there, babe. You'll get into the Zen of it one of these days."

She went back into her whisper, "What the fuck is that supposed to mean, McLeod?"

"It's not something I can explain beyond what I just told you. You'll know it when it happens. After that, it will get easier and easi-er." He asked her why she was whispering.

She was still speaking in a half-whisper. "We don't have phones in our rooms. There are just two phones that the patients are allowed to use. One's in the rec room. The other one's at the nurse's station. I'm at the station. There's not a lot of privacy around here, probably for very good reasons. I have to watch what I say."

"Jan, I have a question to ask. I called your social worker, Anne, today. So she knows what I'm about to ask." He paused. "How would you feel about coming up here for Christmas?" She didn't respond. "I could pick you up Christmas Eve day and bring you back either on Christmas evening or the day after."

"Oh, Andy, I don't know." She was starting to cry. "I don't know if I'm ready for that. I don't want to ruin everyone's Christmas."

In a gentle tone he said, "be careful, Brady, you're getting awful-ly close to the self-pity line." Apparently one of the nurses gave her some tissues. She thanked the nurse. "Tell you what. Think about it. You can have until Monday afternoon to decide whether you want to give it a try." She agreed to those terms.

It snowed all day on Saturday but it was bright, sunny and cold when Andy got up on Sunday. It took him over an hour to clear the driveway. He had just gotten a fire started in his studio when the phone rang. It was Jan. In a tentative voice she asked, "Andy, does your invitation still stand?" He told her it did. "I've talked with Anne and Doctor Jordan. They both think it would be a good idea for me to spend Christmas with you. If I say yes, will you promise to bring me back to the hospital if I find I just can't handle it?" He agreed. "I obviously haven't been able to do any Christmas shopping. I feel really uncomfortable about not having any presents to give."

"That's okay, Jan. At the risk of sounding sappy, just having you here will be a gift in and of itself. I'm pleased with your decision. I'm looking forward to you being here with us. How about I pick you up at 10:00 o'clock tomorrow?"

She asked if he would mind keeping her car at his place. "It's probably buried under a ton of snow at the Justice Center. It needs to be run every once-in-a-while." He told her they could pick it up on the way home.

He truly was pleased with her decision. From past experience he remembered how the psych wards encouraged most of their patients to spend holidays with family, if at all possible. There were always a few who remained on the unit. Even the staff was reduced to just a few orderlies and nurses. It had always seemed to him a pitifully lonely way to have to spend Christmas.

He was working in his studio when Brian and his girlfriend arrived early that afternoon. Cassidy barked and Andy let him out to greet them. Andy put on his coat and followed. Brian's girlfriend's name was Michelle. She let it be known right away that everyone called her Mike. She was a tall, attractive, athletic looking young woman with long, sandy brown hair that she wore drawn back into a French roll. She exuded confidence. She was delighted to meet Cassidy. She shook Andy's hands, using both of hers, telling him how glad she was to finally meet him. "Come on, let's bring your stuff in. It's really cold out here," Andy said. It took two trips to haul luggage and packages into the house. Mike was immediately enthralled with the house, telling Brian that this was just exactly the kind of place she wanted some day. Andy took her on a tour.

The next thing she wanted to see was Andy's studio and the statue he was working on. He estimated that he was half done with it. Mike had several technical questions. He told her that his biggest concern was in doing the face. "Faces are the nemesis of most artists," she told him. "I'd love to help you with that." He welcomed her assistance.

They all went for a walk later that afternoon. Even though there was over a foot of snow on the ground, Andy had a well-worn trail through the woods. Mike was awestruck with the beauty of the property. "I'll show you some pictures I took of this place when I first came here. This was all open meadow back then," Andy told her.

"My neighbor down the road, who's now in his eighties, came by one day while I was planting trees. He wears those bib overalls most of the time. So, he's standing there watching me with his hands tucked into his bibs. He says to me, 'ya know, Andy; our forefathers busted their asses to clear all of this land. Now, here you are putting all these trees back in'."

"You never told me that story, Pops," Brian said. "Do you even know how many trees you've planted over the years?"

"Well over twelve-thousand. The older ones have matured to where they're planting themselves now." Mike wanted to see the rest of the property before she left. "There's a couple pair of snowshoes upstairs in the barn. There's some cross country skis, too, if you prefer them. Brian can take you on a tour tomorrow."

They were sitting around relaxing and conversing that evening. Brian asked about how Jan was doing. It was apparent that he had shared information about Jan with Mike. "I hope you don't mind," Andy said. "I invited her to spend tomorrow evening and Christmas with us. I'm going to Green Bay in the morning to pick her up at the hospital." Brian's only concern was whether Jan, herself, was ready to be out of the hospital yet. "We'll just have to see," Andy replied. He told them about the agreement he had with her. Mike and Brian volunteered to accompany him to the Justice Center. They would dig her car out and bring it back here. Andy liked that suggestion. He had been uncomfortable with the idea of Jan driving from the Justice Center to his place.

In bed that night, Andy thought to himself, 'I really like Mike. She's not only good looking and talented but she's got more poise than most women twice her age. He was pleased that his son had found his way to someone of her caliber. A dark thought crossed his mind. 'God, I hope Jan isn't threatened by her'. He put the thought aside. Walking on egg-shells with her was the last thing she needed from anybody. If she was that easily threatened, then she wasn't ready to manage in the real world yet.

They got an early start the next morning. When they arrived at the Justice Center, they found Jan's car fairly easily. It was not as buried as Andy had expected. He made sure her car started before he continued on his way. At the hospital, Jan was waiting for him in the reception area. She had let her hair grow out and had it done nicely. Although apprehensive at first, she was at the same time glad to see Andy. They hugged. She apologized for her clothing. It was what she was wearing the day she had been brought to the hospital. Andy told her that she had clothes at his place, but they could stop at her apartment on the way home if she preferred. As Jan approached the truck, Cassidy yelped and pranced with excitement at seeing her. He kept nuzzling her to pet him as they drove. By the time they were half-way home, she managed to trade places with Cassidy so that she could sit next to Andy. She took a hold of his arm. "Andy, I'm really sorry for everything I've put you through. I've behaved badly. It's no way to treat a friend."

He patted her hand. "Apology accepted," he told her. "I've thought a lot about you since you left. I had no idea you were going through such a monumental struggle. It just seemed to happen so fast, like a bolt out of the blue. I was caught completely off guard." He asked her when she had sensed that it was coming on.

She thought about the question. "I don't know for sure. Maybe it started well before we met one another and I just didn't want to see it. I was in denial. I've experienced fits of jealousy that bordered on downright paranoia about you for months, Andy. In my mind it wasn't a matter of if, but when you were going to toss me aside for someone else. You were right about me making a preemptive move. I decided to be the one to end the relationship. The night I broke up with you I was starting to take a dive into the worst depression I've ever experienced. I couldn't bring myself to turn around and come back. In my mind that would have been too humiliating. Instead, I tried to cling to a couple of mantras. I kept telling myself that, as painful as my decision was, you'd be better off without me in the long run. The second thing I tried to hold onto was the notion that 'this too would pass.' I decided that I'd either get over you or I would opt-out."

"At the point I called Sheriff Cummings," Andy held up his hand with his forefinger and thumb barely apart. "I thought you were this close to quitting. I will be forever grateful to him for listening to me and taking the steps he did to get you into the hospital. He saved your life."

"Both of you did," she said. "He wouldn't have done what he did if you hadn't gone to him and impressed on him that I was in such desperate shape."

Andy asked, "Are you still mad at me for doing that?"

"It was a confidence that needed to be broken." She told him that in one of her sessions with her social worker, Anne asked me what I would have done if the situation was reversed. As they talked, Andy began to relax. He felt much more confident that Jan had made the decision to come down on the side of life. This was going to be a very good Christmas.

Chapter 23

Jan was more than a little nervous about encountering Brian and meeting Mike. When they arrived home, the two of them came out to greet her. Brian gave her a long hug and kissed her on the cheek, telling her how glad he was to see her again. As Mike and Jan shook hands, Jan turned to Andy saying, "She's even prettier than what you described."

Andy had spent over four hours cleaning the house on Saturday. It was uncluttered and immaculate. Jan commented on the tidiness. Then she apologized, "I'm sorry, Andy, I didn't mean that to sound like you're sloppy. You're anything but." Mike told Jan how much she liked the design of the house.

Eventually they all went to the studio. Jan was amazed when she saw the statue and the pictures Andy was working from. "God, you really bit off a chunk when you took on this project, Andy. Wow! No wonder you were so reluctant." The four of them went for the walk later on. Jan asked Andy where the deer he shot had fallen. He pointed to the spot. "Jesus, that was a long shot. It looks like it was over two hundred yards. I'm impressed."

It was agreed that they would open presents that evening. Andy had wrapped a couple of things he had made and labeled them to Brian and to Mike from Jan. Brian had consulted with Andy in purchasing a nice set of carving tools for Mike. Andy made a jewelry/music box with a carved top for Jan, an oak computer desk for Brian, and a tool box for Mike to go along with the carving set.

Brian and Mike were tired and went to bed before ten. Andy and Jan sat up for awhile longer visiting. Before they retired, Andy told her that she could have the other guest bedroom. "I found a used dresser at a garage sale. I moved all of your things into that room. It's all set up for you." She seemed relieved and not at all disappointed. He commented, "I've decided that friendships between men and women are complicated. I sometimes wonder if they are even possible because of the sex thing."

Andy got up before everyone else on Christmas morning. After starting coffee, he and Cassidy quietly slipped out of the house and got in the truck. When they returned half-an-hour later, Brian was up. Andy kept his coat on and went to Jan's bedroom door and knocked, asking if he could come in. She gave him permission. She was curled up on her side under a large comforter. She saw Cassidy and patted the bed, inviting him to jump up on it. He gave her face a few licks. "How come you've got your coat on?" She asked.

"I needed to keep this little gal warm," he said. A puppy's face protruded from the front of his coat. "Merry Christmas, Jan." He lifted a golden retriever puppy out.

"Oh, my. Oh, my." Jan squealed. She bolted up to a sitting position and reached out from under the covers. He handed her the puppy. "Oh, my." She brought it to her neck to cuddle it. Cassidy worked his way up to sniff the pup. He looked at Andy, then Jan, then back at the pup. Brian and Mike knocked on the open door. "Can we come in?" She relinquished the puppy to Mike and hugged Andy.

"Oh, Andy, she's beautiful. Does she have a name?"

"No, you can choose a name for her." Brian agreed that she really was beautiful. Mike handed the pup back to Jan. "Hey, Merry Christmas everyone," Andy said. "How about some blueberry pancakes?" He got up from the bed. "Do you want me to take her while you get dressed?" Jan handed her over. Andy had saved a large carton that he had lined with towels. He set that in the kitchen for the pup. He'd also purchased bowls and a small collar for her. Brian took her while Andy and Mike made breakfast.

"What possessed you to get Jan a puppy for Christmas, Pops?" Brian asked.

"It's something she's always wanted. I debated doing it. I made the mistake of going to see the litter and fell in love. There were only two pups left that weren't spoken for. The other one was a dark red male. I had the feeling he was going to grow up to be huge."

When Jan appeared, she put her arms around Andy. "What a complete surprise." Brian handed her the pup. "I want to call her Sandy. She's the color of sand. What do you think?" She pulled Andy's bandana from his back pocket and blew her nose.

"I like it. You can always change it if something else pops up that you like better."

"No, I like Sandy."

"Speaking of names," Andy said. "I have wondered for almost as long as I have known you what your real first name is. Is it Janet or Janice?"

Jan smiled at him. "Neither. It's Janelle."

Mike commented on what a nice name she thought that was. "I didn't exactly choose to be called Mike." She revealed, "I've got four older sisters. My dad wanted a son so bad. Even before I was born he and mom came up with Michelle so that he could nickname me Mike. I like both names."

Andy told Jan there were some cans of moist dog food in the utility room. Jan put the puppy down to fetch them. The pup immediately squatted and peed. Jan started to snatch it up. She had an expression of near panic. Andy quickly stepped over to her. "It's okay. That's what puppies do. It's okay." Brian tore off some paper towel and quickly sopped up the puddle. Andy put an arm around Jan. "It's going to take a few weeks before she's completely house broken. There's one more present for you under the tree." He got it for her. It was a book on raising puppies.

"I don't know anything about puppies. I was afraid I screwed-up and did something wrong," Jan said. Andy was relieved that Jan hadn't let the incident throw her. He was faced with the realization that both of them were engaged in some confidence rebuilding, with themselves and with one another.

"You didn't do anything wrong, Jan. When you see her sniffing that's usually a sign that she's looking for a place to do her duty. You'll get so you're able to tell when she needs to go out."

It was such a nice day Brian decided to take Mike sight-seeing after breakfast. Jan and Andy donned snowshoes to go for a long cross country walk. Andy brought a day pack. "The puppy will probably get tired. We can put her in this." Jan carried her until they got into the woods where the snow wasn't so deep or drifted. To their surprise, Sandy stayed close. She stopped frequently to sniff things. Cassidy checked on her occasionally as he cruised about the woods. After they had gone some distance Sandy sat down. "She's tired. Do you want to carry her or should I?" Jan wanted to. He helped her on with the pack. He slipped the puppy into it, allowing her face to protrude. He had a towel in the bottom to act as padding and to absorb pee. He also had brought his camera and took several pictures along the way.

Andy and Jan left early the next morning to return her to the hospital. She asked to stop by her apartment on the way to pick up a few things. When they got there, Andy went with her. As soon as they got to the door of her apartment she knew something was wrong. The door was slightly ajar. "Andy, do you have your gun?" He told her it was in the truck. He immediately left to get it. When they let themselves in, they discovered that the entire apartment had been trashed. Everything belonging to Jan had either been slashed or broken into small pieces. Violent threats and sick graffiti had been scrawled on the walls, using an indelible marking pen. 'U cunt. Wer gonna butt fuk u' til u cant shit. One of her bras was on the kitchen counter. The intruder(s) had poured ketchup in both cups. Scrawled on the counter was, 'u wont ned this wen wer dun wit u'. The phone in the kitchen had been ripped off the wall. The one in the bedroom was smashed. Andy insisted that they get out of the apartment. He drove directly to the nearby city police station. Jan knew the desk officer. He had two patrols dispatched immediately to her apartment. Andy called Sheriff Cummings. He was put through immediately. The Sheriff told him that he would be there in a few minutes. When they got back to the apartment, a third patrol car had just arrived. One of the officers was already stringing crime scene tape around the front entrance to the building. Sheriff Cummings pulled up minutes later.

Despite the fact that Jan was visibly shaken by what had happened, she insisted on participating in going through her apartment. It was impossible to even approximate when the break-in had occurred. The only clue was that the surface of the ketchup in the bra was crusted, meaning that it had probably happened several days before. Only one of the eight building tenants was home during the day. Because he worked nights and slept during the day, he had not heard or seen anything. It seemed almost certain that the vandals had struck during the day. Sheriff Cummings was his usual avuncular self toward Jan. He promised to contact her insurance agent. He knew the apartment owner. He would see if he could persuade the owner to have the door replaced with a steel door and jam. He put a hand on Jan's shoulder. "I'm sorry, Jan. Don't worry about the cleanup. We'll get someone in here to put the place back together. Maybe the perpetrator made a mistake that will give us some clues. You just concentrate on yourself. We miss you."

When they arrived at the hospital Andy went in with her. He promised to call her a couple of times each week. "I'm awfully damn glad that you weren't in your apartment when this happened, Jan." She hugged him and thanked him for such a nice Christmas and especially for the puppy. "I'll take good care of her, you know that," Andy told her. "I'll be sure to take lots of pictures." He thought about Jan most of the way home.

That afternoon he called and left a message for Jan's social worker, asking for her to call him when she returned to work. Anne returned his call first thing the next morning. Andy told her about what had happened to Jan's apartment. "Sweet Jesus," Anne muttered. "I'll call Doctor Jordan as soon as we hang up. I'm going to alert the staff to keep a close eye on her. I'm sorry, Andy. What a terrible thing to happen. I hope this doesn't cause her to take a nosedive. I appreciate you letting me know. I saw Jan just briefly when I arrived today. She didn't mention a thing about it. As matter of fact she seemed to be in good spirits." If Andy was glad about anything, it was that the discovery had happened on the way back to the hospital, not on the way from.

Brian and Mike had been out roaming and sight-seeing while Andy was gone. They joined him in his studio after they returned. Andy had put a second box for Sandy in the studio, not far from the stove. Brian sensed that something was wrong. He asked his father if he was all right. Andy's emotions were catching up with him. He told them about Jan's apartment. Neither of them could believe, nor understand, how anyone could be so viciously cruel. Mike commented, "It's a damn good thing you didn't stop at her apartment on your way here and discover that mess. You would have had to take her straight back to the hospital. I may be wrong but I got the impression that this was one of the best Christmases she's ever had." Andy had to agree. After talking about the situation for awhile longer, Mike turned to the statue. She wanted to try out her new tools. She and Andy consulted about what needed to be done with the face and they spent the next two hours working on it together. By walk time, both of them were satisfied with the expression. It was serene with a subtle hint of sadness. Andy had laid out the folds of the sleeves of the statue's arms using chalk. They decided they would begin the task of working on the garments tomorrow. Mike complimented him on the way the hands had turned out.

During their walk, Andy asked Mike about what she hoped to do after she finished school. "I think Brian and I should move up here and you and I should become partners doing sculptures."

"She's serious, Pops. She hasn't had a chance to see all that much of Door County and she's already in love with this place. If I could find a job in one of the schools up here, we'd move in here in a nanosecond. We both hate living in the city. It's so expensive. It would be a lot cheaper to live up here." He went on with a list of reasons for moving. Andy listened without comment. He had Sandy on a leash and had to keep urging her along. She was distracted by just about everything.

Because of Andy's lack of comment, Mike asked him if he thought it would be foolish of them to move here. "Nope, you're young. You've got nothing to lose, but time. It's worth a try. If it turns out that this isn't where you want to be, you can always pick up and go elsewhere. As for me, I hope to die here at a ripe old age. I love it here."

Brian smiled and turned to Mike, "Pops is an expert at starting over. He does love it here, but, if he had to, he'd start anew someplace else. He's not afraid of change."

"That's not entirely true." Andy said. "I've found my place in the world. I'm a happy man. I'd hate having to give any of this up. I think most people are capable of starting over if they have to. I sure hope it never comes to that again in my own life." He pointed out that the two of them were in the process of making fresh starts in their own lives. He wanted to ask how serious they were about one another, but decided that would be putting them on the spot and might cause some embarrassment. He was surprised when Brian said, "Pops, Mike and I are practically living together. I spend most nights at her place. Her's is nicer than mine."

Mike smiled and looked at Andy. "Actually, we're talking about getting married when we're done with school."

Andy looked at Mike. "Has he met your family yet?" She nodded. "Do they like him?"

"They think he's okay," she teasingly said. "I'm just kidding. They all like Brian. My dad thinks he walks on water. I think dad would disown me if I broke up with him."

Andy turned to Brian. "Well, first-born, that's exactly how I feel about Mike." The puppy was getting tired. Andy lifted her up and snuggled her. "You are beautiful," he told her before tucking her inside his jacket, leaving her face exposed.

Almost all of the carving on the statue was complete by the time Mike and Brian had to leave to return to Illinois. In many ways, Andy hated to see them go. It had been an enjoyable respite from his solitude. He enjoyed their company and he had learned several things from working with Mike. It had always bothered him that his sons had grown up without both parents present. He had divorced their mother when the boys were quite young. They had not had the opportunity to witness parents who loved one another. In his studio Andy looked at the statue. He was faced with numerous hours of sanding and scraping before the statue would be ready to receive the finishing coats of tongue oil.

Anne, the social worker, called Andy regularly to keep him informed of Jan's progress. Both of them were surprised by her response to what had happened to her apartment. Rather than regressing, Jan was showing continued progress. Andy kept his promise to Jan. He called her at least twice-a-week. Whenever he photographed the statue, he took a couple pictures of Sandy. It was turning out to be a brutal winter, both in terms of snowfall and below normal temperatures. Many days he had to force himself to go out to his studio to work on the statue. He was grateful for Cassidy who took it upon himself to baby-sit the puppy. Cassidy's herding instincts emerged. His purpose in life now was to look after Sandy.

Andy was sure that Sandy would probably surpass Cassidy in size within a few months.

It was a bitterly cold, windy morning near the end of January. Andy decided not to even try to work in his studio that day. It would be a waste of his time, energy and firewood. He chose instead to stay in the house to compile his tax information. It was mid-morning when the phone rang. A pleasant, but somber sounding woman asked, "Is this Mr. Andrew McLeod?" He said that it was. "You don't know me. My name is Sarah Standish; I'm with the Bay Area Hospice. I'm calling you from San Francisco, California at the request of a Ms. Stephanie Brandt." He stiffened at the mention of Stephanie's name. The lady asked if this was a bad time for her to be calling. He told her that it was not. "I was assigned to Stephanie in mid-December. I'm terribly sorry to have to tell you this. Stephanie passed away yesterday. You were the only person she asked to be contacted. She gave me an envelope and asked me to send it to you, but only if I obtained your permission." Andy asked what the cause of death was. "Stephanie was diagnosed with pancreatic cancer early in September. By the time it was detected it had already metastasized and spread to other organs. She chose not to submit to any kind of medical intervention. She entered hospice care before Christmas." He asked if anyone had been there with her. "No one other than me," she said. "It wasn't until the very end that she mentioned you. She preferred that you not be told until after she was gone." He asked if she had been in terrible pain. "One of the main goals of hospice is to relieve people from as much pain and suffering as possible. Are you aware that she had a medical background in nursing?" He said that he was. "She knew that she was terminal and she knew what to expect. Stephanie was an extremely brave woman. She bore her suffering with a great deal of grace and dignity. In the weeks that I spent with her, we became friends. I confess I will miss her." She hesitated momentarily. "I don't know if I should say this. Stephanie spoke of you on a few occasions, always positively and with great admiration and respect. I wondered why she refused to let you know of her whereabouts and condition. I concluded that she wished to spare you from having to see her in such a state of illness. She was quite fragile and barely mobile at the end. Still, I felt a great sense of sadness that her life ended without anyone familiar by her side."

Even if had he known about what was happening, Andy couldn't tell this woman that he wouldn't have tried to be there. He asked, "what about funeral arrangements?" He hoped he wasn't sounding cold and callused.

"That's the other reason I have for calling you. Stephanie gave instructions for instant cremation. She has requested that her ashes be sent to you, again only if you grant permission to do so." Without hesitation, Andy gave her permission to send both the envelope and her remains. He asked whom he needed to contact about sending the ashes. "You don't need to contact anyone, Mr. McLeod. Stephanie gave me power of attorney to see to her few final requests. She has already been cremated and the expenses are paid for in full. I will contact the mortuary to inform them of your decision. They will send her ashes to you directly. Stephanie had just a few articles of clothing. She asked that those be donated." She concluded the conversation by asking if Andy had any questions. He did not. She gave him a telephone number where he could reach her if anything occurred to him later. "Again, I'm sorry to be presenting you with this news." Andy thanked her and hung up.

He poured another cup of coffee. He checked on Sandy who was sound asleep in her box. He added wood to the stove and sat down at the counter where he had all of his tax stuff spread out. He looked out the window. It seemed like there were fifty or sixty pine siskins flocking to the large fly-through bird feeder on the front deck. The birds ate voraciously in this cold weather. He needed to fill the feeder twice-a-day. He thought about Stephanie. She had left here a little more than a year ago. She hadn't died in a car accident in Mexico. He had been fairly certain of that all along. He wondered if she had stayed, would she have ended up with cancer and dying just the same. He questioned whether he was doing the right thing by allowing the envelope and her ashes to be sent to him. He gave some consideration to what Jan's reaction would be if she were here. He wouldn't withhold telling her about the call. If 'Draco' was still listening in on him, was this going to re-arouse the dragon? 'The envelope might contain the information Draco has been looking for all along'. He went through a gamut of emotions about the news of Stephanie's death. It was hard for him to believe there was no one other than himself she had been close to. She must have had a few friends. 'How sad that she ended up all alone. Was that because she felt that she needed to protect others from being associated with her'?

He picked Sandy out of the box and stood in front of the stove, cuddling the fast-growing puppy and talking to her. He poured out what was left of the coffee and unplugged the coffee maker. He decided that he'd take Stephanie's ashes out to Thorsen Point in the spring. He would spread them on the water there. Over a period of time, his feelings toward her had gone through several changes. Thinking back about her now, he regarded her as a good and decent person. Her leaving had been an act of love. It had been painful for both of them. She had acted bravely and honorably'. He was able to empathize. 'Her life must have been hellish from then on. She must have constantly been on the go, knowing she couldn't risk befriending anyone. Her suffering is finally over with'. He remembered feeling the same way when his long-ailing mother had died. It was sad but at the same time he had felt a sense of relief.

Corey called Andy that day. It was already ten p.m. in Afghanistan. It was late afternoon here in the central time zone. Corey made a point of calling home every couple of weeks. Sometimes the connection was so poor it limited their conversations. Corey, like most of his comrades, was counting the days left of his deployment. After the initial culture shock of being plunked down in a truly alien environment, he seemed to have adjusted. "The politicians and bureaucrats aside, the Afghans are amazing people, Pops. They have so little and yet they seem happier than most Americans. Maybe it's because they're not tied to all the stupid stuff we think we can't live without." Andy remembered feeling the same way about the Vietnamese peasants he had encountered. When he had first returned home he found himself feeling hyper-critical and downright repulsed by Americans' preoccupation with consumption. Corey expected to be home sometime in mid-January next year. Andy wondered if his own parents had felt the same anxiety about him as he felt about Corey. It wasn't a consuming, pervasive worry for him. But it was always there, needing to be managed.

The next morning Andy was listening to National Public Radio while he was working out. One of the news segments told of an anonymous donor who had bequeathed fifteen million dollars to the American Cancer Foundation and another five million dollars to Habitat for Humanity. Andy said aloud, "if you're listening Draco, I hope the donor they're talking about was Stephanie. If so, she gave your money away. You're screwed, big guy. She won."

The envelope arrived in the next day's mail. It contained statements from a bank in the Cayman Islands showing a deposit of sixteen million dollars five years previously. It showed six withdrawals that were highlighted. One of them was made three days after Stephanie had left here. All told, the withdrawals totaled a hundred and fifty thousand dollars and covered a period of four years. The original deposit had earned over four million dollars in interest during the five years. It showed a withdrawal of twenty million dollars on December 31st. There were two receipts for cashier's checks. One was to the American Cancer Foundation for fifteen million dollars. The other was for five million to Habitat for Humanity. There was a cashier's check for fifteen hundred dollars made payable to Andrew

McLeod labeled "House warming present."

Andy called Jan that evening. She pretty much echoed his sentiments about Stephanie's death. She made an additional comment.
"Assuming 'Draco' is aware of her demise; your troubles may be over
with for once and for all, McLeod. You're a free man at last." He
hoped so. "I have some good news," she told him. "They had a staff
meeting this afternoon and it looks like I'm going to be released from
here on Friday." Andy asked how she felt about the decision. Did she
think she was ready? He listened carefully to her answer. "I think so,
Andy. Doctor Jordan seems to have come up with the right combination of drugs. I feel like I'm on pretty solid ground at last. I'm as
ready as I'm ever going to be. Returning to the real world is the ulti-
mate test." She sounded as confident as any would-be adventurer
could be. Andy told her he'd pick her up on Friday morning. She was
going to call Sheriff Cummings in the morning to see if her apartment
was habitable yet. Andy offered his place if it wasn't.

Friday was bright, sunny, and very cold. The early February
wind was strong out of the northwest, causing the surface snow to
swirl around like dervishes. It had warmed up considerably for three
days the week before. It was the proverbial January thaw. A cold
front had swept in over the weekend, bringing in some fresh light
snow and a new round of bitter cold.

When Andy arrived at the hospital Jan was ready. She seemed
ebullient. Anne was there to see her off. They hugged and Jan
thanked Anne for everything. Anne wished her the very best. When
they got in the truck, Jan couldn't get over how much Sandy had
grown in just over a month. "She's big into the chewing stage right
now," Andy warned her. "I have to make sure I don't leave anything
lying around or she'll shred it. I keep her supplied with toys but she
prefers my socks. She regards my work boots as a delicacy."

Jan's apartment was taking longer to restore than expected. It still
wasn't ready. Andy asked if she had suffered the loss of anything
valuable. She was sure she had not. "I don't have much. I keep all my
important papers in a lock box at the bank. My gun and my purse are
in the trunk of my car. I've got enough clothing at your place to get
me by for the time being." He asked her about going back to work. "I
talked to Charlie. I asked about starting back slowly. You know him.
He bends over backwards for his staff. He's welcoming me with open
arms."

When they got home, Jan wanted to go out to the workshop to
see the statue. While she was examining it, he got a fire started in the
stove. "God, Andy, this is beautiful. I can't believe how nicely this
turned out. You didn't know you had this in you, did you?" She

asked him when he thought that he'd have it done and ready to deliver. He hoped that it would be entirely finished by the end of the month.

Jan said that she had some errands to run and business to take care of. She left saying that she would be back in time for supper. He suggested that they go out for a fish fry that evening. For the next week Jan was out and about every day, usually for the entire day. She seemed in such good spirits that he had no reason to be concerned about her. Midway into the next week she announced that she was going to Chicago for two or three days. She said she had a couple of friends she wanted to see. She planned to leave on Thursday and be back on Sunday. Andy expressed concern for her. "I'll be fine, Andy. Can I bring anything back for you?" He couldn't think of a thing. He thought about her after she left. He had never seen her so consistently cheerful and upbeat. He wondered if her mood was the result of the medication Doctor Jordan had her on. He liked seeing her so cheerful but he was admittedly a bit skeptical. He decided not to risk rocking the boat. He said nothing.

When she returned on Sunday, he was almost stunned to see her new hair style. She laughed and plucked a blond wig off her head to reveal an almost bald head. "My girlfriend talked me into it. She's been wearing wigs for years. She says that it saves her endless hours of screwing around with her hair. She's got a wig for every day of the week." She put the wig back on and adjusted it. She laughed, "You'll get used to it, McLeod. It's the new me."

In order to avoid sounding critical he asked. "What about the summer? Don't those things get uncomfortable when it's hot?" She told him that if it did, she'd just run around bald. She left again the next Thursday. This time she said she was going to the Twin Cities to attend a Law Enforcement conference. She said she'd be back either late Sunday or sometime Monday morning. When she returned from that trip she had a present for him. He opened it to discover a brand new Colt Defender forty-caliber pistol. "I know that you like that cannon of yours, Andy. One of the cops I met at the conference is a licensed gun dealer. He cut me a hell-of-deal on this. A lot of police departments are switching to the forty-caliber. It's got the stopping power of a forty-five without the recoil." She also presented him with two boxes containing a hundred rounds of ammunition each. He asked her how much all of this had cost. "Don't worry about it. I just want my Smith & Wesson back." He went and got her gun and the ammunition. She checked the pistol. It was fully loaded. She praised him for having taken such good care of it. "I missed this gun. I had some second thoughts about loaning it to you. It would be a hard weapon to replace."

Andy was having trouble adjusting to the change in her appearance, as well as her light-hearted demeanor. He had never seen her this jovial and friendly ever before. It was like all the nastiness of the past had been surgically removed. He'd never seen anyone transform this much in all the years he had counseled people. It was like someone had flipped a switch to turn off all the bad stuff and another one to turn on the good. He liked what he saw. It just didn't seem credible.

He finished the statue sooner than he had anticipated, in part due to the lack of any interruptions and the lengthening days. He had put in long hours working on it and was proud of his accomplishment. Jan was able to move back to her apartment the third week in February. He was sorry to see her go but he took comfort in knowing that she seemed to be on such solid ground emotionally. Before Andy was scheduled to deliver the statue, Jan borrowed one of the large format cameras that were used to photograph crime scenes. She took a number of pictures of it. She asked to go with him to deliver the statue and photographed it in the church. Father Byron was extremely pleased with it. He asked if Andy would attend a dedication service for it in later on in March. He told the priest he would be honored to do so.

He submitted the bill for the statue and Father Byron wrote a check right then. The check he handed Andy was for five hundred dollars more than the agreed upon price. "It's worth every penny we're giving you and more, Andy. We all felt that you had underestimated the project. If we had bought a similar statue from a religious supply house it would have been almost double the amount you're charging. Most importantly, we have a unique and exquisite addition to our church, AND we know the artist."

When they left the church, Jan patted Andy on the back. "You done good, McLeod. Aren't you happy now that you took the risk? Look at all you learned in the process. I'm really proud of you." They had both dogs in the truck with them. Sandy had grown to the point that it was getting crowded having them both there. Andy dropped Jan off at the Justice Center shortly after noon. She told him she'd see about getting the film developed today and she'd get the pictures to him. He called her that evening and they had a lengthy conversation. He had sensed a shift in their relationship ever since her discharge from the hospital. He had felt it even more strongly today but he couldn't put his finger on it. The most obvious sign was her positive encouragement of him. She had always been supportive but this was different. Two days later part of the mystery would be solved. When he went to get his mail that afternoon he found a large brown envelope in the mailbox. Inside were the photographs that Jan had taken of the statue in the church. There was a handwritten note. It read, "Andy, I'm going to be gone for quite awhile. I don't know if our paths will cross again. You've been a good friend. I will miss you. I wish I could bring Sandy with me, but I know she's got a good home. Take care of yourself, sweet man. Love, Jan." He realized that what he had been sensing was that she was a fledgling about to leave the nest. She had been trying to reassure him that she was ready and that everything was going to be okay.

He didn't know how to react. He tried to call her at work. The person he talked to said that he was transferring the call to Sheriff Cummings. When the sheriff came on the line, Andy asked straight out what was happening with Jan. "I wish I knew Andy. She came in here late yesterday and told me that she was leaving. She didn't say why or where she was going. I asked her if she was in some kind of danger. All she said was that she had to take care of some things and she doubted that she would be back. Hell, I don't even know where to send her paycheck. I'm at as much of a loss as you about what's happening." They talked back and forth about Jan for several minutes. Andy was beginning to have some suspicions about where she had gone, but he kept them to himself.

In the course of the next several weeks, there was a rash of murders in the city of Chicago. At first the authorities thought they were gang and/or drug related. In time the gang-intelligence unit reported that the killings seemed to be systematic, but unidentifiable. In other words, no one was claiming responsibility. Theories were quick to circulate. Some of them suggested that there was a war for dominance between the gangs. The gang leaders claimed that they didn't know who the assassin or assassins were. Therefore, they didn't know where to direct either their retaliation or their defenses. Some of the gangs began negotiating alliances for the purpose of self-defense. Many of the victims were Hispanic, but not necessarily upper echelon gang members or drug merchants. Two deaths occurred at Statesville Penitentiary in Joliet, Illinois. Authorities expressed the opinion that they appeared to be related to what was happening on the Chicago's streets.

Law enforcement officials and politicians were ambivalent. While they secretly applauded the wave of gang-specific genocide sweeping through the community, they were at a total loss as to who was involved and what their motive was. They were beginning to panic. They had no control over the situation. They were afraid that this might spread to the point of threatening public safety. From a statistical standpoint, Chicago was earning the unwanted reputation of being one of the most dangerous cities in America. It was being compared to Mexican border communities like Juarez or Tijuana. The murder rate was drawing national attention. The media was having a field day speculating. It was suggested that the killers were a cult of religious fanatics (probably Muslim), a group of neo-Nazi's, a sect of vigilante Minute Men, a cult of religious fanatics (possibly Gnostics), the Russian Mafia, a cult of religious fanatics (probably Evangelical Christians), a group of right wing anti-immigrationists, one of the Mexican drug cartels, a group of American Iraq War veterans, a cult of religious fanatics (probably Southern Baptists), Al Qaeda... the list went on-and-on.

The unique thing about the wave of violence was that it was restricted to people with long histories of criminal violence aimed almost entirely at women. At the end of May, the number of such deaths had reached seventeen. Then they suddenly stopped. Everyone involved on both sides of the law held their breath, wondering if this was just a lull. By the end of June it looked like things were getting back to normal. As summer progressed even further, it appeared that the overall number of murders, related to gang violence, was dipping to an all-time low. Chicago ended up experiencing one of the most peaceful summers on record.

Just before Labor Day, Sheriff Cummings called Andy to ask if he had heard anything from Jan. Neither of them had. "Well, I received an interesting phone call from the regional director of the FBI yesterday. I'm sure you heard about that rash of killings that took place in Chicago." Andy had. "Apparently, when they first started, the feds immediately suspected that Jan was somehow connected to what was happening. Many of the victims were on the list of people who had done harm to her in the past. When the killings finally stopped, all of the people on the list were dead. It took the Feds awhile to run her down. Guess where they found her?" Andy could feel his heart sinking." Ireland," the sheriff said. "It turns out that our girl moved to Ireland about five months ago." Andy felt a tremendous sense of relief. "That of course leaves her out as a murder suspect, almost entirely." Andy asked what the sheriff meant by 'almost entirely'. The sheriff sounded like he was smiling. "The FBI's theory is that Jan may have planted a nasty rumor, claiming that certain individuals were snitches. The feds think what happened is that, as the rumor started to spread, these people started going after one another." Andy repeated his question about 'almost entirely'. "Oh yeah, I got ahead of myself. Apparently something happened back in the beginning. Something went wrong and she may have ended up groin-shooting one of the vics. That would have been like mid-February." Andy remembered that was about the time she had gone to Chicago while she was staying at his place. "She may have shot him in self-defense. The bullet severed his femoral artery and the guy bled to death." Andy asked if they were going to try to go after her for that. "Not according to the regional director," the sheriff told him. "The shooter's description didn't match her." Andy smiled. That explained the short hair and the wigs.

"Where in Ireland," Andy asked? "Did he tell you where she went?"

"I thought you'd never be askin', lad," Sheriff Cummings said in a modest brogue. "She purchased a bed and breakfast in a small town on Achill Island, wherever the hell that is. I'll see if I can get an address and phone number for you. Incidentally, she changed her name from Miller to Brady. I don't know if her first name is still the same."

Andy called Brian at his place of employment. He was the new high school principal that served the northern end of Door county. "I just got off the phone with Sheriff Cummings. You'll never guess what he told me. Jan is alive and well and living in Ireland." Brian was pleased for his father's sake. It was good to know that she was alright.

After hanging up with Brian, Andy received a call from his friend Rob, who was now living near Homer, Alaska. He hadn't heard from Rob since Carla and he had left for Alaska over a year ago. "Hey, Amigo, how are you?" Andy immediately recognized Rob's voice.

"That's my line," Andy said. "How are you? Christ, it must be getting close to the time of the year that you have to have the lights on most of the day."

"Not quite, we still have almost six hours of daylight each day." Rob told Andy about their life in Alaska. "Last winter was pretty hard on both of us. Three months of almost total darkness gives new meaning to the term 'cabin fever'." He and Carla were married now. She was teaching in a one-room school. "Her students are all bilingual," Rob told him. "They speak fluent English, as well as Russian. Carla really likes her job. The kids and their parents really appreciate her. Most of their social life revolved around the school and their church. They're all Russian Orthodox." Rob had spent the past year putting up a two-story, 3500 square foot log home. They planned to use part of it as a B& B during the summer months. It also was serving as a model home. Rob already had contracts to build two log homes next summer. "Carla has made it known that we're coming back to Door County for Christmas this year. Most of her family lives there. We'll be sure to stop by for a visit." Rob was saddened to learn that Stephanie had died. He was pleased that Andy was enjoying his new, 'livable' house.

After hanging up, Andy thought about how adventurous both Rob and Carla were. He admired their courage in pulling up stakes to make such a bold move.

Brian and Mike were renting an old farmhouse with an option to buy. It was a mile from Andy's place. They had moved there after completing their master's degrees last spring. Mike was working at a cooperative art gallery where she had some of her pottery on display and for sale. She also taught a couple of pottery-making classes at a summer art school. Andy gave Jan's dog, Sandy, to them. She was turning out to be a beautiful dog with a nice disposition. However, whenever she was left un-tethered, she made for Andy's place to visit Cassidy. Unless Brian or Mike came to pick her up, she often stayed the night.

On a nice evening in mid-September, Andy invited Brian and Mike to meet him at the marina to go sailing. When the sails were up and they each had a glass of wine in hand Mike asked, "So, when are you leaving for Ireland, Pops?"

"I've pretty much decided not to," Andy said. "Jan left here on a mission. She's completed it and moved on with her life. If she had wanted me in it, she would have contacted me." Andy showed a sad smile. "It was last summer when Jan told me her maiden name was Brady. Maybe she went to Ireland to reclaim her heritage. Whatever her reason for leaving here, I hope she's at peace with herself."

"Don't you miss her?" Mike asked.

"I do. This boat was hers as much as mine. We spent almost three weeks sailing together last year. We shared some wonderful times on it. I think of her just about every time I get on 'Desperado'. The two of us chose that name for the boat. It was apropos to the circumstances we were in at the time." Andy proceeded to tell them the story of how they had come to own the boat.

"What a great story, Pops,'" Mike said.

Brian asked, "So, what happens next for you, Pops?"

"I'm not planning on going anywhere. I'm where I want to be, doing what I want to do. I'm at peace with myself. I'm not planning on remaining a goddamn monk if that's what you're asking. Maybe someone will come along that can stand being with me. The worst thing I could do is to try to make it happen."

Brian took the tiller and Andy went below to pour more wine for the three of them. Standing in the companion way, he handed them their wine and asked, "so when are you two going to start a family."

Mike smiled at him. "We already have." She told him. "I just found out yesterday that I'm pregnant. Would you care to offer any suggestions for names?"

Andy congratulated them. They toasted the news. He thought about the question. "How about Daniel Angus if it's a boy? My father's surname was Angus."

"And if it's a girl," Mike asked? "Danielle Allison. Your mother's first name is Allison."

"Good, Pops, D.A.M.," Brian said. "I might have guessed you'd come up with something like that."

<u>Coming Soon!</u>
The Sequel to "Starting Over"
"The Dog Who Took His Man for a Walk"